WALLBANGER

alice clayton

"*Wallbanger* is an instant classic, with plenty of laugh out loud moments and riveting characters—highly recommended!"

~NYT and USA Today Bestselling Author Jennifer Probst

"Hilarious, romantic, and compulsively readable, *Wallbanger* delivers the perfect blend of sex, romance, and baked goods."

~Ruthie Knox, best-selling author of *About Last Night*

"Alice Clayton strikes again, seducing me with her real woman sex appeal, unparalleled wit and addicting snark; leaving me laughing, blushing, and craving knock all the paintings off the wall sex of my very own."

~Brittany Gibbons, brittanyherself.com

"Caroline Reynolds. Finally a woman who knows her way around a man and a KitchenAid Mixer. She had us at zucchini bread!"

~Curvy Girl Guide

OMNIFIC PUBLISHING
DALLAS

Omnific Publishing
10000 North Central Expressway, Dallas, TX 75231
www.omnificpublishing.com

First Omnific eBook edition, xxx 2012
First Omnific trade paperback edition, xxx 2012

The characters and events in this book are fictitious.
Any similarity to real persons, living or dead,
is coincidental and not intended by the author.

Library of Congress Cataloguing-in-Publication Data

Clayton, Alice.
  Wallbanger / Alice Clayton – 1st ed.
  ISBN 978-1-623420-02-4
  1. San Fransisco — Fiction. 2. Contemporary Romance — Fiction.
  3. Interior Design — Fiction. 4. Romantic Humor — Fiction. I. Title

10 9 8 7 6 5 4 3 2 1

Cover Design by Micha Stone and Amy Brokaw
Interior Book Design by Coreen Montagna

Printed in the United States of America

To my mom, for letting me have coconut on my birthday cake
even though no one else likes it.
To my dad, for reading me Garfield comics
until we laughed so hard we were both crying.
Thank you

chapter one

"**O**h, God."

Thump.

"Oh, God."

Thump thump.

What the...

"Oh, God, that's so good!"

I scrambled up out of sleep, confused as I looked around the strange room. Boxes on the floor. Pictures propped against the wall.

My new bedroom, in my new apartment, I reminded myself, placing both hands on the duvet, grounding myself with the luxurious thread count. Even half asleep, I was aware of my thread count.

"Mmmm...Yeah, baby. Right there. Just like that...Don't stop, don't stop!"

Oh boy...

I sat up, rubbed my eyes, and turned to look at the wall behind me, beginning to understand what had woken me up. My hands still stroked the duvet absently, catching the attention of Clive, my wonder cat. Butting his head under my hand, Clive demanded to be soothed. I stroked him as I looked around and oriented myself in my new space.

I'd moved in earlier that day. It was a gorgeous apartment: spacious rooms, wood floors, arched doorways—it even had a fireplace! I had no clue how to actually build a fire, but that was neither here nor there. I was aching to put things on the mantel. As an interior designer, I had a habit of mentally placing things in almost every space, whether it belonged to me or not. It drove my friends a wee bit mad at times, as I was constantly restaging their knickknacks.

I'd spent the day moving in, and after soaking in the incredibly deep, claw-foot tub until well past prune, I settled myself into bed and enjoyed the creaks and squeaks of a new home: light traffic outside, some quiet music, and the comforting click-click of Clive exploring. The click-click came from his hangnail, you see...

My new home, I'd thought contentedly as I slipped into an easy sleep, which is why I was so surprised to be woken at...let's see... two thirty-seven a.m.

I found myself gazing stupidly at the ceiling, trying to return to a relaxed state, but I was startled again as my headboard moved—banged into the wall was more like it.

Are you kidding me? Then I heard, very distinctly:

"Oh, Simon, that's so good! Mmm..."

Aw, jeez.

Blinking, I felt more awake now and a little fascinated by what was clearly going on next door. I looked at Clive, he looked at me, and if I wasn't so tired I'd have been pretty sure he winked. *I guess someone should be getting some.*

I'd been in a bit of a dry spell for a while. A very long while. Bad, rapid-fire sex and an ill-timed one-night stand had robbed me of my orgasm. She'd been on vacation for six months now. Six long months.

The beginnings of carpal tunnel were threatening to set in as I tried desperately to get myself off. But O was on seemingly permanent hiatus. And I don't mean Oprah.

I pushed the thoughts of my missing O away and curled up on my side. All seemed quiet now, and I began to drift back to sleep, Clive purring contentedly beside me. Then all hell broke loose.

"Yes! Yes! Oh, God...*Oh, God!*"

A painting I'd propped on the shelf above my bed fell off and rapped me soundly on the head. That'll teach me to live in San Francisco and not make sure everything is securely mounted. *Speaking of mounted...*

Rubbing my head and cursing enough to make Clive blush—if cats could blush—I looked back at the wall behind me again. My headboard was literally banging against it as the ruckus continued next door.

"Mmm…yes, baby, yes, yes, yes!" the loudmouth chanted…and concluded with a contented sigh.

Then I heard, for the love of all that's holy, *spanking*. You can't misinterpret the sound of a good spanking, and someone was receiving one next door.

"Oh, God, Simon. *Yes*. I've been a bad girl. Yes, *yes!*"

Unreal…More spanking, and then the unmistakable sound of a male voice, groaning and sighing.

I got up, moved the entire bed a few inches away from the wall, and huffed back under the duvet, glaring at the wall the whole time.

I fell asleep that night after swearing I would bang back if I heard one more peep. Or groan. Or spank.

Welcome to the neighborhood.

chapter two

The next morning, my first official morning in my new place, found me sipping a cup of coffee and munching a leftover donut from yesterday's moving-in party.

I wasn't quite as awake as I'd hoped to begin unpackingpalooza, and I silently cursed last night's antics next door. The girl was plowed, spanked, she came, she slept. The same for Simon. I assumed his name was Simon, as that was what the girl who liked to be spanked kept calling him. And really, if she was making up a name there were hotter ones than Simon to be screaming out in the throes.

The throes…*God, I missed the throes.*

"Still nothing, huh, O?" I sighed, looking down. During month four of The Missing O, I'd started to talk to my O as though she were an actual entity. She felt real enough when she was rocking my world back in the day, but sadly, now that O had abandoned me, I wasn't sure I'd recognize her if she saw her. *'Tis a sad, sad day when a girl doesn't even know her own orgasm,* I thought, looking wistfully out the window at the San Francisco skyline.

I unfolded my legs and padded to the sink to rinse out my coffee mug. Placing it in the sink to drain, I pushed my light blond hair back into a sloppy ponytail and surveyed the chaos that surrounded me. No matter how well I planned, no matter how well I labeled those boxes, *no matter how often I told that idiot moving guy that if it said KITCHEN it did not belong in the BATHROOM*, it still was a mess.

"What do you think, Clive? Should we start in here or the living room?" He was curled up on one of the deep windowsills. Admittedly, when I was scouting new places to live, I always looked at the windowsills. Clive was fond of looking out on the world, and it was nice seeing him waiting for me when I came home.

Right now he looked at me, and then seemed to nod toward the living room.

"Okay, living room it is," I said, realizing I'd only spoken three times since waking up this morning, and every word uttered had been directed at a pussy. Ahem...

About twenty minutes later Clive had started a stare-off with a pigeon and I was sorting DVDs when I heard voices in the hallway. My noisy neighbors! I ran to the door, almost tripping over a box, and pressed an eye to the peephole only to see the doorway across the hall. *What a pervert I am, honestly.* But I made no attempt to stop peeping.

I couldn't see very clearly, but I could hear their conversation: the man's voice low and soothing, followed by unmistakable sighing from his companion.

"Mmm, Simon, last night was fantastic."

"I thought this *morning* was fantastic too," he said, planting what sounded like one helluva kiss on her.

Huh. They must have been in another room this morning. I hadn't heard a thing. I pressed my eye back to the peephole. *Dirty pervert.*

"Yes, it was. Call me soon?" she asked, leaning in for another kiss.

"Of course, I'll call you when I'm back in town," he promised, swatting her on her bottom as she giggled again and turned away.

It seemed she was on the short side. *Bye-bye, Spanx.* The angle was wrong for me to see this *Simon*, and he was back in his apartment before I could get any sort of sense of him. *Interesting. So this girl does not live with him.*

I hadn't heard any "I love yous" when she left, but they did seem very comfortable. I chewed absently on my ponytail. They'd have to be, what with the spanking and all.

Pushing thoughts of spanking and Simon from my mind, I went back to my DVDs. *Spanking Simon. What a great name for a band...*I moved on to the Hs.

An hour later I was just placing *Wizard of Oz* after *Willy Wonka* when I heard a knock. There was scuffling in the hallway as I approached the door, and I stifled a grin.

"Don't drop it, you idiot," a sultry voice chided.

"Oh, shut up. Don't be so damn bossy," a second voice snapped back.

Rolling my eyes, I opened the door to find my two best friends, Sophia and Mimi, holding a large box. "No fighting, ladies. You're both pretty." I laughed, raising an eyebrow at them.

"Ha ha. Funny," Mimi answered, staggering inside.

"What the hell is that? I can't believe you guys carried it up four flights of stairs!" My girls did not do manual labor when they could get someone else to do it.

"Believe me, we waited outside in the cab for someone to walk by, but no luck. So we schlepped it ourselves. Happy housewarming!" Sophia said. They set it down, and she fell into the easy chair by the fireplace.

"Yeah, quit moving so much. We're tired of buying you stuff." Mimi laughed, lying down on the couch and placing her arms over her face dramatically.

I poked at the box with my toe and asked, "So what is it? And I never said you had to buy me anything. The Jack LaLanne Juicer was not necessary last year, truly."

"Don't be ungrateful. Just open it," Sophia instructed, pointing at the box with her middle finger, which she then turned upright and displayed in my general direction.

I sighed and sat on the floor in front of it. I knew it was from Williams Sonoma, as it had the telltale ribbon with the tiny pineapple tied to it. The box was heavy, whatever it was.

"Oh, no. What did you two do?" I asked, catching a wink from Mimi to Sophia. Pulling at the ribbon and opening the box, I was pleased as punch with what I found. "You guys, this is too much!"

"We know how much you miss your old one," Mimi laughed, smiling at me.

Years before, I'd been given an old KitchenAid mixer from a great aunt who passed away. It was over forty years old, but still worked great. Those things were built to last, by God, and it had lasted until just a few months ago, when it finally bit it in a big way. It smoked and went wonky one afternoon while mixing a batch of zucchini bread, and as much as I hated to do it, I tossed it out.

Now as I stared into the box, a shiny, new, stainless steel KitchenAid stand mixer staring back at me, visions of cookies and pies began dancing in my head.

"You guys, it's beautiful," I breathed, gazing with delight at my new baby. I lifted it out gently to admire. Running my hands over it, splaying my fingers to feel the smooth lines, I delighted in the cold metal against my skin. I sighed gently and actually hugged it.

"Do you two want to be alone?" Sophia asked.

"No, it's okay. I want you to be here to witness our love. Besides, this is the only mechanical instrument that will likely bring me any pleasure in the near future. Thanks, guys. It's too expensive, but I really appreciate it," I said.

Clive came over, sniffed the mixer, and promptly jumped into the empty box.

"Just promise to bring us yummy treats, and it's all worth it, dear." Mimi sat up, looking at me expectantly.

"What?" I asked warily.

"Caroline, can I please start on your drawers now?" she asked, stutter-stepping her way toward the bedroom.

"Can you start doing what to my drawers?" I answered, pulling my drawstring a little tighter around my waist.

"Your kitchen! I'm *dying* to start placing everything!" she exclaimed, running in place now.

"Oh, hell yes. Have at it! Merry Christmas, freakshow," I called as Mimi ran triumphantly into the other room.

Mimi was a professional organizer. She'd driven us crazy when we were all at Berkley together—with her OCD tendencies and her insane attention to detail. One day Sophia suggested she become a professional organizer, and after graduation, she did just that. She now worked all over the Bay Area helping families get their shit together. The design firm I worked for sometimes had her consult, and she'd even appeared on a few HGTV shows filming in the city. The job suited her to perfection.

So I just let Mimi do her thing, knowing my stuff would be so perfectly arranged I'd be astounded. Sophia and I continued to putz in the living room, laughing over DVDs we'd watched throughout the years. We paused over each and every Brat Pack movie from the eighties, debating whether Bender ended up with Claire once they all went back to school on Monday. I voted no, and I further bet she never got that earring back…

Later that night, after my friends left, I settled on the couch in the living room with Clive to watch reruns of *The Barefoot Contessa* on the Food Network. While dreaming of the creations I'd be whipping up with my new mixer—and how one day I wanted a kitchen like Ina Garten's—I heard footsteps on the landing outside my door, and two voices. I narrowed my eyes at Clive. Spanx must be back.

Springing from the couch, I pressed my eye against the peephole once more, trying to get a look at my neighbor. I missed him again, only seeing his back as he entered his apartment behind a very tall woman with long, brown hair.

Interesting. Two different women in as many days. Manwhore.

I saw the door swing shut and felt Clive curl around my legs, purring.

"No, you can't go out there, silly boy," I cooed, bending down and scooping him up. I rubbed his silky fur against my cheek, smiling as he lay back in my arms. Clive was the manwhore around here. He would lie down for anyone who rubbed his belly.

Returning to the couch, I watched as Barefoot Contessa taught us all how to host a dinner party in the Hamptons with simple elegance—and a Hamptons-size bank account.

A few hours later, with the imprint of the couch cushion pressed firmly into my forehead, I made my way back to my bedroom to go to sleep. Mimi had organized my closet so efficiently that all I had left to do was to hang pictures and arrange a few odds and ends. I quite deliberately removed the pictures from the shelf above my bed. I was taking no chances tonight. I stood in the center of the room, listening for sounds from next door. All quiet on the western front. So far, so good. Maybe last night was a one-time thing.

As I got ready for bed, I looked at the framed pictures of my family and friends: My parents and I skiing in Tahoe. My girls and I at Coit Tower. Sophia loved to take pictures next to anything phallic. She played the cello with the San Francisco Orchestra, and even though she'd been around musical instruments all her life, she could never pass up a joke when she saw a flute. She was twisted.

All three of us were unattached at the moment, something rare. Usually at least one of us was dating someone, but since Sophia had broken up with her last boyfriend a few months ago, we'd all been in a dry spell. Luckily for my friends, their spell wasn't quite as dry as mine. As far as I knew they were still on speaking terms with their Os.

I thought back with a shudder to the night when O and I had parted ways. I'd had a series of bad first dates and was so sexually frustrated that I allowed myself to go back to the apartment of a guy I had no intention of ever seeing again. Not that I was averse to the one-night stand. I'd made the walk of shame many a morning. But this guy? I should have known better. Cory Weinstein, blah blah blah. His family owned a chain of pizza parlors up and down the West Coast. Great on paper, right? Only on paper. He was nice enough, but boring. But I hadn't been with a man in a while, and after several martinis and a pep talk in the car on the way, I relented and let Cory "have his way with me."

Now, up until this point in my life, I'd shared that old theory that sex was like pizza. Even when it's bad, it's still pretty good. I now hated pizza. For several reasons.

This was the worst kind of sex. This was machine-gun style: fast, fast, fast. This was thirty seconds on the tits, sixty seconds on something that was about an inch above where he should have been, and then in. And out. And in. And out. And in. And out.

But at least it was over quick, right? Hell, no. This horrible went on for months. Well, no. But for almost thirty minutes. Of in. And out. And in. And out. My poor hoohah felt like it had been sandblasted.

By the time it was over, and he yelled, "So good!" before collapsing on top of me, I had mentally rearranged all my spices and was starting on the cleaning supplies under the sink. I dressed, which didn't take that long as I was still almost fully clothed, and departed.

The next night, after letting Lower Caroline recover, I decided to treat her to a nice long session of self-love, accented by everyone's favorite fantasy lover, George Clooney, aka Dr. Ross. But to my great regret, O had left the building. I shrugged it off, thinking maybe she just needed a night away, still experiencing a little PTSD from Pizza Parlor Cory.

But the next night? No O. No sign of her that week, or the next. As the weeks became a month, and the months stretched on and on, I developed a deep, seething hatred for Cory Weinstein. That machine-gun fucker…

I shook my head, clearing my O thoughts as I crawled into bed. Clive waited until I was situated before snuggling into the space behind my knees. He let out one last purr as I turned out the lights.

"'Night, Mr. Clive," I whispered and fell right to sleep.

Thump.

"Oh, God."

Thump Thump.

"Oh, God."

Unbelievable…

I woke up faster this time, because I knew what I was hearing. I sat up in bed, glaring behind me. The bed was still pulled safely away from the wall, so I felt no movement, but there was sure as hell something moving over there.

Then I heard…hissing?

I looked down at Clive, whose tail was at full puff. He arched his back and paced back and forth at the foot of the bed.

"Hey, mister. It's cool. We just got a noisy neighbor, that's all," I soothed, stretching my hand out to him. That's when I heard it.

"Meow."

I cocked my head sideways, listening more intently. I studied Clive, who looked back as if to say, "T'weren't me."

"Meow! Oh, God. Me-yow!"

The girl next door was meowing. What in the world was my neighbor packing to make that happen?

Clive, at this point, went utterly bonkers and launched himself at the wall. He was literally climbing it, trying to get to where the noise was coming from, and adding his own meows to the chorus.

"Oooh yes, just like that, Simon…Mmmm…meow, meow, *meow!*"

Sweet Lord, there were out-of-control pussies on both sides of this wall tonight. The woman had an accent, although I couldn't quite place it. Eastern European for sure. Czech? Polish? Was I seriously awake at, let's see, one sixteen a.m. and attempting to discern the national origin of the woman getting plowed next door?

I tried to get a hold of Clive and calm him down. No luck. He was neutered, but he was still a boy, and he wanted what was on the other side of that wall. He continued to caterwaul, his meows mixing with hers until it was all I could to do to not to cry at the hilarity of this moment. My life had become theater of the absurd with a cat chorus.

I pulled myself together because I could now hear *Simon* moaning. His voice was low and thick, and while the woman and Clive continued to call to each other, I listened solely to him. He groaned, and the wall banging began. He was bringing it home.

The woman meowed louder and louder as she undoubtedly climbed toward her climax. Her meows turned into nonsensical screaming, and she finally yelled out, "Da! Da! Da!"

Ah. She was Russian. For the love of St. Petersburg.

One last thump, one last groan—and one last meow. Then all was blessedly silent. Except for Clive. He continued to pine for his lost love until four mother-loving a.m.

The cold war was back on…

chapter three

By the time Clive finally settled down and stopped his cat screaming, I was thoroughly exhausted and wide awake. I had to get up in one more hour anyway, and I realized I'd already gotten whatever sleep I was going to get. I might as well get up and make some breakfast.

"Stupid meower," I said, addressing the wall behind my head, and I padded out into the living room. After switching on the TV, I turned on the coffee maker and studied the pre-dawn light just starting to peek in my windows. Clive curled around my legs, and I rolled my eyes at him.

"Oh, now you want some love from me, huh? After abandoning me for Purina last night? What a jerk you are, Clive," I muttered, stretching out my foot and rubbing him with my heel.

He flopped onto the ground and posed for me. He knew I couldn't resist when he posed. I laughed a little and kneeled next to him. "Yeah, yeah, I know. You love me now because I'm the one that keeps you in vittles," I sighed, scratching his belly.

I headed back into the kitchen, Clive at my heels, and poured some food into a bowl. Now that he had what he needed, I was quickly forgotten. As I headed for the shower, I heard movement in the hallway. Like the Peeping Caroline I was quickly becoming, I pressed my eye to the peephole to see what was happening with Simon and Purina.

He stood just inside his doorway—far enough inside that I couldn't see his face. Purina stood in the hall, and I could see his hand running through her long hair. I could practically hear her purring through the goddamned door.

"Mmm, Simon, last night was…mmmm," she *purred*, leaning into his hand, which was now pressed against her cheek.

"I agree. A fine way to describe the evening *and* this morning," he said quietly as they both chuckled.

Nice. Another twofer.

"Call me when you're back in town?" she asked as he swept her hair back from her face. Her freshly done face. I miss that face.

"Oh, you can count on that," he answered, and then pulled her back into the doorway for what I can only assume was a kiss that killed. Her foot came up like she was posing. I started to roll my eyes, but that hurt. The right one was pressed so firmly against the peephole, you see.

"*Do svidaniya*," she whispered in that exotic accent. It sounded much nicer now that she wasn't caterwauling like a kitten in heat.

"See ya," he laughed, and with that, she gracefully walked away.

I strained to see him before he went back inside, but nope. Missed him again. I had to admit, after the spanking and the meowing, I was dying to see what he looked like. There was some serious sexual prowess going on next door. I just didn't see why it had to affect my sleep habits. I pried myself away from the door and made for the shower. Under the water, I pondered what in the world might be required to make a woman meow.

As seven thirty rolled around, I hopped a cable car and reviewed the day ahead of me. I was meeting a new client, finishing up some details on a project I'd just completed, and having lunch with my boss. I smiled when I thought about Jillian.

Jillian Sinclair headed her own design firm, where I'd had the good fortune to intern during my last year at Berkley. In her late thirties, but looking in her late twenties, she'd made a name for herself in the design community early in her career. She challenged convention, was one of the first to sweep Shabby Chic off the map, and had been an early trendsetter in bringing back the quiet neutrals and geometric prints of the "modern" look that was all the rage now. She hired me after my internship was over, and she'd provided the best experience a young designer could ask for. She was challenging, discerning, had a killer instinct and an even more killer eye for detail. But the best part about working for her? She was fun.

As I jumped off the cable car, I caught sight of my "office." Jillian Designs was in Russian Hill, a beautiful part of town: fairy tale mansions, quiet streets, and a fantastic view from the taller peaks.

Some of the larger old homes had been converted to commercial space, and our building was one of the nicest.

I breathed a sigh when I entered my office. Jillian wanted each designer to make their space their own. It was a way to show potential clients what they could expect, and I'd put a lot of thought into my work space. Deep gray walls were accented by plush, salmon pink curtains. My desk was dark ebony with a chair draped in soft gold and champagne silks. The room was quietly distinguished — with a touch of whimsy coming from my collection of Campbell's Soup ads from the thirties and forties. I'd found a bunch of them at a tag sale, all clipped from old issues of *Life* magazine. I had them mounted and framed, and I still chuckled every time I looked at them.

I spent a few minutes throwing out the flowers from last week and arranging a new display. Every Monday I stopped in a local shop to choose flowers for the week. The blooms changed, but the colors tended to fall within the same palette. I was particularly fond of deep oranges and pinks, peaches and warm golds. Today I had chosen hybrid tea roses of a beautiful coral color, the tips tinged raspberry.

I stifled a yawn and sat down at my desk, preparing for the day. I caught sight of Jillian as she breezed past my door and waved at her. She came back and stuck her head in. Always pulled together, she was tall, lean, and lovely. Today, clad in black top to bottom but for the fuchsia peep-toe pumps she was rocking, she *was* chic.

"Hey, girl! How's the apartment?" she asked, sitting in the chair across from my desk.

"Fantastic. Thank you again so much! I can never repay you for this. You are the best," I gushed.

Jillian had sublet her apartment to me, which she'd had since she moved into the city years ago. Now she was refinishing a house in Sausalito. Rents being what they were in the city, it was a no brainer. The rent control made the price obscenely low. I prepared to gush further when she stopped me with a wave of her hand.

"Shush, it's nothing. I know I should get rid of it, but it was my first grown-up place in the city, and for the rent it would just break my heart to let it go! Besides, I like the idea of it being lived in again. It's such a great neighborhood."

She smiled, and I stifled another yawn. Her sharp eyes caught it.

"Caroline, it's Monday morning. How can you be yawning already?" she chided.

I laughed. "When's the last time you slept there, Jillian?" I looked at her over the rim of my coffee cup. It was my third already. I'd be cruising soon.

"Oh boy, it's been a while. Maybe a year ago? Benjamin was out of town, and I still had a bed over there. Sometimes when I was working late I'd stay in the city overnight. Why do you ask?"

Benjamin was her fiancé. Self-made millionaire, venture capitalist, and knockout gorgeous. My friends and I had a killer crush.

"Did you hear anything from next door?" I asked.

"No, no. I don't think so. Like what?"

"Hmm, just noises. Late-night noises."

"No, not when I was there. I don't know who lives there now, but I think someone moved in last year, maybe? The year before? Never met him. Why? What did *you* hear?"

I blushed furiously and sipped my coffee.

"Wait a minute. *Late-night noises?* Caroline? Seriously? Did you hear some sexy times?" she prodded.

I thumped my head on the desk. Oh, God. Flashbacks. No more thumping. I peeked up at her, and she had her head thrown back in laughter.

"Aw jeez, Caroline. I had no idea! The last neighbor I remember was in his eighties, and the only noise I ever heard coming from that bedroom was reruns of *Gunsmoke*. But come to think of it, I *could* hear that TV show remarkably well..." she trailed off.

"Yes, well, *Gunsmoke* isn't what's coming through those walls now. Straight up sex is coming through those walls. And not sweet, boring sex either. We're talking...interesting." I smiled.

"What did you hear?" she asked, her eyes lighting up.

I don't care how old you are, or what background you come from, there are two universal truths. We will always laugh at...*gas* if it happens at the wrong time, and we are always curious about what goes on in other people's bedrooms.

"Jillian, seriously. It was like nothing I've ever heard before! The first night, they were banging the wall so hard a picture fell off and hit me on the head!"

Her eyes widened, and she leaned forward on my desk. "Shut up!"

"I will not! Then I heard...Jesus, I heard spanking." I was discussing spanking with my boss. Do you see why I love my life?

"Nooo," she breathed, and we giggled like schoolgirls.

"Yeesss. And he made my bed move, Jillian. Made it move! I saw her the next morning, as Spanx was leaving."

"You call her Spanx?"

"You bet! And then last night—"

"Two nights in a row! Spanx got spanked again?"

"Oh no, last night I was treated to a freak of nature I've named Purina," I continued.

"Purina? I don't get it." She frowned.

"The Russian he made *meow* last night."

She laughed again, causing Steve from accounting to stick his head in the door.

"What are you two hens clucking about in here?" he asked, shaking his head.

"Nothing," we answered at the same time, then cracked up again.

"*Two* women in *two* nights, that's impressive," she sighed.

"Come on, impressive? No. Manwhore? Yes."

"Wow, do you know his name?"

"I do, in fact. His name is Simon. I know this because Spanx and Purina kept screaming it over and over again. I could make it out over the banging...Stupid wall banger," I muttered.

She was silent for a moment, and then she grinned. "Simon Wallbanger—I love it!"

"Yeah, you love it. You didn't have your cat trying to mate with Purina through the wall last night." I chuckled ruefully and laid my head back on the desk as we continued to giggle.

"Okay, let's get to work," Jillian finally said, wiping the tears from her eyes. "I need you to land these new clients today. What time are they coming in?"

"Ah, Mr. and Mrs. Nicholson are here at one. I've got the presentation and the plans all ready for them. I think they'll really like the way I redesigned their bedroom. We're going to be able to offer an *en suite* sitting room and an entirely new bathroom. It's pretty great."

"I believe you. Can you run through your ideas with me at lunch?"

"Yep, I'm all over it," I answered as she headed for the door.

"You know, Caroline, if you can land this job, it would be huge for the firm," she said, eying me over her tortoiseshell glasses.

"Just wait until you see what I came up with for their new home theater."

"They don't have a home theater."

"Not yet they don't," I said, arching my eyebrows and grinning devilishly.

"Nice," she appraised and left to start her day.

The Nicholsons were definitely a couple I wanted—everyone did. Mimi had done some work for Natalie Nicholson, blueblood and well heeled, when she reorganized her office last year. She referred me when interior design hit the table, and I immediately started plans for their bedroom remodel.

Wallbanger. Pffft.

"Fantastic, Caroline. Simply fantastic," Natalie raved as I walked her and her husband to the front door. We'd spent almost two hours going through the plans, and while we'd compromised on a few key points, it was going to be an exciting project.

"So, you think you're the right designer for us?" Sam asked, his deep brown eyes twinkling as he wrapped his arm around his wife's waist and played with her ponytail.

"You tell me," I teased back, smiling at the two of them.

"I think we would love to work with you on this project," Natalie said as we shook hands.

I internally high-fived myself, but kept my face composed. "Excellent. I'll be in touch very soon, and we can get started on a schedule," I said as I held the door for them.

I stood in the doorway as I waved them off, then let the door close behind me. I glanced over at Ashley, our receptionist. She raised her eyebrows at me, and I raised mine right back.

"So?" she asked.

"Oh yeah. Nailed it," I sighed, and we both squealed. Jillian came down the stairs as we danced about, and she stopped short. "What the hell happened down here?" she asked, grinning.

"Caroline got hired by the Nicholsons!" Ashley squealed again.

"Nice." Jillian gave me a quick hug. "Proud of you, kid," she whispered, and I beamed. I freaking beamed.

I danced back to my office, putting a little bump and grind in it as I made my way around the desk. I sat down, twirled in my chair, and looked out onto the bay.

Well played, Caroline. Well played.

That night when I went out to celebrate my success with Mimi and Sophia, I may have imbibed more than a few margaritas. I continued with tequila shots, and I was still licking at the now-nonexistent salt on the inside of my wrist as they walked me up my stairs.

"Sophia, you're so pretty. You know that, right?" I cooed, leaning on her as we crawled up the stairs.

"Yes, Caroline, I'm pretty. Good grasp on the obvious," she said. At almost six feet tall with fiery red hair, Sophia was keenly aware her looks.

Mimi laughed, and I turned to her.

"And you, Mimi, you're my best friend. And you're so tiny! I bet I could carry you around in my pocket," I giggled as I tried to find my pocket. Mimi was a petite Filipino, with caramel skin and the blackest hair.

"We should have cut her off after the guacamole left the table," Mimi muttered. "She is never allowed to drink again without food present." She dragged me up the last few steps.

"Don't talk about me like I'm not here," I complained, taking off my jacket and starting in on my shirt.

"Okay, let's not get naked here in the hallway, huh?" Sophia shot back, taking my keys from my purse and opening my door. I tried to kiss her on the cheek, and she pushed me off.

"You smell like tequila and sexual repression, Caroline. Get off me." She laughed and opened my door. As we traveled to the bedroom, I caught sight of Clive on the windowsill.

"Hey there, Clive. How's my big boy?" I sang.

He glared at me and stalked off to the living room. He disapproved of my alcohol use. I stuck my tongue out at him. I flopped down on the bed and surveyed my girls in the doorway. They smirked in that you-are-drunk-and-we-are-not-so-we-judge way.

"Don't act all high and mighty, ladies. I've seen you more drunk than this on many an occasion," I noted, my pants going the way of my blouse. Ask me why I kept my heels on, and I will never be able to tell you.

The two of them pulled down the duvet, and I crawled under the covers and glared. They tucked me in so well that the only things sticking out were my eyeballs, my nostrils, and my messy hair.

"Why is the room spinning? What the hell did you guys do to Jillian's apartment? She'll kill me if I mess up her rent control!" I cried, moaning as I watched the room move.

"The room isn't spinning. Settle down," Mimi chuckled, sitting next to me and patting my shoulder.

"And that thumping, what the hell is that thumping?" I whispered into Mimi's armpit, which I then sniffed and complimented her deodorant choice.

"Caroline, there's no thumping. Jesus, you must have had more than we thought!" Sophia exclaimed, settling down at the end of the bed.

"No, Sophia, I hear it too. You can't hear that?" Mimi said in a hushed voice.

Sophia was quiet, and all three of us listened. There was a distinct thump, and then an unmistakable groan.

"Kittens, lay back. You are about to get Wallbanged," I stated.

Sophia and Mimi's eyes grew wide, but they stayed quiet.

Would it be Spanx? Purina? Anticipating the latter, Clive entered the room and jumped up on the bed. He stared at the wall with rapt attention.

The four of us sat and waited. I can barely describe what we were subjected to this time.

"Oh, God."

Thump.

"Oh, God."

Thump thump.

Mimi and Sophia looked at Clive and me. We just shook our heads—both of us, really. A slow smile spread across Sophia's face. I focused on the voice coming through the wall. It was different... The pitch was lower, and, well, I couldn't really make out exactly what she was saying. It wasn't Spanx *or* Purina...

"Mmm, Simon—" *giggle* "—right—" *giggle* "—there!" *giggle.*
Huh?

"Yes, yes—" *snort* "—yes! Fuck, fuck—" *giggle-hee haw* "—fuck, yes!"

She was giggling. She was a dirty, dirty giggler.

The three of us tittered along with her as she giggled and snorted her way toward what sounded like one helluva climax. Clive, realizing quickly that his beloved wasn't making an appearance, beat a hasty retreat to the kitchen.

"What the hell is this?" Mimi whispered, her eyes as wide as apple pies.

"This is the sexual torture I've been listening to for the last two nights. You have no idea," I growled, feeling the effects of the tequila.

"LaughyPants has been getting done like this for the last two nights?" Sophia cried, slapping her hand over her mouth as more moaning laughter filtered through the wall.

"Oh, hell no. Tonight is the first night I've had the pleasure of this one. The first night was Spanx. She was a naughty, naughty girl and needed to be punished. And last night Clive met the love of his life when Purina made her debut—"

"Why do you call her Purina?" Sophia interrupted.

"Because she meows when he makes her come," I said, hiding under the covers. My buzz was beginning to fade, replaced by the distinct lack of sleep I'd experienced since moving into this den of debauchery.

Sophia and Mimi peeled the covers from my face just as the chick screamed, "Oh, God that's...that's—" *hahahaha* "—so good!"

"The guy next door can make a woman meow?" Sophia asked, raising an eyebrow.

"Apparently so," I chuckled, feeling the first wave of nausea wash over me.

"Why is she laughing? Why would anyone be laughing while they're getting done like that?" Mimi asked.

"No idea, but it's nice to hear she's enjoying herself," Sophia said, laughing herself at a particularly loud guffaw. *Guffaw my aunt Fanny...*

"Have you seen this guy yet?" asked Mimi, still staring at the wall.

"Nope. My peephole is getting a workout, though."

"Glad to hear at least one hole is getting some around here," Sophia muttered.

I glared at her. "Charming, Sophia. I've seen the back of his head, and that's it," I answered, sitting up.

"Wow, three girls in three nights. That's some kind of stamina," Mimi said, still looking in wonder at the wall.

"It's some kind of disgusting is what it is. I can't even sleep at night! My poor wall!" I wailed as I heard a deep groan from *him*.

"Your wall, what does your *wall* have to do—" Sophia began, and I held up my hand.

"Wait for it, please," I said. He began to bring it on home.

The wall began to shake with the rhythmic banging, and the woman's giggles got louder and louder. Sophia and Mimi stared in wonder, as I just shook my head.

I could hear Simon moaning, and I knew he was getting close. But his sounds were quickly drowned out by this evening's friend.

"Oh—" *giggle* "—that's—" *giggle* "—it—" *giggle* "—don't—" *giggle* "—stop—" *giggle* "—don't—" *giggle* "—stop—" *giggle* "—oh—" *giggle-snort* "—God—" *giggle-giggle snort-snort* "—don't—" *giggle* "—stop!" *giggle*.

Please. Please. Please, stop, I thought.

Giggle-sniffle.

And with one last giggle and groan, silence fell across the land. Sophia and Mimi looked at each other, and Sophia said, "Oh."

"My," added Mimi.

"God," they said together.

"And *that's* why I can't sleep," I sighed.

While the three of us recovered from the Giggler, Clive returned to play in the corner with a cotton ball.

Giggler, I think I hate you most of all...

chapter four

The next few nights were blissfully quiet. No thumping, no spanking, no meowing, and no giggling. Admittedly Clive was a little forlorn from time to time, but everything else around the apartment was great. I met some of my neighbors, including Euan and Antonio who lived downstairs. I hadn't heard or seen Simon since that last night with the Giggler, and while I was grateful for the nights of perfect sleep, I was curious about where he'd disappeared to. Euan and Antonio were only too glad to fill me in.

"Darling, wait until you see our dear Simon. What a specimen that boy is!" Euan exclaimed. Antonio had caught me in the hall on my way home and had a cocktail in my hand within seconds.

"Oh my, yes. He is exquisite! If only I were a few years younger," Antonio crooned, fanning himself as Euan looked over his Bloody Mary at him.

"If you were a few years younger you'd what? Please. You'd never have been in Simon's league. He is filet while—face it, love—you and I are tube steaks."

"You would know," Antonio cackled, sucking pointedly on his celery stalk.

"Gentleman, please. Tell me about this guy. I admit, after the show he put on last week, I'm a little intrigued about the man behind the wall banging."

I'd broken down and told them about Simon's late-night antics after realizing that unless I dished the dirt, they would not reciprocate. They clung to every word like fat kids at a buffet. I told them about the ladies he made the sweet love to, and they filled in a few more blanks.

Simon was a freelance photographer who traveled all over the world. They guessed he was currently on assignment, which explained my quality sleep. Simon worked on projects for The Discovery Channel, The Cousteau Society, *National Geographic*—all the bigwigs. He'd won awards for his work and even spent some time covering the war in Iraq a few years ago. He always left his car behind when he was traveling: an old, beat-up, black Range Rover Discovery, like the kind you'd find in the African bush. The kind people drove before the yuppies got a hold of them.

Between what Euan and Antonio told me, the car, the job, and the international house of orgasms from the other side of the wall, I was beginning to piece together a profile of this man, who I still had yet to see. And I'd be lying if I said I wasn't more and more intrigued by the day.

Late one afternoon, after dropping off some tile samples at the Nicholsons, I decided to walk home. The fog had burned off, revealing the city, and it was a nice evening for a stroll. As I rounded the corner to my apartment, I noticed the Range Rover was absent from its usual place behind the building. Which meant it was out and about.

Simon was back in San Francisco.

Although I braced myself for another round of wall banging, the next few days were uneventful. I worked, I walked, I Clived. I went out with my girls, I made a great zucchini bread in my now well-broken-in KitchenAid, and I spent time researching my vacation.

Each year, I took a week and vacationed somewhere totally alone. Somewhere exciting, and I never went to the same place twice. One year I spent a week hiking in Yosemite. One year I went zip-lining through a rain forest canopy at an ecolodge in Costa Rica. Another year I spent a week scuba diving off the coast of Belize. And this year…I wasn't sure where I was going to go. Going to Europe was becoming prohibitively expensive in this economy, so that was out. I was considering Peru, as I'd always wanted to see Machu Picchu. I had plenty of time, but often half the fun was deciding where I wanted to spend my vacation.

I also spent an inordinate amount of time at my peephole. Yes, it's true. Whenever I heard a door close, I actually ran to my door. Clive looked on with a smirk. He knew exactly what I was up to. Why he was judging me, however, I will never know, as his ears perked up every time he heard noises coming up the stairs. He was still pining for his Purina.

I still hadn't actually *seen* Simon. One day I got to the peephole in time to see him going into his apartment, but all I caught was a black T-shirt and a mess of dark hair. And even that could've been dark blond—hard to tell in the muted hallway light. I needed brighter lighting for better sleuthing.

Another time I saw the Range Rover pulling away from the curb as I came around the corner on my way home from work. It was going to pass right by! Just as I was about to get the first peek at him, actually *see* the man behind the myth, I tripped and went ass over applecart on the sidewalk. Luckily Euan spotted me and helped me, my bruised ego, and my bruised bum off the concrete and inside for some Bactine with a whiskey chaser.

But all remained quiet at night. I knew Simon was home, and I could hear him occasionally: a chair leg moving across the floor, a quiet laugh or two. But no harem, and therefore no wallbanging.

However, we did sleep together most nights. He played Duke Ellington and Glenn Miller on his side of the wall, and I lay in bed on my side listening shamelessly. My grandpa used to play his old records at nighttime, and the pop and crackle of a needle on vinyl was comforting as I fell asleep, Clive curled up at my side. I'll say this for Simon: he had good taste in music.

But this calm and quiet was too good to last, and all hell broke loose again a few nights later.

First, I was treated to another round of Spanx. She had once again been a very bad girl and certainly deserved the resounding spanking she received—a spanking that lasted almost half an hour and ended with calls of, "That's it! Right there. God, yes, right there!" before the actual walls began to shake. I'd lain awake that night, rolling my eyes and growing more and more frustrated.

The next morning, from my post at the peephole, I saw Spanx leaving and got my first really good look at her. Pink-faced and glowing, she was a soft, round little bit of a girl with curvy hips and thighs, and packing some serious junk in the trunk. She was short—really short—and a little plump. She had to stand on tiptoes as she kissed Simon goodbye, and I missed seeing him because I watched her walk away. I marveled at his taste in women. She was the total opposite of what I'd seen of Purina, who looked like a model.

Anticipating that Purina was soon up on the roster, the following night I gave Clive a sock full of catnip and a bowlful of tuna. My hope was to get him wasted and passed out before the action started. The treats had the opposite effect. My boy was ready to party down when the first strains of Purina came shrieking through the walls about one fifteen in the morning.

If Clive could have put on a mini smoking jacket, he would have.

He stalked the room, pacing back and forth in front of the wall, playing it cool. When Purina began her meows, though, he couldn't contain himself. He once again launched toward the wall. He jumped from nightstand to dresser to shelf, scaling pillows and even a lamp to get closer to his beloved. When he realized he would never be able to burrow under the plaster, he serenaded her with some weird kind of kitty Barry White, his yowls matching hers in intensity.

When the walls began to shake, and Simon was bringing it on home, I was amazed they could maintain their control and focus with the racket going on. Clearly, if I could hear them, they must have been able to hear Clive and all his carrying on. Although if I were impaled on the Wallbanger Wondercock, I imagine I could compartmentalize as well…

For now, though, I was impaled on nothing and getting angry. I was tired, I was horny with no release in sight, and my cat had a Q-Tip sticking out of his mouth that looked frighteningly like a tiny cigarette.

After an abbreviated night's sleep, the next morning I dragged myself to the peephole for another round of HaremWatch. I was rewarded with a brief side profile of Simon as he leaned in to kiss Purina goodbye. It was quick, but it was enough to see the jaw: strong, defined, good. He gave great jaw. The best thing about that day was the jaw sighting. The rest of the day was shit.

First, there was a problem with the general contractor over at the Nicholson house. It seems he was not only taking extremely long lunch breaks, he was actually blazing it up in their attic every day. The whole third floor smelled like a Dead concert.

Then, an entire pallet of tiles for the bathroom floor arrived cracked and chipped. The amount of time needed to reorder and reship would set the entire project back at least two weeks, leaving no possibility of finishing on time. Any time major construction takes place, the project end date is an *estimated* time of completion. However, I had never missed a deadline, and this being such a high-profile job, it made me very warm (not in a good way) to realize there was nothing I could do to speed things up short of flying to Italy and bringing back those tiles my damn self.

After a quick lunch, during which I spilled an entire soda all over the floor and thoroughly embarrassed myself, I headed back toward work and stopped in a store to look at some new hiking boots. I had plans to go hiking over in the Marin headlands this weekend.

As I examined the selection, I felt warm breath in my ear that I instinctively flinched against.

"Hey you," I heard, and I froze in terror. Flashbacks poured over me, and I saw spots. I felt cold and hot at the same time, and the single most horrifying experience of my life passed through my mind. I turned and saw...

Cory Weinstein. The machine-gun fucker who'd hijacked the O.

"Caroline, lookin' good in the neighborhood," he crooned, channeling his inner Tom Jones.

I swallowed back bile and struggled to keep my composure. "Cory, good to see you. How are you?" I managed.

"Can't complain. Just touring restaurants for the old man. How are you? How's the decorating business treating you?"

"Design business, and it's good. In fact, I was just on my way back to work, so if you'll excuse me," I sputtered, beginning to push past him.

"Hey, no rush, pretty thing. Have you had lunch? I can get you a discount on some pizza just a few blocks away. How does five percent off sound to you?" he said. If it was possible for a voice to swagger, his did.

"Wow, five percent. As much as that does sweeten the pot, I'm gonna pass," I chuckled.

"So, Caroline, when can I see you again? That night...damn. It was pretty great, huh?" he winked, and my skin begged me to tear it from my body and throw it at him.

"No. No, Cory. And hell no." I blurted, the bile rising again. Flashes of in and out and in and out and in and out. My hoohah shrieked in its own defense. Granted, the two of us were not on great terms, but nevertheless I knew how afraid she was of the machine gun. Not on my watch.

"Oh, come on, baby. Let's make some magic," he cooed.

He leaned in, and I could tell he'd had sausage recently. "Cory, you should know I'm about to vomit on your shoes, so I'd back up if I were you."

He blanched and stepped away.

"And for the record, I'd rather staple my head to the wall than make *magic* with you again. You and me and your five-percent discount? Not going to happen. Bye-bye now," I said through clenched teeth and stalked out of the store.

I stomped back to work, angry and alone. No Italian tiles, no hiking boots, no man, and no O.

I spent the night on the couch in a funk. I didn't answer the phone. I didn't make dinner. I ate leftover Thai from the takeout container and growled back at Clive when he tried to sneak a shrimp. He flounced to the corner and glared at me from under a chair.

I watched Barefoot Contessa, which usually cheered me up. Tonight she made French onion soup and took it to the beach for lunch with her husband, Jeffrey. Normally watching the two of them made me all warm and fuzzy inside. They were so cute. Tonight they made me nauseous. *I* wanted to be sitting on the beach in South Hampton, wrapped in a blanket and eating soup with Jeffrey. Well, not Jeffrey per se, but a Jeffrey equivalent. My own Jeffrey.

Fucking Jeffrey. Fucking Barefoot Contessa. Fucking lonely takeout.

When it was late enough that I could justify going to bed and putting this terrible day behind me, I dragged my sad-sack self back to my bedroom. I went to get my pjs, and realized I hadn't done any laundry. Dammit. I dug around in my jammies drawer, looking for something, anything. I had plenty of sexy little numbers, from back in the day when O and I were on the same page.

I grumbled and fumed and finally pulled out a pink baby doll nightie. It was frilly and sweet, and while I used to love to sleep in beautiful lingerie, I currently hated it. It was a physical reminder of my missing O. Although, it had been a while since I'd attempted to contact her. Maybe tonight would be the night. I was certainly tense. No one could use the release more than me.

I shooshed Clive out and closed the door. No one needed to see this.

I turned on some INXS, since tonight I needed all the help I could get. Michael Hutchence always got me close. I climbed into bed, arranged the pillows behind me, and slipped between the sheets. In the tiny nightie, my bare legs slid along the cool cotton. There's nothing like the feeling of freshly shaved legs on high-thread-count sheets. Maybe this was a good idea after all. I closed my eyes and tried to slow my breathing. The last few times I'd attempted to find the O, I was so thoroughly frustrated that by the end I was near tears.

Tonight I began with the usual fantasy roundup. I started with a little Catalano, allowing my hands to slip under the bottom of my nightie and come up to my breasts. As I thought of Jordan Catalano/Jared Leto kissing Angela Chase in the basement of the school, I imagined it was me. I felt his kisses thick and heavy on my lips, and it became his hands sliding up my skin toward my nipples. As my/Jordan's fingers began to massage, I felt that familiar tug low in my tummy, getting warm all over.

With my eyes still closed, the image changed to Jason Bourne/Matt Damon attacking my skin. With the two of us on the run from the government, only our physical connection kept us alive. My/Jason's fingers trailed lightly down my belly, sliding inside my matching panties. I could feel it working. My touch was waking something, stirring something inside. I gasped when I felt how ready I was for Jason, and for Jordan.

Jesus. The thought of the two of them together, working to bring back the O made me actually twitch. I moaned and went for the big guns.

I went Clooney. Flashes of Clooney came to me as my fingers teased and twirled, twisted and taunted. Danny Ocean...George from *Facts Of Life*...

And then, I went for it.

Dr. Ross. Third season of *ER*, after the Caesar haircut had been rectified. Mmmm...I moaned and groaned. It was working. I was actually getting really turned on. For the first time in months, my brain and the rest of me seemed to be in tune. I rolled onto my side, hand between my legs as I saw Dr. Ross kneeling before me. He licked his lips and asked me when was the last time anyone had made me scream.

You have no idea. Make me scream, Dr. Ross.

Behind tightly closed eyes, I saw him lean toward me, his mouth getting closer and closer. He gently pressed my knees farther apart, placing kisses on the inside of each thigh. I could actually feel his breath on my legs, which made me shiver.

His mouth opened, and that perfect Clooney tongue flickered out to taste me.

Thump.

"Oh, God."

Thump thump.

"Oh, God."

No. No. *No!*

"Simon...mmm—" *giggle.*

I couldn't believe it. Even Dr. Ross looked confused.

"So—" *giggle* "—fucking—" *giggle* "—good...hahahaha!"

I groaned as I felt Dr. Ross leaving me. I was wet, I was frustrated, and now Clooney thought someone was laughing at him. He began to back away...

No, don't leave me, Dr Ross. Not you!

"That's it! That's it! Oh...oh...hahahahaha!"

The walls began to shake, and the bed-thumping began.

That's it. Giggle this, bitch...

I scrambled to my feet, the Catalano and the Bourne and the ever-loving Clooney fading away in wisps of testosterone-laden smoke. I threw back the covers, whipped open the door, and stalked out of my bedroom. Clive held out a paw and started to reproach me for shutting him out, but when he saw my face, he wisely let me pass.

I stomped to my front door, my heels pounding into the hardwood floor. I was beyond angry. I was livid. I'd been *so* close. I opened my front door with the strength of a thousand angry Os, denied release for centuries. I began to pound on his door. I pounded hard and long, like Clooney had been about to pound into me. I banged again and again, never relenting, never letting up. I could hear feet slapping toward the door, but still I didn't let up. The frustration of the day and the week and the months without an O unleashed itself in a tirade the likes of which no one had ever seen.

I heard locks rattling and chains coming undone, but still onward I banged. I began to yell. "Open this door, you asshole, or I will come through the wall!"

"Take it easy. Quit that banging," I heard Simon say.

Then the door swung open, and I stared. There he was. Simon.

Silhouetted by soft light from behind, Simon stood with one hand grasping the door and the other hand holding a white sheet around his hips. I looked him over from top to bottom, my hand still hanging the air, clenched into a fist. It was pulsing, I'd been banging so hard.

He had jet black hair that stood straight up, likely from the Giggler's hands buried in it as he plowed into her. His eyes were piercing blue, and cheekbones just as strong as the jaw. Completing the package? Kiss-swollen lips, and what looked like about three days of scruff.

Jesus, there was scruff. How had I missed that this morning?

I gazed down his long, lean body. He was tan, but not a premeditated tan — outdoorsy tan, weathered tan, *manly tan*. His chest rose and fell as he panted, his skin coated in a thin sheen of sex sweat. As my eyes traveled down further I saw a smattering of dark hair low on his torso, which led below the sheet. Below the six pack. Below that V that some men have, and which on him didn't look weird or BowFlexed.

He was stunning. Of course he was stunning. And why did there have to be scruff?

I inadvertently gasped as my gaze dropped lower than I had intended. But my eyes were drawn, as if by a magnet, lower and lower. Beneath the sheet — which was already lower on his hips than should be legal —

He

Was

Still

Hard.

chapter five

"**O**h, God."

Thump.

"Oh, God."

Thump thump.

I was traveling up the bed with the strength of his thrusts. He drove into me with unflinching force, giving me exactly what I could take, then pushing me just past that edge. He stared down at me, hard, flashing a knowing smirk. I closed my eyes, letting myself feel how deeply I was being affected. And by deep, I mean deep...

He grasped my hands and brought them above my head to the headboard.

"You're gonna wanna hold on tight for this," he whispered and threw one of my legs up over his shoulder as he altered the rhythm of his hips.

"Simon!" I shrieked, feeling my body begin to spasm. His eyes, those damnable blue eyes, bore into mine as I shook around him.

"Mmm, Simon!" I screamed again. And promptly woke up—with my arms over my head, hands tightly grasping the headboard.

I closed my eyes for a moment and forced my fingers to uncurl. When I looked again I could see dents in my hands from gripping so tightly.

I struggled to sit up. I was covered in sweat and panting. I was actually panting. I found the sheets in a ball at the foot of the bed with Clive buried underneath, just his nose peeking out.

"Oh, Clive, are you hiding?"

"Meow," came the angry reply, and a tiny face followed the kitty nose.

"You can come out, silly. Mommy's done screaming. I think." I chuckled, running a hand through my damp hair.

I had charmingly sweated through my pjs, so I got up to stand over the A/C vent, cooling off and beginning to calm down. "That was close, huh, O?" I grimaced, pressing my legs together and feeling a not-unpleasant ache between my thighs.

Ever since the night Simon and I "met" in the hallway, I couldn't stop dreaming about him. I didn't want to, *really* didn't want to, but my unconscious mind had taken over and was having her way with him. Nocturnally. My body and brain were separate on this one: Brain knew better, Lower Caroline was not so sure...

Clive pushed past me and ran into the kitchen to do his little dance next to his bowl.

"Yah yah yah, settle down," I croaked as he threaded himself in and out of my ankles. I dumped a scoop of kibble in his bowl and hit the coffee. I settled against the counter and tried to collect myself. I was *still* breathing a little hard.

That dream had been...well, it had been intense. I thought again of his body perched over mine, a bead of sweat rolling off his nose and dropping onto my chest. He'd lowered himself and dragged his tongue up my stomach, toward my breasts, and then...

Ping! Ping!

Mr. Coffee brought me back from my saucy thoughts, and I was grateful. I could feel myself getting worked up again. *Is this going to be a problem?*

I poured a cup of coffee, peeled a banana, and looked out the window. I ignored my compulsion to massage the banana and thrust it into my mouth. Oh, sweet Christ, the thrusting! This was headed south fast. And by south I mean...

I slapped myself in the face and forced my mind to think of something besides the manwhore I was currently sharing a wall with. Inane things. Innocuous things.

Puppy dogs...doggy style.

Ice cream cones...licking his cone and two scoops.

Children's games…damn, did I want to do whatever Simon Says…Okay, enough! *Now you aren't even trying.*

While showering I sang *The Star Spangled Banner* over and over again to keep my hands from doing anything other than washing up. I needed to remember what an asshole he was—not how he looked in only a sheet and a grin. I closed my eyes and leaned into the spray, remembering that night again. Once I'd stopped staring at his, well, his below the sheet, I'd opened my mouth to speak:

"Now look here, mister, do you have any idea how loud you are? I need my sleep! If I have to listen to one more night, one more *minute*, in fact, of you and your harem banging away on my wall, I'll go insane!"

I yelled to release all the tension that would have, could have, *should* have been released already in a very Clooney way.

"Just settle down. It can't be that bad. These walls are pretty thick." He grinned, pumping his fist against the doorframe and trying to unleash a little charm. He was clearly used to getting what he wanted. With abs like that, I could see why.

I shook my head to impart focus. "Are you out of your mind? The walls are not nearly as thick as your head. I can hear everything! Every spank, every meow, every giggle, and I have had it! This shit ends now!" I screeched, feeling my face burn with fury. I'd even used air quotes to emphasize the spank, meow, and giggle.

As I spoke of his harem, he began to downshift from charm to chastise. "Hey, that's about enough!" he shot back. "What I do in my home is my business. I'm sorry if I disturbed you, but you can't just come over here in the middle of the night and dictate what I can and can't do! You don't see me coming across the hall and banging on your door."

"No, you just bang on my damn wall. We share a bedroom wall. You're right up against me when I'm trying to sleep. Have some common courtesy."

"Well, how come you can hear me and I can't hear you? Wait, wait, there's no one banging on your walls, is there?"

He smirked, and I felt the color drain from my face. I crossed my arms tightly across my chest, and as I looked down, I remembered what I was wearing.

Pink baby doll nightie. What a way to establish credibility.

As I fumed, his eyes drifted down my body, unabashedly taking in the pink and the lace and the way my hip jutted out as I tapped my foot angrily.

His eyes finally came back up, and he met my stare, not backing down. Then with a twinkle in those baby blues, he winked at me.

I saw red. "*Oooohhh!*" I'd screamed and slammed back into my apartment.

Mortified now, I let the water wash away my frustration. I hadn't seen him since, but what if I did? I thumped my head against the tiles.

When I opened the front door forty-five minutes later, I tossed a goodbye to Clive over my shoulder and prayed silently that there'd be no random harem girls in the hallway. All clear.

I pushed my sunglasses on as I walked out the door of the building, barely noticing the Range Rover. And by barely, I mean I barely noticed that *rover* rhymed with *over*, as in bend me *over* the chair in my family room and—

Caroline!

I might have a problem here.

Later that afternoon Jillian stuck her head inside my office. "Knock, knock," she said, smiling.

"Hey! What's going on?" I leaned back in my chair.

"Ask me about the house in Sausalito."

"Hey, Jillian, how's the house in Sausalito?" I asked, rolling my eyes.

"Done," she whispered and threw her arms in the air.

"Shut up!" I whispered back.

"Totally, completely, absolutely done!" She squealed and sat down across from me.

I offered a fist bump across the desk. "Now *that* is some good news. We need to celebrate." I reaching into a drawer.

"Caroline, if you pull out a bottle of scotch, I'm going to have to consult human resources," she warned, a grin twitching.

"First of all, you *are* human resources. And second of all, like I would keep scotch in my office! Obviously that's in a flask lashed to my thigh," I giggled, producing a Blow Pop.

"Nice. Watermelon even. My favorite," she said as we unwrapped and began to suck.

"So, tell me all about it," I prompted.

I'd been consulting a little with Jillian as she chose the final touches on the house she and Benjamin has been renovating, and I knew it was just the kind of house I'd been dreaming of for years. Like Jillian, it would be warm, inviting, elegant, and filled with light.

We talked shop for a while, and then she let me get back to work.

"By the way, housewarming next weekend. You and your posse are invited," she said on her way out the door.

"Did you just say posse?" I asked.

"I might have. You in?"

"Sounds great. Can we bring anything, and can we stare at your fiancé?"

"Don't you dare, and I would expect nothing less," she fired back.

I smiled as I went back to work. Party in Sausalito? Sounded promising.

"You don't seriously have a crush on him do you? I mean, how many dreams have you had about him?" Mimi asked, sucking on her straw.

"A crush? No, he's an asshole! Why would I—"

"Of course she doesn't. Who knows where that dick has been? Caroline would never," Sophia answered for me, tossing her hair over her shoulder and stunning stupid a table of businessmen who'd been staring since she walked in. We'd met for lunch at our favorite little bistro in North Beach.

Mimi settled back into her chair and giggled, kicking me under the table.

"Piss off, pipsqueak." I stared hard at her, blushing furiously.

"Yeah, piss off, pipsqueak! Caroline knows better than to…" Sophia laughed then trailed off, finally taking off her sunglasses and switching her gaze to me.

The cellist and the pipsqueak watched me fidget. One smiled and the other swore.

"Ah, jeez, Caroline, do not tell me you are crushing on that guy? Oh no, you are, aren't you?" Sophia huffed as the waiter set down a bottle of Pellegrino. He stared at her as she ran her fingers through her hair, and she waved him away with a carefully aimed wink. She knew how men looked at her, and it was fun to watch her make them squirm.

Mimi was different. She was so tiny and cute that initially men were drawn in by her innate charm. Then they really got a look at her and realized she was lovely. Something about her made men want to take care of her and protect her—until they got her to the bedroom. Or so I'd been told. Crazytown that one was…

I'd been told I was pretty, and on some days I believed it. On a good day I knew I could work it. I never felt as hot as Sophia or as perfectly pulled together as Mimi, but I cleaned up good. I knew when the three of us went out we could really work a scene, and until recently we'd used this to our advantage.

We each had very distinct types, which was good. We rarely went for the same guy.

Sophia was very particular. She liked her men long, lean, and pretty. She liked them not too tall, but taller than her. She wanted her men polite and smart, and preferably with blond hair. It was her true weakness. She also was a sucker for a southern accent. Seriously, if a guy called her "sugar," she'd wet herself. I had firsthand knowledge of this because I'd messed with her one night when she was wasted using my best Oklahoma accent. I had to fight her off the rest of the evening. She *claimed* it was college, and she wanted to experiment.

Mimi, on the other hand, was particular, but not with a specific look. She went for overall size. She liked her men big, huge, tall, and strong. She loved when they had to pick her up to kiss her, or stand her on a stool so they didn't get neck cramps. She liked her men a little on the sarcastic side and hated condescending. Because she was small, she had a tendency to draw types that wanted to "protect." But girlfriend had been taking karate since she was a kid, and she needed no one's protection. She was a badass in a retro skirt.

I was harder to pin down, but I knew him when I saw him. Like the Supreme Court and pornography, I was aware. I did have a tendency toward outdoorsy guys—lifeguards, scuba divers, rock climbers. I liked them clean cut, but a little shaggy, gentlemanly with a touch of bad boy, and making enough money that I didn't have to play mommy. I'd spent a summer with a hotter-than-hell surfer who couldn't afford his own peanut butter. Even Micah's round-the-clock orgasms couldn't save him when I found out he'd been using my AmEx to pay for his sex wax. And his cell phone bill. And his trip to Fiji that I wasn't even invited on. To the curb, surfer boy. To the curb.

I might have taken one more for the road before he left though. Ahh, the days before O's departure. Round-the-clock orgasms. Sigh.

"So, wait a minute, have you seen him since the hallway encounter?" Sophia asked after we'd ordered and I'd come back from my surfer memories.

"No," I groaned.

Mimi patted my arm soothingly. "He's cute, isn't he?"

"Dammit—yes! Too cute for his own good. He's such an asshole!" I slammed my hand down on the table so hard I made the silverware bounce. Sophia and Mimi exchanged a glance, and I showed them my middle finger.

"And then that morning, he's in the hallway with Purina, kissing on her! It's like some sick, twisted orgasm town going over there, and I want no part of it!" I said, chewing furiously on my lettuce after telling them the story for the third time.

"I can't believe Jillian didn't warn you about this guy," Sophia mused, pushing her croutons around on her plate. She was on a no-bread thing again, terrified of the five pounds she claimed she'd put on in the last year. She was full of it, but there was no arguing with Sophia when she set her mind to something.

"No, no, she says she doesn't know this guy," I reported. "He must've moved in since the last time she was there. I mean, she hardly ever stayed in that place. They just kept it so they always had a place to stay in the city. According to the neighbors, he's only been in the building a year or so. And he travels all the time." As I spoke, I realized I'd compiled quite a dossier on this guy.

"So has he been wall banging at all this week?" Sophia asked.

"Relatively quiet, actually. Either he really listened to me and is being neighborly, or his dick finally broke off in one of them and he's sought medical attention," I said, a little too loudly. The table of businessmen must've been listening pretty closely as they all choked a little just then and shifted in their seats, perhaps crossing their legs in unwitting sympathy. We giggled and continued our lunch.

"Speaking of Jillian, you guys are invited out to the house in Sausalito next weekend for their housewarming party," I informed them.

They both immediately fanned themselves. Benjamin was the one guy we all agreed on. Whenever we'd plied Jillian with enough liquor, we'd confess our crush to her and make her tell us stories about him. If we were lucky and had managed to get an extra martini into her…well, let's just say it was nice to know sex continued to be worth doing even after your man was well into his forties. The one about Benjamin and the Tonga Room at the Fairmont Hotel? Wow. She was a lucky woman.

"That'll be cool. Why don't we come over and get ready at your place, like the old days?" Mimi squealed as Sophia and I plugged our ears.

"Yes, yes, that's fine, but no more squealing or we'll leave your ass with the bill," Sophia scolded as Mimi settled back into her seat, eyes sparkling.

After lunch, Mimi walked toward her next appointment around the corner, and Sophia and I shared a cab.

"So, naughty dreams about your neighbor. Let's hear it," she began, to the great delight of the cab driver.

"Eyes on the road, sir," I instructed as I caught him looking at us in the rear view mirror.

I let my thoughts drift to the dreams, which had come every night for the past week. I, on the other hand, had not — ratcheting up my sexual frustration to a critical point. When I could ignore the O, I was okay. Now that I was treated to dreams of Simon every night, O's absence was even more pronounced. Clive had taken to sleeping on top of the dresser, safer with my flailing legs, you see.

"The dreams? The dreams are good, but he's such an asshole!" I exclaimed, thumping my fist on the door.

"I know. That's what you keep saying," she added, looking at me carefully.

"What? What is that look?"

"Nothing. Just looking at you. You're awfully worked up over someone who's an asshole," she said.

"I know." I sighed, looking out the window.

"You're poking me."

"I am not."

"Seriously, what the hell is in your pocket, Mimi? Are you packing?" Sophia exclaimed, jerking her head away as Mimi pressed the curling iron through her hair.

I smiled from my place on the bed, lacing up my sandals. I'd put my own hair up in rollers before the girls got here, so I'd been spared the full treatment. Mimi fancied herself some kind of beauty school dropout, and if she could've opened a shop in her bedroom, she'd have given it some careful thought.

Mimi produced a brush from her pocket and showed it to Sophia before starting to tease. With the brush, that is.

We were pre-partying just like we did at Berkeley, right down to the frozen daiquiris. Although we'd upgraded to the good alcohol and freshly squeezed lime juice, it still made us a little hyper and slaphappy.

"Come on, come on—you never know who you might meet tonight! You don't want to meet Prince Charming with flat hair, do you?" Mimi reasoned as she forced Sophia to flip her hair over to "get some lift at the crown." You didn't argue—you just let her do it.

"I'm not flat anywhere. If these girls are on display, Prince Charming won't even notice I *have* hair," Sophia muttered, which sent me into another gale of giggles. Then over our laughter, I heard voices from next door. I got up off the bed and went closer to the wall where I could hear better. This time instead of just Simon, there were two other distinctly male voices. I couldn't make out what they were saying, but suddenly Guns N' Roses came blaring through the walls loud enough to make Sophia and Mimi stop what they were doing.

"What the hell is that?" Sophia snapped, looking wildly around the room.

"Simon's a GN'R fan, I guess." I shrugged, secretly enjoying being welcomed to the jungle. I put a headband low on my forehead and did Axl's crab dance back and forth, much to the delight of Mimi and the scorn of Sophia.

"No, no, no—that's not it, fool," Sophia scolded over the music and grabbed another headband. Mimi screamed with laughter as Sophia and I Axl-battled. Until, of course, Sophia started to mess up her hair. Then Mimi lunged. Sophia jumped on the bed to get away from her, and I joined her. We jumped up and down, shrieking the lyrics now and dancing wildly. Mimi finally gave in, and all three of us danced like mad fools. I started to feel the bed moving underneath us, and I realized it was banging merrily against the wall—Simon's wall.

"Take that! And *that!* And a little of…that! No one's banging on my walls, huh? Hahahahaha!" I shrieked crazily as Mimi and Sophia watched in amazement. Sophia climbed off the bed, and she and Mimi clutched each other as they laughed and I thumped. I rocked back and forth like I was surfing, driving my headboard into the wall again and again.

The music cut off suddenly, and I dropped like I'd been shot. Mimi and Sophia clasped their hands over each other's mouths while I lay flat on the bed, biting my own knuckle to keep from laughing. The frenzy in the room was like when you got caught TP-ing someone's house, or laughing in the back of church. You couldn't stop, and you couldn't *not* stop.

Bang bang bang.

No way. He was banging at me?

Bang bang bang.

He *was* banging at me…

Bang bang bang! I gave as good as I got. I couldn't believe he had the balls to try to get me to quiet down. I heard male voices chuckling.

Bang bang bang came once more, and my temper flared.

Oh, he really *was* an asshole…

I looked at the girls incredulously, and they jumped back on the bed with me.

Bang bang bang bang we pounded, six furious fists raining down on the plaster.

Bang bang bang bang came back to us—much, much louder this time. His boys must have gotten in on the action.

"Give it up, mister! No sex for you!" I yelled at the wall as my girls cackled maniacally.

"Tons of sex for me, sister. None for you!" he yelled all too clearly through the wall.

I raised my fists to bang once more. Bang bang ba-bang bang rang out from my side.

Bang bang! A single fist answered back, and then all was silent.

"Oooohhhhh!" I screamed at the wall, and I could hear Simon and his boys laughing.

Mimi, Sophia, and I stared wide-eyed at each other until we heard a tiny sigh from behind us.

We turned to see Clive sitting on the dresser. He stared back at us, sighed again, and proceeded to lick his bum.

"The nerve, I mean, the mother-loving nerve of that guy! He has the balls to actually bang on my wall, on *my* wall? I mean, God what an—"

"Asshole, we know," Mimi and Sophia said in unison as I continued my rant.

"Yes, an asshole!" I continued, still worked up. We were in the car on the way to Jillian's party. The car service had arrived promptly at eight thirty, and we were soon headed over the bridge.

As I looked out at the twinkling lights of Sausalito, I began to calm down a little. I refused to let that guy upset me. I was out with my two best friends, about to attend a fantastic housewarming hosted by the best boss in the world. And if we were lucky, her fiancé would let us see the pictures of him when he was a swimmer in college, back when swimmers still just wore tiny Speedos. We would sigh and gaze endlessly until Jillian made us put them away. And then she would usually put Benjamin away too—for the night.

"I'm telling you, I have a really good feeling about tonight. I feel like something's going to happen," Mimi mused, staring thoughtfully out the window.

"Something's going to happen, all right. We'll have a great time, drink way too much, and I'll probably try to cop a feel off Caroline on the car ride home," Sophia said, winking at me.

"Mmm, sugar," I teased, and she blew me a kiss.

"Oh, would you two forget your pseudo-lesbian romance? I'm being serious here," she continued, sighing in the Harlequin romance voice she used sometimes.

"Who knows? Not sure about me, but maybe *you'll* meet your Prince Charming tonight," I whispered, smiling back at her hopeful face. Mimi was certainly the most romantic of the three of us. She was steadfast in her belief that everyone had a soulmate.

Eh…I'd just settle for my Soul-O.

When we pulled up to Benjamin and Jillian's house, there were cars parked everywhere along the winding street, and Japanese lanterns and luminary bags lined the property. Like most houses set into the hilly landscape, from the street there was nothing to look at. We giggled as we made our way through the gate, and I smiled when the girls stared at the contraption before us. I'd seen the plans for this, but had yet to take a ride.

"What kind of fucked-up rickshaw is this?" Sophia blurted, and I couldn't help but laugh. Jillian and Benjamin had designed and installed a hillevator, basically an elevator that went up and down the hill. Very practical when you considered the amount of steps it took to reach the house. Their hillside front yard was blanketed with terraced gardens and benches and various garden scenes, all artfully arranged on flagstone paths lit with tiki torches that led down the hill to the house. But for grocery shopping and other less-leisurely approaches, the hillevator made for a much easier ride.

"Would you ladies care to use the lift or make your way down the path?" an attendant asked, appearing from the other side of the carriage.

"You mean, ride in that thing?" Mimi squeaked.

"Sure, that's what it's made for. Come on," I encouraged, stepping through the little door that he'd opened in the side. It really felt like a ski lift, except that it was going down a hill instead of up in the air.

"Yeah, okay, let's do it," said Sophia, climbing in behind me and plopping down on the seat. Mimi shrugged and followed.

"There'll be someone at the bottom waiting for you. Enjoy the party, ladies." He smiled, and we were off.

As we rode down the hill, the house rose up to meet us. Jillian had created a purely magical world here, and as there were huge windows throughout the house, we could see into the party as we continued our descent.

"Wow, there's a lot of people here," Mimi noted, her eyes huge. The sounds of a jazz band on one of the many patios below came tinkling up to us.

I felt a little fluttering in my tummy as the cart came to a stop and another attendant came to open the door. As we filed out and our heels click-clacked across the flagstone, I could hear Jillian's voice from inside the house and immediately smiled.

"Girls! You made it!" she called as we walked in.

I turned in the space, taking it all in at once. The house was almost like a triangle, set into the hillside and sprawling outward. Deep mahogany wood floors spread out beneath us, and the clean lines of the walls contrasted beautifully. Jillian's personal taste was a comfortable modern, and the colors in the house reflected the colors of the surrounding hillside: warm leafy greens, rich earthy browns, soft muted creams, and hints of deep marine blue.

Almost the entire back of the two-story house was glass, taking advantage of the spectacular view. The moonlight danced on the water in the bay, and in the distance you could see the lights of San Francisco.

Tears sprang to my eyes as I saw the home she and Benjamin had created for themselves and as I looked back at her, I saw the excitement in her eyes. "It's perfect," I whispered, and she hugged me tightly.

Sophia and Mimi gushed to Jillian as a waiter brought us each a glass of champagne. When Jillian left to go mingle, the three of us made our way out onto one of the many terraces to take stock. Waiters passed trays, and as we munched on roasted prawns and sipped our bubbly, we scanned the crowd for anyone we knew. Of course many of Jillian's clients were there, and I knew I'd be mixing in a bit of work tonight, but right now I was content to eat my fancy shrimp and listen to Sophia and Mimi size up the men.

"Oooh, Sophia, I see a cowboy for you right over there—no, no, wait, he's taken by another cowboy. Moving on." Mimi sighed as she continued her search.

"I got him! I spotted your boy for tonight, Mimi!" Sophia squealed in a whisper.

"Where, where?" Mimi whispered back, hiding her mouth behind a prawn. I rolled my eyes and grabbed another glass of bubbly as the waiter passed.

"Inside—see? Right over there by the island in the kitchen, black sweater and khaki pants? Jesus, he is a *tall* drink of water…Hmmm, nice hair too," Sophia mused, narrowing her eyes.

"With the curly brown hair? Yes, I could definitely work with that," Mimi said, her target acquired. "Look how tall he is. Now, who is that yummy he's talking to? If that bimbo would just move out of the way," Mimi murmured, raising an eyebrow until the alleged bimbo finally moved on, giving us a clearer shot of the man in question.

I looked as well, and as a path opened up, we could now see both of the chatting men. The big guy was, well, big. Tall and broad—linebacker shoulders almost. He filled out his sweater quite nicely, and as he laughed his face lit up. Yeah, he was exactly Mimi's type.

The other gentleman had wavy blond hair that he constantly pushed behind his ears. He wore bookish glasses that really worked for him. He was long and lean and intense looking, almost classical in his beauty. Make no mistake, this guy was geeky gorgeous, and Sophia drew in a quick breath at the sight of him.

As we continued to watch the scene unfold, a third man joined them, and we all smiled. Benjamin.

We headed for the kitchen immediately to say hi to our favorite man on the planet. No doubt Sophia and Mimi were also delighted to have Benjamin handle their introductions. I glanced at the two as they simultaneously worked themselves over. Mimi surreptitiously pinched both cheeks, a la Scarlett O'Hara, and I saw Sophia sneak a quick boob prop. These poor guys didn't stand a chance.

Benjamin caught sight of us on our way across to him and smiled. The guys opened their circle to let us in, and Benjamin enveloped all three of us in a giant hug.

"My three favorite girls! I was wondering when you were going to turn up. Fashionably late as always," he teased, and we all giggled. Benjamin did that—he made us into silly schoolgirls.

"Hi, Benjamin," we said in unison, and it struck me how much we sounded like Benjamin's Angels at that moment.

Big Guy and Glasses stood there grinning as well, perhaps waiting for an introduction as the three of us just stared at Benjamin. He really was aged to perfection: wavy brown hair, just barely beginning to silver by his temples; jeans, a dark blue shirt, and pair of old cowboy boots. He could have walked right off a Ralph Lauren runway.

"Allow me to make some introductions here. Caroline works with Jillian, and Mimi and Sophia are her, oh, what do you call it—BFFs?" Benjamin smiled, gesturing to me.

"Wow, BFFs? Who's been teaching you the lingo, daddy-o?" I laughed and extended my hand to Big Guy. "Hi, I'm Caroline. Nice to meet you."

He engulfed my hand with his paw. It actually was like a paw. Mimi was gonna lose her mind with this one. His eyes were full of fun as he smiled down at me.

"Hey, Caroline. I'm Neil. This tool here is Ryan," he said, nodding over his shoulder at Glasses.

"Thanks, remind me of that next time you can't remember your email password." Ryan laughed good-naturedly and extended his hand to me. I shook it, noticing how scorchingly green his eyes were. If Sophia had kids with this guy, they would be illegally beautiful.

I made sure to handle the continued introductions as Benjamin stepped away. We began to small talk, and I chuckled as the four of them began their little getting-to-know-you dance. Neil spotted someone he knew behind me and shouted, "Hey, Parker, get your pretty-boy ass over here and meet our new friends."

"I'm coming, I'm coming," I heard a voice say behind me, and I turned to see who was joining our group.

The first thing I saw was blue. Blue sweater, blue eyes. Blue. Beautifully blue. Then I saw red as I recognized who belonged to the blue.

"Fucking Wallbanger," I hissed, frozen on the spot.

His grin slid off as well as he played place-the-face for a moment.

"Fucking Pink Nightie Girl," he finally concluded. He grimaced.

We stared, seething as the air literally turned electric between us, snapping and crackling.

The four behind us had fallen silent, listening to this little interchange. Then they caught up.

"That's Wallbanger?" Sophia screeched.

"Wait a minute, that's Pink Nightie Girl?" Neil laughed, and Mimi and Ryan snorted.

My face flamed bright red as I processed this information, and Simon's sneer became that damnable smirk I'd seen that night in the hallway—when I'd banged on his door and made him quit giving it to the Giggler and yelled at him. When I'd been wearing…

"Pink Nightie Girl. *Pink Nightie Girl!*" I choked out, beyond pissed. Beyond angry. Well into Furious Town. I stared at him, pouring all of my tension into that one look. All of the sleepless nights and lost Os and cold showers and banana thrusting and merciless wet dreams went into that one look.

I wanted to level him with my eyes, make him beg for mercy. But no...Not Simon, Director of the International House Of Orgasms.

He

Was

Still

Smirking.

chapter six

We stood staring at each other, waves of anger and annoyance pinging back and forth between us. We glared, he with the smirk and me with the sneer, until I noticed that our very own peanut gallery had fallen silent again, along with every other guest in the kitchen. I looked past my neighbor and saw Jillian standing with Benjamin with an inquisitive look on her face—no doubt wondering why her protégé was squaring off in the middle of her housewarming.

Wait a minute—how the hell did she know Simon? Why was he even here?

I felt a tiny hand on my shoulder and spun quickly to see Mimi.

"Easy, Trigger. You don't need to go nuclear at Jillian's, 'kay?" she whispered, smiling shyly at Simon. I tossed her a look and turned back to him, finding him joined by our hosts.

"Caroline, I didn't realize you knew Simon. What a small world!" Jillian exclaimed, clasping her hands together.

"I wouldn't say I *know* him, but I'm familiar with his work," I replied through clenched teeth. Mimi danced in a circle around us like a little kid with a secret.

"Jillian, you won't believe this but—" she started, her voice bubbling over with barely concealed mirth.

"Mimi…" I warned.

"Simon is Simon from next door! Simon Wallbanger!" Sophia cried, grasping Benjamin's arm. I'm sure she only did it so she could touch the Benjamin.

"Dammit," I breathed as Jillian took in this information.

"No fucking way," she breathed, hand clapping over her mouth as she dropped the f-bomb. Jillian always tried to be such a lady. Benjamin looked confused, and Simon had the decency to blush a little.

"Asshole," I mouthed to him.

"Cockblocker," he mouthed back, the smirk returning in full force.

I gasped. I clenched my fists and prepared to tell him exactly what he could do with his cockblocker when Neil burst in.

"Benjamin, check this out—this little hottie here is the Pink Nightie Girl! Can you stand it!" He laughed as Ryan struggled to keep a straight face. Benjamin's eyes widened, and he raised an eyebrow at me. Simon swallowed a laugh.

"Pink Nightie Girl?" Jillian asked, and I heard Benjamin lean in and tell her he'd explain later.

"Okay, that's it!" I shouted and I pointed at Simon. "You. A word, please?" I barked and grabbed him by the arm. I yanked him outside and pulled him down one of the paths that led away from the house. He scrambled along after me, my heels ringing out angrily on the flagstone.

"Jesus, slow down, will you?"

My response was to dig my nails into his arm, which made him yelp. Good.

We reached a little enclave set away from the house and the party—far enough away that no one would hear him scream when I removed his balls from his body. I released his arm and rounded on him, pointing a finger in his surprised face.

"You've got some nerve telling everyone about me, asshole! What the hell? *Pink Nightie Girl?* Are you kidding me?" I whisper-yelled.

"Hey, I could ask you the same question! Why do all those girls in there call me Wallbanger, huh? Who's telling tales now?" he whisper-yelled right back.

"Are you kidding me? Cockblocker? Just because I refused to spend another night listening to you and your harem does not make me a cockblocker!" I hissed.

"Well, due to the fact that your door-banging blocked my cock, it actually *does* make you a cockblocker. Cockblocker!" he hissed back. This entire conversation was beginning to sound like something that might have happened in fourth grade—except for all the nighties and the cock talk.

"Now, you listen here, mister," I said, trying for a more adult tone. "I'm not going to spend every night listening to you try to crash your girl's head through my wall with the force of your dick alone! No way, buddy." I pointed a finger at him. He grabbed it.

"What I do on my side of that wall is my business. Let's get that straight right now. And why are you so concerned about me and my dick anyway?" he asked, smirking at me again.

It was the smirk, that damn smirk, that made me go ballistic. That and the fact that he was still holding my finger.

"It *is* my business when you and your sex train come knocking on *my* wall every night!"

"You're really fixated on this, aren't you? Wish you were on the other side of that wall? Are you lookin' to ride that sex train, Nightie Girl?" He chuckled as he wagged his finger in my face.

"Okay, that's it," I growled. I grabbed his finger in defense, which instantly locked us together. We must have looked like two loggers trying to cut down a tree. We struggled back and forth—beyond ridiculous. We both huffed and puffed, each trying to get the upper hand, each refusing to relent.

"Why are you such a manwhoring asshole?" I asked, my face inches from his.

"Why are you such a cockblocking priss?" he asked, and when I opened my mouth to tell him exactly what I thought, the fucker kissed me.

Kissed me.

Placed his lips on mine and kissed me. Under the moon and the stars, with the sounds of the waves crashing and the crickets cricketing. My eyes were still open, furiously looking back into his. His eyes were so blue, it was like looking at two angry oceans.

He pulled away, our fingers still gripping each other's like pliers. I released his hand and slapped him across the face. He looked shocked, even more so as I grabbed his sweater and pulled him closer. I kissed him, this time closing my eyes and letting my hands fill with wool and my nose fill with warm boy smell.

God *damn*, he smelled good.

His hands crept around to the small of my back, and as soon as he touched me, I realized where I was and what I was doing. "Dammit," I said, and pulled away. We stood looking at each other, and I wiped at my lips. I started to walk away and then turned back quickly.

"This never happened, got it?" I pointed at him again.

"Whatever you say." He smirked, and I felt my temper flare again.

"And cool it with the Pink Nightie stuff, okay?" I whisper-yelled and turned to walk back down the path.

"Until I get to see your *other* nighties, that's what I'm calling you," he shot back, and I almost tripped. I smoothed my dress and headed back to the party.

Unbelievable.

"So I told the guy, there is no way I'm organizing your 'play room'. You can arrange your own riding crops!" Mimi shrieked, and we all laughed. She can tell a story like nobody's business. She has a knack for bringing a group together, especially when it's new people just getting to know each other.

As the party began to wind down, my girls and Simon's guys were gathered around a fire pit on one of the terraces. Dug deep and lined with flagstone, it had benches all around. While the fire crackled merrily, we laughed and drank and told stories. And by that I mean Mimi, Sophia, Neil, and Ryan told stories while Simon and I glared at each other over the flames. With the sparks flying, if I squinted my eyes a little I could imagine him roasting in the fires of hell.

"So, are we gonna address the elephant in the room here?" Ryan asked, drawing his knees up and placing his beer on the bench next to him.

"Which elephant would that be?" I asked sweetly, sipping my wine.

"Oh, please—the fact that the guy thumping the headboard off your bed is the hottie across the way, girl!" Mimi squealed, almost tossing her drink in Neil's face. He laughed along with her, but pried the glass out of her hand before she could do any real damage.

"There really isn't anything to talk about," Simon said. "I have a new neighbor. Her name is Caroline. That's it." He nodded, eyeing me across the fire. I raised my eyebrow and sipped my wine.

"Yeah, it's nice to know Pink Nightie Girl has a name. The way he described you…wow! I wasn't sure you were real, but you're as hot as he said you were!" Neil hooted at me appreciatively, trying for a moment to fist bump Simon through the flames before he realized how hot they were.

My eyes shot to Simon. He grimaced at the description. *Interesting…*

"So, you were the guys banging back at us tonight? Listening to the Guns N' Roses?" Sophia asked, nudging Ryan.

"You were the girls singing along, I suppose, yes?" he nudged back, smiling.

"Small world, isn't it?" Mimi sighed, gazing up at Neil. He winked at her, and I saw quickly where this was going. She had her giant, Sophia had her pretty boy, and I had my wine. Which was disappearing by the second.

"Excuse me," I muttered and stood up to find a waiter.

I made my way through the dwindling crowd, nodding at a few faces I recognized. I accepted yet another glass of wine and strolled back outside. I'd started back toward the fire pit when I heard Mimi say, "And you should have heard Caroline when she told us about the night she banged on his door."

Sophia and Mimi leaned together and said breathlessly, "He…was…still…hard!"

They all dissolved into laughter. I needed to remember to kill those girls tomorrow, with pain.

I groaned at my public humiliation and spun around to stomp off into the gardens when I saw Simon in the shadows. I tried to back away before he saw me, but he waved.

"Come on, come on, I don't bite," he scoffed.

"Yeah, sure, I guess," I answered, walking toward him.

We stood quietly in the night. I looked out over the bay, enjoying the silence. Then he finally spoke.

"So I was thinking, since we're neighbors and all—" he started.

I turned to look at him. He was giving me a sexy little grin, and I knew that's what he used to make the panties drop. Ha—little did he know I wasn't wearing any.

"You were thinking what? That I'd want to join you some night? See what all the fuss is about? Hop on the welcome wagon? Honey,

I have no interest in becoming one of your girls," I answered, glaring at him.

He said nothing.

"Well?" I asked, tapping my foot angrily. The nerve of this guy…

"Actually, I was going to say, since we're neighbors and all, maybe we could call a truce?" he said quietly, looking at me in a very irritated way.

"Oh," I said. It was all I could say.

"Or maybe not," he finished and started to walk away.

"Wait, wait, wait, Simon," I groaned grabbing him by the wrist as he pushed past me.

He stood there, glaring.

"Yes. Fine. We can call a truce. But there will have to be some ground rules," I replied, turning to face him. He crossed his arms over his chest.

"I should warn you now, I don't enjoy women telling me what to do," he answered darkly.

"Not from what I've heard," I said under my breath, but he caught it anyway.

"That's different," he said, the cockiness beginning to reappear.

"Okay, here's the thing. You enjoy yourself, do your thing, hang from the ceiling fans, I don't care. But late at night? Can we keep it down to a dull roar? Please? I gotta get some sleep."

He considered for a moment. "Yes, I can see where that might be a problem. But you know, you don't really know anything about me, and you certainly don't know anything about me and my 'harem,' as you call it. I don't have to justify my life, or the women in it, to you. So no more nasty judgments, agreed?"

I considered it. "Agreed. By the way, I appreciated the quiet this week. Something happen?"

"Happen? What do you mean?" he asked as we walked back to the group.

"I thought maybe you were injured in the line of duty, like your dick broke off or something," I joked, proud to use my zinger again.

"Unbelievable. That's all you think I am, isn't it?" he retorted, his face angry again.

"A dick? Yes, in fact," I snapped back.

"Now look—" he started, and Neil appeared out of nowhere.

"Nice to see you two have kissed and made up," he chided, pretending to hold Simon back.

"Can it, anchorman," Simon muttered as the rest of the newly paired-off reappeared.

"Cool it with the anchorman, huh?" Neil said, and Sophia whirled on him.

"Anchorman! Wait a minute, you're the local sports guy on NBC, right? Am I right?" she asked.

I watched his eyes light up. Sophia may have been a classical music kind of girl, but she was also a huge 49ers fan. I was pretty sure the 49ers were a football team.

"Yeah, that's me. You watch a lot of sports?" he asked, leaning toward her, bringing Mimi along. The way she was clinging to his arm, it was unavoidable. She stumbled a little, and Ryan swooped in to steady her. They smiled at each other as Sophia and Neil continued their football talk. I coughed, reminding them that I was, in fact, still here.

"Caroline, we're taking off!" Sophia giggled, now leaning on Ryan's arm. I glared at Simon one more time and stalked toward the girls.

"That's good. I've had enough fun for tonight. I'll call for the car, and we can head out in a few," I replied, reaching into my bag for my phone.

"Actually, Neil was telling us about this great little bar, and we were going to go that way. Do you two want to come?" Mimi interrupted, stopping my hand. She squeezed it, and I saw her shake her head almost imperceptibly.

"No?" I asked, raising both eyebrows.

"Great! Ol' Wallbanger here'll make sure you get home okay," Neil said, clapping Simon roughly on the back.

"Yeah, sure," he said through clenched teeth.

Before I could even blink, the four of them were on their way to the hillevator, saying sloppy goodbyes to Benjamin and Jillian, who just laughed and shared a high five.

Wallbanger and I stared at each other, and I suddenly felt exhausted. "Truce?" I said tiredly.

"Truce," he said, nodding.

We left the party together. We drove back across the bridge, with the late-night fog and silence enveloping us. He'd opened the door for me when I approached the Rover, probably some ingrained training from his mother. His hand had rested on the small of my back as I climbed in, and then it was gone and he was around to his side before I even had a chance to make a snarky remark. Maybe it was best; we *had* called a truce. The second truce within the span of mere minutes. This was going to end badly, I could tell. Still, I would try. I could be neighborly, right?

Neighborly. Ha. That kiss was all kinds of neighborly. I was trying as hard as I could not to think about it, but it just kept bubbling up. I pressed my fingers to my lips without even realizing it, remembering the feeling of his mouth on mine. His kiss was almost a dare, calling my bluff—a promise of what would follow if I allowed it.

My kiss? Straight up instinct that frankly surprised me. Why had I kissed him? I had no idea, but I did. It must have looked ridiculous. I'd slapped him, then kissed him like some scene from an old Cary Grant movie. I'd thrown my entire body into my kiss, letting my soft places curve against his strong. My mouth had sought his, and his kiss had grown as eager as mine. There was no fairy tale music, but there was something there. And it had quickly hardened against my thigh...

His messing about with the radio brought me back to the present. He appeared quite focused on the music as we drove across the bridge, which made me quite nervous.

"Can I help you with that? Please?" I asked, looking nervously at the water below.

"No thanks, I got it," he said, glancing at me. He must have noticed the way I was peering over the side of the bridge, and he chuckled. "Okay, sure, go ahead. I mean, you knew every word to 'Welcome to the Jungle,' so you might pick out something good," he challenged.

He returned his eyes to the road, but even from the side, I could see the approving grin. Which, and I hated to admit it, made his jaw look like it had been chiseled out of the hottest piece of granite ever unearthed.

"I'm sure I can find something," I sassed, reaching over his hand and leaning toward him. His hand grazed against the side of my breast, and we both flinched. "What, you tryin' to cop a feel there?" I snapped, selecting a song.

"Did you or did you not just place your tits in the path of my hand?" he sniped back.

"I think your hand just moved in front of the girls' trajectory, but don't sweat it. You're hardly the first that these celestial beings have brought into their orbit." I sighed dramatically, looking at him sideways to see if he could tell I was joking. The corner of his mouth rose into a grin, and I allowed myself a small smile as well.

"Yes, celestial. That's the word I was going to use—as in, not of this earth. As in, suspended in the heavens. As in, courtesy of Victoria's Secret." He grinned, and I pretended to be shocked.

"Oh my, you know of the Secret? And here I thought we silly girls had you all fooled." I laughed and settled back into my seat. We'd crossed the bridge and now returned to the city.

"It takes a lot to fool me, especially when it comes to the opposite sex," he replied, as the music came on. He nodded at my choice. "Too Short? Interesting selection. Not many women would have chosen this," he mused.

"What can I say? I'm feeling very Bay Area tonight. And I should tell you now, I am not like most women," I added, feeling another smile sneak across my face.

"I'm beginning to get that," he said.

We were quiet for a few minutes, then suddenly both started to speak at once.

"So what do you think about—" I began.

"Can you believe that they all—" he said.

"Go ahead," I chuckled.

"No, what were you going to say?"

"I was going to say, so what do you think about our friends tonight?"

"That's actually what I was going to say. I couldn't believe they just up and left us!" He laughed, and I couldn't help but laugh along with him. He had a great laugh.

"I know, but my girls know what they want. I couldn't have painted two better guys for them. They're exactly what they look for," I confided, leaning against the window so I could watch him as we navigated the hilly streets.

"Yeah, Neil has a weakness for Asian girls—and I swear that sounded less pervy in my head. And Ryan loves him some leggy redheads," he laughed again, glancing over to see if I was okay with his leggy redhead comment.

I was. She was.

"Well, I'm sure I'll hear all about it tomorrow—what kind of impression they made on my ladies. I'll get the full report, don't you worry." I sighed. My phone would be ringing off the hook.

Silence crept back in, and I wondered what to say next.

"So how do you know Benjamin and Jillian?" he asked, saving me from small talk fever.

"I work for Jillian at the firm. I'm an interior designer."

"Wait. Hold up, you're *that* Caroline?" he asked.

"I have no idea what that means," I answered, wondering why he was now staring at me.

"Damn, it really *is* a small world," he exclaimed, shaking his head from side to side as though trying to clear it.

He was silent as I sat there in limbo.

"Hey, wanna clear that up a bit? What did you mean, *that* Caroline?" I finally questioned, slapping his shoulder.

"It's just that…well…huh. Jillian has mentioned you before. Let's leave it at that," he said.

"Hell no, we *won't* leave it at that! What did she say?" I pushed, slapping again at his shoulder.

"Would you cut that out? You're really rough, you know that?" he said.

There were simply too many ways I could go with that comment, so I wisely kept quiet.

"What did she say about me?" I asked quietly, now worried that perhaps she'd said something about my work. My nerves were already shot, and now they were pinging.

He looked over at me. "No, no, it's not like that," he said quickly. "It's nothing bad. It's just that, well, Jillian adores you. And she adores me—of course, right?"

I rolled my eyes, but played along.

"And well, she might have…mentioned a few times…that she thought I should meet you," he dragged out, only to wink at me when I met his eyes.

"Oh. Ohhhh," I breathed as I realized what he meant. I blushed. Jillian, that little matchmaking shit. "Does she know about the harem?" I asked.

"Would you quit with that? Don't call them the harem. You make it sound so shady. What if I told you those three women were incredibly important to me? That I care a lot about them. That the relationships I have with them work for us, and no one else needs to understand it—got it?" he said, pulling the Rover to an angry stop at the curb outside our building.

I was quiet as I studied my hands and watched him rake his through his already messed-up hair.

"Hey, you know what? You're right. Who am I to say what's right or wrong for anyone else. If it works for you, great. Hit it. Mazel tov. I'm just surprised Jillian would want to set you up with me. She knows I'm a pretty traditional girl, that's all," I explained.

He grinned and turned the force of his blue eyes on me.

"As it happens, she doesn't know everything about me. I keep my private life private—with the exception of my neighbor with the thin walls and the devastating lingerie," he said in a low voice that could melt, well, anything.

My brain was most certainly among those things, seeing as I suddenly felt it oozing out of my ears and on down to my collar.

"Except for her," I muttered, thoroughly scrambled.

He let out a dark laugh and opened his door. He kept his eyes on mine as he strode around the car and opened my door.

I climbed down, taking the hand he offered me, and almost not noticing that he traced a tiny circle on the inside of my left hand with his right thumb. *Almost didn't notice it, my ass.* It made my skin pebble and Lower Caroline sit up straight. Nerves? Shooting like fireworks all over the place.

We walked inside the building, and he once again opened the door for me. He really was charming, I had to give him that.

"So how do you know Benjamin and Jillian?" I asked, walking up the stairs ahead of him. I knew for certain he was checking out my legs, and why wouldn't he? I had great stems, currently flattered by my flouncy little dress.

"Benjamin's been a friend of my family's for years. I've known him practically my whole life. He also manages my investments," Simon answered as we rounded the first floor and started on the second.

ALICE CLAYTON

I looked over my shoulder and confirmed him peeking at my legs. Ha! Caught him. "Oooh, your investments. Have a few savings bonds left over from birthdays there, moneybags?" I teased.

He chuckled. "Yeah, something like that."

We continued up the stairs.

"It's curious, don't you think?" I offered.

"Curious?" he asked, his voice slipping over me like warm honey.

"Well, I mean, Benjamin and Jillian both knowing us, us meeting at a party like this, and you being the one that's been keeping me nocturnally amused all these weeks. Small world, I suppose?" We rounded the top stair, and I got my keys out.

"San Francisco's a big city, but it can feel like a small town in some ways," he offered. "But yes, it's curious. Intriguing even. Who knew that the nice designer Jillian wanted to set me up with was actually Pink Nightie Girl? Had I known, I might have taken her up on it," he replied, that damnable grin back on his beautiful face.

Dammit, why couldn't he have stayed an asshole?

"Yes, but Pink Nightie Girl would have said no. After all, thin walls and all…" I winked, making a fist and thumping on the wall next to my door. I could hear Clive prattling around behind the door, and I needed to get inside before he began to wail.

"Ah yes, thin walls. Hmmm…Well, good night, Caroline. Truce is still on, right?" he asked, turning toward his door.

"Truce is still on, unless you do something to make me mad again," I laughed, leaning in the doorway.

"Oh, count on that. And Caroline? Speaking of thin walls?" he said, as he opened his door and looked back at me. He leaned in his own doorway, thumping his fist on the wall.

"Yes?" I asked, a little too dreamily for my own good.

The smirk reappeared and he said, "Sweet dreams."

He thumped the wall one more time, winked, and went inside.

Huh. Sweet dreams and thin walls. Sweet *dreams* and thin walls…

Mother of pearl. He'd heard me.

chapter seven

*P*oke.

"Grrr."

Poke. Knead, knead. Poke.

"Enough."

Knead, knead, knead. Head butt.

"I realize you don't know how to read a calendar, but you should know when it's Sunday. Seriously, Clive."

Hard head butt.

I rolled over, away from Clive's head butts and persistent poking, and pulled the covers over my head. Flashes of the night before kept appearing. Simon in Jillian's kitchen with the intro heard round the world. His friends calling me Pink Nightie Girl. Benjamin putting two and two together when he learned *I* was the Pink Nightie Girl. Kissing Simon. Mmm, kissing Simon.

No, no kissing the Simon! I snuggled deeper under the covers.

*Sweet dreams and thin walls...*Sheer mortification washed over me as I remembered his parting words. I burrowed farther under the covers. My heart beat faster, thinking about how embarrassed I'd been. Heart, pay no attention to that girl below the covers.

Last night had been decidedly dream free, but to make sure no one (Simon) could hear me screaming in passion, I'd slept with the TV on. The revelation that Simon had heard me dreaming of him had thrown me for such a loop that I flipped endlessly through the channels, trying to find something that would *not* sound like me having my own version of the Simon Wet Dream. I ended up on the all-infomercial channel, which, of course, kept me up later that I'd planned. Everything they sold was fascinating. I had to pry the cell phone out of my own hand at three thirty a.m. when I almost ordered the Slap Chop—to say nothing of the half hour I will never get back after watching Bowser try to sell me the Time Life collection of songs from the fifties.

All this was in addition to listening to the sounds of Tommy Dorsey coming through the wall. They made me smile. I can't lie.

I stretched lazily under the sheet, stifling a giggle as I watched the shadow of Clive stalking me, trying to figure out a way in. He tried every angle as I deflected his advances. Finally, he resumed his poke-poke-knead approach, and I popped my head back up to laugh at him.

I could handle this thing with Simon. I didn't have to be totally embarrassed. Sure, my O was gone, maybe for forever. Sure, I'd been having sex dreams about my overly attractive and overly confident neighbor. And sure, said neighbor had heard these dreams and commented on them, getting the last word in an already extremely bizarre evening.

But I could handle this. Of course I could. I'd just acknowledge it before he could—take the wind out of his sails, as it were. He didn't always have to have the last word. I could recover from this and keep our ridiculous little truce going.

I'm totally screwed.

Just then I heard the alarm go off next door, and I froze. Then I recovered and slipped back under the covers, leaving just my eyes peeping over.

Wait, why was I hiding? He couldn't see me.

I heard him slap at the alarm clock, and his feet hit the floor. Why was he up so early? When all was quiet, you truly could hear through these walls. How the hell did I not realize before that if I could hear him, he could obviously hear me. I felt my face color as I thought of my dreams again, but then I got control. This was further aided by Clive head butting the small of my back in an attempt to physically push me from the bed to give him his breakfast.

"Okay, okay, let's get up. God, you're such a little jerk sometimes, Clive."

He fired back a reply over his cat shoulder as he stalked toward the kitchen.

After getting Mr. Clive fed and running myself through the shower, I headed out to meet the girls for brunch. I was leaving the building while looking at my phone, answering a text from Mimi, when I collided with a wet, hot wall of Simon.

"Whoa," I cried as I teetered backward. His arm shot out and caught me just before I went from flustered to flat-out wrong and on my bottom.

"Where are you running off to this morning?" he asked, as I took him in. Sweaty white T-shirt, black running shorts, damp curly hair, iPod, and a grin.

"You're sweaty," I word-vomited.

"I *am* sweaty. It happens," he added, sweeping the back of his hand across his forehead, making his hair stand straight up. I had to physically block the neurons from my brain trying to get to my fingers with instructions to lift and nestle. Lift and nestle.

He stared down at me, his blue eyes twinkling. He'd make this painful if I didn't go ahead and out the giant sex elephant in the room.

"So listen, about last night," I started.

"What about last night? The part where you were berating me about my sex life? Or the part where you were sharing my sex life with your friends?" he asked, raising an eyebrow and raising his T-shirt to wipe his face. I drew in a breath that sounded like a wind tunnel as I stared at abs that could almost be speedbumps. Why couldn't he be a soft, fat neighbor?

"No, I mean the crack you made about the sweet dreams. And the…well…the thin walls," I stammered, avoiding all eye contact. I was suddenly fascinated by my new shade of toenail polish. It was lovely…

"Ah, yes, the thin walls. Well, they work both ways, you know. And if someone were to, say, have a very interesting dream some night, well, let's just say it would be quite entertaining," he whispered. My knees went a little wobbly. Damn him and his voodoo…

I had to get back in control. I backed up a step.

"Yes, you may have heard something I would have preferred you not hear, but that's not the way things always go down. So, you got me. But you won't actually ever *have* me, so let's move on. You got that? And brunch, by the way," I finished, concluding my diatribe.

He looked confused and amused at the same time. "Brunch, by the way?"

"Brunch. You asked where I was off to this morning, and my answer is brunch."

"Ah, got it. And are you meeting your girls that were out with my guys last night?"

"I am, and I will gladly share the scoop with you if it's any good," I laughed, twirling a piece of hair around my finger. *Nice. Flirting 101. What the hell?*

"Oh, I'm sure it's good scoop. Those two look like man-eaters," he said, rocking back on his heels as he began to stretch a bit.

"Are we talking Hannibal?"

"No, more like Hall & Oates." He laughed, looking up at me as he stretched his hamstrings.

Christ, hamstrings.

"Yes, well, they can definitely work a room when they need to," I said thoughtfully, beginning to back away again.

"And how about you?" he asked, standing straight.

"How about me what?"

"Oh, I bet Pink Nightie Girl can work any room she wants." He chuckled, his eyes twinkling.

"Eh, work this," I fired back and walked away with a twinkle of my own.

"Nice," he added when I shot him a look over my shoulder.

"Oh, please, like you're not intrigued," I called back from about ten feet away.

"Oh, I'm intrigued," he shouted as I walked backward, shaking my hips while he applauded.

"Too bad I don't work well with others! I ain't no harem girl!" I yelled, practically at the corner.

"Truce still on?" he yelled.

"I don't know, what does Simon say?"

"Oh, Simon says, hell yes. It's on!" he shouted back as I rounded the corner.

I twirled about, actually doing a little pirouette. I smiled big as I bounced along, thinking a truce was a very good thing.

"Egg-white omelet with tomatoes, mushrooms, spinach, and onions."

"Pancakes—four stack, please—with a side of bacon. And I'll need the bacon very crispy, please, but not blackened."

"Two eggs sunny side up, rye toast with butter on the side, and the fruit salad."

After ordering, we settled in for a morning of coffee and gossip.

"Okay, so tell me what happened after we left last night," Mimi said, placing her chin in her hands and blinking prettily at me.

"After you left? You mean after you left me with my jerky neighbor to drive me home? What were you thinking? And telling everyone the he-was-still-hard story? Seriously? I'm writing you both out of my will," I snapped, swallowing coffee that was too hot and instantly searing off a third of my taste buds. I let my tongue hang out of my mouth to cool.

"First of all, we told that story because it's funny, and funny is good," Sophia began, fishing a piece of ice out of her water glass and handing it to me.

"Thanh ooo," I managed, accepting the cube.

She nodded. "And second, you have nothing to leave me anyway, as I already have the entire set of Barefoot Contessa cookbooks, which you bought me yourself. So write me out of the will. And third, the two of you were being such downers there was no way we were taking you out with our new boys," Sophia finished, smiling wickedly.

"New boys. I love new boys," Mimi clapped, looking like a Disney cartoon.

"How was the ride home?" Sophia asked.

"The ride home. Well, it was interesting." I sighed, now sucking on the cube with wild abandon.

"Interesting good?" Mimi squealed.

"If you call schtupping someone on the Golden Gate Bridge interesting, then yes," I replied, calmly drumming my fingers on the table. Mimi's mouth began to fall from her face when Sophia placed her right hand over Mimi's left, which was about to squeeze her fork into something unrecognizable.

"Sweetie, she's kidding. We would know if Caroline had been schtupped last night. She'd have better skin tone," Sophia soothed.

Mimi nodded quickly and released the fork. I pitied any guy who pissed her off during a handjob.

"So, no dish?" Sophia asked.

"Hey, you know the rules. You dish, I dish," I answered, eyes widening as our breakfast was served. After we dug in, Mimi fired the first shot.

"Did you know that Neil played football for Stanford? And that he always wanted to go into sports broadcasting?" she offered, methodically separating her melon from her berries.

"Good to know, good to know. Did you know Ryan sold some kind of amazing computer program to Hewlett Packard when he was just twenty-three? And that he put all the money in the bank, quit his job, and spent two years teaching English to kids in Thailand?" Sophia provided next.

"That's very good to know as well. Did you know that Simon doesn't consider his lady friends a 'harem', and Jillian at one point actually told *him* about *me* as a potential girl he should be dating?"

We all hmm-ed and chewed. Then began Round Two.

"Did you know that Neil loves to windsurf? And he has tickets to the symphony benefit next week? When he found out I was already going with you, Sophia, he suggested we double."

"Mmm, that sounds fun. I was thinking of asking Ryan. Who, by the way, also loves to windsurf. They all do — they surf in the bay whenever they can. And I can also report that he now runs a charity that puts computers and educational materials into inner city schools all over California. It's called — " Sophia began.

"No Child Left Offline?" Mimi quickly finished.

Sophia nodded.

"I love that charity! I give to that organization every year. And Ryan is the one who runs it? Wow...small world," Mimi mused as she began to cut her eggs.

Quiet descended while we chewed again, and I tried to come up with something else to say about Simon that didn't have anything to do with him kissing me, me kissing him, or him being aware of my nocturnal verbal emissions.

"Um, Simon has Too Short on his iPod," I mumbled, which was met with hmms, but I knew my dish wasn't as good.

"Music is important. Who was that guy you were dating who had his own album out?" Mimi asked.

"No, no. He didn't have an album out. He was trying to sell his own CDs out of the back of his car. Not the same thing." I laughed.

"You dated another singer too—Coffee House Joe, remember him?" Sophia snorted into her breakfast.

"Yes, he was about fifteen years too late for the flannel, but he got an A for angst. And was more than decent in bed," I sighed, thinking back.

"When is this self-imposed dating hiatus going to be over?" Mimi asked.

"Not sure. I kinda like not dating anyone."

"Please, who are you kidding?" Sophia snorted again.

"You need a tissue over there, Miss Piggy? Seriously, there have been too many Coffee House Joes and Machine Gun Corys. I'm not interested in just dating any more. It's too much of a merry go round. I'm not investing any more time and effort until I know it's going somewhere. And besides, O's off in no-man's land. I might as well join her," I added, trying some coffee again and avoiding their eyes.

They had their Os, and now they had new boys. I didn't expect anyone to join me on my dating sabbatical. But now their faces just looked so sad. I needed to turn this back to them.

"So last night was good for you guys, huh? Any kisses at the door? Any spit swapping?" I asked, smiling cheerfully.

"Yes! I mean, Neil kissed me," Mimi sighed.

"Oooh, I bet he's a good kisser. Did he wrap you up tight and run his hands up and down your back? He has great hands. Did you notice his hands? Damn fine hands," Sophia rambled, face in her pancake stack. Mimi and I exchanged a glance and waited for her to come up for air. When she saw us staring, she blushed a little.

"What? I noticed his hands? They're huge. How could you not?" she stammered and crammed her mouth full so we would move on.

I giggled and turned my attention back to Mimi. "So, did Mr. Great Hands use his great hands?"

It was Mimi's turn to blush. "Actually, he was very sweet. Just a little peck on the lips and a nice hug at my door," she answered with a giant smile.

"And you, Miss Thing? Was the computer genius charitable with his goodnight kiss?" I giggled.

"Um…yes, he was. He gave me a great goodnight kiss," she replied, licking syrup off the back of her hand. She didn't seem to notice the way Mimi's eyes burned a little when she mentioned the goodnight she'd received, but I did.

"So, you escaped last night unscathed, I take it?" Mimi asked me, sipping her coffee. I was still nursing the sore tongue, so I chose to stick with juice.

"I did. We came to a truce and will try to be more neighborly."

"What exactly does that mean?" she asked.

"That means he'll try to curtail his activities to earlier in the evening, and I'll try to be more understanding about his sex life, as lively as it is," I answered, digging into my purse for some money.

"One week," Sophia muttered.

"Come again?"

"You wish. One week. That's how long I give this truce. You can't keep your opinions to yourself, and he can't keep that Giggler quiet. One week," she said again as Mimi smiled away.

Huh, we'll see…

Monday morning, bright and early, Jillian came waltzing in to my office.

"Knock knock," she called. She was the picture of casual chic: hair swept back into a loose bun, little black dress on her little tan body, legs that went on for miles ending in red pumps. Pumps that would probably constitute almost a week's pay for me. She was my mentor in every way, and I made a mental note to make sure I someday obtained the quiet confidence she carried with her.

She smiled when she saw the new flowers in the vase on my desk. This week I'd chosen orange tulips, three dozen.

"Morning! Did you see that the Nicholsons have added a home theater? I knew they'd come around." I smiled as I sat back in my chair. Jillian settled herself in the chair across from me and just smiled back.

"Oh, and Mimi is coming over for dinner tonight. We're hoping to finalize the plans for the new closet system she's designing. She wants to add carpet now." I shook my head and sipped coffee from the mug on my desk. My tongue had almost healed.

Jillian just continued to smile. I began to wonder if I had a Cheerio stuck to my face. "Did I tell you I got the glass company in Murano to give me a deal on the pieces I ordered for the bathroom chandelier?" I forged ahead. "It's going to be beautiful. I think we'll definitely want to use them again." I added, smiling hopefully.

She finally sighed and leaned forward with a cat-that-ate-the-canary-and-went-back-for-the-feathers-to-play-with grin.

"Jillian, did you have dental work done this morning? Are you try-ing to show me your new dentures?" I asked, and she finally flinched.

"As if I would ever need dentures, pffft. No, I'm waiting for you to tell me about your neighbor, Mr. Parker. Or should I say Simon Wallbanger?" She laughed, finally sitting back in her chair and giving me a look that said I would not be allowed to leave my office until I told her everything she wanted to know.

"Hmm, Wallbanger. Where to start? First of all, you can't tell me you didn't know he lived next door. How the hell could you have lived there as long as you did and *not* know he was the one thump-ing away every night?" I inquired, looking back at her with my best detective sneer.

"Hey, you know I hardly ever stayed there, especially the last few years. I knew he was in that neighborhood, but I had no idea it was next door to the apartment I was subletting! When I see him, it's always with Benjamin, and we usually go out for drinks or we have him over to our place. Regardless, it's the beginnings of a great story, don't you think?" she tempted, grinning again.

"Oh, you and your matchmaking. Simon said you'd mentioned me to him before. You are so busted."

She held up her hands in front of her. "Wait, wait, wait, I had no idea he was so, well, active. I never would have suggested you if I'd known he had so many girlfriends. Benjamin must have known… but it's a guy thing, I guess," she replied.

I was the one to lean forward now. "So tell me, how does he know Benjamin?"

"Well, Simon isn't originally from California. He grew up in Philadelphia and only moved out here when he went to Stanford. Benjamin has known him most of his life — he was really close to his dad. He's kind of watched out for Simon—favorite uncle, big brother, surrogate father, that kind of thing," she said, her face growing soft.

"*Was* really close to his dad? Did they have a falling out or something?" I asked.

"Oh, no, no, Benjamin was always great friends with Simon's dad. He was the one who mentored him early in his career. He was very close with the entire family," she said, her eyes growing sad.

"But now?" I pressed.

"Simon's parents were killed when he was a senior in high school," she said quietly.

My hand flew to my mouth. "Oh no," I whispered, my heart full of sympathy for someone I barely knew.

"Car accident. Benjamin says they went really quickly, almost instantly," she replied.

We were quiet for a moment, lost in our own thoughts. I couldn't even process what that must have been like for him.

"So after the funeral, he stayed in Philadelphia for a while, and he and Simon began to talk about him going to school at Stanford," she continued after a moment.

I smiled at the image of Benjamin doing everything he could to help.

"I can imagine it was probably a good idea for him to get away from everything," I said, wondering how I would deal with something like that.

"Mm-hmm. I think Simon saw the chance, and he took it. And knowing that Benjamin was close by if he needed anything? I think that made it easier," she added.

"When did *you* meet Simon?" I asked.

"His senior year of college. He'd spent some time in Spain the summer before, and when he came home that August he came into the city to have dinner with us. Benjamin and I had been dating for a while by then, so he knew *of* me, but hadn't actually met me," she said.

Wow, Simon does Spain. Those poor flamenco dancers—they never stood a chance.

"We met for dinner, and he charmed the waitress by ordering in Spanish. Then he told Benjamin that if he was ever stupid enough to leave me that he would be quite happy to—now what was it he said?—ah, yes, he would be quite happy to warm my bed." She giggled, her face growing pink.

I rolled my eyes. This matched what I knew of him already. Although, as brash as my girls and I were when flirting with Benjamin, it was the pot calling the kettle forward.

"And that's how I met Simon," she finished, her eyes far away. "He really is pretty great, Caroline, all banging aside."

"Yes, banging aside," I mused, running my fingertips back and forth across the tops of the flowers.

"I hope you get to know him a little better," she said with a grin, matchmaker once again.

"Settle down there. We've called a truce, but that's all," I laughed, shaking my finger at her.

She got up and started for the door. "You're very sassy for someone who's supposed to be working for me," she said, trying to look severe.

"Well, I'd get a lot more work done if you'd let me get back to it and stop with your nonsense!" I said, looking severely back at her.

She laughed and looked out to reception.

"Hey, Maggie! When did I lose control of this office?" she called.

"You never actually had it, Jillian!" Maggie yelled back.

"Oh, go make coffee or something! And you," she said, turning to me and pointing. "Design something brilliant for the Nicholsons' basement."

"Again, all things I could've been doing while you were yakking away in here..." I murmured, tapping my pencil on my watch.

She sighed. "Seriously, Caroline, he's really sweet. I think you two could be great friends," she said, leaning in the doorway.

What's with everyone leaning in doorways lately?

"Well, I can always use another friend, now, can't I?" I waved as she disappeared.

Friends. Friends who called a truce.

"Okay, so we know the floors in the bedroom are going to be reclaimed, honey-toned wood, but you for sure want carpet in the closet?" I asked, settling on the couch next to Mimi and starting on my second Bloody Mary. We'd been going through her plans for almost an hour as I tried to get her to see that I was not the only one who would have to compromise on her designs. She would as well. As long as we'd been friends, Mimi had believed she won every argument. Mimi saw herself as a badass that could strong-arm anyone into anything. Little did she know Sophia and I had figured out that we only had to let her *think* she was getting her way, which made her much more tolerable.

The truth was, I always knew I wanted carpet in the closet—just not for the same reasons she did.

"Yes, yes, yes! It *has* to be carpet—really thick and luxurious carpet! It will feel so good under cold toes in the morning," she cried, almost shaking in her excitement. I really hoped Neil would be around long enough to romance her right. She needed to release some of this excess energy.

"Okay, Mimi, I guess you're right. Carpet in the closet. But for that, you have to give me back those two feet you wanted from the bathroom for the rotating shoe rack that I vetoed." I spoke carefully, wondering if she would go for it.

She thought for a moment, looked at her plans again, took a long pull from her cocktail, and nodded. "Yes, take back the two feet. I get my carpet, and I can live with that." She sighed, offering me her hand.

I shook it solemnly and offered her my celery stalk. Clive came sauntering in and began to pace by the front door, pawing under the crack.

"I bet our Thai is almost here. Let me get my money," I said, pointing toward the door as I headed for my purse on the kitchen counter. Just as I spoke, I could hear steps in the hallway.

"Mimi, get the door, that'll be the takeout guy," I called, rummaging through my purse.

"Got it," she yelled, and I heard the door open. "Oh, hey there, Simon!" she said, and then I heard the strangest sound.

I would swear, on a stack of Bibles in a court of actual law, that I heard my cat speak.

"Porrrrreeeennnnnya," Clive said, and I whirled about.

In the span of five seconds, a thousand things happened: I saw Simon and Purina in the hallway, bags from Whole Foods in hands, key in front door. I saw Mimi at the door, barefoot and leaning (again with the leaning) in the doorway. I saw Clive rear back on his hind legs preparing to jump in a way that I'd only ever seen him do once when I hid the catnip on the top of the fridge. Babies were born, old people died, stocks were traded, and someone faked an orgasm. All in those five seconds.

I launched myself at the door in a slow-motion run reminiscent of every action movie ever made.

"*Noooooooooo!*" I cried as I saw a look of panic cross Purina's face and a look of pure lust cross Clive's as he prepared to woo. If I'd started for the door any earlier, maybe even a second earlier, I could've prevented the pandemonium that ensued.

Simon pushed his door open and smiled a confused smile at me as I caught his eye. No doubt he was wondering why I was charging the door and screaming noooooo. Just then Clive jumped. Leapt. Charged. Purina saw Clive jumping directly at her, and she did the worst thing she could've done. She ran. She ran into Simon's apartment. Of course the girl who meows when she has an orgasm is afraid of cats.

Clive gave chase, and as I stood in the hallway with Simon and Mimi, we heard shrieking and meowing echoing back to us. It sounded oddly familiar, and I was reminded of Simon bringing it on home. I shook my head and took over.

"Caroline, what the hell was that? Your cat just—" Simon was saying, and I placed my hand over his mouth as I hurried past him.

"We don't have time, Simon! We have to get Clive!"

Mimi followed me into his apartment, Ned Nickerson to my Nancy Drew. I followed the shrieks and meows to the back of the apartment, noticing that Simon's place was an exact mirror image of mine. It was very single guy, with the flat screen TV and the amazing sound system. I didn't really have time for a proper shakedown, but I did notice the mountain bike in the dining room, as well as beautiful framed photographs all over the walls lit by retro sconces. I couldn't admire for long, as I could hear Clive getting worked up in the bedroom.

I paused by the door, listening to Purina scream. I looked back at Simon and Mimi, who wore twin expressions of fear and confusion—although Mimi's also showed quite a bit of merriment.

"I'm going in," I said in a low, brave voice. With a deep breath I pushed the door open, and saw the Bedroom of Sin for the first time. Desk in the corner. Dresser on one wall, with top covered in loose change. More photographs on the wall, black and whites. And there it was: his bed.

Cue trumpets.

Pushed up against the wall, my wall, was a giant California king, complete with a padded, leather headboard. Padded. It would have to be, now wouldn't it? It was immense. And he had the power to move that thing with his hips alone? Once again Lower Caroline sat up straight and took notice.

I centered, I focused, and I pried my eyes away from Orgasm Central. I scanned and acquired the target: there at the leather club chair in front of the window. Purina perched on the back of this chair, hands in her hair, moaning and wailing and crying. Her skirt was shredded, and there were tiny claw marks in her stockings. She attempted with every fiber of her being to shrink away from the cat on the floor in front of her.

And Clive?

Clive was strutting. Strutting back and forth in front of her, giving it his all. He turned like he was on a runway, pacing along a line on the floor and glancing at her nonchalantly.

If Clive could wear a blazer, he would have taken it off, draped it casually over his kitty shoulder, and pointed at her. It was all I could do not to fall down laughing. I stepped toward him, and Purina shouted something at me in Russian. I ignored her and focused all my attention on my cat.

"Hey, Clive. Hey. Where's my good boy?" I crooned, and he turned. He glanced at me, and then jerked his head in Purina's direction as though he were making the first round of introductions. "Who's your new friend?" I crooned again, shaking my head at Purina when she tried to say something. I held my finger up in front of my lips. This would require great finesse.

"Clive, come here!" Mimi yelled and barreled into the room. She always had trouble containing her excitement.

Clive made for the door as Mimi made for Clive. Purina made for the bed as I raced after Mimi, who collided with Simon just outside the bedroom door, who was still holding his damn Whole Foods bags. Thoughtfully chosen sustainable organic produce rained down on both of them as I pushed past, hurdling over limbs and a wheel of Brie on my way back to the front door. I caught Clive just as he made a break for the stairs and held him close.

"Clive, you know better than to run away from mommy," I chastised, as Simon and Mimi finally caught up to us.

"What the hell are you doing, Cockblocker? Are you trying to kill me?" he shouted.

Mimi rounded on him. "Don't you call her that you…you…you wallbanger!" she fired back, smacking his chest.

"Oh, you two shut up!" I yelled. Here came Purina down the hallway toward us, wearing only one shoe and a furious look. She began to shout in Russian.

Mimi and Simon continued to yell, Purina screamed, Clive struggled to get loose and be reunited with his one and only, and I stood in the middle of the chaos trying to figure out what the hell had happened in the last two minutes.

"Get control of your damn cat!" Simon yelled, as Clive tried to spring free.

"Don't you yell at Caroline!" Mimi yelled, smacking him again.

"Look at my skirt!" Purina cried.

"Did someone order pad thai?" I heard above the chaos. I looked and saw a petrified delivery boy standing on the top step, reluctant to come any further.

Everyone stopped.

"Unbelievable," Mimi muttered and walked into my apartment, motioning for the delivery boy to follow her. I set Clive just inside the door and pulled it shut, cutting off his cries. Simon ushered Purina into his place, telling her softly to find something in his room to put on.

"I'll be there in just a minute," he said and nodded again for her to go inside. She glared at me once more and turned in a huff, slamming the door.

He turned back to me and we stared at each other, both starting to laugh at the same time.

"Did that really just happen?" he asked through his chuckles.

"I'm afraid it did. Please tell Purina I am sooo sorry," I answered, wiping tears from my eyes.

"I will, but she needs to cool off for a while before I will attempt that—wait, what did you just call her?" he asked.

"Umm, Purina?" I replied, still chortling.

"Why do you call her that?" he asked, no longer laughing.

"Seriously? Come on, you can't figure it out?" I said.

"No, tell me," he said, running his hands through his hair.

"Oh, man, you're gonna make me say it? Purina...because she, God, because she *meows!*" I blurted, laughing again.

He blushed deep red and nodded. "Right, right, of course you would've heard that." He laughed. "Purina," he said under his breath and smiled. I could hear Mimi arguing with the delivery guy in my apartment, something about missing spring rolls.

"She's a little scary, you know?" Simon said, gesturing toward my door.

"You have no idea," I said. I could still hear Clive wailing behind the door. I pressed my face to the edge and opened it just an inch.

"Shut it, Clive," I hissed. A paw came out through the crack, and I swear he flipped me off.

"I don't know a lot about cats, but is that normal feline behavior?" Simon asked.

"He has a rather odd attachment to your girl there—ever since the second night I lived here. I think he's in love."

"I see. Well, I'll make sure I convey his sentiments to *Nadia*," he said. "When the time is right, of course." He chuckled and prepared to go back inside.

"You better keep it down over there tonight, or I'll send Clive back," I warned.

"Jesus, no," he said.

"Well, then turn some music on. You gotta give something," I pleaded. "Or he'll be climbing the walls again."

"Music I can do. Any requests?" he asked, turning to face me from inside the doorway. I backed up to mine and put my hand on my door.

"Anything but big band, okay?" I answered softly. Heart moved down low in my tummy, flitting about.

A look of disappointment crossed his face. "You don't like big band?" he inquired, his voice low.

I pressed my fingers to my collarbone, my skin feeling warm under his gaze. I watched as his eyes followed my hand, further heating me with the intensity of his gaze.

"I love it," I whispered, and his eyes jerked back to mine in surprise. I smiled a shy smile and disappeared into my apartment, leaving him smiling back at me.

Mimi was still yelling at the delivery guy as I came inside to school Clive, a simpering look on both our faces. Five minutes later, with a mouthful of noodles, I heard Purina yelling something in indecipherable Russian on the landing and his door slammed. I tried to hide my grin, instead playing it off as a particularly spicy bite. No wallbanging tonight, I guess…Clive would be so depressed.

At around eleven thirty that night, as I was settling into bed, Simon played me some music through our shared wall. Wasn't big band, but it was pretty good. Prince. "Pussy Control."

I smiled in spite of myself, delighted at his wicked sense of humor.

Friends? Definitely. Maybe. Possibly.

"Pussy Control." I thought of it again and snorted.

Well played, Simon. Well played.

chapter eight

The next evening I was headed out to yoga when I found myself face to face with Simon once again. He was coming up the stairs as I went down.

"If I said, 'we have to stop meeting like this,' would it sound as trite as it sounds in my head?" I offered.

He laughed. "Hard to say. Give it a try."

"Okay. Wow, we have to stop meeting like this!" I exclaimed.

We both waited a beat and then laughed again.

"Yep, trite," he said.

"Maybe we can work out some kind of schedule, share custody of the hallway or something." I shifted my weight from one leg to another. *Great, now it looks like you have to pee.*

"Where are you off to tonight? I seem to always catch you when you're leaving," he said as he propped himself up on the wall.

"Well, clearly I am headed somewhere very fancy." I gestured to my yoga pants and cami. I then showed him my water bottle and yoga mat.

He pretended to think very carefully, and then his eyes widened. "You're going to pottery class!"

"Yes, that's where I'm headed…ass."

He grinned that grin at me. I smiled back.

"So you never gave me the scoop on what you heard at brunch the other day. What's going on with our friends?" he asked, and I didn't *at all* feel a flutter in my belly at the mention of the word *our.* Not at all…

"Well, I can tell you that my girls were quite taken with your boys. Did you know they're all going to the symphony benefit next week?" I said, instantly horrified that I went there that quickly.

"I heard that. Neil gets tickets every year. Perks of the job, I suppose. Sportscasters always go to the symphony, right?"

"I would assume, especially when one is trying to cultivate a certain man-about-town persona," I added with a wink.

"You caught that, huh?" He winked back, and we found ourselves smiling again. Friends? Definitely a stronger possibility.

"We'll have to compare notes afterward, see how the Fantastic Four are doing. Did you know they've been going out on double dates all week?" I said. Sophia had confided that they'd been going out constantly, but always as a foursome. Hmm…

"I did hear something about that. They all seem to be getting along well. That's good, right?"

"It's good, yes. I'm actually going out with them next week. You should come along," I tossed out casually. *It's all for the truce, just the truce…*

"Oh, wow. I'd love to, but I'm heading overseas. Leaving tomorrow, actually," he said.

If I didn't know better, I'd say he almost looked disappointed.

"Really? On a shoot?" I said, and realized my mistake. That knowing smirk came back with a vengeance.

"A shoot? Checking up on me?"

I felt my face go from pink to a lovely tomato red. "Jillian mentioned what you do for a living, yes. And I noticed the pictures in your apartment. When my pussy was chasing your Russian? Ring any bells?"

He seemed to shift his weight a little at my choice of words. *Hmmm, weak spot?*

"You noticed my pictures?" he asked.

"I did. You've got a great set of sconces." I smiled sweetly and looked directly at his crotch.

"Sconces?" he mumbled, clearing his throat.

"Occupational hazard. So where are you headed, anyway? Overseas, I mean." I dragged my eyes deliberately back up to his, and noticed his were nowhere near my face. *Heh, heh, heh…*

"What? Oh, um, Ireland. Shooting a bunch of coastal spots for *Condé Nast*, and then going into some of the smaller towns," he answered, bringing his gaze back to mine.

It was nice to see him a bit flustered. "Ireland, nice. Well, bring me back a sweater."

"Sweater, got it. Anything else?"

"A pot of gold? And a shamrock?"

"Great. I won't have to leave the airport gift shop," he muttered.

"And then when you come home, I'll do a little Irish dance for you!" I cried and started laughing at the lunacy of this conversation.

"Aw, Nightie Girl, did you just offer to dance for me?" he said in a low voice, stepping a little closer.

And just like that, the balance of power shifted.

"Simon, Simon, Simon," I exhaled, shaking my head. Mainly to clear it from the effect of him being so near. "We've been over this. I have no desire to join the harem."

"What makes you think I'd ask you?"

"What makes you think you wouldn't? Besides, I think that would mess with the truce, don't you?" I laughed.

"Mmm, the truce," he said.

Just then I heard steps on the stairs below. "Simon? Is that you?" a voice called up.

At that he leaned back, away from me. I looked down and realized we'd been inching toward each other on the landing throughout our exchange.

"Hey, Katie, up here!" he called down.

"A haremette? I'll watch my walls tonight." I said softly.

"Stop it. She had a hard day at work, and we're heading out to a movie. That's it."

He smiled sheepishly at me, and I laughed. If we were going to be friends, I might as well meet the harem, by God.

A moment later we were joined by Katie, who I, of course, knew as Spanx. I muffled a laugh as I smiled at her.

"Katie, this is my neighbor, Caroline," Simon said. "Caroline, this is Katie."

I offered my hand, and she looked curiously between Simon and me.

"Hi, Katie. Nice to meet you."

"You too, Caroline. You the one with the cat?" she asked, a twinkle in her eye. I looked at Simon, and he shrugged.

"Guilty, although Clive would argue that, in fact, he is an actual person."

"Oh, I know. My dog used to watch TV and bark until I put on something she liked. What a pain in the ass she was." She smiled.

We all stood for a moment, and it was beginning to get a little awkward.

"Okay, kids, I'm off to yoga. Simon, have a safe trip, and I'll fill you in on the gossip from the new couples when you get back."

"Sounds good. I'll be gone a while, but hopefully they won't get in too much trouble while I'm away." He chuckled as they started up the stairs.

"I'll keep my eyes on them. Nice to meet you, Katie," I said, headed down.

"You too, Caroline. 'Night!" she called back to me.

As I walked down the stairs, more slowly than necessary, I heard her say, "Pink Nightie Girl's pretty."

"Shut it, Katie," he fired back, and I swear he swatted her on the butt.

Her yelp a second later confirmed it.

I rolled my eyes as I pushed the door open and headed out to the street. When I got to the gym, I switched my class from yoga to kickboxing.

"I'll have a vodka martini, straight up with three olives, please." The bartender got to work as I looked around the crowded restaurant, taking a break from the Fantastic Four. After two weeks of hearing about all these fabulous double dates, I'd agreed to go out with them and turn them into a Fantastic Five. It was fun, and I was having a great time, but after being with two new couples all night I needed a break. People-watching at the bar was a great way to get some time off. To my left was an interesting couple: silver-haired gentleman with a woman younger than I was who had newly purchased tits. Good girl! You get yours. I mean, if I had to look at flabby, old-man buns I'd want bigger boobs too.

I never thought I'd enjoy being alone, but lately I was finding I did pretty well without a man in my life. I was alone, but I wasn't lonely. Orgasms aside, I did occasionally miss the companionship of a boyfriend, but I liked going places solo. I could travel alone, so why not? Nevertheless, the first time I took myself out to a movie I thought it was going to be weird—the likelihood of running into someone I knew while out and about in the jungles of Costa Rica was slim to none, but running into someone at the movies in the jungles of San Francisco? Odds were greater—but it was great! And a restaurant alone was also just fine. Turns out I'm a great date all by myself.

Still, dinner tonight with my friends had been quite entertaining. The way these two new couples circled each other was fun to watch. Mimi and Sophia had both snagged themselves the men they'd cultivated in their heads as the perfect match. Just then I spotted Sophia in the crowd, her height and gorgeous red hair setting her apart even among hundreds. Hot restaurant, and even hotter bar, this place was packed with people and pretention.

I could see her chatting with someone, and off to the side I found Mimi and Ryan. What was odd? *Neil,* not Ryan, seemed to be Sophia's conversation partner. *Ryan* appeared completely captivated by Mimi, her hands moving through the air and punctuating statements with her toothpicked olive as he listened, fascinated. From where I stood, the distance afforded me perfect clarity. I couldn't help but smile. They'd found the boys they always thought they wanted, but now they each seemed fascinated by the other one...ah well, the grass was always cuter, right?

Sophia glanced over and spotted me at the bar, and shortly thereafter, she excused herself and headed my way.

"Having fun?" I asked as she perched on the stool next to me.

"I'm having a great time," she mused. She then told the bartender exactly how to make her cocktail.

"How's Neil tonight?"

Her eyes lit up briefly, and then she seemed to catch herself.

"Neil? Good, I guess. Ryan looks great, doesn't he?" she covered, gesturing over to where we'd left our group, and where Mimi and Ryan were still deep in conversation. Ryan did indeed look good in jeans and a shirt that exactly matched his icy blue eyes—the eyes fixed delightedly on Ms. Mimi.

How could they not see it?

"Neil looks pretty good tonight too," I tossed out, refocusing on the brawny sportscaster. Charcoal sweater, chinos—he was every inch the man about town.

"Yep," she said icily, licking a bit of salt from the rim on her glass.

I giggled and placed a hand on her arm.

"Come on, pretty girl, let's get you back to your perfect man," I said, and we rejoined the group.

I departed a little before my friends did, tired but happy. Once again I'd spent an evening alone and lived to tell the tale. I wondered if other single women understood the delight that came from fifth-wheeling it. To not have to make small talk with some guy you'd been set up with, to not have to worry about some idiot with peppercorn-encrusted-filet breath trying to force his wiggly tongue down the back of your throat, and to not have to explain to that same idiot why you insist on taking a cab home when his super-fast Camaro is parked right over there.

I'd enjoyed—or should I say *mostly* enjoyed—an assortment of relationships since high school, but hadn't really been in love for a long time. Not since senior year of college. And since that fell apart, I'd had just a series of casual flings, never really feeling fully invested in anyone. Hence my current hiatus from dating. Getting all the parts to line up seemed more and more difficult for me as I got older, and the process could be exhausting. Lower Caroline might be on board, but Brain and Heart always seemed to have reservations. Plus, now that my O was also absent, for who knew how long, I was finding my solitary lifestyle more and more appealing.

As I mused over these thoughts, headed home in a cab, my phone beeped. I had a text from a number I didn't recognize.

Have a good time tonight?

Who the hell is texting me?

Who the hell is texting me?

As I waited for the reply, I leaned down and slipped off my shoes. Fantastic heels, but damn, they hurt my feet. My phone beeped again, and I read.

Some people call me Wallbanger.

I hated myself a little for the way my now-naked toes curled. Stupid toes.

Wallbanger, huh?
Wait a minute—how did you get my number?

I knew it was either Mimi or Sophia. Damn girls. They were really pushing it lately.

I can't reveal my sources.
So, did you have a good time tonight?

Okay, I can play this game.

In fact I did. On my way home now.
How is the Emerald Isle? Lonely yet?

It's beautiful actually, just having breakfast.
And I am never lonely.

I believe that. Did you buy my sweater?

Working on it, want to get just the right one.

Yes, please give me a good one.

Not going to respond to that one…how's that pussy of yours?

Really not going to respond to that one.
Is there something you wanted?

This not responding thing is getting harder…

I know what you mean. It's hard not to touch that one.

Okay, officially ending this round.
The innuendos are too thick to see straight.

Oh, I don't know, it's better when it's thick…

Wow. I'm enjoying this truce more than I expected.

I have to admit it's good for me too.

Are you home yet?

Yep, just pulled up in front of our building.

Okay, I'll wait until you're inside.

Bet you can't wait to get inside.

You're a demon, you know that?

I have been told. Okay, inside. Just kicked your door, btw.

Thanks.

Just being a good neighbor.

Goodnight, Caroline.

Good morning, Simon.

I laughed as I turned the key in my lock and went inside. I sank into my couch, still laughing. Clive quickly jumped into my lap, and I petted his silky fur as he purred his welcome home. My phone beeped once more.

Did you really kick my door?

Shut up. Go eat your breakfast.

I laughed again as I silenced my phone for the night and lay back onto the couch. Clive perched on my chest as I relaxed for a bit, thoughts of that damn wallbanger in my head. It was shocking how clearly I could picture him: soft faded jeans, hiking boots a la Jake Ryan from *Sixteen Candles*, off-white Irish cable knit turtleneck sweater, hair all in disarray. Standing on a rocky coast somewhere, ocean in the background. A little tan, slightly weathered, hands in pockets. And that grin…

chapter nine

Text between Caroline and Simon:

You had a package delivered.
I signed for it and it's at my place.

Thanks. I'll pick it up when I'm back. How are you?

Good, just working. How are the Irish?

Lucky. How's that insane cat?

Lucky. I caught him trying to climb the walls.
He's still looking for Purina. Misses her.

I don't think a romance is in the cards for those two.

Probably not…he won't be over it anytime soon tho.
Might have to bump up his catnip ration.

Don't overmedicate.
No one likes a pussy that can't hold a conversation.

I'm actually a little scared of you.

LOL. Don't be scared. Wait until I offer you candy for that.

If I catch you in a trench coat I'm running the other way!
When are you coming home btw?

Missing me a little?

No, I wanted to re-hang some pictures on the wall behind my
headboard and I'm wondering how much time I have.

Be home in 2 weeks. If you can wait that long,
I'll help you. It's the least I can do.

The very least, and I'll wait. You provide the hammer,
I'll provide the cocktails.

Curious about my hammer, are you?

Going across the hall right now to kick your door.

Text between Mimi and Caroline:

Girl, guess what? Sophia's grandparents' house is available
next month. We're on our way to Tahoe, baby!

Sweet! That'll be nice.
I've been dying to get away with my girls.

We were thinking of inviting the boys…is that cool with you?

That's fine. The four of you will have a great time.

Idiot, obviously you're still invited.

Aw thx! I'd love to go along on a romantic weekend
with 2 couples. FANTASTIC!

Don't be an asshole. You're totally still coming. You won't be
a 5th wheel. It'll be so fun! Did you know Ryan plays guitar?
He's gonna bring it, and we can sing along!

What is this…camp? No thx!

Text between Mimi and Neil:

Hey, Big Man, what are you doing middle of next month?

Hey, Shortie. No plans yet. What's up?

Sophia's grandparents are gonna let us have
the Tahoe house. You in? Ask Ryan…

Hells yes! I'm there. I'll ask the nerd if he's in.

Trying to talk Caroline in to coming along too.

Great! The more the merrier.
We still meeting for drinks with Sophia and Ryan tonight?

Yep, see you then.

You got it, kiddo.

Text between Simon and Neil:

Quit fucking asking me about Lucky Charms.

That little guy cracks me up every time!
Hey, when are you home?
We're headed up to Tahoe for a weekend next month.

I'll be home next week. Who's going?

Sophia and Mimi, me and Ryan. Maybe Caroline.
That girl's pretty cool.

Yah, she's pretty cool when she's not cockblocking.
Tahoe, huh?

Yep, Sophia's grandparents have a house there.

Nice.

Text between Simon and Caroline:

You going to Tahoe?

How the hell did you hear about that already?

Word gets around…Neil is pretty excited.

Oh, I'm sure he is.
Sophia in a hot tub—isn't too hard to figure out.

Wait, I thought he was dating Mimi.

Oh, he is, but he is def thinking about Sophia in a hot tub,
trust me.

What the hell?

Strange things afoot in San Francisco.
They're each dating the wrong person.

What?

It's shocking. Mimi can't stop talking about Ryan, who's usually staring like a sad puppy dog at her. And Sophia is so busy mooning over Neil's giant man hands she can't see that he's staring right back at her. Pretty funny.

Why don't they swap?

Says the guy with the harem…it's not always that easy.

Wait until I get home, I'll take care of it.

Okay, Mr. Fix-It. Before or after you hang my pictures?

Don't worry, Nightie Girl.
I'm all about getting into your bedroom.

Sigh

Did you really just type the word sigh?

Sigh…

Are you going to Tahoe?

Not if I can help it. Although it would almost be worth it to watch the chaos when they finally figure this out.

Indeed.

Text between Caroline and Sophia:

What's this I hear about you not coming to Tahoe?

Ugh! What's the big deal?

Easy, Trigger. What crawled up your ass?

I just don't know why it's essential that I accompany all of you on a romantic weekend. I'm perfectly happy to go next time. Going out with you guys here is one thing. Tagging along to Tahoe? I don't think so.

It won't be like that. I promise.

I already have to hear Simon banging on the walls when he's home. I don't need to hear Ryan drilling you in the next room, or Mimi getting manhandled.

Do you think he's manhandling her?

What?

Neil. Do you think he's manhandling her?

Is he what?

Oh, you know what I mean…

*Are you actually asking me if our dear friend Mimi
is having sex with her new boy toy?*

Yes! I'm asking!

*As it happens, no. They're not manhandling yet. Wait, why are
you asking? You've slept with Ryan right? Right????*

Gotta go.

Text between Sophia and Ryan:

*Is it weird that we only ever go out on double dates
with Mimi and Neil?*

What?

Is it weird?

I don't know. Is it?

*Yes. Tonight you're coming over, alone,
and we're watching a movie.*

Yes, ma'am.

And btw, ask your buddy Simon to come to Tahoe.

Any specific reason I'm doing this?

Yep.

Care to share?

Nope. Bring popcorn.

Text between Ryan and Simon:

Are you sick of green yet?

I'm ready to come home, yes. My flight gets in late tomorrow night. Or tonight. Shit, I don't know.

Sophia asked me to officially ask you if you want to come along to Tahoe. You in?

Tahoe, huh?

Yep. I think Caroline is going.

I thought she wasn't going.

Have you been talking to the Cockblocker?

Some. She's pretty cool. The truce seems to be holding.

Hmmm. So, Tahoe?

Let me think about it. Windsurfing this weekend?

Yep.

Text between Simon and Caroline:

So I got invited to the Tahoe thing. Are you going?

You got invited? Ugh…

I take it you're still not sold on the idea?

I don't know. I love going up there, and the house is pretty fantastic. Are you going?

Are you going?

I asked you first.

So what?

Child. Yes, I suppose I will end up going.

Great! I love it up there.

Oh, you're going now?

Might as well. Sounds like fun.

Hmm, we'll see. Home tomorrow, yes?

Yep, late flight in and then sleeping for at least a day.

Let me know when you're up. I've got that package for you.

Will do.

*And I'm baking zucchini bread tonight. I'll save some for you.
You probably have no groceries at all, right?*

You make zucchini bread?

Yep

Sigh…

I woke up suddenly and heard music coming from next door. Duke Ellington. I looked at the clock. It was after two in the morning. Clive poked his head out from under the covers and hissed.

"Oh, shut up. Don't be jealous," I hissed back.

He glared at me, showing me his bum as he turned and wiggled his way back under the covers, head first.

I snuggled in deeper myself, smiling as I listened to the music.

Simon was home.

The next morning I woke up so happy it was Saturday. I was caught up on everything: no laundry to do, no errands to run. Just a day to enjoy and relax. Fantastic.

I decided to start with a nice long bath, and then I'd decide what to do with my day. I was thinking of a run at Golden Gate Park that afternoon. Fall in San Francisco was so pretty when the weather held. I just might take a book and spend the entire afternoon there.

I started the bath and Clive came in to keep me company. He weaved in and out of my legs as I dropped my PJs on the floor and meowed as he explored the top of the tub. He loved to balance on the edge while I took a bath. He'd never fallen in, although sometimes he would dip his tail. Silly cat—one of these days he was gonna dip more than his tail.

I tested the water. It was just beginning to make its way up the side of the giant tub when I decided I needed a little coffee before I settled in. I padded out to the kitchen—naked as the day is long—to make myself a cup. I yawned as I measured the beans for the grinder.

I tossed a few spoonfuls into the filter and went to get water. As soon as I turned on the faucet, the screeching began.

First I heard Clive meow like never before. Then I heard splashing. I started to smile, thinking he'd finally fallen in, when the water from the sink shot straight in my face.

I blinked furiously, confused until I realized water was shooting out the top of the faucet, spraying the entire kitchen. *"Shit!"* I screamed, trying to turn it off. No luck.

I ran to the bathroom, still swearing and found Clive hiding behind the toilet, soaking wet, and the tub faucet spraying wildly all over the bathroom. "What the—?" I cried, trying again to turn off the water. Then I began to panic. It was like the entire apartment had gone haywire at the same moment. There was water spraying everywhere, and Clive was still screeching at the top of his lungs.

I was naked, sopping wet, and freaking out.

"Motherfuckingcocksuckershitdamndamn!" I screamed and grabbed a towel. I tried to think, tried to calm down. There must be a shut-off valve somewhere. I'd redesigned bathrooms, for Christ's sake. *Think, Caroline!*

About this time I heard the banging coming from somewhere else in the apartment. Of course I thought it was the bedroom first—naturally. But no, it was the front door.

Wrapping the towel around myself and still cursing enough to make a sailor blush, I stomped across the floor, fortunately not slipping in the collecting water, and angrily swung the door open.

Of course it was Simon.

"Are you out of your goddamned mind? What's with all the screaming?"

I practically didn't notice the green plaid boxers, the sleep hair, or the speedbump abs. Practically.

Survival mode kicked in, and I grabbed him by the elbow as he was rubbing his eye and dragged him forcibly into the apartment. "Where the hell is the shut-off valve in these apartments?" I shrieked.

He looked around at the chaos: water spraying from the kitchen, water on the floor from the bathroom, and me in my Camp Snoopy towel, which was the first one I grabbed.

Even in a crisis Simon took 2.5 seconds to look at my nearly naked body. Okay, I might have taken 3.2 to look at his.

Then we both snapped into action. He ran into the bathroom like a man on a mission, and I could hear him knocking around. Clive hissed and ran out, straight into the kitchen. Realizing it was just as wet in there, he leapt across the room in an acrobatic fit and landed high atop the fridge. I started to run to the bathroom to help and collided with Simon as he ran to the kitchen. Undeterred, he slid across the floor and opened the doors under the sink. He began throwing my cleaning supplies all over the floor, and I assumed he was trying to get at the shut-off valve. I tried not to notice the way the back of his boxers clung to his buns. I tried *so* very hard. He was covered in water as well now, and just then his feet slipped out from under him, crashing him to the floor.

"Ow," he said from under the sink, his legs now splayed out across my wet kitchen floor. Then he rolled over. He was soaking wet and a tad bit glorious.

"Get over here and help me. I can't get this one turned off," he requested over the rushing water and the cat meowing.

Remembering that I was only wearing a towel, I gingerly knelt next to him and tried to avoid looking at his body—his wet, long, lean body that was dangerously close to my own. One more random jet of water straight into my eyeball was enough to pull me from my stupor, and I renewed my focus.

"What do you want me to do?" I yelled.

"Do you have a wrench?"

"Yes!"

"Can you go get it?"

"Sure!"

"Why are you yelling?"

"I don't know!" I sat there, trying to see underneath the sink.

"Well, go get it, for God's sake!"

"Right. Right!" I yelled and ran for the hall closet.

When I came back, I slipped a little on the wet tile and slid into his side.

"Here!" I yelled and thrust the wrench under the sink.

I watched him work, his face hidden. His arms strained, and I saw how strong he really was. I watched in amazement as his stomach hardened and revealed six little packs. Oops, make that eight. And then the V showed up. Hello, V...

He grunted and groaned and as he strained to turn off the valve, his entire body caught up in the struggle. I watched as he fought the Battle of the Valve and was finally triumphant. I also kept a close eye on those green plaid boxers, which when wet, clung to him like a second skin. Skin that was wet, and probably warm, and—

"Got it!"

"Hurray!" I clapped as the water finally stopped. He let out one last groan, which sounded oddly familiar, and relaxed. I watched as he slid out from under the sink.

He lay next to me on the floor, soaked and in his boxers.

I sat next to him, soaked and in a towel.

Clive sat on top of the fridge, soaked and angry.

Clive continued to yell/meow, and we continued to stare at each other, breathing heavily—Simon because of his battle and I... because of his battle. Clive finally jumped down from the fridge to the counter and skidded across in the puddle. He hit my radio, bounced off, and fell to the floor. Loud Marvin Gaye poured into the wet kitchen as Clive shook himself and ran for the living room.

"*Let's get it on...*" Marvin sang it like he meant it, and Simon and I looked at each other, our faces stained crimson red.

"Are you kidding me?" I said.

"Is this for real?" he said, and we both started to laugh—at the chaos, at the ridiculousness, at the sheer insanity of what had just happened and the fact that we were now lying half naked in my kitchen, covered in water, listening to a song that encouraged us to, in fact, "get it on," and laughing our asses off.

I finally straightened up, wiping tears from my eyes. He sat up next to me still holding his stomach.

"This is like a bad episode of *Three's Company*," he chuckled.

"No kidding. I hope someone called Mr. Furley." I giggled, drawing my towel tighter around me.

"Shall we get this cleaned up?" he asked, standing.

I noticed that his boxers, and anything that might be contained inside, were now at eye level. *Settle, Caroline.*

"Yes, I suppose we should." I laughed again as he held out his hand to help me up. I couldn't gain any traction, so I hung on to his hands, my feet slipping all over the floor.

"This is never going to work," he muttered and swooped me up. He carried me into the living room and set me down. "Watch it there. Snoopy is drooping a little," he noted, gesturing to the part covering the girls.

"You'd love that, wouldn't you?" I sassed, pulling things tighter.

"I'm going to get changed, and I'll bring you back some dry towels. Try to stay out of trouble." He winked and headed back to his place. I laughed again and went to the bedroom where Clive was now just a bump under the covers.

I looked in the mirror over my dresser as I dug for something to put on. I was positively glowing. *Huh.* Must have been all that cold water.

An hour later things were back under control. We'd cleaned up the water, alerted the people downstairs in case there was leakage below, and placed a call to the maintenance guy.

We began to move toward my front door, mopping up the last little bit of water with the towels Simon had generously provided.

"What a disaster!" I cried, pulling myself up off the floor and sinking down on the couch.

"Could have been worse. You could have had to deal with this after only three hours' sleep, and being woken up by some woman screaming at the top of her lungs," he said, coming to sit on the arm of the couch.

I arched one eyebrow, and he recanted.

"Okay, bad example since that scenario is something you're familiar with. What are you going to do now?"

"I dunno. I need to stay here and wait for the guy to fix this mess. In the meantime, I'm without water, which means no coffee, no shower, no nothing. Sucks," I muttered, crossing my arms across my chest.

"Well, I guess I'll be across the hall, drinking coffee and thinking about my shower, if you need anything," he said, starting for the door.

"Ass, you are totally making me coffee."

"Are you taking me up on the shower, too?"

"You won't be in there with me, you know."

"I guess you can take one anyway. Come on, you little cock-blocker," he huffed, pulling me up off the couch and leading me across the hall. Clive tossed one last angry cry at me from the bedroom, and I shushed him.

"Oops, wait. Let me grab breakfast." I snatched a foil-wrapped package from the table.

"What's that?" he asked.

"Your zucchini bread."

I swear he almost bit through his bottom lip. He must really like zucchini bread.

Thirty minutes later, I sat at Simon's kitchen table, legs curled underneath me, drinking French-pressed coffee and towel-drying my hair. He seemed really relaxed and happy, and he'd devoured the entire loaf of zucchini bread. I barely managed half a slice before he took it away from me, the entire chunk disappearing in his mouth.

He pushed away from the table and groaned, patting his full belly.

"You want another loaf? I baked plenty, you little piggy." I wrinkled my nose at him.

"I will take anything you want to give me, Nightie Girl. You have no idea how much I love homemade bread. No one's made anything like this for me in years." He winked and let out a tiny burp.

"Now that's sexy." I frowned and took my coffee cup into the living room, glancing out into the hallway to see if the maintenance guy had shown up yet.

Simon followed me in and sat down on his big, comfy couch. I wandered around, looking at all his pictures. He had a series of black and whites on one wall, several prints of the same woman on a beach. Hands, feet, tummy, shoulders, back, legs, toes, and finally one of just her face. She was gorgeous.

"This is beautiful. One of your harem?" I asked, looking back at him.

He sighed and ran his hand through his hair. "Not every woman has made a trip to my bed, you know."

"Sorry. I'm kidding. Where were these taken?" I asked, sitting down next to him.

"On a beach in Bora Bora. I was working on a travel photography series—the most beautiful beaches of the South Pacific, very retro styled. She was on the beach one day, local girl, and the light was perfect, so I asked if I could take some shots of her. They came out great."

"She's gorgeous," I said, sipping my coffee.

"Yes," he agreed with a sweet smile.

We sipped silently, being okay with being quiet.

"So what were you planning to do today?" he asked.

"You mean before my pipes revolted?"

"Yes, before the attack," he smiled over the rim of his mug, blue eyes twinkling.

"I didn't have a lot planned, actually, and that was a good thing. I was gonna go for a run, maybe sit outside and read this afternoon." I sighed, feeling warm and comfortable and cozy. "What about you?"

"I was planning on sleeping the entire day before tackling a mountain of laundry."

"You can go sleep, you know. I can wait in my own apartment." I started to get up. Poor guy, he'd gotten in late, and I was keeping him from sleep.

But he waved me off and pointed to the couch. "I know better, though. If I sleep I'll have jet lag all week. I need to get back on Pacific time as soon as I can, so it's probably a good thing your pipes attacked."

"Hmm, I guess. So how was Ireland? Good times?" I asked, settling back.

"I always have a good time when I'm traveling."

"God, what an amazing job. I'd love to travel like that, living out of a suitcase, seeing the world, amazing…" I trailed off, looking around again at all the pictures. I spotted a slender shelf on the far wall with tiny bottles on it. "What's that?" I asked, heading for the curious little shelf. They each contained what looked like sand. Some were white, some gray, some pink, and one was almost pitch black. They each had a label. As I looked I felt, rather than saw, him move behind me. His breath was warm in my ear.

"Every time I visit a new beach, I bring back a little sand—like a reminder of where I was, when I was there," he answered, his voice low and wistful.

I looked more closely at the bottles and marveled over the names I saw: *Harbour Island–Bahamas, Prince William Sound–Alaska, Punaluu–Hawaii, Vik–Iceland, Sanur–Fiji, Patura–Turkey, Galicia–Spain.*

"And you've been all these places?"

"Mmm-hmm."

"And why bring back sand? Why not postcards, or better yet, the pictures you take? Isn't that enough of a souvenir?" I turned to look at him.

"I take pictures because I love it, and it happens to be my job. But this? This is tangible, it's tactile, it's real. I can *feel* this, this is sand I was actually standing on, from every continent on the planet. It brings me back there, instantly," he said, his eyes going all dreamy.

From any other guy, in any other setting, it would have been pure cheese. But from Simon? The guy had to be deep. Dammit.

My fingers continued to trail over all the bottles—almost more than I could count. My fingertips lingered on the few from Spain, and he noticed.

"Spain, huh?" he asked.

I turned to look at him. "Yep, Spain. Always wanted to go. I will someday." I sighed and crossed back to the couch.

"Do you travel much?" he asked, sinking down next to me again.

"I try to go somewhere each year—not as fancy as you, or as frequent, but I try to take myself somewhere every year."

"You and the girls?" he smiled.

"Sometimes, but the last few years I've enjoyed traveling by myself. There's something nice about being able to set your own pace, go where you want, and not have to run it by a committee every time you want to go out for dinner, you know?"

"I get it. I'm just surprised," he said, frowning slightly.

"Surprised that I'd want to travel alone? Are you kidding? It's the best!" I cried.

"Hell, you'll get no argument from me. I'm just surprised. Most people don't like to travel alone—too overwhelming, too intimidating. And they think they'll get lonely."

"Do you ever get lonely?" I asked.

"I told you, I am never lonely," he said, shaking his head.

"Yes, yes, I know, Simon says, but I have to say I find that a little hard to believe." I twisted a lock of almost-dry hair around my finger.

"Do you get lonely?" he asked.

"When I'm traveling? No, I'm great company," I answered promptly.

"I hate to admit it, but I'd agree with that," he said, raising his mug in my direction.

I smiled and blushed slightly, hating myself as I did it. "Wow, are we becoming friends?" I asked.

"Hmm, friends…" He appeared to think carefully, examining me and my current state of blush. "Yes, I think we are."

"Interesting. From cockblocker to friend. Not bad." I giggled and clinked his mug with my own.

"Oh, it remains to be seen whether you're lifted from cockblocker status yet," he said.

"Well, just give me a heads up before Spanx comes over next time, okay, *friend?*" I laughed at his confused expression.

"Spanx?"

"Ah, yes, well, you know her as Katie." I laughed.

He finally had the decency to blush and smile sheepishly. "Well, as it happens, Ms. Katie is no longer part of what you so kindly refer to as my harem."

"Oh no! I liked her! Did you paddle her too hard?" I teased again, my giggling beginning to get out of control.

He ran his hands through his hair frantically. "I have to tell you, this is frankly the strangest conversation I've ever had with a woman."

"I doubt that, but seriously, where did Katie go?"

He smiled quietly. "She met someone else and seems really happy. So we ended our physical relationship, of course, but she's still a good friend."

"Well, that's good." I nodded and was quiet a moment. "How does that work, actually?"

"How does what work?"

"Well, you have to admit, your relationships are unconventional at best. How do you do it? Keep everyone happy?" I prodded.

He laughed. "You're not seriously asking how I satisfy these women, are you?" He grinned.

"Hell, no. I've heard how you do that! There doesn't seem to be any question about that. I mean, how does no one get hurt?"

He thought for a moment. "I guess because we were honest going into this. It isn't like anyone sets out to create this little world, it just happens. Katie and I had always gotten along great, especially in that way, so we just fell into that relationship."

"I like Spanx—I mean Katie. So was she the first? In the harem?"

"Enough with the harem—you make it sound so sordid. Katie and I went to college together, tried dating for real, didn't work out. She's great though, she's...wait, are you sure you want to hear all this?"

"Oh, I am all ears. I've been waiting to peel this onion since you first knocked that picture off my wall and clocked me on the head." I smiled, settling back on the couch and curling my knees underneath me.

"I knocked a picture off your wall?" he asked, looking amused and proud at the same time. What a guy.

"Focus up, Simon. Gimme the skinny on your ladies in waiting. And spare no details—this shit is better than HBO."

He laughed and put on his storyteller face. "Well, okay, I guess it started with Katie. We didn't work out as a couple, but when we ran into each other after college a few years ago, coffee turned into lunch, lunch turned into drinks, and drinks turned into...well, bed. Neither of us was seeing anyone, so we started getting together whenever I was in town. She's great. She's just...I don't know how to explain it. She's...soft."

"Soft?"

"Yeah, she's all rounded edges and warm and sweet. She's just... soft. She's the best."

"And Purina?"

"Nadia. Her name is Nadia."

"I have a cat that says otherwise."

"*Nadia* I met in Prague. I was doing a shoot one winter. I usually never do fashion photography, but I got asked to shoot for *Vogue*—very artsy, very conceptual. She had a house outside the city. We spent a naked weekend together, and when she moved to the States she looked me up. She's getting her masters now in international relations. It's crazy to me that at twenty-five she's on the tail end of her career, in modeling, that is. So she's working hard to do something else. She's very smart. She's traveled the entire world, and she speaks five languages! She went to the Sorbonne. Did you know that?"

"How would I know that?"

"Easy to make snap judgments when you don't know someone, isn't it?" he asked, eyeing me.

"Touché," I nodded, nudging him with my foot to go on.

"And then Lizzie. Oh boy, that woman is insane! I met her in London, piss drunk in a pub. She walked up to me, grabbed my collar, kissed me stupid, and dragged me home with her. That girl knows exactly what she wants and isn't afraid to ask for it."

I remembered some of her louder moments in great detail. She really was rather specific about what she wanted, provided you could get past the giggling.

"She's a solicitor—attorney—and one of her main clients lives here in San Francisco. Her business is based in London, but when we're both in the same city, we make sure to see each other. And that's it. That's all she wrote."

"That's it? Three women, and that's it. How do they not get jealous? How are they all okay with this? And don't you want more? Don't they want more?"

"For now, no. Everyone is getting exactly what they want, so it's all good. And yes, they all know about each other, and since no one's in love here, no one has any real expectations beyond friendship—with the best possible benefits. I mean, don't get me wrong, I adore each of them, and love them in their own way. I'm a lucky guy. These women are amazing. But I'm too busy to date anyone for real, and most women don't want to put up with a boyfriend who's across the globe more often than home."

"Yes, but not all women want the same thing. We don't all want the picket fence."

"Every woman I've ever dated has said she doesn't, but then she does. And that's cool—I get it—but with my schedule being so crazy, it got to be very difficult for me to be involved with anyone who needed me to be something I'm not."

"So you've never been in love?"

"I didn't say that, did I?"

"So you have been in a relationship before, with just one woman?"

"Of course, but as I said, once my life became what it is today—the constant traveling—it's hard to stay in love with that kind of guy. At least that's what my ex told me when she started dating some accountant. You know, wears a suit, carries a briefcase, home every night by six—it's what women seem to want." He sighed, setting his coffee down and relaxing further into the couch. His words said he was okay with all this, but the wistful look on his face said otherwise.

"It's not what all women want," I countered.

"Correction, it's what the women I have dated all wanted. At least until now. That's why what I have works great for me. These women I spend my time with when I'm home? They're great. They're happy, I'm happy—why would I rock the boat?"

"Well, you're already down to two now, and I think you'd feel differently if the right woman came along. The right woman for you wouldn't want you to change anything about your life. She wouldn't rock your boat, she'd jump right in and sail it with you."

"You're a romantic, aren't you?" He leaned in, bumping my shoulder.

"I'm a practical romantic. I can actually see some appeal in having a guy who travels a lot, because, frankly? I like my space. I also take up the entire bed, so it's difficult for me to sleep with anyone." I shook my head ruefully, remembering how quickly I used to kick my one-nighters to the curb. Some of my past wasn't all that different from Simon's. He just had his sexcapades tied up in a much neater package.

"A practical romantic. Interesting. So what about you? Dating anyone?" he asked.

"Nope, and I'm okay with that."

"Really?"

"Is it so hard to believe a hot, sexy woman with a great career doesn't need a man to be happy?"

"First of all, bully for you for calling yourself hot and sexy—because it's true. It's nice to see a woman give herself a compliment instead of fishing for one. And second, I'm not talking about getting married here, I'm talking about dating. You know, hanging out? Casually?"

"Are you asking me if I'm fucking anyone right now?" I shot at him, and he spluttered into his coffee.

"Definitely the strangest conversation I've ever had with a woman," he muttered.

"A hot and sexy woman," I reminded him.

"That's for damn sure. So, how about you? Ever been in love?"

"This feels like an ABC mini-series, with all the coffee and the love talk," I said. I might have been stalling.

"Come on, let's celebrate this moment in our lives," he snorted, gesturing with his coffee mug.

"Have I ever been in love? Yes. Yes, I have."

"And?"

"And nothing. It didn't end in a very good way, but what ending is ever good? He changed, I changed, so I got out. That's all."

"You got out, like…"

"Nothing dramatic. He just wasn't who I thought he was going to be," I explained, setting my coffee down and playing with my hair.

"So what happened?"

"Oh, you know how it goes. We were together when I was a senior at Berkley, and he was finishing up law school. It started out great, and then it wasn't, and so I left. He did teach me how to rock climb, so I'm grateful for that."

"A lawyer, huh?"

"Yep, and he wanted a little lawyer wife. I should have caught on when he referred to my future career plans as a 'little decorating business.' He really just wanted someone who looked good and picked up his shirts from the cleaners on time. Not for me."

"I don't know you that well yet, but I can't really see you in the suburbs somewhere."

"Ugh, me either. Nothing wrong with the 'burbs, just not for me."

"You can't move to the 'burbs. Who would bake for me?"

"Pfft, you just want to see me in my apron."

"You have no idea," he said, winking.

"It's hard to get everything you need from one person. You know what I mean? Wait, of course you do. What was I thinking?" I laughed, gesturing to him.

We both jumped at the knocking on my door across the hall. The maintenance guy had finally arrived.

"Thanks for the coffee, and the shower, and the pipe rescue," I said, stretching as I walked toward the door. I nodded at the guy in the hallway and held up one finger to let him know I'd be right there.

"No problem. It wasn't the nicest way to wake up, but I suppose I deserved that one."

"Indeed. But thank you anyway."

"You're welcome, and thanks for the bread. It was great. And if another loaf happens to make its way over here, that would be okay."

"I'll see what I can do. And hey, where's my sweater?"

"Do you know how expensive those are?"

"Pffft, I want my sweater!" I cried, slapping him in the chest.

"Well, as it happens, I did bring you something—a sort of thanks-for-kicking-my-door present."

"I knew it. You can drop it off later." I walked across the hall to let the guy in. I directed him toward the kitchen and turned back to Simon. "Friends, huh?"

"Looks that way."

"I can live with that." I smiled and closed the door.

As the maintenance guy went about fixing the problem, I wandered to my bedroom to check on Clive. Just as I entered, my phone buzzed. A text from Simon already? I grinned and flopped down on the bed, snuggling a still-freaked-out kitty to my side. He began to purr instantly.

You never answered my question…

I felt my skin heat up as I realized what he was referring to. I was suddenly warm and a little tingly, like when your foot falls asleep, but all over. And in a good way. *Damn*, he gave great text.

About whether I'm fucking anyone?

Jesus, you're crass. But yes, friends can ask that, can't they?

Yes they can.

So?

You're kind of a pain in the ass. You know this, right?

Tell me. Don't get shy on me now.

As it happens, no. I'm not.

I heard a thud from next door,
and then a slight but constant banging on the wall.

What the hell are you doing? Is that your head?

You're killing me, Nightie Girl.

As soon as I finished reading, the banging resumed. I laughed out loud as he thumped his head against the wall. I placed my hand on the wall over my bed where the thumping was concentrated and chuckled again. *What a strange morning...*

chapter ten

I sat in my office, gazing out the window. I had a list of things to do in front of me—and it wasn't a small list either. I needed to run by the Nicholson house. The renovation was almost complete. The bedroom and bathroom were finished, and just a few details remained. I needed to get some new sample books from the design center. I had a meeting with a new client Mimi had referred to me, and on top of all that, I had a folder full of invoices to go through.

But still, I gazed out the window. I might have had Simon on the brain. And for good reason. Between the pipe explosions, the head banging, and the constant texting all day Sunday asking for more zucchini bread, my brain simply could not expunge him. And then last night, he brought out the big guns: he Glenn Miller-ed me. He even knocked on the wall to make sure I was listening.

I put my head down on the desk and banged it a few times to see if it helped. It had seemed to help Simon…

That night I went straight to yoga after work and was climbing the stairs to my apartment when I heard a door open from above.

"Caroline?" he called down to me.

I grinned and continued up the stairs. "Yes, Simon?" I called up.

"You're home late."

"What, are you watching my door now?" I laughed, rounding the last landing and staring up at him. He was hanging over the railing, hair in his face.

"Yep. I'm here for the bread. Zucchini me, woman!"

"You're insane. You know this, right?" I climbed the last stair and stood in front of him.

"I've been told. You smell nice," he said, leaning in.

"Did you just sniff me?" I asked incredulously as I opened the door.

"Mmm-hmm, very nice. Just get back from a workout?" he asked, walking in behind me and closing the door.

"Yoga, why?"

"You smell *great* when you're all worked up," he said, waggling his eyebrows at me like the devil.

"Seriously, you pick women up with lines like that?" I turned away from him to take off my jacket and squeeze my thighs together maniacally.

"It's not a line. You do smell great," I heard him say, and I closed my eyes to block out the Simon Voodoo currently making Lower Caroline curl in on herself.

Clive came bounding out of the bedroom when he heard my voice and stopped short when he saw Simon. Unfortunately, he had little traction on the hardwood floor and skidded rather ungracefully under the dining room table. Trying to regain his dignity, he executed a difficult four-foot leap from a standing position onto the bookshelf and waved me over with his paw. He wanted me to come to him — typical male.

I dropped my gym bag and sauntered over. "Hi, sweet boy. How was your day? Hmm? Did you play? Did you get a good nap? Hmm?" I scratched behind his ear, and he purred loudly. He gave me his dreamy cat eyes and then turned his gaze to Simon. I swear he cat-smirked at him.

"Zucchini bread, huh? You want some more, I take it?" I asked, throwing my jacket on the back of a chair.

"I know you have more. Simon says gimme it," he deadpanned, making his finger into a gun.

"You're oddly into your baked goods, aren't you? Support group for that?" I asked, walking into the kitchen to locate the last loaf. I might have been saving it for him.

"Yes, I'm in BA. Bakers Anonymous. We meet over at the bakery on Pine," he replied, sitting down on the stool at the kitchen counter.

"Good group?"

"Pretty good. There's a better one over on Market, but I can't go to that one anymore," he said sadly, shaking his head.

"Get kicked out?" I asked, leaning on the counter in front of him.

"I did, actually," he said, and then curled his finger to get me to lean in closer.

"I got in trouble for fondling buns," he whispered.

I giggled and gave his cheek a light pinch. "Fondling buns," I snorted as he pushed my hand away.

"Just fork over the bread, see, and no one gets hurt," he warned.

I waved my hands in surrender and grabbed a wine glass from the cupboard over his head. I raised my eyebrow at him, and he nodded.

I handed him a bottle of Merlot and the opener, then grabbed a bunch of grapes from the colander in the fridge. He poured, we clinked, and without another word, I started making us dinner.

The rest of the evening happened naturally, without me even realizing it. One minute we were discussing the new wine glasses I'd purchased from Williams Sonoma, and thirty minutes later we were sitting at the dining room table with pasta in front of us. I was still wearing my workout clothes, and Simon was in jeans and a T-shirt and his stocking feet. He'd taken off his Stanford sweatshirt before draining the pasta, something I didn't even have to ask him to do. He'd simply wandered into the kitchen behind me, and had it drained and back in the pot just as I finished the sauce.

We'd talked about the city, his work, my work, and the upcoming trip to Tahoe, and now we headed over to the couch with coffee.

I leaned back against the pillows with my legs curled underneath me. Simon was telling me about a trip he'd taken to Vietnam a few years before.

"It's like nothing you've ever seen — the mountain villages, the gorgeous beaches, the food! Oh, Caroline, the food." He sighed, stretching his arm along the back of the couch. I smiled and tried not to notice the butterflies when he said my name that way: with the word *Oh* right in front of it...Oh me, oh my.

"Sounds wonderful, but I hate Vietnamese food. Can't stand it. Can I bring peanut butter?"

"I know this guy—makes the best noodles ever, right on a houseboat in the middle of Ha Long Bay. One slurp and you'll throw your peanut butter right over the side."

"God, I wish I could travel like you do. Do you ever get sick of it?" I asked.

"Hmmm, yes and no. It's always great to come home. I love San Francisco. But if I'm home too long I get the itch to get back out on the road. And no comments about the itch—I'm starting to get to know your mind there, Nightie Girl." He patted my arm affectionately.

I tried to feign offense, but the truth was I *had* been about to make a joke. I noticed he still had his hand on my arm, absentmindedly tracing tiny circles with his fingertips. Had it really been so long since I'd let a man touch me that fingertip circles sent me into a mental tizzy? Or was it that *this* man was doing it? *Oh, God, the fingertips.* Either way, it was doing things to me. If I closed my eyes, I could almost imagine O waving at me—still far away, but not as far as she'd been before.

I glanced at Simon and saw that he was watching his hand, as if curious about his fingers on my skin. I breathed in quickly, and my intake of breath drew his eyes to mine. We watched each other. Lower Caroline was, of course, responding, but now Heart began to beat a little wildly as well.

Then Clive jumped up on the back of the couch, put his bum right in Simon's face, and killed that real quick. We both laughed, and Simon moved away from me as I explained to Clive that it was not polite to do that to company. Clive seemed oddly pleased with himself, though, so I knew he was up to something.

"Wow, it's almost ten! I've taken up your entire evening. I hope you didn't have plans," Simon said, standing and stretching. As he stretched, his T-shirt came up, and I bit down hard on my tongue to stop myself from licking the bit of skin showing above his jeans.

"Well, I did have a rather exciting night of watching Food Network planned, so damn you, Simon!" I shook my fist in his face as I stood up next to him.

"And you even made me dinner, which was great, by the way," he said, searching for his sweatshirt.

"No problem. It was nice to cook for someone other than myself. It's what I do for any guy who shows up demanding bread." I finally handed him the loaf I'd left out for him.

He grinned as he grabbed his sweatshirt off the floor next to the couch. "Well, next time, let me cook for you. I make a fantastic—huh, that's weird," he interrupted himself, grimacing.

"What's weird?" I asked, watching as he unfolded his sweatshirt.

"This feels damp. Actually, it's more than damp, it's…wet?" he asked, looking at me, confused. I looked from the sweatshirt to Clive, who sat innocently on the back of the couch.

"Oh no," I whispered, the blood draining from my face. "Clive, you little shit!" I glared at him.

He jumped off the couch and darted quickly between my legs, headed for the bedroom. He'd learned I couldn't reach him behind the dresser, and that's where he hid when he'd done a bad, bad thing. He hadn't done this in a long time.

"Simon, you might want to leave that here. I'll wash it, dry clean it—whatever. I am so, so sorry," I apologized, horrifically embarrassed.

"Oh, did he? Oh man, he did, didn't he?" His face wrinkled as I took the sweatshirt from him.

"Yes, yes, he did. I'm so sorry, Simon. He has this thing about marking his territory. When any guy leaves clothes on the floor—oh, God—he eventually pees on them. I'm so sorry. I am so, so sorry. I'm so—"

"Caroline, it's okay. I mean, it's gross, but it's okay. I've had worse things happen to me. It's all good, I promise." He started to put his hand on my shoulder, but seemed to think better of it, probably when he realized the last thing he'd touched.

"I'm so sorry, I—" I began again as he started for the door.

"Stop it. If you say sorry one more time I'm gonna go find something of yours and pee on it, I swear."

"Okay, that's just gross." I finally laughed. "But we had such a nice night, and it ended in pee!" I wailed, opening the door for him.

"It *was* a nice night, even with the pee. There'll be others. Don't worry, Nightie Girl." He winked and crossed the hall.

"Play me something good tonight, huh?" I asked, watching him go.

"You got it. Sleep tight," he said, and we closed the doors at the same time.

I leaned back against the door, hugging the sweatshirt in my arms. I'm sure I had the goofiest grin on my face, as I remembered the feeling of his fingertips. And then I remembered I was hugging a pee-stained sweatshirt.

"Clive, you asshole!" I yelled and ran for my bedroom.

Fingers, hands, warm skin pressed against mine in an effort to get closer. I felt his warm breath, his voice like wet sex in my ear. "Mmm, Caroline, how can you feel this good?"

I moaned and rolled over, twisting legs with legs and arms with arms, pushing my tongue into his waiting mouth. I sucked on his bottom lip, tasting mint and heat and the promise of what was to come when he pushed into my body for the first time. I moaned as he groaned, and in a flash I was pinned beneath him.

Lips moved from my mouth to my neck, licking and sucking and finding the spot—that spot underneath my jaw that made my insides explode and my eyes cross. A dark laugh against my collarbone, and I knew I was done for.

I rolled on top of him, feeling the loss of his weight but the gain of my legs on either side of him, feeling him twitch and throb exactly where I needed him to be. He pushed my hair from my face, gazing up at me with those eyes—the eyes that could make me forget my name but scream his own.

"Simon!" I cried, feeling his hands grab my hips and push me against him.

I sat straight up in bed, my heart racing as the last dreamy images left my brain. I thought I heard a low chuckle from other side of the wall, where the strains of Miles Davis came through.

I lay back down, skin tingling as I tried to find a cool spot on my pillow. I thought about what was on the other side of that wall, inches away. I was in trouble.

Later that morning I sat at my desk getting ready to meet a new client—one who'd specifically requested to work with me. Still a new designer, much of my work came from referrals, and whoever had referred this guy to me I owed big time. All new interiors for some fancy apartment—it was practically a gut remodel, a dream project. Whenever I prepped for a new client I pulled pictures from other projects I'd designed and had sketchbooks ready, but today I did it with particular intensity. If I let my mind wander for a second, Brain immediately returned to the dream I'd had last night. I blushed every time I thought of what I'd let Dream Simon do to me, and what Dream Caroline had done to him as well…

Dream Caroline and Dream Simon were some naughty kids.

"Ahem," I heard from behind me. I turned to find Ashley in the doorway. "Caroline, Mr. Brown is here."

"Excellent, I'll be right out." I nodded, standing and smoothing my skirt. My hands pressed my cheeks, hoping they were not too red.

"And he is cute, cute, cute!" she murmured as she walked beside me down the hall.

"Oh, really? Must be my lucky day." I laughed, rounding the corner to greet him.

He certainly was cute, and I would know. He was my ex-boyfriend.

"Oh, my God! What are the chances?" Jillian exclaimed at lunch, two hours later.

"Well, considering my entire life now seems ruled by odd coincidences, I figure it's right on track." I broke off a piece of flatbread and chewed determinedly.

"But I mean, come on! What are the chances, really?" she wondered again, pouring us another glass of Pellegrino.

"Oh, there's nothing chance about this. This guy doesn't leave things to chance. He knew exactly what he was doing when he approached you at that benefit last month."

"No," she breathed.

"Yep. He told me. He saw me, and when he found out I worked for you? Bam! He needs an interior designer." I smiled, thinking of how he'd always arranged things exactly the way he wanted them. Well, almost everything.

"Don't worry, Caroline. I'll move him over to another designer, or I'll even take him myself. You don't have to work with him," she said, patting my hand.

"Oh, hell no! I already told him yes. I'm totally doing this." I crossed my arms over my chest.

"Are you sure?"

"Yep. No problem. It wasn't that we had a bad breakup. In fact, as far as breakups go, it was mild. He didn't want to accept the fact that I was leaving him, but eventually he came around. He didn't think I had the balls to do it, and boy, was he surprised." I played with my napkin.

I'd dated James most of my senior year at Berkeley. He was already in law school, steadily moving through it on his way to a future of perfection. My goodness, he was beautiful — strong and handsome, and very charming. We met at the library one night, had coffee a few times, and it grew into a solid relationship.

The sex? Unreal.

He was my first serious boyfriend, and I knew he wanted to marry me at some point. He had very specific ideas about what he wanted from his life, and that definitely included me as his wife. And he was everything I'd ever *thought* I wanted in a husband. Engagement was inevitable. But then I began to notice things, small at first, but over time they revealed the big picture. We went where he wanted to for dinner. I never got to pick. I overheard him telling someone that he figured my "decorating" phase wouldn't last long, but it'd be nice to have a wife who could make a pretty home. The sex was still great, but I was irritated with him more and more, and I stopped going along to get along.

When I began to realize he was no longer what I wanted for *my* future, things got a little strained. We fought constantly, and when I decided to end the relationship, he tried to convince me I was making the wrong choice. I knew better, and he finally accepted that I was really done — and not just pitching a "feminine fit," as he liked to call them. We didn't keep in contact, but he'd been a major part of my life for a long time, and I cherished the memories we had together. I cherished what he'd taught me about myself.

Just because we didn't work out as a couple didn't mean we couldn't work together, right?

"You sure about this? You really want to work with him?" Jillian asked one more time, but I could tell she was ready to let it go.

I thought about it again, replaying the flash of memory I'd had when I saw him standing in the lobby. Sandy blond hair, piercing eyes, charming smile: I'd been hit with a wave of nostalgia and grinned as he crossed to me.

"Hey there, stranger," he'd said, offering me his hand.

"James!" I gasped, but recovered quickly. "You look great!" We hugged—to gawking Ashley's surprise.

"Yes, I'm sure," I told Jillian. "It'll be good for me. Call it a growth experience. Plus, I don't want to give up the commission. We'll see what happens tonight."

At that she looked up from her menu. "Tonight?"

"Oh, I didn't tell you? We're going for drinks to get caught up."

I stood in front of the mirror, fluffing my hair and checking my teeth for wayward lipstick. The rest of the workday had gone quickly, and I now found myself at home getting ready for tonight. We'd agreed to just drinks, very casual, although I was leaving the option open for dinner. But skinny jeans, black turtleneck, and cropped gray leather jacket was as fancy as I was gonna get.

The time I'd spent this morning with James at the office was pleasant, and when he'd asked me to go for drinks to catch up, I agreed instantly. I was anxious to learn what he'd been up to, as well as make sure we'd be able to work together. He'd been a huge part of my life at one time, and the idea of being able to work with someone I'd once been so close to felt good to me. It felt mature. Closure? Not sure what to call it, but it seemed like the natural thing to do.

He was picking me up at seven, and I planned to meet him outside. Parking on my street was ridiculous. A glance at the clock told me it was time to get going, so I gave a quick kiss goodbye to Clive, who'd been on his best behavior since the pee incident, and let myself into the hallway.

And straight into Simon, who was in front of my door.

"Okay, you are officially my stalker! There's no more zucchini bread, mister. I hope you made that loaf last because there is no more for you," I warned, pressing him back from my front door with my pointer finger.

"I know, I know. I'm actually here on official business," he laughed, throwing up his arms in defeat.

"Walk with me?" I asked, nodding toward the stairs.

"I'm headed out as well. Going to rent a movie," he explained as we started down.

"People still rent movies?" I joked, rounding the corner.

"Yes, people still rent movies. Just for that you're gonna have to watch whatever I pick out," he replied, raising an eyebrow.

"Tonight?"

"Sure, why not. I was coming over to see if you wanted to hang out. I owe you for dinner from the other night, and I got an urge to watch something spooky…" He launched into *The Twilight Zone* theme.

I couldn't help but laugh at his claw hands and crossed eyes. "Last time someone asked me to rent a movie it was code for 'let's make out on the couch.' Am I safe with you?"

"Please! We've got that truce, remember? I am all about the truce. So, tonight?"

"I wish I could, but I have plans tonight. Tomorrow night?" We rounded the last stair and entered the entryway.

"Tomorrow I can do. Come on over after work. But I get to pick the movie, and I'm making you dinner. Least I can do for my little cockblocker." He smirked, and I punched him in the arm.

"Please stop calling me that. Otherwise I won't bring dessert," I said, lowering my voice and batting my eyelashes like a fool.

"Dessert?" he asked, holding the door open as I walked out into the night.

"Mmm-hmm. I picked up some apples yesterday while I was out, and I've been craving pie all week. How does that sound?" I asked, scanning the street for James.

"Apple pie? Homemade apple pie? Christ, woman, are you trying to kill me? Mmm…" He smacked his lips and looked at me hungrily.

"Why, sir, you look like you've seen something you'd like to eat," I offered in my best Scarlett.

"You show up with apple pie tomorrow night, and I may not let you leave," he breathed, his cheeks rosy and his messy hair blowing in the cool air.

"That would be terrible," I whispered. *Wow.* "Okay, so, go get your movie," I said, playfully shoving the six feet of hot in front of me. *Remember the harem!* I shouted inside my head.

"Caroline?" a concerned voice came from behind me, and I turned to see James walking toward us.

"Hey, James," I called out, stepping away from Simon with a giggle.

"You ready to go?" he asked, looking at Simon carefully. Simon straightened to his full height and looked back, just as carefully.

"Yep, ready to go. Simon, this is James. James, Simon." They leaned in to shake hands, and I could see that they both exerted a little extra force, neither seeming to want to be the one to let go first. I rolled my eyes. Yes, boys. You can both write your names in the snow. The question is, who would make bigger letters?

"Nice to meet you, James. It was James, right? I'm Simon. Simon Parker."

"That's correct. James. James Brown."

I saw the beginnings of a laugh on Simon's face.

"Okay, James, we should get going. Simon, I'll talk to you later," I interrupted, ending the handshake of the century.

James turned toward where his car was double-parked, and Simon looked at me.

"Brown? James Brown?" he mouthed, and I squelched my own laugh.

"Shush," I mouthed back, smiling at James when he turned back to me.

"Nice to meet you, Simon. See you around," James called, steering me to the car with his hand on the small of my back. I didn't think twice about it, as that's how we always used to walk together, but Simon's eyes widened a little at the sight.

Hmm…

James opened the door for me, then headed around to his side. Simon was still standing in front of our building when we drove away. I rubbed my hands together in front of the heater and grinned at James as he steered through the traffic.

"So, where are we headed?"

We made ourselves comfortable in the swanky bar he'd selected. It seemed very James: chic and sophisticated, and laced with hidden sexuality. The deep red leather banquettes, thinly cushioned and cool, ensconced us as we settled in and began the process of getting to know each other after so many years apart.

As we waited for a server to come by, I studied his face. He still looked the same: closely cropped sandy blond hair, intense eyes, and a lean frame folded in on itself like a cat's. Age had only improved his good looks, and his carefully torn jeans and black cashmere sweater clung to a body I could see was in great shape. James had been a rock climber, relentless in his pursuit of the sport. He viewed each boulder, each mountain as an obstacle to overcome, something to be conquered.

I'd gone climbing with him a few times towards the end of our relationship, even though I grew up skittish about heights. But watching him climb, seeing the sinewy muscles stretch and manipulate his body into positions that seemed unnatural, was a heady experience, and I'd pounced on him those evenings in the tent like a woman possessed.

"What are you thinking about?" he asked, interrupting my musings.

"I was thinking about how much you used to climb. Is that something you still do?"

"It is, but I don't get as much free time as I used to. They keep me pretty busy at the firm. I try and get out to Big Basin as often as I can," he added, smiling as our waitress approached.

"What can I get you two?" she asked, placing napkins in front of us. "She'll have a dry vodka martini, three olives, and for me bring three fingers of Macallan," he answered. The waitress nodded and left to fill our order.

I studied him as he sat back, then turned his gaze to me.

"Oh, Caroline, I'm sorry. Is that still your drink?"

I narrowed my eyes at him. "As it happens, yes. But what if I didn't want that tonight?" I answered primly.

"My mistake. Of course, what did you want to drink?" He waved the waitress back over.

"I'll have a dry vodka martini with three olives, please," I told her with a wink.

She looked confused.

James laughed loudly, and she walked away, shaking her head.

"Touché, Caroline. Touché," he said, studying me again.

"So, tell me what you've been up to the last few years." I put my elbows on the table and chin in hands.

"Hmm, how to encapsulate years in a few sentences? Finished law school, signed on with the firm here in the city, and worked like a dog for two years. I've been able to ease up a bit, only around sixty-five hours a week now, and it's nice seeing daylight again, I admit." He grinned, and I couldn't help but smile back. "And of course working as much as I do leaves me very little time for a social life, so it was just blind luck that I saw you at the benefit last month," he finished, leaning forward on his elbows as well. Jillian attended many social events around town, and I accompanied her on occasion. Good for business. I should've known I'd eventually run into James at one of those shindigs.

"So you saw me, but you didn't come talk to me. And now here you are, weeks later, asking me to work on your condo. Why is that, exactly?" I accepted my drink as it arrived and took a long pull.

"I wanted to talk to you, believe me. But I couldn't. So much time had passed. Then I realized you worked for Jillian, who a friend had recommended to me, and I thought, 'how perfect.'" He inclined his glass toward mine for a clink.

I paused for a moment, then clinked him. "So you're serious about working with me? This isn't some kind of ploy to get me into bed, is it?"

He looked at me evenly. "Still direct as ever, I see. But no, this is professional. I didn't like the way we left things, admittedly, but I accepted your decision. And now here we are. I *needed* a decorator. You *are* a decorator. Works out well, don't you think?"

"Designer," I said quietly.

"What's that?"

"Designer," I said, louder this time. "I'm an interior designer, not a decorator. There's a difference, Mr. Attorney Man." I took another sip.

"Of course, of course," he replied, signaling for the waitress.

Surprised, I looked down to find my glass empty.

"Care for another?" he asked, and I nodded.

As we small talked for the next hour, we also began to discuss what he needed in his new home. Jillian had been right. He was pretty much asking me to design his entire place, from area rugs to lighting fixtures and everything in between. It would be a huge commission, and he'd even agreed to let me photograph it for a local design magazine Jillian had been wanting me to submit to. James came from a wealthy family—the Browns of Philadelphia, don't you know—and I knew they must be footing the bill for most of this. Young lawyers didn't make enough to afford the kind of place he had, let alone in one of the most expensive cities in America. But trust funds live on, and he had a large one. One of the perks of dating him in college had been that we could actually afford real dates, not just cheap takeout all the time. I'd enjoyed that aspect of being with him. Not gonna lie.

And I would enjoy that aspect of this project. A basically unlimited budget? I couldn't wait to get started.

In the end, it was a nice evening. As with all old flames, there was a feeling of knowing, a nostalgia you can only share with someone who has known you intimately—especially at that age when you're still forming. It was great to see him again. James has a very strong personality, intense and confident, and I was reminded why I'd been attracted to him in the first place. We laughed and told stories about things we'd done as a couple, and I was relieved to find that his charm remained. We could get along quite well in a social setting. There was none of the awkwardness that *could* have accompanied this.

As the evening wound down and he drove me home, he got around to the question I knew he'd been dying to ask. He pulled the car to a stop in front of my building and turned to me.

"So, are you seeing anyone?" he asked quietly.

"No, I'm not. And that's hardly a question a client would ask me," I teased and looked toward my building. I could see Clive sitting in the front window in his usual post, and I smiled. It was nice to have someone waiting for me. I couldn't stop myself from glancing next door to see if there was a light on in Simon's apartment, and I also couldn't stop my tummy from doing a little flippity-flop when I saw his shadow on the wall and the blue light of his television.

"Well, as your client, I'll refrain from asking those kinds of questions in the future, Ms. Reynolds," he chuckled.

I turned back to face him. "It's okay, James. We passed designer/ client relationship a long time ago." I felt triumphant as I saw a blush carve a chink in his careful façade.

"I think this is gonna be fun." He winked, and it was my turn to laugh.

"Okay, you can call me tomorrow at the office, and we'll get started. I'm gonna fleece you blind, buddy, Get ready to work that credit card," I taunted as I stepped out of the car.

"Oh hell, I'm counting on it." He winked and waved goodbye.

He waited until I was inside, so I tossed another wave his way as the door closed. I was glad to see I could handle myself with him. Upstairs, as I turned the key in my lock I thought I heard something. I looked over my shoulder, and there was nothing there. Clive called to me from inside, so I smiled and stepped in, scooping him up and whispering softly in his ear as he gave me a tiny cat hug with his big paws around my neck.

The next evening I was rolling out the pie crust when the text came in from Simon.

Come on over whenever. I'll start dinner once you're here.

I'm still working on the pie, but I'll be over soon.

Need any help?

How are you with peeling apples?

The next thing I heard was a knock on the door. I walked over, hands covered in flour, and elbowed the door open. "Well, hello there," I said, holding the door open with my foot.

"Looks like the end of Scarface in here," he observed, reaching out to touch my nose and show me the flour on the end.

"I tend to lose control when there's pie crust involved," I said as he shut the door.

"Duly noted. That's good information for me to have," he responded, swatting at my hand as I tried to slap him.

He took a good long look at me then, blue eyes dropping from my face and traveling across my body. "Hmm, you weren't kidding about the apron, I don't know how long I'll be able to hang in here without trying a little grab-ass."

"Get in there and grab an apple, buddy," I said and walked toward the kitchen, adding a little extra swish to my hips. I heard him sigh heavily. I glanced down at my outfit, noting my tank top, old jeans, bare feet, and chef's apron that said, *You should see my scones…*

"Now when you said 'grab an apple,' what exactly were you referring to?" he asked from the kitchen where he'd started taking off his sweater.

I shook my head at the sight of Simon in a black T-shirt and weathered jeans. He was in his stocking feet once again, and I marveled at how at ease he seemed in my kitchen.

I walked around the kitchen counter and picked up my rolling pin. "You know, I won't think twice about whacking you over the head with this if you continue this borderline sexual harassment," I warned, running my hand up and down the rolling pin suggestively.

"I'm gonna have to ask you not to do that if you're serious about me peeling apples here," he said, eyes widening.

"I never joke about pie, Simon." I sprinkled a little more flour on the marble.

He was silent while he watched me pat out the pie crust, breathing through his mouth. "So, what are you gonna do with that?" he asked, his voice low.

"With this?" I asked, leaning over the board, and perhaps arching my back a little as I did.

"Mmm-hmm," he replied.

"I'm gonna roll this crust out. See, like this?" I teased again, thrusting the pin back and forth over the dough, making sure I arched my back each time and the forward action pushed my girls together.

"Oh my," he whispered, and I grinned naughtily at him.

"You gonna be okay over there, big guy? This is just the top crust, I still need to work on my bottom," I said over my shoulder.

His hands clutched at the edge of the counter. "Apples. Apples. Gonna peel me some apples," he told himself and turned away toward the colander filled with apples in the sink.

"Let me just get you the peeler," I said, coming up behind him and pressing myself against him as I curled around his side to grab the vegetable peeler from the other sink. This was fun.

"Peeling apples, just peeling apples. Didn't feel your boobs. No, no, not me," he chanted as I openly laughed at him.

"Here, peel this," I said, taking pity on him and removing myself from his cooking space. I might have sniffed his T-shirt.

"Did you just sniff me?" he asked, keeping himself turned away.

"I might have," I admitted, going back to my rolling pin, which I squeezed mightily.

"I thought so."

"Hey, if you can sniff, I can sniff," I shot back, taking out my sexual frustration on a defenseless *Pâte Brisée*.

"Only fair. So how do I rate?"

"Good. Very good, actually. Downy?"

"Bounce. I lost my Downy ball," he confessed.

I laughed, and we continued to roll and peel. Within fifteen minutes, we had a bowlful of peeled and sliced apples, a perfectly rolled-out pie crust, and we'd both consumed our first glass of wine.

"Okay, what's next?" he asked, wiping up flour and generally tidying.

"Now we spice things up and add a little citrus," I answered, lining up cinnamon and nutmeg, my sugar bowl, and a lemon.

"Okay, where do you want me?" he asked, taking care to show me his hands, now covered in flour.

Visions ran through my head, and I had to bite back an invitation to show him exactly where I wanted him. "First dust yourself off, and then we'll get started. You can be my assistant."

He looked around for a dishtowel, and I turned to look for the one I knew I'd left out. I'd already started for it on the counter when I felt two very strong and very specifically placed hands on my ass.

"Um, hi?" I said, freezing in place.

"Hi," he answered cheerfully, not releasing his hands.

"Explain yourself, please," I ordered, trying not to notice how my heart was trying to leave my body by way of my mouth.

"You told me to find something to clean my hands with," he stuttered, trying hard not to laugh as he gave each cheek a little squeeze.

"And you took that to mean my ass?" I laughed back and turned to face him, removing his hands with my own.

"What can I say? I take liberties with my neighbors," he replied, his eyes darting back and forth now between my lips and my eyes.

"We have a pie to make, mister. I'll thank you to remember your manners. No one touches my ass without an invitation." I giggled, still holding his hands. I felt his thumb trace little circles on the inside of my palm, and my head got swimmy. This guy was going to be the death of me. "Get over there, handsy, and behave," I instructed.

He smirked and turned away, which gave me the opportunity to mutter, "Oh my Jesus Lord," to no one in particular before meeting him back at the apple bowl.

"Okay, you do what I tell you, got it?" I said, sprinkling sugar into the bowl.

"Got it."

I started tossing the apples with my hands and Simon followed my instructions to the letter. When I asked for more sugar, he sugared. When I asked for more cinnamon, he complied. When I asked him to squeeze the lemon, he lemoned so well I had trouble keeping my tongue in my mouth and off his throat.

I tossed and tasted, and when they were finally right, I lifted a wedge to his mouth. "Open up," I said, and he leaned in.

I placed an apple on his tongue, and he snapped his mouth shut before I had to chance to remove my fingers. He let his lips close around two, and I slowly withdrew them, feeling his tongue wrap around them delicately and deliberately.

"Delicious," he said softly.

"Gah," I answered, eyes crossing a little at the sex on two legs displayed in front of me.

He chewed. "Sweet. Sweet, Caroline."

"Gah," I managed again. Brain knew this was bad, Heart was beating out of our chest.

"Good for you?" he asked, that knowing smile treading dangerously close to smirk territory.

"Good for me," I answered, on fire after the fingerlatio. Truce schmuce, harem schmarem. Who cared if there was no actual O? I needed to be in contact with this man in the very worst way.

My sexual wall had been hit, and as I prepared to rip the clothes from his body, throw him to the ground, and ride him amid a pile of apples and cinnamon with only a rolling pin to guide us, my phone rang.

Thank you, Jesus.

I looked at the blue-eyed devil and launched myself across the room, away from the brain-scrambling voodoo. I saw his face as I ran, and he looked a little disappointed.

"Girl, what are you up to tonight?" Mimi screeched into the phone. I held it away from my ear before the bleeding started. Mimi had three sound levels: Normal Loud, Excited Loud, and Drunky Loud. She was leaving Excited and on her way to Drunky.

"I'm getting ready to have dinner. Where are you?" I asked, nodding at Simon who had started pouring the apples into the pie dish.

"I'm out for drinks with Sophia. What are you doing?" she screamed.

"I just told you, getting ready to have dinner!" I laughed.

Simon came out into the living room with the pie in his hands. "Should I put this in the oven?" he asked.

"Hang on, Mimi. Not yet, I still need to brush it with a little cream," I told him, and he ducked back into the kitchen.

"Caroline Reynolds, that was a man! Who was that? Who are you having dinner with? And what are you brushing with cream?" she fired at me, her voice growing even louder.

"Settle down. My goodness, you're loud! I'm having dinner with Simon, and we're making an apple pie," I explained, which she immediately screamed out to Sophia.

"Shit," I muttered as I heard the phone yanked away from Mimi.

"Reynolds, what are you doing? Are you baking pies with your neighbor? Are you naked?" Sophia yelled, taking her turn to grill me.

"Okay, no, and you all need to seriously settle down. Hanging up now," I yelled over her yelling at me. I could hear Mimi squealing nasty things about pies and cream. Sophia was in the middle of threatening me not to hang up on her, when I did just that.

I sighed and went to find Simon, with his hands full of pie. I snorted in spite of myself.

"Oh, my God, that's so good," I whimpered, closing my eyes and losing myself to the sensations.

"I knew you'd like it, but I had no idea you'd enjoy it this much," he whispered, staring at me with rapt attention.

"Stop talking, you're going to ruin it for me," I moaned, stretching and feeling myself respond to everything he was giving me.

"Did you want another one?" he offered, raising up on his elbows.

"If I have another, I won't be able to walk tomorrow."

"Go ahead, be a bad girl—you deserve it. I know you want it, Caroline," he teased, leaning closer.

"Okay," I managed, opening up to him once again. I closed my eyes and heard him fumbling about before putting it in. Sighing as I felt it, I closed my lips around what he offered.

"I've never seen a woman who could take so much in one sitting," he marveled, watching me come undone once more.

"Yes, well, you've never met a woman who likes meatballs as much as me," I moaned around another mouthful, feeling stuffed beyond belief but not wanting the meal to end.

Simon had just cooked me quite possibly the most perfect meal ever, hitting every single taste bud that needed to be hit. He'd learned how to make the most amazing meatballs from a woman in Naples, and he'd sworn they'd be the best I'd ever had. After no less than seven jokes about balls and mouths, I had to agree they were the best balls I had ever had in my mouth.

God, he have great meatball.

I then proceeded to eat almost a pound of pasta myself, as well as all of my meatballs, plus half of his. I insisted he eat the last one, but he refused and brought the perfection that was his meatball to my willing mouth.

Simon was a great host, insisting that I sit, drink wine, and watch rather than help. He entertained me with stories about his travels as he got everything ready, and while the food was simple, it was good.

"Nonni made me promise if she showed me how to make her *polpette* I would only serve them with her special sauce. If I dared serve these with a jar of Prego, she would cross the ocean to break her wooden spoon against my backside."

"She made you call her Nonni?" I laughed, leaning back in my chair and unbuttoning the top button on my jeans. I had no shame. I'd eaten an obscene amount.

"You know what Nonni means?" he asked, surprised.

"I had an Italian great-grandmother. She insisted everyone call her Nonni." I laughed again when his eyes went to my hands massaging my stomach.

"You gonna be okay there?" He raised his eyebrows as he got up to clear.

"Yep, just need to breathe a little." I groaned, pulling myself up from the table.

"No, no, you don't have to help," he said, rushing to my side and grabbing my plate.

"Oh, no, I wasn't. I was gonna drop this off and pass out on that couch right there," I said, nodding toward the living room.

"You go relax. Anyone who just had that many balls in their mouth deserves a rest," he teased, and I flicked his ear.

"I said no more ball jokes! You've had your fun, now let me go die in peace." I shuffled into the living room. I really had made quite a little piggy of myself, but it was seriously good. I reclined and popped open another button on my jeans, relaxing into the cushions and replaying some of the finer points of the evening.

Watching Simon cook was, in a word, hot. He was really at home in a kitchen, his earlier fussing about with the pie aside. Even his salad — simple greens dressed lightly with lemon and olive oil, salt, pepper, and good Parmesan — was easy and perfect.

"Pink Himalayan salt, thank you very much," he'd said proudly, producing a bag from his pantry. He'd brought it back from one of his many trips and had me taste a little before sprinkling it on the salad. Could have been pretentious, but it fit Simon. The many facets of this guy were astounding. My earliest assumptions about him were proving to be completely wrong. As assumptions tend to be...

I could hear him tending to the dishes, and as much as I probably should have gone to help him, I simply couldn't remove myself from the couch. I snuggled on my side and looked around his living room again, my eyes drawn back to the tiny bottles of sand from all over the world. I marveled at how traveled he was, and how he seemed to enjoy it still. I gazed at the pictures of the woman in Bora Bora—her dark, beautiful skin and the smooth planes of her body—and thought about how different the three of the women in his harem were. Oops, make that two now that Katie/Spanx was with her new man.

Suddenly I could smell the apple pie and heard the oven door clank shut. I'd put it in his oven as soon as we came over so it would be ready after dinner.

"Don't you dare try to serve me pie now. I am stuffed, I tell you, stuffed!" I yelled.

"Quiet, it's just cooling," he scolded, coming around the corner from the kitchen. "You're gonna have to scooch over, sister. It's movie time," he instructed, pushing me with his big toe as I struggled to sit up straight.

"What is it that we're watching?"

"*The Exorcist*," he whispered, turning off the light on the end table and leaving the room quite dark.

"Are you freaking kidding me?" I screeched, leaning over him to turn it back on.

"Don't be a wuss. You're watching it," he hissed, turning it back off.

"I'm not a wuss, but there is stupid and not stupid, and stupid is watching a movie like *The Exorcist* with the lights off! That's just asking for trouble!" I hissed back, turning it back on.

It was starting to look like a disco in here...

"Okay, I'll make a deal with you. Lights off, but—" He shushed me with is finger as he saw me begin to interrupt. "If you get too scared, lights go back on. Deal?"

I was still leaning across him on my way to turn the light back on again when I noticed how close I was to his face. And how I was angled across him like a girl waiting to get a spanking. And I knew he was capable of delivering one...

"Fine," I huffed as the opening credits came on. I returned to a normal, seated position.

He smiled triumphantly and gave me a thumbs up.

"If you show me that thumb one more time I'll bite it off," I growled, pulling an afghan off the back of the couch and curling it protectively around me. One minute into the movie, and I was already spooked.

I was tense from that moment on, and any idea I might have had about girls being ridiculous around guys when they watched scary movies went by the wayside when Regan peed herself at the dinner party.

By the time the priest came for a little visit, I was practically sitting on Simon's lap, my right hand had a death grip on his thigh, and I was viewing the movie through the holes in the afghan, which I had draped entirely over my head.

"I actually, literally, hate you for making me watch this movie," I whispered in his ear, which was right in my face as I refused to leave any space between us. I'd even accompanied him to the bathroom earlier when we took a break. He insisted I stay out in the hallway, but I stood just outside the door, eyes glancing around furtively, still with the afghan over my head.

"Do you want me to stop? I don't want you to have nightmares," he whispered back, his eyes on the screen.

"Just no banging on the walls for a few nights, please. I won't be able to take it," I said, looking at him through one of my eyeholes.

"Have you heard any banging lately?" he asked, rolling his eyes as he did every time he looked at me with the ridiculous afghan on my head.

"No, I haven't actually. Why is that?" I asked.

He took a breath. "Well, I — " he started, and then the most maniacal scary noises started coming from the TV, and we both jumped.

"Okay, maybe this movie is a little scary. You wanna sit closer?" he asked, pressing pause on the remote.

"I thought you'd never ask," I cried, launching myself fully into his lap and settling between his thighs. "Do you want some afghan?" I offered, and he laughed.

"No, I can take it like a man. You stay under there, though," he teased.

I narrowed my eyes at him through the eyeholes and poked one finger through the weave. "Guess which finger this is," I said, waving it at him.

"Shhh, movie," he answered, wrapping his arms around me and pulling me back against his chest.

He was warm and strong and powerful, but absolutely no match for terror that was *The Exorcist*. What had we been talking about? Now I couldn't think about any walls banging except the one Regan was currently banging the shit out of and spraying down with pea soup. We watched the rest of that damn movie wound around each other like pretzels, and he finally succumbed to the false security that an afghan eyehole can provide.

Click. Click. Click.

What the hell is that?

Click. Click. Click.

Oh no.

I lay paralyzed in my bed, every light in my entire apartment blazing.

Click. Click. Click.

I pulled the covers up higher, covering my face up to my eyes, which kept a constant vigil around the bedroom. Brain knew we were safe and secure, but also kept replaying scenes from that terrible, terrible movie, making it impossible to shut off for the night and go to sleep. Nerves had everything on lockdown, blazing a trail of fiery adrenaline throughout my body. I hated Simon with every fiber of my being in that moment. I also wished he was here.

Click. Click. Click.

What is *that?*

Click. Click.

Nothing.

Then Clive leaped on the bed, and I screamed bloody murder. Clive puffed out his tail and hissed at me, wondering why the hell mommy was screaming at him, I'm sure. The click-click-click was his goddamned kitty hangnail.

My phone vibrated an instant later, shaking the entire nightstand and eliciting another scream from me. It was Simon.

"What the hell is wrong? Why are you screaming? Are you okay?" he yelled when I answered, and I could hear him through the phone and through the wall.

"Get your ass over here right now, you motherfucking scary movie pusher," I seethed and hung up. I pounded on the wall and ran out to unlock the door. In much the same way I'd run up the last few steps of the basement stairs when I was a kid, I hightailed it back into my room, jumping the last few feet and landing in the center of my bed. I wrapped the covers around me and peered out, waiting. He knocked, and I heard the door push open.

"Caroline?" he called.

"Back here," I yelled. Sad that I'd been reduced to this, but I was glad to see him.

"I brought the pie," he said with an embarrassed grin. "And this," he added, producing the afghan from behind his back.

"Thanks." I smiled at him from behind my pillow shield.

A few minutes later we were settled on my bed, each balancing a plate and a glass of milk. We'd been too full, then too terrified to eat pie earlier. Clive and his phantom hangnail retired to the other room after rolling his eyes at Simon and swishing his tail.

"How old are you?" I asked, cutting into my pie.

"Twenty-eight. How old are you?"

"Twenty-six. We are twenty-eight and twenty-six years old and terrified of a movie," I mused, poking in a bite. The pie was good.

"I wouldn't say I'm terrified," he countered. "Spooked? Yes. But I only came over to stop you from screaming."

"And to taste my pie," I added, winking.

"Shut it, you," he warned, and then he went ahead and tasted my pie.

"Jesus, that's good," he breathed, eyes closed as he chewed.

"I know. What is it about apples and homemade pie crust? Is there anything better?"

"If we were eating this naked, then it would be better," he grinned, opening one eye.

"No one is getting naked here, buddy. Just eat your pie." I pointed at his plate with my fork.

We chewed.

"I feel better," I added a few minutes later, drinking my milk.

"Me too. Not too spooked anymore."

He smiled as I took his plate and set it on the nightstand. I sighed contentedly and lay back against my pillows, sated and less scared.

"So, I gotta ask…James Brown? I mean, *James Brown?*" He laughed, and I kicked him as he lay down next to me. We turned on our sides to face each other, arms curling under the pillows.

"I know, I know. I can't believe you held it in as long as you did! I know you've been dying to make jokes since last night."

"Seriously, who is this guy?" he asked.

"He's a new client."

"Ah, got it," he said, looking pleased.

"And an old boyfriend," I added, watching for his reaction.

"I see. New client but old boyfriend—wait, the lawyer?" he asked, trying to keep his expression neutral, but failing.

"Yep. Haven't seen him in a few years."

"How's that gonna work?"

"Don't know yet. We'll see."

I really didn't know how things were going to go with James. I was glad to see him, but it was going to be tough to keep things professional if he wanted more. And every instinct I had told me he wanted more. In the past he'd had more control over me than I was comfortable relinquishing. I'd found myself sucked into the gravitational pull that was James Brown—lawyer, not Godfather of Soul.

"Anyway, we're just going to be working together. It'll be a great job for me. He wants his entire place redone." I sighed, already planning the palette. I rolled onto my back and stretched. I'd really abused my stomach tonight and was starting to get sleepy.

"I don't like him," Simon said suddenly, after a long pause.

I turned and saw him scowling.

"You don't even know him! How could you possibly not like him?" I laughed.

"I just don't," he said, now turning his gaze to mine and unleashing the power of the baby blues.

"Oh, please, you're just a stinky boy." I laughed, ruffling his hair. Wrong move. It sure was soft…

"I don't stink. You said yourself I was April fresh," he protested, lifting his arm and sniffing.

"Yes, Simon, you smell delicious," I deadpanned, sniffing the air around me.

He left his arm up higher on the pillow, and I knew if I rolled just a little I could slide right on into the nook. He looked at me, raising his eyebrows ever so slightly. Was he thinking what I was thinking?

Did he want to nook me?

Did I want to nook him?

Oh the hell with it…

"I'm coming into the nook," I announced and went full snuggle: head nestled in, left arm over chest, right arm tucked under his pillow. Legs I kept to myself—I wasn't a total fool.

"Well, hello there," he said, sounding surprised. Then he curled himself around me immediately. I sighed again, wrapped in boy and voodoo.

"What brought this on, *friend?*" he whispered into my hair, and I shivered.

"Delayed reaction to Linda Blair. I need some nook time. Friends can nook, can't they?"

"Sure, but are *we* friends who can nook?" he asked, tracing circles on my back. Him and his demon finger circles…

"I can handle it. You?" I held my breath.

"I can handle just about anything, but…" he started, and then stopped.

"What? What were you going to say?" I asked, leaning up to look at him. One piece of hair uncurled from my ponytail and fell down between us. Slowly, and with great care, he pushed it back behind my ear.

"Let's just say that if you were wearing that pink nightie? You'd be in a heap of trouble."

"Well, it's a good thing we're just friends then, right?" I forced myself to say.

"Friends, yes."

He stared into my eyes.

I breathed in, he breathed out. We traded actual air.

"Just nook me, Simon," I said quietly, and he grinned.

"Come on back down here," he said and coaxed me back to his chest. I slid down, resting where I could hear his heart beat. He folded the afghan over us, and I noticed again how soft it was. It had served me well tonight, this afghan.

"I love this afghan, but I have to say it doesn't really fit your apartment—the cool-dude motif you have going on," I mused. It was orange and pea green and very retro. He was silent, and I thought maybe he had fallen asleep.

"It was my mom's," he said quietly, and his grip on me became infinitesimally tighter.

There was nothing to say after that.

Simon and I slept together that night, with every light in the entire place on.

Clive and his hangnail stayed away.

chapter eleven

I woke up a few hours later, startled by the warmth of the body next to me, which was decidedly bigger than the cat usually nestled against my side. I rolled carefully onto my back and away from Simon so I could see him. I could see him just fine as the lamps, along with all my other lights, continued to blaze away into the night, fighting back the evils of that awful movie.

I rubbed my eyes and inspected my bedmate. He lay on his back, arms curled as though I was still in them, and I thought of how good it felt to nook with Simon.

But I shouldn't be nooking with Simon. Brain knew better. Nerves were in agreement. That was definitely a very, very slippery slope. And though the images of climbing a slippery Simon that immediately came to mind were far from innocent, I pushed them aside. I looked away and noticed the terribly wonderful afghan tangled between his legs—and mine, for that matter.

It had been his mom's. Heart broke each time I thought of his sweet, timid voice sharing that little nugget with me. He didn't know I'd talked to Jillian about his past, that I knew his parents were no longer alive. The idea that he still clung to his mother's afghan was inexorably sweet, and once again my heart broke open.

I was close with my parents. They still lived in the same house where I'd grown up, in a small town in southern California. They were great parents, and I saw them as often as I could, which is to say holidays and an occasional weekend. A typical twenty-something, I enjoyed my independence. But my parents were there when I needed them, always there. The idea that I would someday have to walk this earth without their anchor and misguided guidance made me wince, to say nothing of losing both of them at only eighteen.

I was glad Simon seemed to have good friends and such a powerful advocate as Benjamin watching out for him. But as close as friends and lovers could be, there was something about belonging to someone completely that gave you roots — roots you sometimes needed when the world battled against you.

Simon stirred slightly in his sleep, and I watched him again. He murmured something that I couldn't quite pick out, but it sounded a little like "meatballs." I smiled and allowed my fingers to slip into his hair, feeling the soft silk tousled on my pillow.

God, he gave good meatball.

As I stroked his hair, my mind wandered to a place where meatballs flowed endlessly and there was pie for days. I giggled to myself as sleepiness began to return, and I nestled back down into the nook. As I felt the comfort that only warm boy arms could provide, a little alarm went off in my head, warning me not to get too close. I had to be careful.

Clearly we were both divinely attracted to each other, and in another space and time, the sex would have been ringing out across the land and around the clock. But he had his harem, and I had my hiatus, not to mention that I did *not* have my O. So friends we would remain.

Friends who meatball. Friends who nook. Friends who were headed to Tahoe very soon.

I pictured Simon soaking in a hot tub with Lake Tahoe spread out in all its glory behind him. Which sight was actually more glorious remained to be seen. I settled back to sleep, rousing only slightly when Simon snuggled me a little closer.

And even though it was barely above a whisper, I heard it. He sighed my name.

I smiled as I slipped back to sleep.

The next morning I felt a persistent poking at my left shoulder. I brushed it away, but it continued.

"Clive, stop it, you asshole," I moaned, hiding my head under the covers. I knew he wouldn't stop until I fed him. Ruled by his stomach, that one. Then I heard a distinctly human laugh—quiet and definitely not Clive.

My eyes sprang open, and the night before came back to me in a rush: the horror, the pie, the nook. I reached backward with my right foot, sliding it along the bed until I felt it stop against something warm and hairy. Although I was now more sure than ever it wasn't Clive, I poked with my toe, inching my way higher until I heard another chuckle.

"Wallbanger?" I whispered, not wanting to flip over. True to form, I was spread-eagled diagonally across the entire bed, head on one side, feet practically on the other.

"The one and only," a delicious voice whispered in my ear.

My toes and Lower Caroline curled. "Shit." I rolled onto my back to take in the damage. He was huddled in the one corner my body had allowed him. My bed-sharing habits had not improved at all. "You sure can fill a bed," he noted, smiling at me from under the little bit of afghan I'd left him. "If we're going to do this again there'll have to be some ground rules."

"This won't be happening again. This was in response to a terrible movie you inflicted on both of us. No more nooking," I stated firmly, wondering how dreadful my morning breath was. I cupped my hand in front of my face, breathed, and gave a quick sniff.

"Roses?" he asked.

"Obviously." I smirked.

I looked at him, exquisitely rumpled and in my bed. He smiled that smile, and I sighed. I allowed myself a moment to indulge in a fantasy where I was then quickly flipped and ravaged to within an inch of my life, but I wisely got control of my inner whore.

"What if you get scared tonight?" he asked as I sat up and stretched.

"I won't," I threw back over my shoulder.

"What if I get scared?"

"Grow up, pretty boy. Let's make coffee, and then I have to get to work." I whacked him with my pillow.

He slid out from under the afghan, taking care to fold it, and carried it with him into the kitchen where he set it gently on the table. I smiled, thinking of him saying my name in the night. What I wouldn't give to know what was running through his mind.

We moved about the kitchen with quiet economy, grinding beans, measuring coffee, pouring water. I put the sugar and cream on the counter while he peeled and sliced a banana. I poured granola, he milked and banana-ed the bowls for us. Within a few minutes we were seated next to each other on barstools, eating breakfast as though we'd been doing so for years. Our simple ease intrigued me. And worried me.

"Plans for the day?" I asked, digging into my bowl.

"I need to stop by the *Chronicle* office."

"Are you working on something for the paper?" I asked, surprised at the level of interest even I could hear in my voice. Would he be in town for a while? Why did I care? Oh boy.

"I'm spending a few days on a piece about quick getaways in the Bay Area—weekend drives kind of thing," he answered through a mouthful of banana.

"When are you going to do that?" I asked, examining the raisins in my bowl and trying not to look too interested in his answer.

"Next week. I leave on Tuesday," he replied and my stomach was instantly queasy. Next week we were supposed to go to Tahoe. Why the hell did my stomach care so much that he wouldn't be going?

"I see," I added, again fascinated by the raisins.

"But I'll be back before Tahoe. I was planning on just driving straight there when I finish my shoot," he said, looking at me over the rim of his coffee mug.

"Oh, well, that's good," I answered quietly, my stomach now bouncing all around.

"When are you headed up, anyway?" he asked, seeming to now be studying his own bowl.

"The girls are driving up with Neil and Ryan on Thursday, but I have to stay in the city to work until at least noon on Friday. I'm gonna rent a car and drive up that afternoon."

"Don't rent a car. I'll swing through to pick you up," he offered, and I nodded without a word.

That settled, we finished our breakfast and watched Clive chase a stray piece of fluff around the table over and over again. We didn't talk much, but whenever we met each other's eyes, we both grinned.

Text between Mimi and Sophia:

Did you know Caroline is working with James?

James who?

James Brown, obviously. Who else?

NO! What the hell?

Remember she mentioned she had a new client? She neglected to mention who he was.

I'm gonna kick her ass when I see her next. She better not cancel on Tahoe. Did Ryan tell you he was bringing his guitar?

Yep, he told me you wanted to have some kind of fucked-up singalong.

He did? Haha. I just thought it would be fun.

Text between Neil and Mimi:

Hey, Tiny, are we still bowling with Sophia and Ryan tonight?

Yep, and you better bring your A game. Sophia and I are pretty severe.

Sophia knows how to bowl? Wow.

Why is that wow?

I just wouldn't have expected her to bowl is all. See you tonight.

Text between Neil and Simon:

You still planning on heading up with us this weekend?

Yep, but I'm coming a little late, have a shoot

When are you coming up?

Fri night sometime, stopping thru the city on my way

Why the hell are you going back into the city? You're doing that shoot in Carmel, right?

I just need to pick up some shit for the weekend.

Dude, pack your shit and get your ass to Tahoe.

I will, but I'm picking up Caroline.

I see.

You see nothing.

I see everything.

You sure about that, Big Boy? What about Sophia?

Sophia? Why is everyone asking me about Sophia?

See you in Tahoe.

Text between Mimi and Caroline:

You have some splainin' to do, Lucy…

Oh no, I hate it when you go Ricardo on me. What the hell did I do?

Explain to me why you didn't tell me about your new client.

Caroline, don't ignore my text! CAROLINE!!

Oh, settle down. This is exactly why I did NOT tell you.

Caroline Reynolds, this is news that obviously I should have known about!

Look, I can handle it okay?? He's my client, nothing more. He's going to spend an obscene amount of money on this project.

I frankly don't care how much he's spending. I don't want you working with him.

Listen to yourself! I will take on whatever new client I damn well please!
I have this under control.

We'll see…Did I hear a rumor that you're driving up to Tahoe with Wallbanger?

Wow, subject change. Yes, I am.

Good. Take the long way.

What the hell is that supposed to mean?

Mimi?? You there??

Damn you, Mimi…HELLO??

Text between Caroline and Simon:

Wallbanger…come in Wallbanger

Wallbanger isn't here, only the exorcist

Not even a little bit funny.

What's up?

What time are you picking me up tom?

I should be back in the city by noon. If you can knock off work we can beat rush hour.

Already told Jillian I'm taking a half day. Where are you right now?

In Carmel, on a cliff overlooking the ocean

Boy, are you a closet romantic…

I'm a photographer. We go where the money shot is.

Oh man, we're not discussing money shots.

Besides, I thought you were the romantic one

I told you, I'm a practical romantic.

Well then practically speaking, even you would appreciate this sight—waves crashing, sun setting, it's nice

Are you alone?

Yep

Bet you wish you weren't.

You have no idea

Pfft…you old softie

There's nothing soft about me, Caroline.

And we're back…

Caroline?

Yep

See you tomorrow

Yep

Text between Caroline and Sophia:

Can you give me the address again to the house so I can plug it into the GPS tom?

No

No?

Not until you tell me WHY YOU'RE HIDING JAMES BROWN.

Jesus, it's like having 2 more mothers…

This isn't about sitting up straight or eating more vegetables, but we do need to have a conversation about your posture.

Unbelievable.

Seriously, Caroline, we just worry.

Seriously, Sophia, I know. Address please?

Let me think about it.

Not gonna ask you again…

Yes you will. You want to see Simon in that hot tub. Don't lie.

I hate you…

Text between Simon and Caroline:

You done with work?

Yep, at home waiting for you.

Now that's a nice visual…

Prepare yourself, I'm taking bread out of the oven.

Don't tease me, woman…zucchini?

Cranberry orange. Mmmm…

No woman has ever done breakfast bread foreplay the way you do.

Ha! When are you coming?

Can't. Drive. Straight.

Can we have one conversation where you're not twelve?

Sorry, I'll be there in 30

Perfect, that will give me time to frost my buns.

Pardon me?

Oh, I didn't tell you? I also made cinnamon rolls.

Be there in 25.

"I'm not listening to this."

"Like hell. It's my car. Driver picks music."

"Actually, you're wrong about that. The passenger always picks music. It's what you get when you give up driving privileges."

"Caroline, you don't even own a car, so how could you ever have driving privileges?"

"Exactly, so we listen to what I pick," I chided, sitting back after changing the radio station for the hundredth time. I hit the iPod and scrolled until I found something that I thought would please us both.

"Good song," he admitted, and we hummed along.

The trip had been great so far. When I first met him—*heard* him—I never would have predicted it, but Simon was quickly turning into one of my favorite people. I'd been wrong about him.

I glanced at him: humming along to the song, drumming his thumbs along the steering wheel. As he was concentrating on the road, I took the opportunity to catalogue some of his more swoonworthy features.

Jaw? Strong.

Hair? Dark and messy.

Stubble? About two days' worth and nice.

Lips? Lickable, but lonely looking. Maybe I could check them out, do my own little tongue inspection…

I sat on my hands to stop myself from launching over the console. He continued to hum and drum.

"What's going on over there, Nightie Girl? You look a little flushed. Need some more air?" He started for the air conditioner.

"Nope, I'm good," I answered, my voice sounding ridiculous.

He looked at me strangely, but resumed his hum drum. "I think it's time we broke out that cranberry-orange bread. Hit me," he said a moment later as I was indulging in a fantasy about how exactly I could maneuver myself into his lap while still maintaining a good highway speed.

"I'm on it!" I hollered, diving into the backseat and surprising us both. I had my legs in the air and my bottom on display as I clasped my upside-down face in my hands behind the seat. I could feel how red my cheeks were, and I gave myself a little slap to snap me back into this world.

"That is one sweet ass, my friend." He sighed, leaning his head on it as though it were a pillow.

"Hey. Ass Man. Pay attention to the road and not my heiney, or no bread for you." I gave his head a bump with my bum and sent myself flailing as he took a turn.

"Caroline, you need to control yourself back there, or I'm pulling over."

"Oh, zip it. Here's your damn bread," I snapped, crawling back into my chair in a graceless way and throwing the bread at him.

"What the hell? Don't throw this. What if you'd bruised it?" he cried, gently stroking the foil-wrapped loaf.

"I worry about you, Simon. I really do," I laughed, watching him struggle to open the end of the wrapper. "You want me to cut you a piece—okay, or you could just do that." I frowned as he took a giant bite out of the end.

"Thif if mine, righ?" he asked, spraying crumbs.

"How do you function in normal society?" I asked, shaking my head as he took another monster bite. He just smiled and continued, eating the entire loaf in less than five minutes.

"You're gonna be so sick tonight. That's meant to be eaten piece by piece, not ingested whole," I said. His only response was to burp loudly and pat his tummy.

I couldn't help but laugh. "You're one twisted man, Simon." I chuckled.

"You're still intrigued though, aren't you?" He grinned, turning the blue eyes loose on me.

My panties actually disintegrated. "Oddly, yes," I admitted, feeling my face flame again.

"I know." He smirked, and we drove on.

"Okay, the turn should be coming up just around this corner—I remember that house!" I cried, bouncing in my seat. It had been a while since I was up here, and I'd forgotten how beautiful it was. I loved Tahoe in the summertime—all the water sports and everything—but in autumn? Autumn was beautiful.

"Thank God. I need to pee," Simon groaned, as he'd been doing for the past twenty or so miles.

"That's your own fault for drinking that Big Gulp," I admonished, still bouncing away.

"Wow, is that it?" he asked as we turned into the drive. Lanterns lit the way to a sprawling, two-story cedar house with a giant stone fireplace up the left side. Cars were already in the driveway, and I could hear the music spilling out from the back deck.

"Sounds like our friends have already got their party on," Simon observed. Squealing and laughter joined the music coming from the back side of the house.

"Oh, I don't doubt it. My guess is they've been drinking since dinner and are half-naked in the hot tub by now." I walked around back to grab my bag.

"We'll just have to catch up, now won't we?" he winked, pulling a bottle of Galliano from his bag. "I thought we could make some Wallbangers."

"Now isn't that interesting. I was thinking the same thing," I countered, pulling an identical bottle from my duffle.

"I knew you were dying to get me inside you, Caroline." He chuckled and grabbed my bag as we headed to the door.

"Please, you would make up a drink and call it a Pink Nightie just to have me in your mouth—and don't even try to lie," I taunted, nudging him with my shoulder.

He stopped midway up the walk and looked at me fiercely. "Is that an invitation? Cuz I'm a hell of a bartender," he stated, the eyes glowing in the darkness.

"I've no doubt," I breathed, the space between us now crackling with tension that was becoming ridiculously hard to ignore. I took a deep breath, and noticed he did as well.

"Come on, let's get sauced and start this weekend," he chuckled, nudging me with his shoulder and breaking the spell.

"Sauce away," I muttered, walking up the path behind him.

Finding the front door open, Simon stashed our bags, and we made our way through the house to the back deck. There the lake spread out before us, just barely lit by the tiki torches dotting the dock and pathways that led to the shore. The entire back of the house was flanked with brick patios and decks, and that's where we found our friends.

"Caroline!" Mimi screeched from the hot tub, where she and Ryan were splashing each other. Ah, we'd made it to Drunky Loud already.

"Mimi!" I squealed back, looking around for Sophia. She and Neil were perched on the stone bench by the firepit, roasting marshmallows. They both waved merrily, and Neil gestured obscenely with his stick.

"Making them see the error of their ways might be easier than we thought, fellow matchmaker," I whispered to Simon, who was already mixing a cocktail at the patio bar.

"You think its gonna be that easy?" he whispered back, giving his friends the international guy head nod that said, "What's up, man?"

"Hell, yes. They're almost already there without our help. All we have to do is show them what's right in front of them."

He handed me a cocktail. "So, how am I?" he asked, winking.

"Is this a Wallbanger?"

"It is."

I took a sip, swirling the taste around my mouth and over my tongue.

"You're as good as I knew you'd be," I whispered, taking a dangerously large swallow.

"To things staring you right in the face," he added, clinking my glass and taking his own large gulp.

"To things staring you right in the face," I echoed, our eyes locking over the rims.

Damn Banger Voodoo.

chapter twelve

"Whose foot is that?"

"It's mine, Neil. Quit rubbing it."

"Dude! Quit trying to play footsie with me, Ryan!"

"You're the one still holding my foot."

Ryan and Neil tried to look nonchalant as they disengaged from their footsie session under the bubbling water. I laughed as I caught Simon's eye across the hot tub, and he grinned back at me.

"Want another?" he mouthed, nodding to my empty glass.

"I have had enough for tonight, don't you think?" I mouthed back, as our friends cackled all around us.

"I thought you were girl who always wanted more," he mouthed. The characteristic smirk returned.

I looked at him, the image of Hot Tub Simon that had been in my head for the last few weeks actually paling in comparison to the real thing. Strong arms stretched across the back of the hot tub, hair wet and artfully swept back. If I thought seeing him wet and half-naked on my kitchen floor was enticing, it was nothing like having him backlit by tiki torches and seen through a strong buzz.

He was now the most singularly handsome man I'd ever seen, and if I wasn't mistaken, he was trying to get me drunk. Brain was getting a bit fuzzy. Heart was beginning to sing Etta James songs.

"Are you trying to get me drunk?" I asked, giggling as I pushed my empty glass away, resolving myself to no more alcohol.

"Nope. A sloppy Pink Nightie Girl gets me nowhere."

He grinned as I splashed water toward his side. Our friends had all quieted and were watching us with undisguised interest.

After Simon and I arrived, we got our drinks, and then I showed him around the rest of the house. I left my bags at the front door, not knowing how the sleeping arrangements had been laid out. We returned to the patio to find that Sophia and Neil had joined Ryan and Drunky Mimi in the hot tub. A quick trip to the pool house left me in nothing but a dark green bikini and a smile as I approached the others. Simon had already jumped in, and I watched him watch me. As I slid under the warm water, I sipped my cocktail and drank in the sight of my neighbor, wet and in board shorts, before me. Sophia actually had to nudge me to stop the staring.

Now we were smack dab in the middle of a sexual soup, bubbling away with two pairs of mismatched lovers and more pheromones than we knew what to do with.

So did I want another cocktail? Didn't matter. I couldn't afford it.

I had to shake my head a little to clear it as I looked around at the rest of the group. Mimi had gotten too hot and was perched on the side, kicking Neil as she swung her feet back and forth. He indulged her in much the same way a big brother indulges his little sister. Sophia and Ryan were huddled on the other side, Sophia scratching Ryan's back as she and Neil talked back and forth about the 49ers' starting lineup or defensive line or something football-ish and, frankly, boring.

"So, what are we doing this weekend?" I asked, focusing my attention on the group at large and not the blue eyes staring at me. Damn those eyes! They would be the death of me.

"We were thinking about going for a hike tomorrow. Who's in?" Ryan asked.

Sophia shook her head. "Count me out. No way am I hiking."

"Why not?" Neil asked.

Simon and I exchanged a quick glance at his sudden interest.

"Can't. Last time I hiked I took quite a spill and sprained my wrist. Can't take the chance during the season," she said, waving and reminding us she made her living with her hands. As a cello player, she could get out of quite a bit. Once she dodged hand jobs all winter. Investment banker Bob was not a happy camper.

"How 'bout you, Tiny?" Neil pulled on Mimi's foot.

"Um, no, Mimi doesn't hike," she replied, adjusting her barely there black bikini. Her *actual* boy toy didn't notice, but I saw Ryan's eyes grow to the size of pies from across the hot tub as her breasts were nearly revealed.

"You gonna take a pass as well?" Simon nodded to me.

"Hell, no. I'm hiking with the boys tomorrow!" I laughed as Sophia and Mimi rolled their eyes. They never understood why I loved "mountain man activities," as they called them.

"Nice," Simon purred, and for a second I calculated the distance between my mouth and his. Then we were all quiet, all six of us lost in our thoughts. I remembered the plan to out the four of them, and I jumped right in.

"So, Ryan, did you know Mimi here gives to your charity every year?" I asked, surprising them both.

"You do?"

"Yep, every year," she said. "I've seen what having access to computers can do, especially for kids who wouldn't otherwise have the opportunity." She looked shyly at him, and they began a conversation about the process he used to determine which schools will receive the scholarships each year.

Simon and I grinned at each other. Looking sideways at Sophia, Simon launched the second wave of the attack. "Hey, Neil, how many seats did you get for the symphony this year?" he asked.

Neil blushed.

"You bought tickets?" Sophia asked.

"*Season* tickets," Simon added, as Neil nodded. Sophia and Neil then launched into a discussion of where his seats were, and Simon raised his foot above the surface of the water.

"Come on, don't leave me hangin'."

"What?"

"Gimme a little high five. I can't reach your hand," he insisted, waving his foot back and forth. I giggled and slid lower on my seat, stretching my foot out and patting his lightly.

"Ugh, pruney." He laughed.

"I'll give you pruney," I warned, dipping my foot and splashing him lightly.

"I could not be more comfortable. Seriously, I literally could not feel more cozy right now if I were actually inside a marshmallow," I mumbled through a thick tongue coated in Bailey's and coffee. I had curled up on top of about fifty pillows next to fireplace—a fireplace with a hearth almost ten feet wide and a chimney almost three stories high. Made out of stone quarried nearby, it was massive. It was the focal point of the entire house, with rooms radiating out from its center. And it gave off massive heat.

We were chilled to the bone when we finally made it back inside. One by one, we all got too warm in the hot tub, so we hoisted ourselves out to cool off a little. By the time we realized how cold the night had gotten, we were shivering and puffing, and wanting nothing more than to curl up next to the fire. As we had yet to pick rooms, I soon learned, the girls snuck into the master bedroom to change into our pjs and rejoin the boys, who were now all decked out in T-shirts and pajama pants. We made a quick pot of coffee, and I sliced up some of the additional cranberry-orange bread I'd wisely hidden from Simon. A couple shots of Bailey's in the coffee cups, and we were all relaxing by the fire like an ad for Currier and Ives.

Simon had reclined regally by the fireplace and patted the stack of pillows next to him. I dove in and a few stray puffs of feathers swirled around our heads. We'd discovered that each boy had a different method of starting a fire—kindling, newspapers, kindling *and* newspapers—when finally Sophia stuck her head up there and declared that the flue was still closed. Brought back down a few pegs, the guys at that point deferred to Ryan, if for no other reason than that he was the one holding the matches. But within minutes, they had a fire blazing, and we were now all seated around the fireplace, sleepy and content.

I breathed deeply. There was nothing like the smell of an actual fire—not a gas fireplace, not a bunch of candles, but an honest to goodness fireplace with snaps and crackles and funny little whizzing screeches when the steam came out of a crack in the wood.

"So, Caroline, have you asked Simon to teach you how to windsurf yet?" Mimi asked suddenly from her perch on the arm of the couch. We'd been quiet for a while, drowsy and almost dreaming, and I started a little when she spoke.

"What? I mean, what?" I asked, startled out of my pillows and back to the present.

"Well, these boys here all windsurf. You want to learn to windsurf, and I bet Simon here would show you, wouldn't you, Simon?" She giggled, polishing off the last of her coffee and sliding off the arm of the chair into Ryan's conveniently placed lap. They smiled at each other for a moment before they realized what they were doing and Ryan jokingly launched her off his own lap and into Neil's. He'd not been awakened by her earlier question, but he now seemed wide awake with a lapful of Scheming Mimi.

"You want to learn to windsurf?" Simon asked, turning toward my pillow pile.

"Actually, yes. I've always wanted to try it."

"It's tough — not gonna lie. But totally worth it." He smiled, and Ryan nodded from across the room.

"Sure, Simon'll show you. He'd love to," Ryan chimed in, earning a wink from Mimi and an eye roll from me.

"We can plan something for when we get back to the city," I suggested.

"No more talk tonight. This girl has had it," Sophia said. "I'm pooped. Where are we all sleeping?" She poked her head over the back of the armchair where she'd been curled up.

"Well, how many rooms we talking about?" Simon asked as I sat up and yawned.

"There are four bedrooms, so take your pick," Sophia answered, then wisely drained an entire bottle of water.

"Are we doing boy-girl, boy-girl?" I asked, laughing when I saw Simon's surprised face.

"We can, sure," Mimi answered, looking a little nervously at Neil.

I stifled a giggle when I saw Sophia and Ryan trade a similar spooked look. Simon caught it as well.

"Yeah, sure! Don't let Caroline and me stand in the way of the lovebirds! Mimi, you and Neil pick a room, Sophia and Ryan can pick a room, and Caroline and I will take the rooms that are left over. Perfect. Right, Caroline?"

"Sounds perfect to me. I'll just rinse out these mugs. Now, off to bed with you all. Scoot! Scoot!" I cried. Simon and I scurried about cleaning up while sneaking peeks over our shoulders at the four of them. They looked like they'd just begun a death march.

"Oh, man, I hope this works out…for my sake." I stood behind Simon as we watched the four become two pairs as they parted ways by the bedroom doors.

"Why for your sake?" he whispered, turning his face just a little to be inches from mine.

"Because right now, behind those doors? Sophia and Mimi are trying to figure out the best way to hurt me. Physically hurt me," I sighed, backing away to rinse the last of the coffee cups and place them in the dishwasher.

Simon added the soap and switched it on. As we walked around, turning lights off for the night, we talked about the hike we'd be taking tomorrow.

"You're not gonna slow me down, are you?" he teased.

I shoved him into the wall. "Please, you will be eating my trail dust tomorrow, bucko," I warned, grabbing my bag and heading for the bedrooms.

"We'll see, Nightie Girl. Speaking of, got any nighties in there for me?" He poked his hand into my bag as he followed me down the hall.

"Stay outta there. Nothing for you in there, or anywhere for that matter." I stopped at the room I was taking.

He went past me to the room next door. "Look at that, sharing a bedroom wall once again." He smirked.

"Well, I know you're in there alone, so I'd better not hear any banging," I warned, leaning in the doorway.

"No, no banging. 'Night, Caroline," he said softly, leaning in his own doorway.

"'Night, Simon," I answered, giving him a little waggle of my fingertips as I closed my door. I placed my bag on my bed and smiled.

"Come on, guys, not that much farther," I yelled behind me as I surged up the final leg of the trail. We'd been hiking for about two hours now, and while everyone stayed together for a while, in the last thirty minutes or so, Ryan had slowed considerably, and Neil hung back with him. Simon and I kept the pace together, and were about to reach the crest of the trail.

I'd managed to avoid being alone with Sophia or Mimi, although the puffy eyes and tired faces on all four of them proved no one had gotten a good night's sleep—except Simon and me.

After breakfast, I dodged the firing squad by changing quickly and waiting outside for the boys before the hike. I knew once I returned to the house I'd be in for it, although I admit I was curious to see how they were planning to rage without acknowledging that sleeping with the guys they'd been seeing for weeks now was not, in fact, what they wanted to do.

But as Simon had said, "Here's to things staring you in the face." Tonight should be interesting.

I pushed up and over the last little ridge and made it to the top. Simon was only a few yards behind me, and I could hear him on his way. I breathed deep, the clear air prickling at my lungs. It was chilly, but I was warm with exertion. It had been a while since I'd gotten out of the city, and my body had missed hiking like this. My legs were burning, my nose was running, I was sweating like a pig, and I couldn't remember when I'd felt better. I laughed out loud as I looked down at the lake below, spying a few hawks gliding on a downdraft. The steely blue of the lake, the deep green of the forest, the clean whites and creams of the rocks: it was beautiful.

And then there was my new favorite blue. Simon appeared at my side, breathing as deeply as I was. He stretched his arms wide and took in the valley below. He'd peeled off layers as we climbed and was now wearing a white T-shirt with a flannel knotted at his waist. Khaki shorts, hiking boots, and a wide grin completed the wet dream I now stared at, instead of looking at the natural wonders all around us. And those blue eyes—I could see them framing each shot as he looked around.

"Beautiful," I breathed, and he turned to me. I got caught staring. "I mean, isn't it beautiful?" I stuttered, gesturing widely with my arm.

He appeared to know exactly what I'd been doing, and I felt the blush come up in my cheeks. Luckily, I was still a bit winded from the climb, and I hoped I was already sufficiently red.

"Yes, it *is* beautiful actually. Very beautiful." He smiled, and we stared at each other. He took a few steps closer, and I felt the air shift and change. I bit my lip. He ran his hand through his hair. We smiled. There were no words, but even the woodland animals could tell there was something about to happen and wisely stayed in their hidey holes.

"Hi," he said quietly.

"Hi," I answered.

"Hi," he said again, taking one last step toward me and stepping inside my little circle. One more step and he'd be practically on top of me. And how.

"Hi," I said once more, tilting my head to the side and letting him know he could take that last step.

Simon leaned toward me, just barely, but almost as if he were going to...

"Parker!" thundered from below, and we both sprang back. "Parker!" It came again, and I recognized Ryan's voice underneath the jungle-man yell.

"Ryan," we both said and smiled.

Now that the voodoo wasn't so concentrated, I could see things clearly again, and I repeated the word *harem* over and over again in my head.

"Up here!" Simon yelled, and Ryan appeared from around a bend.

"Hey there! Neil is done, kaput, thrown in the towel, so to speak. You guys about ready to head back down?" he called, jumping from rock to path to rock again with the ease of a mountain goat. He didn't even appear to be winded. *Hmmmm...*

"Yep, we were just about to come looking for you guys," I said, kicking my leg up behind me for a quick stretch.

"Is he really pussing out so close to the top?" Simon asked, heading back down the trail.

"He's lying straight across the trail like he owns the place, refusing to go any higher." Ryan laughed, bounding ahead and calling down to Neil to let him know we were on our way.

"You sure you didn't want to stay up here a little longer? I mean, we worked so hard to get all the way here," Simon asked, reaching out to stop me running down the mountain after Ryan.

I felt the warmth of his hand on my shoulder and willed my hormones to flee to the other side of my body. "I'm sure. We should get back. Looks like a storm is coming." I nodded toward the horizon where a group of dark clouds had begun to build. His eyes followed mine, and he frowned.

"You're probably right. We don't want to get caught out here all alone," he muttered.

"Besides, if we don't hurry, we can't tease Neil about getting beat up the mountain by a girl." I grinned, and he laughed loudly.

"Hell, we don't want to miss that. Let's go."

And down the trail we went.

"So how was your gangbang, Caroline?" Sophia sang sweetly as she found us all in the kitchen drinking water after our hike. The three guys each did different versions of a spit take, but I calmly continued sipping like a lady.

"Fantastic, thanks. Neil especially. We practically had to carry him back down the mountain after I finished with him," I replied just as sweetly.

The boys recovered their game faces, but Neil could barely stop staring at Sophia's tight tank top. Her actual suitor? Playing Spot The Mimi, his head rotating so fast I could have sworn he was an owl. I shook my head and put him out of his misery.

"Where's Mimi?" I asked.

"Shower, which you four clearly need. It's freezing outside. How could you have gotten so sweaty?" she asked, wrinkling her nose.

"We worked hard making it up that mountain. Hiking is harder than you think," Neil puffed, and the rest of us wisely kept silent about the heart attack he almost had fifty feet from the summit.

I grabbed an apple and headed in the direction of my room with Sophia hot on my tail, as expected. I smirked a little and contemplated going easy on her—just asking her about it, giving her an out.

"Those shorts look terrible on you, Caroline," she remarked as she followed me into my room.

Nope. Not going to happen. No easy out. "Thank you, dear. Should I have packed a little cat food for you when I packed Clive's travel bag?" I sneered.

She collapsed on my bed, curling her body around one of the giant pillows. "Where is he anyway? Who's watching him this weekend?"

"He's staying with Uncle Euan and Uncle Antonio. That cat is lounging on a silk bed being handfed tuna rolls right about now. He's living the life."

"He has the life, that's for sure," she said, her face clouding briefly as she got comfortable.

I peeled off my sweaty clothes and wrapped up in a terrycloth robe hanging on the back of the door. She complimented my choice of sports bra and laughed when she saw that I'd paired it with leopard panties, but then she went back to her previous wistful expression.

"What's up, Sophia?" I asked, lying on the bed next to her and wrapping myself around a pillow as well.

"Nothing, why?" she asked.

"You look like a sad sack."

"Eh, I just didn't sleep well, I guess."

"Oh really? Mr. Ryan keeping you up late at night, hmm? He didn't have a lot of energy on the mountain today..." I nudged her with my elbow.

"No, no, nothing like that. I just...I dunno. I just couldn't get settled last night. Normally I sleep really well up here, but it was so quiet last night, I just..." She beat her pillow a little with her fist, forcing it into a new shape.

"I see. Well, I slept great!" I laughed, and she starting trying to force my *head* into a new shape with her fist.

"You wanna get drunk tonight?" she asked when we finally settled down.

"Hell, yes. You?"

"Yes, ma'am."

There was a knock at the door, and Mimi poked her towel-covered head in. "Is this a private session, or can a non-lesbian get into this bed?" she called.

We waved her in, and she vaulted from the floor to the bed and landed on top of both of us.

"What are we doing in here, ladies? Foreplay or just going for it?" she asked.

"Please say foreplay," a male voice said from the now-open door. We rolled over to see the men in the doorway, different versions of the same oh-my-goodness-girls-in-bed-together look on their faces.

"Oh, get over yourselves. Like we'd ever need a guy to tell us whether we needed foreplay or not," Sophia giggled, kicking a foot in the air and waving at them from over my shoulder. They shifted their weight from one foot to the other and cleared their throats. So predictable.

"We're planning on getting drunk tonight. You boys up for it?" Mimi yelled. Even though no alcohol was currently present in her system, Drunky Mimi's volume level was already making an encore appearance.

"Done and done," Ryan answered, giving us a weird little salute that made us giggle even harder.

"Now run away, boys, and let us have our girl time," Sophia tossed over her shoulder, lifting my robe a little and giving my ass a quick smack. I squealed and tried to cover myself, but it was too late.

"Dude. Leopard print," Neil whispered to Simon in the kind of whisper that's actually louder than just speaking.

"I know, I know," Simon countered, then drew his hand down his face as though he were trying to physically remove the image from his brain.

Simon liked animal prints. Duly noted.

"Come on, guys. The ladies have requested a little alone time, so let's leave them to it." Ryan tugged them out into the hallway and closed the door behind them with a wink that made Mimi's entire neck turn bright red. Sophia examined her fingernails.

I was really going to have fun with these two tonight.

"Where the hell did you learn to cook like this? Jesus, this is good!" Neil exclaimed, taking his third helping of paella from the giant pan in the center of the table.

"Thank you, Neil." I laughed as he dug into another pile of rice.

Simon nodded toward my wine glass, and I nodded back.

I'd thought about making a quick version of paella when I saw all the wonderful seafood on sale at the local market, and when I saw their special on Spanish Rosé and Cava, my plans came together. We'd started in on the Cava while prepping in the kitchen. The sparkling Spanish wine went perfectly with the wedge of Manchego I'd picked up, as well as the little salty olives. Once again, Simon was my helper, and we moved together in the kitchen. The other four settled on bar stools across from us while we cooked, someone popped an old Otis Redding record on the ancient turntable, and we were in business.

The wine flowed as freely as the conversation, and I could tell this had the potential to become a tight-knit group. Similar interests, similar senses of humor, but everything just different enough to keep it lively.

Speaking of lively, as the alcohol was inhaled, the walls came down. Mimi and Sophia were barely hiding their misplaced interests anymore. Not that the boys were minding. In fact, they were encouraging it. Ryan currently examined Mimi's foot for what she insisted was a spider bite. The fact that he'd been inspecting it for several minutes, and that said inspection included a calf massage did not escape my attention, or Simon's.

He grinned and motioned for me to move closer. I slid across the bench and inclined my head to his. He put his mouth next to my ear, and I inhaled. Wine, heat, and actual sex ran straight up my nostrils and invaded my brain, turning everything a bit fuzzy.

"How long before they kiss?" he whispered, his mouth so close I swear I felt lips brush my ear.

"What?" I asked, beginning to giggle the way I did when I'd had a little too much to drink and a little too much sexy dangled in front of me.

"How long? You know, before they kiss the wrong person?" he asked as I turned to look into his eyes.

Those eyes, oh, those eyes were now calling to me.

"You mean the right person?" I whispered.

"Yeah, the right person," he answered, scooting a little closer on the bench.

"I don't know, but if the kiss doesn't come soon, I'm gonna burst," I admitted, knowing full well I was no longer talking about our friends. And knowing full well that he knew full well I was no longer talking about our friends.

"Hmm, I wouldn't want you to burst." He was now mere inches from my face.

Harem. Harem. Harem. I repeated this mantra over and over.

"I wanna go in the hot tub."

The whining pulled me away from the voodoo and back to the kitchen. Where there were people present.

"I wanna go in the hot tub," I heard again and turned to address Mimi. Imagine my surprise when I saw that Sophia was actually the whiner, and she was now hanging on Neil like a backpack.

"Okay, so go in the hot tub. No one's stopping you," I insisted, sliding away from Simon and back in front of my plate where I began separating my peas from my lobster. I was full, but I would never leave lobster on the plate. I had standards, after all.

"You have to come too," Sophia whined again as I began to comprehend. Sophia was drunk. Sophia got clingy when she got drunk. Oh boy.

"Go ahead. I'll clean up the kitchen a little and then meet you guys out there," Simon said, taking my plate and starting to stand.

"Hey, hey, hey! Lobster bite, hello," I protested as I grabbed my fork.

"Here, I would never get between a woman and her lobster." He smiled, offering me my fork back. I accepted the bite with a smile and stood up. I was a little more drunk than I thought, and this fact made itself known as gravity began tease me.

"Whoa there, you okay?" he asked, steadying me as Sophia started off for the bedroom.

"Yeah, I'm fine, I'm fine," I answered, planting my feet and winning the battle.

"Maybe you outta slow down?" he asked, taking my wine glass.

"Oh, lighten up, it's a party," I cried, beginning to giggle. Suddenly everything was funny.

"Okay, party on." He smiled as I headed to the bedroom to change into my suit. Which proved harder than I thought. String bikinis are difficult to tie when you're more than a little buzzed.

"Okay, Caroline's next. Truth or dare," Mimi yelled, once again proving that Drunky Mimi only had one volume level.

"Truth," I yelled back, splashing Sophia in the face accidentally as I reached behind me for my glass of wine. We'd brought out the last bottle of Cava and were steadily working our way through it. And it was steadily working its way through us, our game becoming more and more dangerous. The sky crackled a bit with far-away lightning, and low rumbles of thunder were just beginning to be heard over the giggling and splashing.

Once we came outside and got settled in the hot tub, it was only minutes before Neil suggested a game of Truth or Dare, and only seconds after that before Sophia agreed to it. I laughed it off at first, saying there was no way I'd play such a childish game. But when Simon implied that I was chicken, the alcohol reared its ugly head and shouted something to the effect of, "I will play Truth or Dare, you sucker, until you can't tell your truth from your dare!"

This statement made perfect sense in my head, and must have seemed logical to Mimi and Sophia as well, as they immediately began offering me high fives and you-go-girls. I'm pretty sure I saw Simon shake his head, but he was smiling, so I let it go. And poured another glass of sparkly.

"Where's the one place you want to travel, and haven't been yet," she asked, humming along to the tunes coming through the French doors.

Sophia had found all of her grandfather's old records, and Simon almost had a fit when he saw the collection. He'd selected a Tommy Dorsey album, and the big band accentuated the night perfectly.

"Boring, make her take a dare!" Simon sang, and I stuck my tongue out at him.

"It's not boring, and she chose truth so she gets truth. Caroline, where is the one place on earth you want to go?" she asked again.

I leaned my head back against the edge of the tub. I looked up at the stars and an image immediately came to mind: soft wind blowing, warm sun on my face, the ocean spread out in front of me dotted with craggy rocks. I smiled just thinking about it.

"Spain," I sighed quietly, the smile lingering as I imagined myself on a beach in *Spain*.

"Spain?" Simon asked.

I turned my face toward his. He was smiling back at me. "Spain. That's where I want to go. But it's so expensive, it's going to have to wait a while," I smiled again, my head still wrapped around the image.

"Hey, wait, Simon, aren't you going to Spain next month?" Ryan asked, and my eyes widened.

"Um, yeah. Yeah, I am actually," he answered.

"Great! Caroline, you can go with him," Mimi decided, clapping her hands and turning to Ryan.

"Ryan, you're next."

"No, no, wait a minute. First of all, I can't just go with Simon to Spain. And second of all, it's my turn," I protested, as Simon sat up.

"Actually, you could 'just go with Simon to Spain,'" he said, turning to me fully. The other side of the hot tub got very quiet.

"Um, no, I can't. You're working. I can't afford a trip like that, and besides, I don't know that I can take time off next month." I felt my heart swell as I processed what he'd just said.

"Actually, I heard Jillian telling you the other day that next month would be a good time to take your vacation before the holiday season," Mimi piped up. She sank back into the shadows as I glared at her.

"Be that as it may, I also can't afford it, so discussion ended. Now then, I believe it's my turn. Let's see, who should I pick?" I looked around at everyone.

"It wouldn't be that expensive. I'm renting a house, so that would be paid for. Airfare and spending money—that's all you'd have to cover," Simon added, not letting this go.

"Hey, that's a pretty good deal there, Caroline," Mimi spouted, her energy making little ripples across the tub.

"Okay, Mimi, truth or dare?" I asked, gritting my teeth and pushing ahead with the game.

"Hey, we're discussing something here. Don't change the subject," she objected.

"Well, I'm done discussing it. Truth or dare, you little shit," I said again, letting her know I meant business.

"Fine. Dare," she pouted.

"Great. I dare you to kiss Neil," I shot back, not missing a beat.

"What?" she shouted, as the entire hot tub erupted in gasps.

"Hey, we're just playing a game, right? And Mimi, really, it's not that shocking that I would dare you to kiss the guy you've been seeing for weeks now, is it?"

"Well, no, I just, I don't like public displays," she sputtered, almost going under. This from the girl who was almost arrested for public nudity when she was found under the bleachers at a football game freshman year at Berkeley.

"Oh, come on, what's the big deal?" Simon chimed in, and I looked at him gratefully.

"Nothing, it's just—" she said again, and Neil interrupted.

"Oh, come here, Tiny," he exclaimed and pulled her over. They stared at each other for a second, and then Neil swept her hair out of her face. He smiled, and she leaned in. I heard Sophia inhale at the same time Ryan did, and we all watched as Mimi kissed Neil.

And it was weird.

They broke away, and Mimi swam back over to her side. Next to Ryan. All was quiet for a moment. Simon and I looked at each other, not sure what to do next. We'd been outsmarted. And I got pissed when I got outsmarted. I began to burn. The fact that I was drunk had *nothing* at all to do with my overreaction.

"Okay, I guess it's my turn. Hmmm...Ryan, truth or dare?" Neil started, and I stood up, splashing everyone around me as I did.

"No, no, no! That's not what was supposed to happen!" I yelled, stamping my foot, losing my balance and going under in the process. Simon's strong hands brought me back to the surface, and I continued my alcohol-induced tirade. Flashes of lightning, now much closer, blazed across the sky.

"*You* were not supposed to let *her* kiss *him!*" I sputtered, spitting out water and pointing at Ryan and then at Mimi. I whirled on Sophia. "And *you* were supposed to get mad at *her!*"

"Why would I get mad at Mimi? For kissing her boyfriend?" Sophia mumbled, taking a sudden interest in her fingernails.

"Argh!" I screamed and turned back to Mimi.

"Mimi, are you even remotely interested in Neil?" I challenged, hands on my hips as I steamed into the night air.

"Neil is exactly what I've always wanted in a man. He is my type to a T," she countered robotically, flinching when Ryan looked at her with hurt in his eyes.

"Blah, blah, blah, have you fucked Neil yet?" I screeched, pointing wildly as I tend to do when I drink.

"Okay, Caroline, you've made your point," Simon soothed, trying to get me to sit back down.

"What point? What are you two talking about?" Sophia asked, leaning forward.

"Oh, please, the four of you are ridiculous! I don't care what you all think you want on paper. In reality, you're doing it all wrong!" I answered, smacking the top of the water for emphasis. Why weren't they getting it? I don't know when I'd gotten so riled up, but in the last sixty seconds or so, I'd become blazing mad.

"Are you kidding?" Mimi cried, jumping to her feet in the hot tub, which kept the water at about the same level.

"Mimi, come on! Anyone with eyes can see the way you and Ryan feel about each other! Why the hell are you wasting time on anyone else?" I pushed.

Simon pulled me back onto his lap and attempted to quiet me.

"Okay, this has gone far enough," Neil said, starting to get out of the tub.

"No, no! Neil, look at Sophia. Can't you see she is totally into you? Why the hell are you all so thick? Seriously? Are Simon and I the only ones that can see clearly here?" I yelled once more, bringing Simon into the conversation whether he wanted it or not.

Neil looked at Ryan, and then at Simon.

"Dude!" Neil exclaimed.

"Dude," Simon answered, gesturing toward Sophia, who stood up like she was going to say something. Neil put his hand on her shoulder, and she stopped and sat back down. Neil nodded at Ryan.

"Dude?" he asked, and Ryan nodded back. Neil took a deep breath and looked at Sophia.

"Sophia, truth or dare?" Neil asked.

"We are not playing any more —" I tried to yell, but Simon took that moment to place his hand over my mouth.

"All clear over here," Simon announced as he pinned me to his lap more securely with his other hand on my waist. Thunder rolled in, blanketing the scene with an ominous air.

"Sophia?" Neil asked again. She was quiet, and not looking in the direction of Mimi and Ryan.

"Dare," she whispered and closed her eyes.

Alcohol made everything *much* more dramatic.

"I dare you to kiss me," Neil said, and all you could hear was the occasional loon over the lake. The loons in the tub were finally quiet. We all watched as Sophia turned to Neil and placed a hand on the back of his head, pulling him toward her. She kissed him, slowly but surely, and it went on for days. I smiled into Simon's hand, and he patted my stomach, which made me giddy.

When they finally broke apart, Sophia was laughing into Neil's mouth, and he answered with his giant, goofy man-giggle.

"Well, it's about freaking time," Simon said, releasing my mouth.

"Mimi, I—" Sophia began, turning toward Mimi and finding an empty hot tub.

Mimi and Ryan were gone. I caught just the edge of Ryan's towel headed into the pool house—with a slippery wet companion on his arm.

"Well, then, I guess we'll call it a night." Sophia sighed, grabbing Neil by the hand.

"'Night." I giggled as she walked into the house with Neil in tow. They cuddled close, already a picture in the making. I looked at the pool house, and noticed no lights had come on yet. They probably would not be coming on in the near future.

"Well, that was a fine bit of matchmaking, although your bull-in-a-china-shop delivery left a lot to be desired," Simon chuckled, letting his head rest against my back. I was still perched on his lap. His hand had left my mouth, and it was now drifting south, while his other hand remained tightly on my waist.

"Yes, I usually leave a lot to be desired," I observed wryly, not wanting to leave this exquisite spot, but knowing I needed to—and soon. Simon was quiet behind me, and I started to move off his lap.

"You leave everything to be desired, Caroline," he said softly, and I froze. It was quiet for another moment, both of us not moving, but still moving toward each other.

Without looking back, I let out a tiny laugh. "You know, I never really got that phrase. Does that mean I *am* desirable or—"

His fingers began to trace tiny circles on my skin. "You know exactly what it means," he breathed into my ear. The air crackled around us, the tension as well as the actual weather. More tiny circles. In the end, it was the tiny circles that finally broke me.

I lost all control. I turned quickly, catching him off guard as I wrapped my legs around his waist and threw caution, and my harem mantra, to the wind. I sunk my hands into his hair, luxuriating in the feel of wet silk around my fingertips as I pulled him toward me.

"Why did you kiss me that night at the party?" I asked, my mouth mere inches from his. Once he realized I was driving this bus, he responded by pressing his hips into mine, bringing us closer together than we'd ever been.

"Why did *you* kiss *me?*" he asked, running his hands up and down my back, settling into the space where his hands spanned my waist exactly—thumbs in front, fingers in back—and pressed me into him further.

"Because I had to," I answered honestly, remembering how I'd reacted instinctively, kissing him when I'd wanted to do anything but. "Why did *you* kiss me?" I asked again.

"Because I had to," he said, the smirk returning. Luckily I didn't see the smirk for too long. Because I'd finally discovered the secret of the ages.

How do you make Wallbanger stop smirking? You kiss him.

chapter thirteen

The sky opened up, pelting us with chilly rain, which mixed with the heat around us, and between us. I looked at Simon underneath me, warm and wet, and there was nothing in the world I wanted more than his lips against mine. So even though every single cowbell in my head was ringing out the alarm, I centered myself, wrapped my legs tighter around his waist, and gazed directly into his eyes.

"Mmm, Caroline, what are you up to?" He smiled, his hands strong on my waist as his fingers dug into my skin. His skin slipped against mine in a way that made me not right in the head, and I could feel—I could actually *feel*—his abs against my tummy. He was so strong, so powerfully delicious that Brain began to burn, and other organs began to make all my decisions.

I think O even popped her head up for a moment, like a groundhog. She took a quick glance around and pronounced it much closer to spring than she'd been in months.

I licked my lips, and he mirrored my actions. I could barely see him through the haze of steam from the hot tub and the lust now brewing in this little cauldron of chlorinated chemistry.

"I'm up to no good, that's for sure," I breathed, rising up just a little. The feeling of my breasts crushing against his skin was unimaginable. As I settled on his lap again, I felt his reaction in a very tangible way, and we both groaned at the contact.

"You're up to no good, huh?" he said, his voice gruff and thick and maple syrup pouring over me.

"No good," I whispered in his ear as he pressed his mouth against my neck. "Wanna be bad with me?"

"You sure about that?" he groaned, hands clutching at my back with delightful abandon.

"Come on, Simon, let's bang some walls," I answered, allowing my tongue to dart out from between my lips and against the skin just underneath his jaw. The scruff scratched my taste buds and gave me a sense of what that very scruff would feel like against other soft places on my body.

O poked her head out just a little more at that point and went straight to Brain, which in turn spoke directly to my hands.

I grasped him firmly at the base of his neck, and positioned him directly in front of me, his eyes flaring wide and turning into tiny little hypnotizers.

His grin was hard, and so was he.

I leaned in and sucked his bottom lip between my teeth, nibbling lightly before biting down and pulling him closer. He came willingly, ceding control as my fingers pulled and pushed at his hair, and my tongue pressed into his mouth as he groaned into mine. Everything in my world now narrowed to just the feeling of this man, this wonderful man in my arms and threaded between my legs, and I kissed him like the world was about to end.

It wasn't sweet and tentative, it was pure carnal frustration spiked with incomprehensible lust and rolled into a giant ball of please-God-let-me-live-in-this-man's-mouth-for-the-forseeable-future. My mouth led his in a dance as old as the mountains that watched over us approvingly, our tongues and teeth and lips smacking and cracking and giving in to the sweet tension that had been building since I showed up at his door wearing the inspiration for my nickname.

I shook as I felt his hands reach lower to grasp my bottom and pull me closer still, my legs scrambling as I panted like a whore in church. The Church Of Simon…where I was dying to kneel before him.

My eyes were closed, my legs were open, and I was now moaning into his mouth like some kind of rabid dog. The idea that a kiss, just a kiss, had turned me into this giant lusting bag of CarolineNeedThat was undeniable, and I knew that if he continued to make me feel this way I was going to invite him straight into my Tahoe. *Great idea.*

"Come into my Tahoe, Simon," I mumbled incoherently into his mouth.

He paused. "Caroline, come into your what? Oh, God," he managed, as I pushed us off the side of the hot tub and vaulted us across the water, emptying half of its contents onto the deck and the other half sloshing us around like it was high tide. He slammed me into the opposite wall, pushing me up against the bench and rewrapping my legs around his waist, as I gamely pushed my mouth back onto his, unwilling to let go of him. At one point, I kissed him so hard, he had to push me off so he could catch a breath.

"Breathe, Simon, breathe," I giggled, stroking his face as he struggled before me.

"You…are…a mad woman," he panted, his hands looping underneath my arms and curling around the tops of my shoulders, keeping me firmly against the side while I dug my heels into his backside, nudging him to exactly where I needed him. He closed his eyes and bit down on his lower lip, an animalistic growl sounding low in his throat as I launched my second wave of the Lower Caroline-commanded attack.

"You feel uncommonly good," I moaned as I began to kiss him again, raining them down across his mouth, his cheeks, his jaw, slipping underneath to suck and bite at his neck as he dropped his head back to allow my assault. His hands were rough on me, dipping down low on my back and catching on my bikini strings, loosening the sides. The thought of my naked breasts against his skin drove me crazy with lust, and I removed my hands from his poor hair to snake back behind my neck and pull on the knot. As I maneuvered, I knocked into one of the empty bottles of Cava, starting a domino effect of bottles crashing to the ground. I giggled as he pulled back, startled at the sound.

His eyes were smoky blue, crowded with lust, but as they focused on me, they began to crystallize. I finally managed to get to the knot untied and could feel the water swirl across my naked skin. I started to drop the strings, when Simon grasped them tightly in his hands. He shook his head as though to clear it, then closed his eyes firmly, cutting off our connection.

"Hey, hey, hey!" I prodded, forcing his eyes open and making him look at me. "Where did you go just now?" I whispered.

He wrapped his hands, still holding my strings, back around my neck. He slowly began to tie my suit back together, and I felt my face flush bright red, all the blood in my body betraying me in that instant.

"Caroline," he began, breathing heavily, but looking at me carefully.

"What's wrong?" I interrupted.

His hands came to rest on my shoulders, and he seemed to be keeping a specific distance between us.

"Caroline, you're amazing, but I...I can't—" he started.

Now I was the one to close my eyes. Emotions whirled behind my eyelids, shame being chief among them. Heart plummeted. I could feel his eyes on me, willing me to open my own.

"You can't," I stated, opening my eyes and looking anywhere but at him.

"No, I mean, I..." he stammered, clearly uneasy as he moved away from me.

I began to shake. "You...can't?" I asked, suddenly feeling icy cold, even in the water. I unlocked my legs from around him, allowing him the room he needed to move away.

"No, Caroline, not you. Not like—"

"Well, don't I feel like a fucking idiot?" I managed, laughing shortly and pulling myself up and out of the water to the side of the hot tub.

"What? No, you don't understand, I just can't—" he started toward me, and I kicked out a leg, pressing my foot square in the center of his chest to keep him away.

"Hey, Simon, I get it. You can't. It's cool. Wow, what a crazy night, huh?" I laughed again, swinging over the side and starting for the house, wanting to get away before he could see the tears I knew were on their way. Of course, as I tried to navigate the steps, I slipped in a wet spot and fell with a big thud. I could feel the back of my eyeballs begin to burn as I scrambled up as quickly as I could, panicked that I was going to cry before I could get inside. Now that I was moving, I could feel the effects of all the alcohol I'd consumed, and the beginnings of a very strong headache.

"Caroline! Are you okay?" Simon cried, starting to get out of the hot tub.

"I'm fine. I'm fine. Just..." I got out, my throat beginning to close as I choked back a sob. I held my hand out behind me, willing him to understand that I did not need his help. "I'm fine, Simon."

I couldn't turn around and see him. I just continued walking away. The cursed big band music still played on the turntable, but I still heard him say my name once more. Ignoring it, I made my way to the door, feeling foolish now in my teeny bikini that was clearly not as enticing as I thought it was.

I didn't even bother to grab a towel. Instead I threw open the glass door and heard it slam shut behind me as I all but ran for my room. I left little puddles along the slate floor down the hallway, trying to ignore the giggles coming from Sophia's room. As the tears finally coursed down my cheeks, I locked the door and stripped off my bathing suit. I stumbled into the bathroom, flicked on the light, and there I stood, reflected back to me. Naked, wet hair streaming down my back, a bruise already beginning to form on my thigh from my drunken spill…and puffy, kiss-swollen lips.

I wrapped my hair in a towel, and then leaned on the countertop, bringing my face within inches of the mirror.

"Caroline, my dear, you just got turned down by a man who once made a woman meow for thirty minutes straight. How do you feel?" the naked woman in the mirror asked me, turning my thumb into a little microphone. She gestured toward me, holding out her thumb.

"Well, I drank enough wine to sustain a small Spanish village, I haven't had an orgasm in a thousand years, and I will probably die old and alone in a beautifully designed apartment with all of Clive's illegitimate children swarming around me…How do you think I feel?" I asked back, offering Mirror Caroline her thumb.

"Silly Caroline, you had Clive neutered," Mirror Caroline answered, shaking her head at me.

"Go fuck yourself, Mirror Caroline, since I can't even do that," I finished, ending the interview and taking my naked ass back into the bedroom. Throwing on a T-shirt, I fell into bed, my drunk self exhausted from the hike and the dinner and the wine and the music and the best make-out session I'd ever engaged in. The thought of it brought my tears to the surface again, and I rolled over to grab some tissues, only to find an empty box, which made me cry even harder.

Stupid Wallbanger voodoo.

Could this night get any worse?

Then my phone rang.

"Pancakes, sweetie?"

"Love some. Thanks, babe."

Jesus.

"Is there still cream for the coffee?"

"I got your cream right here, honeybunch."

Sweet Jesus.

Listening to a new couple, much less *two* new couples was sometimes vomit-worthy. Add that to a hangover, and this was going to be a long morning.

After talking to James on the phone last night, I'd fallen into a deep sleep, aided, no doubt, by all the wine I'd consumed. I woke with a thick tongue, a splitting headache, and a queasy stomach—made even more queasy by the knowledge that I'd have to see Simon this morning and have that weird we-totally-made-out-last-night conversation.

James had made me feel better, though. He'd made me laugh, and I remembered how well he took care of me back in the day. It was a nice memory, and an even nicer feeling. He'd called under the pretense of checking with me about a paint color, which I quickly called as a bluff. Then he'd admitted he just wanted to talk to me, and fresh off the Great Hot Tub Rejection, I was happy to talk to someone I *knew* wanted my attention. *Damn you, Simon.* When James asked me to dinner next weekend, I agreed immediately. We'd have a great time...and since my O was back in her hidey-hole, I might as well enjoy a night on the town.

Now, I was seated at the breakfast table, surrounded by two new couples who were filling the kitchen with enough sexual satisfaction to make me scream. I didn't though. I kept it to myself as Mimi perched happily on Ryan's lap, and Neil fed Sophia melon balls as though he was put on the earth for this reason and this reason alone.

"How was the rest of your evening, Ms. Caroline?" Mimi chirped, raising a knowing eyebrow. I pressed the tines of my fork into her hand and told her to zip it.

"Wow, grumpy. Someone must have spent the night alone," Sophia murmured to Neil.

I looked up at her in surprise. The casualness with which they were treating this was really starting to bother me.

"Well, of course I spent the night alone. Who the hell do you think I spent the night with? Huh?" I asked, slamming back from the table and knocking my orange juice glass over. "Ah, fuck it all to hell," I muttered, stomping off toward the patio, tears threatening for the second time in less than twelve hours.

I sat in one of the Adirondack chairs, looking out over the lake. The cool of the morning soothed my heated face, and I wiped clumsily at my tears as I heard the girls footsteps follow me outside.

"I don't want to talk about it, okay?" I instructed, as they took the seats opposite me.

"Okay...but you gotta give us something. I mean, I thought for sure when we left last night, I mean...you and Simon are just—" Mimi started, and I stopped her.

"Me and Simon nothing. There is no me and Simon. What, you thought we'd pair off just because you four finally figured your shit out? You're welcome for that, by the way," I snapped, pulling my ball cap down lower on my face, hiding my continuing tears from my best friends.

"Caroline, we just thought—" Sophia began, and I cut her off as well.

"You thought since we were the ones left over we'd just magically become a couple? How storybook—three sets of perfectly matched couples, right? Like that ever happens. This isn't some romance novel."

"Oh, come on, you two are perfect for each other. You called *us* blind last night? Hi, pot. It's me, kettle," Sophia snapped back.

"Hi, kettle, you have about thirty seconds before this pot kicks your ass. Nothing happened. Nothing is going to happen. In case you forgot, he has a harem, ladies. A harem! And I'm not about to become his third chippie. So you can forget it, okay?" I yelled, pushing out of the chair, turning for the house, and running right into a quiet Simon.

"Great! You're here too! And I see you two peeking through the blinds, idiots!" I cried as Neil and Ryan backed away from the window.

"Caroline, can we talk, please?" Simon asked, grasping me by the arms and spinning me toward him.

"Sure, why not? Let's make the embarrassment complete. Since I know you're all dying to know, I threw myself at this guy last night, and he turned me down. Okay, secret's out. Now can we please drop it?" I wiggled out of his grip and walked toward the trail to the lake. I heard nothing behind me and turned to see all five of them, wide eyed and evidently unsure what to do next.

"Hey! Come on, Simon. Let's go," I snapped my fingers, and he started after me, looking a little afraid.

I stomped down the trail and tried to slow my breathing. My heart was pounding, and I didn't want to talk when I was this riled up. No good could come of it. As I breathed in and out, I took in the beautiful morning all around and tried to let that lighten my heart a bit. Did I need to make this more awkward that it already was? No. I had the control here, last night notwithstanding. I could make it so last night never happened, or I could certainly try.

I breathed again, feeling a bit of the tension leave my body. Despite everything that happened, I enjoyed Simon's company and had to come to think of him as my friend. I still stomped along the path, but eventually eased back into a moderately pissy stroll.

I left the trees behind and didn't stop until I reached the end of the dock. The sun peeked out after last night's storm, casting a silver light on the water.

I heard him approach and stop just behind me. I took one more deep breath. He was silent.

"You're not going to push me in, are you? That would be a bad move, Simon." He exhaled a laugh, and I smiled a little, not wanting to, but not able to help it.

"Caroline, can I explain about last night? I need to you know that —"

"Just don't, okay? Can't we just chalk it up to the wine?" I asked, whirling about to face him and trying to beat him to the punch.

He stared down at me with the strangest look on his face. He looked like he'd gotten dressed in a hurry: white thermal, well worn jeans, and hiking boots that weren't even laced up, the strings now damp and muddy from the trek through the woods. Still, he was stunning, the early morning sun illuminating the strong planes of his face and that scruff that was so delicious.

"I wish I could, Caroline, but —" he started again.

I shook my head. "Seriously, Simon, just —" I began, but stopped when he pressed his fingers against my mouth.

"You have to shut up, okay? You keep interrupting me, and watch how fast you get tossed in that very lake," he warned with the twinkle in his eye I'd become so used to.

I nodded, and he removed his hand. I tried to ignore the flames that licked at my lips, brought to the surface by just that little touch.

"So, last night we came really close to making a very big mistake," he said, and when he saw my mouth begin to open, he wagged his finger at me.

I zipped my lip, miming throwing the key into the water. He smiled sadly and continued.

"Obviously I'm attracted to you. How could I not be? You're amazing. But you were drunk, I was drunk, and as great as it would have been, it would have—ah, it would have changed things, you know? And I just can't, Caroline. I can't allow myself to…I just…" He struggled, running his hands through his hair in a gesture I'd come to understand as frustration. He stared at me, willing me to make this okay, to tell him we were okay.

Did I want to lose a friend over this? No way.

"Hey, like I said, it's cool—too much wine. Besides, I know you have your *arrangement*, and *I* can't…Things just got away from me last night," I explained, trying to sell it to him.

He opened his mouth to comment, but after a moment he nodded and sighed a great sigh. "We still friends? I don't want this to get weird for us. I really like you, Caroline," he asked, looking as though his world was about to come to an end.

"Of course friends. What else would we be?" I swallowed hard and forced a smile. He smiled too, and we began to walk back up the trail. Okay, that wasn't too bad. Maybe this could work. He stopped to pick up a handful of sand from the beach and put it in a little plastic baggie.

"Bottles?"

"Bottles." He nodded, and we started up the path.

"So it looks like our little plan worked," I began, searching for conversation.

"With those guys? Oh yeah, I think it worked well. They seem to have found what they needed."

"That's all anyone's trying to do, right?" I laughed as we crossed the patio to the kitchen. Four heads disappeared from the window and began to assume positions of nonchalance around the table. I chuckled.

"Always good when what you need and what you want are the same things," Simon said, holding the door open for me.

"Boy, did you say a mouthful." A pang of sadness hit me again, but I didn't have to force the smile once I saw how happy my friends were.

"You want some breakfast? There are still some cinnamon buns, I think," Simon offered, walking over to the counter.

"Um, no. I think I'm gonna go pack, get my stuff together," I said, noticing a flash of disappointment cross his face before he smiled bravely.

Okay, so this wasn't great. Well, that's what happens when two friends kiss. Things are never the same. I nodded at my girls and headed for my room.

Spurred by my insistence about getting back to the city, within two hours we were all packed and deciding who was going to ride with whom. I didn't want to ride alone with Simon, so I pulled Mimi aside and instructed her to bring Ryan along with us. Now we were all outside arranging bags. As Simon piled everything into the Range Rover, I shivered a little, realizing too late that I'd packed my fleece jacket into my bag, which was now buried. As he turned back toward me, he noticed.

"You cold?"

"A little, but it's fine. My bag's at the bottom, and I don't want you to have to rearrange everything," I answered, stamping my foot to keep warm.

"Oh! That reminds me, I have something for you," he exclaimed, rummaging in his bag, which was on top. He handed me a lumpy package, wrapped in brown paper.

"What's this?" I asked, as he blushed deeply. Simon does blush? I rarely saw that…

"You didn't think I forgot this, did you?" he replied, his hair falling into his eyes a little as he smiled a boyish smile. "I was going to give it to you last night, but then—"

"Hey, Parker! Could use a little help over here!" Neil called as he struggled to load all of Sophia's luggage. Yesterday, this would have been Ryan's job. Now it was Neil's. Yesterday. How the world had changed in one day.

He backed away from me as Mimi and Ryan got themselves settled in the backseat.

I opened the package to find a very thick, very soft Irish sweater. I lifted it out of the paper, feeling the weight and the nubbly texture of the weave. I pressed it against my nose, inhaling the scent of wool and unmistakable Simon that clung to it. I grinned into the sweater, then quickly slipped it over my T-shirt, admiring the way it hung loose and low, yet still wrapped me in a comforting way. I turned to see Simon watching me from over at Neil's truck. He smiled as I twirled for him.

"Thank you," I mouthed.

"You're welcome," he mouthed back.

I gave my sweater a long, deep sniff, hoping no one noticed.

chapter fourteen

Inside a black Range Rover on the way back to San Francisco...

Caroline: Okay, I can do this...It's only a few hours back into the city. I can be the bigger person here. I can act like he didn't pull an all stop at the thought of seeing my tatas last night—and what the hell? What man says no to tatas? I mean, they're nice tatas. They were pushed up nice and tight, and they were wet, for Christ's sake...Why didn't he want my tatas? Caroline, just settle down...Just smile at him and act like everything is fine. Wait, he's looking over here. Smile! Okay, he smiled back...Stupid tata turner-downer...I mean, what's up with that? And he was hard!

Simon: She's smiling at me...I can smile back at her, right? I mean, we're acting natural, right? Okay, done. I hope that looked more natural than it felt. Jesus, who knew a giant sweater would look so good on a girl...But everything looks pretty good on Caroline—especially that green bikini. Did I really turn her down last night? God, it would have been so easy to just...But then I couldn't. *Why couldn't I???* Jesus, Simon. Well, we were drunk...Correction, she was drunk. Would she have regretted it? She might have. Couldn't risk it? Might have been a bit of a disaster...Or was it the girls? I shouldn't do that to the girls either. But it's not even really working so well with the girls these days, now is it? Huh, I didn't think about them once this weekend...because I couldn't stop thinking about Caroline. She's looking at me again...What the hell are we going to talk about the whole way back to the city? Ryan isn't even paying attention. Bastard. I told him he needed to help me out...He's helping himself to a handful of Mimi. I'm almost sorry Caroline and I worked so hard to push them together. Hmm...Caroline and I...Caroline and me in a hot tub where bikinis are outlawed...Jesus, wait a minute—yep, now I've got a semi...

Caroline: Why is he twitching like that? Jesus, does he have to pee? Maybe I have to pee. Maybe this would be a good time to suggest a pee break...Then I can grab Mimi and make sure she knows the reason they're riding with us is not so they can suck face the whole way, but to run interference for me with Scared of Tatas over there. Okay, just ask him to pull over at the next gas station. Wow, he really does have to pee, I guess. I hope this gas station has Gardetto's.

Simon: Thank God she wanted to stop. Now I can adjust without looking like a pervert...oh, who am I kidding? I am a pervert. I'm riding in a car with a woman who was straddling me last night and just the thought of it makes me hard. Pervert, pervert, pervert. I hope this gas station has Gardetto's.

Mimi: Ooh! We're stopping! I hope this gas station has bubble gum!

Ryan: Oh, man, we're stopping already? We're not going to make it back to the city before dark. Mimi wants me to see her place, and I'm really hoping that means walk around naked and let me watch...I hope this gas station has condoms.

Caroline: Okay, you could have handled that a little better. Mimi suggesting you and Simon split the big bag of Gardetto's was not that big of a deal. Am I a little sensitive today? Yes, I suppose I am...But I know for a fact that Simon was checking out my ass as I walked away from the car. Why the hell is he checking out my ass now? Last night he didn't even want to peek under my bikini. Is he really that complicated? Why the hell is he looking at me? He's reaching his hand out. Stay still, Caroline, stay still...Oh, sesame seed on my chin. Well, if you weren't looking at my mouth, Mr. Mixed Messages, you wouldn't even have noticed it. You will never get this sesame seed now, buddy. Damn! Why does this sweater have to smell so good? I hope he hasn't noticed me sniffing this sweater the whole way.

Simon: She's really sniffly today. I hope she isn't catching a cold. We spent so much time outside this weekend…I would hate for her to come down with something. She just sniffled again. Should I offer her a Kleenex?

Mimi: Busted, Caroline. I totally knew you were sniffing that sweater.

Ryan: I wonder if Mimi has any more of that bubble gum? I hope she didn't notice me buying those condoms. I mean, I don't want to be presumptuous. But I definitely want to be under her again sometime very, very soon. Who knew someone so tiny could be so loud…and now I'm hard.

Mimi: Ryan Hall…Mimi Reyes Hall…Mimi Hall…Mimi Reyes-Hall…

Caroline: Okay, Caroline, time to have that difficult conversation—with yourself. Why exactly did you throw yourself at Simon last night? Was it the wine? Was it the music? The voodoo? Was it the combination of all those things? Okay, okay, no more bullshit. I did it because…because…Fuck, I need some more Gardetto's.

Simon: She's so pretty. I mean, there's pretty and then there's pretty… What a pussy I am. Fuck pretty—she's beautiful…pussy… And she smells good…pussy…Why do some girls just smell better? Some girls smell like flowery, fruity bullshit. I mean, why would some girls want to smell like a mango? Why should a girl smell like mango? Maybe if I think the word mango enough I won't think about pussy anymore. Caroline…mango… Caroline…pussy…*God!* And now I'm hard…

Caroline: He looks like he needs to pee again…He's drinking too much coffee. He's had like six cups already from that thermos. That's funny…He never has a second cup at home. Why the hell do I know how many cups of coffee he drinks? Face it, Caroline, you know so much about him because…because…

Ryan: Dude, we're stopping again? We are never gonna make it home. My boy is having some serious issues today…I should probably see if he wants to get a beer or something when we get back—in case he wants to come clean about what really happened last night. Should I offer? Wow, Mimi looks fantastic in those pants…I wonder if she's buying more bubble gum.

Mimi: Stop sniffing your sweater, Caroline! Seriously, girl. If I could just get her alone…Okay, Simon seems to be hobbling toward the men's room. I can get her alone by the beef jerky.

Caroline: Ugh…I can't believe Mimi knew I was sniffing the sweater. I wonder if Simon noticed.

Simon: She seems better…She's not sniffling any more.

Mimi: I need to text Sophia. She needs to know the Simon/Caroline situation is not getting any better. What the hell are we gonna do with these two? I mean, seriously…sometimes people just can't see what's right in front of them. Aawww…Ryan wants me to scratch his back. I adore him…And damn, are his fingers long…

Ryan: Mmmm…back…scratch…back…scratch…Mmmm…

Caroline: Okay, no more avoiding it in your own head, Reynolds. And now I'm serious because I'm using my last name. Now listen up, Reynolds…Heeheehee…I sound like such a badass!

Simon: So…she's giggling? Inside joke, she says. So maybe she is okay with how this is going—oops, grabbed the wrong bag of Gardetto's. Did she just growl at me?

Caroline: Turn my tatas down and then try to steal my Gardetto's? I don't *think* so, buddy. Okay, Reynolds, no more giggling. You can't avoid this forever, even in your own mind. Here are the questions on deck: 1. Why did you throw yourself at Simon last night? And you're not allowed to blame alcohol or music or vacation vibes or Nerves or Heart or anything. 2. Why did he turn you down? If he didn't want to go there, why has he been flirting with you for weeks, and not just in the neighborly way? He's got a harem, for God's sake. He's not a Puritan. Agh!! 3. Does being rejected by Simon have anything to do with the date you agreed to with James? 4. How the hell do Simon and I go back to being just friends when we know what the inside of each other's mouths taste like? And his tastes very, very, very good. Okay, yes. You can sniff the sweater one more time—just don't let anyone see you.

Simon: I have to figure this shit out with Caroline. She's so great, and I mean so great…Has there ever been a woman who's possessed every single quality I've been looking for? Except for Natalie Portman, of course. But Caroline? I have to stop watching so much Lifetime—I mean what guy in his own mind even thinks in sentences like: "Has there ever been a woman who's possessed every single quality I've been looking for?" Wait, have I been looking for that woman? No, I haven't. I don't have time for that, space for that—and my girls don't want the picket fence. They keep away the picket fencers. Caroline says she isn't a picket fencer...Katie found her picket fence, and I'm happy for her. When's the last time I even talked to Nadia or Lizzie? Maybe they're not right for me anymore. I don't want them the way I might want...could want Caroline. You're such a pussy, Parker...Jesus, Caroline—she's a fucking keeper...Wait a minute. What the hell? Are you really entertaining the idea of a...gulp...relationship? And why the fuck did I actually think the word "gulp"? That was a little dramatic, Parker. Come on, think about this...If I recall correctly, you invited her to Spain! Don't run away from it. Dude, did she just sniff her sweater?

Ryan: Mmmm...my girl likes beef jerky—could I be any luckier? She scratches my back and eats beef jerky. I have died and gone somewhere like heaven.

Mimi: I can't believe he ate all my beef jerky. What a jerky. Heehee.

Caroline: Question 1 is too hard. I can't start with that one. I'll answer them in reverse order. 4. I don't know if we can be friends, but I really want to be—and not in the fake way. I really like Simon, and even though what happened last night sucked major balls, I think we can figure this out...And I would like to have some of whatever I'm smoking. 3. OF COURSE I AGREED TO GO OUT WITH JAMES BECAUSE OF WHAT HAPPENED WITH SIMON! It's funny how that shows up in all caps even in my head. 2. If I knew why he turned me down, I'd be a fucking genius. Bad breath? No. Because I was drunk? Possibly... But if it's because we were drunk that's the worst timing for chivalry in the history of the universe. He did keep saying "I can't" and that it was a "mistake." Now, mistake perhaps. But might have been worth it...Maybe he was just being faithful to his harem? Which in an odd way is quite sweet. I know he really does care about them. Dammit, he's even great when it comes to them! But I know "I can't" wasn't accurate. "Can't" implies some kind of erectile dysfunction. And I felt that junk on my thigh. Sigh. Sigh for thigh. This sweater is doing things to my head. Sniff...

Simon: She just sniffed it again—why does she keep doing that? When I wore it I didn't notice it smelling like anything other than wool. Girls are weird…weirdly wonderful…Pussy…Caroline's pussy…Aaand I'm hard. Why the hell am I even pretending I'm not totally and completely over the moon for this girl? And it has nothing to do with her pussy…and now I'm harder.

Caroline: Stop trying to get out of answering this question. Face it head on! Why did you throw yourself at Simon, forgetting about the friendship and the harem and the O drought and all of the very good reasons you had for staying away from him and his banger voodoo??? Come on, Caroline. Suck it up and say it. What was it he said when you asked him why he kissed you that night you met? "Because I had to." Jesus, even in my head he sounds amazing saying that…There's your answer, Caroline: because you had to. And now you have to figure this shit out. I kissed him, and he kissed me because we had to. And the choices we made were ours and ours alone…And the fact that he stopped it and said he couldn't? Even after all the ridiculous weeks of flirting? After he invited me to Spain? Motherfucking Spain! And I want to go to motherfucking Spa—wait, do I want to go to Spain with him? Argh! Spain Schmain. Anyway, he better have a damn good reason because I am a fucking catch—O or no O—I am a fucking catch. Yeah, you are, Reynolds. Weird how you flip back and forth between first and third person during your inner monologues, though…Thank Christ, the Bay Bridge! Enough introspection…

Simon: Shit, the Bay Bridge. We're almost home, and I have no idea how this is going to go with Caroline. We've barely said anything the entire way—although I'm glad to be almost home. I smell like beef jerky, and I need to jerk off like you wouldn't believe…

Mimi: Yay! The Bay Bridge! I wonder if Ryan would mind spending the night at my place!

Ryan: Thank fuck, the Bay Bridge. We're almost home. I wonder if Mimi knows I'm spending the night at her place—and planning on making her call in sick tomorrow? Little girl, the things I plan to do to you…But I'm never eating that much beef jerky again. This has been the quietest road trip ever.

We dropped off the new couple at Mimi's—not that they particularly noticed—they were in their own bubble gum world—and continued on to our apartments. Though we'd mostly just been lost in our thoughts, the tension had grown during the drive, and it was even more noticeable now that we were alone in the car. Simon and I had always had things to talk about, but now that we had so much to discuss, we were silent. I didn't want things to be weird, and I knew I'd have to be the one to make sure he knew I was okay now. He'd already done his part to have a mature conversation, and once again my bull-in-a-china-shop delivery seemed to have taken care of that.

A vision of me announcing on the deck, at full volume, that I'd made a pass at Simon flashed across my mind, and while my cheeks certainly heated in embarrassment, I also had a mental chuckle at how odd I must have looked, arms flailing, mouth set as though I could spit nails. And then barking at frightened Simon to follow me to the beach. He must have wondered if I was going to thrash him and dump his body in the lake.

Looking at his hands on the steering wheel, the very hands that were on me in a very pronounced way the night before, I marveled at his ability to stop himself, because I know for a fact he had been in to it. Or his body had been, at least, if not his head.

The thing is, though, I *did* think his head was in it, at least until he thought about it too much. I glanced over at him once more, noticing we were pulling down our street. As we stopped at the curb, he looked over at me, biting down on the same lower lip that less than twenty-four hours ago I'd had the good fortune to be biting on.

He sprang from the car and ran around to my side before I even had my seatbelt unbuckled.

"Um, I'm just gonna…get the bags," he stammered, and I studied him closely. He ran his left hand through his hair while his right drummed against the side of the car. Was he nervous?

"So, yeah," he stammered again, disappearing around the back.

Yep, he was nervous, just as nervous as I was. He worried my bag out of the car, and we slogged up the three flights of stairs to our apartments. We were still not talking, so the only sound was our keys jangling in the locks. I couldn't leave it like this. I had to square with him. I took a deep breath, and turned. "Simon, I—"

"Look, Caroline—"

We both laughed a little.

"You go."

"No, you go," he said.

"Nope. What were you gonna say?"

"What were *you* gonna say?"

"Hey, spit it out, bucko. I got a pussy to rescue from two queens downstairs," I instructed, hearing Clive call to me from the apartment below.

Simon snorted and leaned against his door. "I guess I just wanted to say I had a really great time this weekend."

"Until last night, right?" I leaned against my own door, watching him flinch as I addressed the elephant in the hot tub.

"Caroline," he breathed, closing his eyes and letting his head fall back.

He looked like he was in actual pain as his face twisted. I took pity. I shouldn't have, but I did.

"Hey, can we just forget it happened?" I said. "I mean, I know we can't, but can we pretend to forget it? I know people say things won't get weird all the time, but then it always does. How can we make sure things don't get weird?"

He opened his eyes and looked hard at me. "I guess we just don't let it. We make sure it doesn't get weird. Okay?"

"Okay." I nodded and was rewarded with the first real smile I'd seen since I unwrapped my sweater back in Tahoe. He gathered up his bag.

"Play me something good tonight, 'kay?" I asked as I headed inside.

"You got it," he answered, and we shut our doors.

But he didn't play me big band that night.

And we didn't speak again that week.

"Who peed in your chili?"

I looked up from my desk to see Jillian, composed as always with her casually elegant chignon, black pencil trousers, white silk blouse, and raspberry cashmere sweater wrap. How did I know it was cashmere from across the room? Because it was Jillian.

I selected one of the five pencils currently stuck in my twisted hair bun and returned my attention to the mess that was my desk. It was Wednesday, and this week was both flying by and dragging simultaneously. No word from Simon. No texts from Simon. No songs from Simon.

But I hadn't reached out to him either.

I was consumed with finishing the last few details on the Nicholson house, ordering expensive knickknacks for James's condo, and starting the sketches for a commercial design project I had lined up for next month. It *looked* like chaos, but sometimes it was the only way I could get work done. There were days that I needed neat and orderly, and days when I needed the mess on my desk to reflect the mess in my head. This was that day.

"What's up, Jillian?" I barked, knocking over my cup of colored pencils as I grabbed for my coffee.

"How much coffee have you had today, Miss Caroline?" She laughed, taking the seat opposite me and handing me the pencils that had spilled on the floor.

"Hard to say…how many cups are in a pot and a half?" I answered, restacking some papers to clear a space for her teacup. The woman walked around drinking tea out of a bone china cup, but it worked for her.

"Wow, I take it you aren't seeing any clients today?" she asked, leaning over the desk and casually removing my coffee cup. I hissed at her, and she wisely put it back.

"Nope, no clients," I answered, shoving the new sketches into color-coordinated folders and stuffing them into their appropriate drawers.

"Okay, sister, what's up?"

"What do you mean? I'm working—what you pay me to do, remember?" I snapped, grabbing for a ring of fabric swatches and knocking my flower vase over. I'd picked out dark purple, almost black tulips for this week, and they were now all over the floor. I sighed heavily and forced myself to slow down. My hands shook from the caffeine arguing through my system, and as I sat and surveyed the state of affairs in my office I felt two fat tears forming in my eyes.

"Damn," I muttered and covered my face with my hands. I sat for a minute, listening to the tick of the retro clock on the wall, and waited for Jillian to say something. When she didn't, I peeked through my hands at her. She was standing by the door with my jacket and purse in her hands.

"Are you throwing me out?" I whispered as the tears launched themselves down my face. She waved her arm and beckoned me toward the door. Grudgingly I stood, and she draped my sweater around my shoulders and handed me my purse.

"Come on, dearie. You're buying me lunch." She winked and pulled me down the hallway.

Twenty minutes later she had me ensconced in an ornate red booth hidden partially behind two gold curtains. She'd brought me to her favorite restaurant in Chinatown, ordered me chamomile tea, and waited in silence for me to explain my semi breakdown. Actually, it was not entirely silent; we'd ordered the sizzling rice soup.

"So, you must've had a helluva weekend in Tahoe, huh?" she finally asked.

I laughed into my sizzle. "You could say that."

"What happened?"

"Well, Sophia and Neil finally got together and—"

"Wait a minute, Sophia and *Neil?* I thought Sophia was with *Ryan?*"

"She was, she was, but truthfully she was always meant to be with Neil, so it all worked out in the end."

"Poor Mimi and Ryan. That must've been weird for them."

"Ha! Oh yes, poor Mimi and Ryan. They got it on in the pool house, for God's sake," I snorted.

Jillian's eyes grew wide. "In the pool house...wow," she breathed, and I nodded.

We sizzled.

"So, Simon went to Tahoe, right?" she asked a few minutes later, looking everywhere but at me. I cracked a small smile at her imagined stealth. Jillian was many, many things, but subtle was not one.

"Yep, Simon was there."

"And how was that?"

"It was great, and then it wasn't, and now it's weird," I admitted, setting aside my soup to drink my tea. It was soothing and non-caffeinated, which Jillian had insisted on.

"So, no pool house for you two?" she asked, still glancing around the restaurant as though she weren't asking me anything of importance.

"No, Jillian, no pool house. We hot tubbed, but we did not pool house," I said emphatically, and then I spilled my guts and told her the entire ridiculous story.

She listened, she hmm'd and groaned in the right places, and she got indignant in the right places too. By the time I was finished, I was in tears again, which was really pissing me off.

"And the stink of it all, I shouldn't have been doing it, but *he* is the one who stopped it, and I don't really think he wanted to!" I huffed, angrily wiping tears away with my napkin.

"So why do you think he did?"

"He's gay?" I offered, and she smiled. I took a deep breath and got control.

Jillian looked at me thoughtfully and then finally leaned in. "You realize we are two smart women who are not acting very smart right now," she said.

"Huh?"

"We know better than to try to figure out what a man is up to. This'll get worked out when it's supposed to. And your tears? These are tension tears, frustration tears—nothing more. I'll tell you one thing, though."

"What's that?"

"As long as I've known Simon, I've never heard of him inviting someone on a shoot with him, ever. I mean, inviting you to Spain? That's very unlike Simon."

"Well, who knows if I'm even invited anymore." I sighed dramatically.

"You're still friends, right?" she asked, raising an eyebrow at me. "Why don't you just ask him?" When I didn't respond she added, "Stick that in your pipe and suck it."

"I think it's smoke it, Jillian. Stick that in your pipe and smoke it."

"Ah, smoke it, suck it, whatever. Eat your fortune cookie, sweetie." She smiled, nudging the cookie across the table. I cracked it open and removed the fortune.

"What does yours say?" I asked.

"Fire all employees who have more than one pencil in their hair," she stated seriously. We laughed together, and I could feel some of the tension finally leaving my body.

"What does yours say?" she asked.

I opened it up, read the words, and rolled my eyes to the ceiling. "Stupid fortune cookie," I sighed, and handed it to her.

She read it and her eyes went wide again. "Oh, man, are you in for it! Come in, let's go back to work."

She laughed, tugging my hand and leading me from the restaurant. She gave the fortune back to me, and I started to throw it away, but then slipped it into my purse:

BE AWARE OF THE WALLS YOU BUILD
AND WHAT COULD BE ON THE OTHER SIDE
Confucius, you kill me.

Text from James to Caroline:

Hey there.

Hey to you.

We still on for Friday night?

Yep, I'm in. Where are we going for dinner?

There's a great new Vietnamese restaurant I've been wanting to try.

Have you forgotten I'm not really big on Vietnamese food?

Come on, you know it's my favorite. You can get soup!

Fine, Vietnamese it is. I'll find something. BTW, the last of your furniture should be delivered Monday. I'll be there to receive and place.

How much longer until the project is finished?

Except for a few pieces in the bedroom, should be all done by next weekend.
Ahead of deadline I might add…

Very good. Will you also be there to finish things in the bedroom?

Stop it, Jamie.

I hate when you call me Jamie.

I know, Jamie. See you Friday night

The day had exhausted me. I literally had nothing left. I had plans to go to yoga, really I did, but as the evening approached all I wanted to do was go home. I wanted Clive, and I could no longer pretend that I didn't also want Simon. Maybe he would be home? As I walked up the stairs I could hear Simon's TV through the door. I was already turning my key in my lock when I thought about my fortune cookie. I could knock on the door, right? I could just say hi, right? As I debated, I heard his phone ring, followed by his voice through the door.

"Nadia? Hey, how are you?" he said, and that made up my mind for me. He had his harem, and I couldn't possibly enter in to something like that. If I wanted Simon, I wanted *all* of Simon. I'd promised myself no more messing around. As I felt tears prick at my eyes for the thousandth time that day, I walked in to find Clive waiting for me, and I smiled through my tears. I picked him up, cuddling him to me as he told me all about his day in cat speak. I interpreted for him, and it would seem that Clive's day consisted of a light snack, a nap, about thirty minutes of grooming, another snack, another nap, and then he watched the neighborhood for the rest of the afternoon and evening. Leftover takeout with Ina and Jeffrey on the couch, a quick shower, and I packed it in early. I simply could not allow this day to go on any longer.

With Clive curled between my legs, I went to sleep, again with no music from the other side of the wall.

The following night I stood in front of my mirror, trying on different shoes for my date/not a date/of course it's a date with James. I'd almost called him twice today to back out, but in the end, I pushed through it and got dressed. Sometimes a girl just needs to get dressed up, and tonight I was dressed to kill: thin, fitted black blouse, tight red pencil skirt, teetery tall heels.

I'd been conflicted about this event, whatever it was, all week long. But I wanted to go. Was I using James a little? Perhaps. But I did have a good time with him, and maybe it wouldn't be the worst thing in the world for us to start back up again.

"Caroline Reynolds, you heartbreaker," I whispered to myself in the mirror. I actually cracked myself up. Clive was embarrassed for both of us and hid his nose behind his paw. I was still laughing when I heard the knock at the door. I slipped into my heels and went for the door, Clive close behind.

I took a deep breath, and opened it. "Hey, James."

"Caroline, you look great," he murmured, stepping inside and catching me into a hug.

As his arms went around me, I knew immediately. This was a date.

He smelled spicy. I don't know why girls always say boys smell spicy, but some do. And it's a good thing, warm and spicy. But not like potpourri…

I hugged him back, enjoying the way my body still fit with his. We always were good at the hugging.

"You ready to go?"

"Yep, let me grab my bag." I knelt to give Clive a quick kiss. He tossed his tail angrily in James's direction and wouldn't let me kiss him.

"What's your problem?" I asked Clive, who turned and showed me his rear end.

"You know, that's starting to become a very rude habit, Mr. Clive," I warned him as I picked up my purse from the table. I stuck my tongue out at Clive, grabbed James, and locked the door behind us.

"Okay, so dinner?" I asked as we stood outside my door.

"Yep, dinner," he replied, standing very close to me. We stared at each other—for only seconds really, but it felt much longer. He stepped a little closer, and my breath caught. Of course, just then Simon decided to open his door.

"Hey, Caroline! I was just—Oh, hi. James, right?" His smile faded slightly when he saw my dinner date. Date, date, date.

"Sheldon, right?" James said, offering his hand.

"Simon, actually." He raised his trash-bag-filled hands and declined the shake. "After you," he nodded to the stairs, and the three of us began to troop down together.

"So, where are you two crazy kids off to tonight?" Simon asked as we walked ahead of him.

I could feel his eyes on the back of my neck, and as I hit the landing I looked back. He had a fake smile plastered across his face, and his voice was colder than I'd ever heard it before.

"Caroline and I are headed out for dinner," James answered.

I smiled back over my shoulder. "Yes, some lovely little Vietnamese restaurant," I cooed, pretending to be thrilled.

"You don't like Vietnamese food," he said, frowning.

This made me smile. "I'm going to try the soup," I answered.

James locked eyes with Simon as he held the door for me. He let it swing right as Simon came through with his hands full of trash bags, but I caught it just in time.

"Well, have a good night," I said as James walked me toward his car with his hand on the small of my back.

"'Night," Simon answered, lips tight. I could tell he was irritated.

Good.

James bundled me into the car, and we were off.

The dinner was fine. I ordered fried rice off of the fusion side of the menu, and when it arrived, for a moment all I could think about was eating noodles on a houseboat in the middle of Ha Long Bay with Simon.

But as I said, dinner was fine, the conversation fine, the man I was with, fine. He was a fine-looking man with a great future ahead, his own adventures to be had, mountains to conquer. And tonight, I was the mountain. I kind of wanted to let him climb.

He walked me upstairs to my door, even though I could have stopped him from coming all the way up. As I dug for my keys, I could hear Simon's phone ringing, and he answered.

"Nadia? Hi. Yep, ready when you are." He laughed.

My heart clenched. Fine. I turned to say goodnight to James, devastatingly handsome and right there. Right there in front of me. O had been gone a long time, and she and James had once been close. Could he? Would he? I was going to find out. I invited him in.

As I pulled a bottle of wine from the fridge, I watched him scan the room, taking stock of everything: the Bose sound system, the Eames chair by the desk. He even checked out my crystal as I handed him his glass. He thanked me, his eyes burning into mine as our fingers slipped past each other.

Nature took over. Hands knew, skin recognized, lips teased and became reacquainted. It was new and old at the same time, and I'd be lying if I said it didn't feel good. His shirt came off. My skirt dropped, I kicked off my heels, and our arms wrapped and tucked in. Eventually and inevitably, we headed to the bedroom.

I bounced lightly on the bed, watching through hazy eyes as he knelt before me on the floor.

"I missed you."

"I know." I pulled him on top of me. Everything was fine, everything was as it should be, and as I mechanically wrapped my legs around his waist, his belt buckle digging cold into my thigh, he looked deeply into my eyes and smiled.

"I'm so glad I needed a decorator."

And just like that, fine was not enough.

"No, James." I sighed, pushing at his shoulders.

"What, baby?"

I hated when he called me baby.

"No, no, just no. Get up." I sighed again as he continued to kiss my neck. Tears sprang to my eyes as I realized what used to make me feel something now made me feel nothing at all.

"You're kidding, right?" He moaned in my ear, and I pushed him again.

"I said get up, James," I said, a little louder this time.

He got the message. Doesn't mean he was happy to hear it. He stood up as I smoothed my shirt, which was thankfully still mostly buttoned.

"You gotta go," I managed, tears beginning to track down my cheeks.

"Caroline, what the—"

"Just go, okay? Just go!" I yelled. It wasn't fair to him, but I had to be fair to myself. I couldn't go backwards, not now.

I clasped my hands to my face and heard him sigh, then stomp off, slamming the door. I couldn't blame him. He must've been in blue-ball hell. I was sad and mad and a little bit tipsy, and I hated my O. My eyes landed on one of my Come Fuck Me shoes on the floor, and I threw it as hard as I could into the living room.

"Ooof!" I heard a deep voice utter, and it was not James Brown's. It was the man I *did* want in my bed, and the one I was most mad at right now. Holding the shoe like some kind of late-night Prince Charming to my slutty O-less Cinderella, Simon appeared in my doorway, barefoot and in his pajama bottoms. The sight of his perfect speedbump abs crossed me over from pissed off to M. A. D.

"What the hell are you doing here?" I asked, angrily wiping my tears from my face. He was going to see me cry.

"Um, I heard you and James…Well, I heard you, and then I heard you yelling, and I wanted to make sure you were okay," he stammered.

"You're not here to rescue me, are you?" I bit back, air-quoting the *rescue*.

He backed away as I crawled off the bed, seeming scared of my impending explosion. Even I knew this was going to be ugly.

"Why do all men seem to think they need to rescue a woman? Are we not capable of rescuing our damn selves? Why do I need to be rescued? I don't need a man to rescue me, and I certainly don't need no wallbanging, Purina-fucking, listening-at-my-wall-like-a-goddamn-psycho coming over here to rescue me! You got that, mister?"

I was pointing and waving my arms around like someone was going to take them away from me. He had every right to look scared.

"I mean, what the hell is with you men? I've got one who wants me back, and one who doesn't want anything to do with me! One who wants to be my boyfriend, but can't even remember that I'm an interior designer. Designer! Not a fucking decorator!"

I was on a roll. At this point I was just ranting, plain and simple. I stalked in a circle around Simon, pacing and shouting while he tried to follow me, finally just standing still and watching me with huge eyes.

"I mean, you shouldn't force someone to eat Vietnamese food if they don't like Vietnamese food, should you? I shouldn't have to eat it, should I, Simon?"

"No, Caroline, I don't think you should—" he started.

"No, of course I shouldn't, so I got the fried rice! Fried rice, Simon! I'm not gonna eat Vietnamese food ever again—not for James, not for you, not for anyone! You got that?"

"Well, Caroline, I think—"

"And for your information," I continued, "I did not need a rescue tonight! I took care of it myself. He's gone. And I know you think James is some kind of psycho, but he isn't," I said, beginning to lose momentum. My lower lip quivered again, and I fought it, but finally let go. "He isn't a bad guy. He just...he just...he just isn't the right guy for me." I sighed, sinking down to the floor in front of my bed and holding my head in my hands.

I cried for a moment, while Simon remained frozen above me. I finally looked up at him. "Hello? Girl crying down here!" I sputtered.

He swallowed a smile and sat down in front of me. He pulled me off the floor and gathered me into his arms. And I totally let him. He settled me onto his lap and held me close as I cried into his chest. He was warm and gentle, and even though I knew better—oh, how I knew better—I tucked into the nook and let him comfort me. His hands ran up and down my back as I sobbed, his fingertips making the tiniest of circles on my shoulder blades as I breathed him in. It had been so long since I'd been held, just held, by a man that between the tiny circles and the scent of his fabric softener I was losing my senses.

Finally my sobs began to quiet as he held me close, cross-legged on my floor. "Why didn't you play me music this week?" I sniffled.

"My needle was broken. I have to get it fixed."

"Oh, I thought maybe...well, I missed it is all," I said shyly.

He smoothed back my hair and brought his hand under my chin, forcing me to look up at him. "I missed *you*." He smiled gently.

"Me too," I breathed, and his sapphires began to spin. Oh no. No voodoo. "How was Purina? Good? Bet she missed you too," I whispered and watched his face change.

"Why do you keep bringing up *Nadia?*"

"I heard you on the phone with her earlier. Sounded like you were making plans."

"Yes, I met her for drinks."

"Please. You expect me to believe she didn't come over?" I asked, noticing I was still on his lap.

"Ask your cat. Did he go crazy tonight?" Simon pointed at Clive, who had returned and was now watching us from the back of the couch.

"No, he didn't, actually."

"That's because she didn't come over. We met for drinks to say goodbye." Simon looked at me carefully.

My heart began to beat so loud there was no way he couldn't hear it. Why did Heart have to be so in to this? "Goodbye?"

"Yep, she's going back to Moscow to finish her degree there."

Heart settled down a bit. "Oh, so you said goodbye because she was *leaving*, not for any other reason. Silly me." I lifted myself off his lap as he held me closer. I struggled.

"She's leaving, yes, but that's not why we said goodbye. I —"

I continued to wiggle. "Wow, only the Giggler left! And then there was one. I guess technically one does not make a harem, so will she be shouldering the load for the others or will you need to be interviewing for some more women? How does that work exactly?" I snapped.

"Actually, I'm going to be having a conversation with Lizzie very soon as well. I think we're going to be just friends from now on," he said, watching me closely. "What used to work for me just doesn't work anymore."

All stop. *What?* "It doesn't work for you anymore?" I breathed, not daring to believe it.

"Mm-hmm," he answered, his nose dipping down to the skin just below my ear and breathing deep.

Would he notice if I licked his shoulder? Just the tiniest taste?

"Caroline?"

"Yes, Simon?"

"I'm sorry I didn't play music for you this week. I'm sorry that I…well, let's just say I'm sorry for a lot of things."

"Okay," I breathed.

"Can I ask you something?"

"No, I don't have any zucchini bread," I whispered, and his laugh echoed through the room. I laughed along, in spite of myself. I'd missed laughing with Simon.

"Come to Spain with me," he whispered.

"Wait, what?" I asked again, my voice wavering. *What, what, what?* "Are you serious?"

"I'm very serious."

I had to remind myself to breathe. Already heady from the voodoo and fabric softener, I shook my head to clear it. He was going Spain on me?

I was glad he seemed focused on the space behind my ear, because I doubted he'd be as interested if he could see how my eyes were now crossed. I needed a moment. I pulled myself away, finally standing up.

"I'm gonna go wash my face. Don't go anywhere," I instructed.

"Sweet Caroline, I'm not going anywhere," he said, his sexy smile returning.

I made myself walk away. Every step I took, every thunk of my heels on the hardwood was like a chant in my head: Spain. Spain. Spain. Once in the bathroom, I splashed some water on my face, most of it going into my mouth because I couldn't stop smiling. New harem head count: two down, one to go? There were times to be cautious, and then there were times when you just needed to go balls-out and take a risk. I needed some backbone. I thought about what Jillian had said earlier today, and I went with my impulse. I steeled myself, took out my figurative balls, and headed back out.

"Okay, it's late, Simon. Time for you to go." I took him by the hand, pulled him off the floor, and led him toward the front door.

"Um, really? You want me to go? Don't you want to, I don't know...talk a little more?" he asked. "I wanted to tell you how—"

I continued to pull him. "Nope. No more talking tonight. I'm tired." I opened my door and ushered him out to the landing. He started to say something else, and I held up two fingers. "I need to say two things, okay? Two things."

He nodded.

"First, you hurt my feelings in Tahoe," I began, and he tried to interrupt me. "Shut it, Simon. I don't want a rehash. But just know you hurt me. Don't do it again," I finished. I couldn't stop my smile when I saw his reaction.

His eyes hit the floor, his entire body contrite. "Caroline, I'm really sorry about all that. You have to know that I just wanted to — "

"Apology accepted." I smiled again and began to close my door.

His head popped up immediately. "Wait, wait. What was the second thing?" he called, leaning into my doorway. I stepped closer to him, bringing my body within inches of his. I could feel the heat of his skin across the tiny space between us, and I closed my eyes against the onslaught of emotions. I breathed deep and opened my eyes to look in to the sexy sapphires gazing down at me.

"I'm coming with you to Spain," I said. And with a wink, I closed the door in his astonished face.

chapter fifteen

"Eggs sunny-side up, bacon, wheat toast with raspberry jelly."

"Oatmeal with raisins, currants, cinnamon, and brown sugar, side of sausage links."

"Belgian waffles, fruit cup, bacon *and* sausage," Sophia said, completing our order and earning a raised eyebrow from both Mimi and me.

"What? I'm hungry."

"Nice to see you getting a real breakfast for a change. Must have been working up an appetite with Mr. Mitchell last night, hmmm?" I teased, winking at Mimi over my orange juice.

The three of us were together for breakfast on a Sunday, something we hadn't done since Tahoe. They'd been busily settling into the life of new coupledom with their recently switched boyfriends, which left me out most of the time. When they were dating the wrong guys they were always more than happy to have me along—the more the merrier they'd say. It helped when there was no real chemistry. But now? Mimi and Sophia were definitely with the right guys and enjoying every second of it.

Initially I'd been a little worried that the Parent Trap shenanigans would make things uncomfortable, but the ladies had made me proud. They took it in stride, and since each wound up with her new better half, all my worries went by the wayside.

We giggled as we got caught up on friendly gossip, waiting until the food arrived for any big news, as was protocol.

"Okay, who's going first? Who has news?" Mimi began, and we settled into our ritual. Sophia paused from shoveling in the waffles, indicating that she would serve the first volley.

"Neil has to go to LA for a sportswriters in television conference, and he asked me to go with him," she offered. Mimi and I nodded.

"Ryan is thinking of letting me reorganize his home office. You should see it—his filing system alone made me break out in hives," Mimi reported, shuddering.

"Natalie Nicholson referred two new clients to me—Nob Hill, very posh, thank you very much," I added, pouring myself more coffee from the carafe as they congratulated me.

We chewed.

"Neil talks in his sleep. It's the cutest thing. He calls out football scores."

"Ryan let me paint his toenails last night."

"I told Simon I'd go to Spain with him."

Here's the thing about a spit take. In the movies, they're hysterical. In real life, they're just messy.

"Wait a minute, wait a goddamn minute...what?" Sophia sputtered, juice still dribbling down her chin.

"Caroline, you told him what?" Mimi managed, still choking as she waved the waiter over for more napkins.

"I told him I'd go to Spain with him. No big deal." I grinned. It was a big deal indeed.

"I can't believe you had the nerve to sit here and talk about random shit all morning and *not* tell us this. When did this happen?" Sophia asked, leaning forward on her elbows.

"The night I went on a date with James." I smiled.

"Okay, that's it. No more dicking around—spill it." Mimi rounded on me with a butter knife and a frown.

"What the hell, Caroline? I can't believe you kept all this from us. When did you go on a date with James? And don't you dare leave anything out. Tell us everything now, or I'll let Mimi loose on you!" Sophia warned. Mimi gestured again in a menacing way with her knife—in a very *West Side Story* menacing way, mind you. I imagined an actual fight with Mimi would involve hitch kicks and barrel turns...

Nevertheless, I took a deep breath and spilled. All of it. Why I went out with James, the feelings that had been percolating with Simon, how James called me a decorator, how I kicked him out. They listened intently, only interjecting occasionally when they needed clarification.

"I'm so proud of you," Sophia said when I'd finished. Mimi nodded in agreement.

"For what?"

"Caroline, there was a time when if James told you to jump, you'd fucking jump. I guess we worried him showing back up in your life would take you back to being that girl again," Sophia explained.

"I know you were worried. You're both sweet, and no one will ever take care of me as well as you, even though you worry like old chickens in a henhouse." I smiled at my fierce ladies.

"So you sent James Brown packing, and then what happened?" Sophia asked, and I finished the last of the story: Simon's entry, his apology, the disappearing Purina, his invitation...

"So you just, had this epiphany in the bathroom, just like that? Go to Spain with Simon?" Mimi finally asked.

"Yep. I didn't really overthink it. I just, I can't explain it...I just know I should go on this trip. I mean, I've always wanted to go to Spain, and I know he'll be a good tour guide, and come on, how much fun will it be? We'll have a blast together!"

"Bullshit," Sophia stated simply.

"Come again?"

"I call bullshit, Caroline. You're going because you want something to happen there with him. Don't deny it." She eyed me severely.

"I deny nothing," I quipped, signaling the waiter for our check.

"No more harem, huh?" Mimi asked.

"So it would seem. I'm not a fool. I know a man like him doesn't change overnight, but if the Giggler is out of the way before Spain? Well, then, that's a Simon of a different color, now isn't it?" I grinned cheekily, wiggling my eyebrows at my girls.

"Why, Caroline Reynolds, I do believe you plan on seducing this man," Sophia said, and Mimi clapped her hands with glee.

"Simon's going to bring back the O!" Mimi cheered, attracting more than a little attention.

"Oh, hush. We'll see. If, and this is a big fat if, ladies. *If* I ever allow anything to happen between Simon and me, it's gonna be on my terms. Which would include no harem, no drinking, and no hot tubbing."

"I don't know, Caroline. No drinking? I think it'd be criminal to be in Spain and not be indulging in a little sangria," Mimi piped up.

"Well, I do enjoy me some sangria," I mused. Visions of Simon and me, sipping sangria while watching the Spanish sunset. Hmmm…

Text between Simon and Caroline:

So are you the type of girl who wears a big floppy hat on the beach?

Pardon me?

You know, those crazy giant beach hats? Do you have one?

As it happens, yes. Is this a concern of yours?

Concern, no. Just trying to get a visual of you on the beach in Spain…

How's that working out for you?

Pretty spiffy.

Spiffy? Did you just say spiffy?

I typed it actually. You got something against spiffy?

This explains the old records…

HEY!

I enjoy the old records. You know this…

I do know this…

Are we really going to Spain together?

Yep.

Are you home? I didn't see the Rover this morning.

Checking up on me?

Perhaps…where are you, Simon?

Have a shoot in LA, driving back in a few days. Can I see you
when I get back?

We'll see…

I'll play records for you.

Spiffy.

"So, since things are all completed on the Nicholson project, I was thinking…since I have a jump on the commercial project I'm starting next, and you mentioned before that I could take some time off before we get busy for the holiday season, that, well, maybe I could…"

"Spit it out, Caroline. You trying to ask me if you can go to Spain with Simon?" Jillian demanded, not trying very hard to hide her smile.

"Maybe," I winced, dropping my forehead to the desk.

"You're a grown woman, capable of making her own decisions. You know I think it's a good time to take vacation, so why should I tell you whether you should go away with Simon or not?"

"Jillian, to clarify, I'm not *going away* with Simon. You make it sound like some illicit affair."

"Right, right, it's just two young people off to enjoy a little Spanish *culture.* How could I forget?" Jillian drawled, insinuation all over her face, as well as a little satisfaction. She was enjoying my squirming.

"Okay, okay, so can I go?" I asked, knowing I would never hear the end of it, but past caring.

"Of course you can. But can I just say one thing?" she asked, eyebrows raised.

"Like I could stop you," I grumbled.

"You couldn't, actually. All I ask is that you have a good time, play hard, but take care of him while you're there, okay?" she asked, her face taking on a seriousness I rarely saw.

"Take care of *him?* What is he, seven?" I laughed, stifling it immediately when I saw she was *not* kidding.

"Caroline, this trip will change things. You must know that. And I love you both. I don't want either of you to get hurt, no matter what transpires while you're there," she said softly. I started to make a joke, but I stopped. I knew what she was asking.

"Jillian, I don't know quite what's going on between Simon and me, and I've no idea what's going to happen in Spain. But I can tell you, I'm excited about this trip. And I get the sense he is too," I added.

"Oh, my dear, he's definitely excited. Just…Oh, never mind. You're both adults. Go crazy on each other in Spain."

"First you tell me to be gentle, and now you tell me to go crazy?" I grumbled.

She reached across the desk to pat my hand affectionately. Then she took a deep breath and changed the mood in the room entirely. "Now then, fill me in on where we stand with James Brown. What's left to be done?"

I smiled and flipped my planner open to the end of the week, when I would be finished with All Things James Brown.

A few nights later I was settling into my couch comfortably with Mr. Clive and Barefoot Contessa when I heard something in the hallway. Clive and I looked at each other, and he jumped off my lap to investigate. I knew Simon wasn't due home for another day or so based on his texts—and the fact that I might have been counting the days—so I followed Clive to my old post: The Peephole.

As I peered out into the hallway, there was a flash of strawberry-blond hair at Simon's door. Who was visiting Simon? Was I wrong to stare? What was that package she had? The woman the hair belonged to knocked once, then twice, and then before I knew it, she whirled about and looked directly at my door, curiously staring at my peephole. Not accustomed to anyone staring at my peephole, I froze, eyes unblinking as she appraised my door. She crossed the tiny landing, and rapped soundly on my door. Surprised, I jumped back a little, bumping into my umbrella stand and letting her know there was, in fact, someone home. I turned my face to the side and shouted, "Coming!" Then I proceeded to walk in place as though I was headed for the door. Clive looked on with interest, tossing his head and assuring me I was not nearly as clever as I thought I was.

I made a great noise of clicking the locks, and then opened the door.

We appraised each other instantly, in the way that women do. She was tall and beautiful in a cold, patrician way. She wore a black suit, severely cut and buttoned up to the collar. Her strawberry blond hair was twisted and pinned back, although one solitary piece had marched away from her sisters and now hung in her face. She pushed it back behind her ear. Her cherry red lips pursed as she finished looking me over and offered a thin smile.

"Caroline, yes?" she asked, a solidly British accent piercing the air as clearly as her attitude. I already knew I didn't care for this woman.

"Yes, can I help you?" I suddenly felt underdressed in my Garfield boxers and tank top. I shifted my weight from one leg to the other, feet clad in giant socks. I shifted my weight again, realizing I probably looked like I had to pee. I also realized at the same time that this woman made me nervous, and I had no idea why. I straightened up immediately, putting my game face on. This all took place in less than five seconds, a lifetime in the world of Woman Figuring Out The Other Woman.

"I need to drop this off for Simon, and he mentioned that if he wasn't at home to leave it at the flat across from his, that *Caroline* would take care of it for him. You're Caroline, so here you go, I suppose," she finished, thrusting a cardboard box at me. I took it, taking my eyes off of hers for a moment.

"What does he think I am, a mailbox?" I muttered, setting it on the table just inside the door and turning back to the woman.

"May I tell him who dropped this off, or will he know?" I asked. She was still looking me over as though I were a great puzzle.

"Oh, he'll know," she answered, her cool tone sounding musical but clipped at the same time. As an American, I'll admit I am always fascinated by a British accent, but could do without this particular side of superiority.

"Okay, well...I'll make sure he gets it." I nodded, leaning my hand on the door. I closed it ever so slightly, but she didn't move.

"Is there anything else?" I asked. I could hear Ina working on her shortbread in the other room, and I didn't want to miss any KitchenAid porn.

"No, nothing else," she replied, still making no move.

"Okay, then, have a good night," I said, almost making it a question as I started to close the door. Just as I did, she stepped forward enough so I was forced to catch the door before it hit her.

"Yes?" I asked, my irritation beginning to show through. This Limey was stopping me from seeing the completion of the pecan squares I'd been waiting for all episode.

"I just, well, I'm really glad to have met you," she answered, her eyes finally softening and a hint of a smile breaking through her façade. "And you really *are* quite lovely," she added. I stared back at her. Her voice sounded oddly familiar, but I couldn't quite place it.

"Um, okay, thank you?" I answered as she started for the stairwell. Her heel caught just slightly, and she stumbled a little. As I closed the door, she began to giggle as she worked her shoe loose. That's when I realized who'd just visited.

My eyes widened, I'm sure to the size of dahlias, and I hurled the door back open. I gaped at her, and her face broke open into the widest cheeky grin. She winked as I blushed. I'd been present for some of this lady's greatest moments.

She wiggled her fingers at me and disappeared down the stairs. Clive brought me back from my stupor by nipping me on the calf, and I closed the door.

I sat on my couch, pecan squares all but forgotten as my brain processed everything.

The Giggler had said I was lovely.

She basically told me Simon had *told* her I was lovely.

Simon thought I was lovely.

Was the Giggler out of the harem?

Was there even a harem left?

What did this mean?

Would I only think in questions now?

And if so, who is Eric Cartman's father?

Text between Simon and Caroline:

> What are you doing?
>
> *What are YOU doing?*
>
> I asked you first.
>
> *You sure did.*

Waiting…

Me too…

Jesus you're stubborn. I'm driving back from LA. Happy now?

Yes, thank you. I'm baking pumpkin bread.

It's a good thing I'm at a gas station right now and not driving or I would have a hard time keeping the car on the road…

Right, the baking gets you worked up, doesn't it?

You have no idea.

So I probably shouldn't tell you I smell like cinnamon and ginger right now?

Caroline.

My raisins are soaking in brandy this very minute.

That's it…

I peered out the window again, scanning the street below, and still no sign of the Rover. The fog was quite thick, and although I didn't want to be a nag, I was becoming a little concerned that he wasn't home yet. Here I sat, with cooling loaves, and no Simon had shown up to inhale them. I picked up my phone to text him, but then called instead. I didn't want him texting while he was on the road. It rang a few times, and then he picked up.

"Hi there, my favorite baker," he purred, and my knees clanked together. He was like the best Kegel exercise ever—instant clench.

"Are you close?"

"Pardon me?" He laughed.

"Close to home. Are you close to home?" I asked, rolling my eyes and unclenching.

"Yes, why?"

"There seems to be a lot of fog tonight. I mean, more than usual… Be careful, okay?"

"That's very sweet of you to be looking out for me."

"Shut up, mister. I always look out for my friends," I scolded, beginning to get ready for bed. I was a multi-tasker from way back. I could do my taxes while getting waxed and not bat an eye. I could certainly get undressed while talking to Simon. *Ahem.*

"Friends? Is that what we are?" he asked.

"What the hell else would we be?" I shot back, pulling off my shorts and grabbing a pair of thick woolen socks. The floor was chilly tonight.

"Hmmm," he muttered as I took off my T-shirt and slipped into a button-down to sleep in.

"Well, while you're hmmming, I have to tell you about a visit I had earlier this week from a friend of yours."

"A friend of *mine?* This sounds intriguing."

"Yep, Julie Andrews accent, buttoned-up Brit? Ring any bells? She dropped off a box for you."

His laughter rang out immediately. "Julie Andrews accent—that's brilliant! That must have been Lizzie. You met Lizzie!" He laughed like this was the funniest thing ever.

"Lizzie Schmizzie. She'll always be the Giggler to me." I smirked, sitting on the edge of my bed and applying some lotion.

"Why do you call her the Giggler?" he asked, playing innocent, and I could tell he was on the verge of absolute hysterics.

"You really need me to tell you? Come on, even you can't be that thick—never mind, walked right into that one." I cut him off before he could regale me with how thick he was, indeed. I'd been pressed up against that very thick in a hot tub, so I was familiar. Kegel. And, thank you, another Kegel.

"I like messing with you, Nightie Girl. It gives me a chuckle."

"First *spiffy,* now a *chuckle?* I worry about you, Simon." I returned to the living room to turn off lights and get the place ready for bed. This included freshening Clive's water bowl and hiding a few Pounce treats around the apartment. He enjoyed playing Big Game Hunter while I slept sometimes, with the Pounce, of course, playing the part of the Big Game. Some nights the pillows were unfortunately involved, as well as any hair ties, loose shoelaces, and pretty much anything else that seemed appealing around two a.m. Some mornings my place looked like *Wild Kingdom* had been filmed overnight.

"Well, no worries. I'll pick it up when I get back. So, did you two have a nice chat?"

"We chatted briefly, yes. But no dirty secrets were shared. Although with the thin walls, I'm already a bit familiar. How is the lonely haremette? Missing her sisters?" I flipped off the lights and padded through the kitchen to fetch the Big Game. I was dying to ask him if he'd actually broken up with the Giggler. Did he, did he not?

"She may be a bit lonely, yes," he said, in what I thought sounded like a careful way. *Hmm...*

"Lonely because..." I led, pausing in my Pounce-scattering.

"Lonely because, well, let's just say, for the first time in a very long time, I am...well...I am...you see..." He stuttered and stalled, dancing around the issue.

"Go on, out with it," I instructed, barely breathing.

"Without...female companionship. Or as you would say, harem free." His words came out in a quiet whoosh, and my legs began a little shimmy shake. This made the Pounce shimmy-shake in their container, alerting Clive that his hunt had begun early.

"Harem free, huh?" I breathed back, visions of Sugar Simons dancing in my head. Single Sugar Simons, Single Sugar Simons in Spain...

"Yeah," he whispered, and we were both silent for what seemed like months, although in actuality it was only enough time for Clive to claim his first victim: the Pounce hidden in my tennis shoe by the front door. I walked over to congratulate him on his catch.

"She said something curious," I mentioned, breaking the spell.

"Oh yeah? What's that?" he asked.

"She told me that I was, and I quote, 'quite lovely.'"

"Did she now?" He laughed, easing back into comfortable.

"Yes, and the thing of it is, she said it like she was agreeing with something someone else had already said. Now, I'm not a girl who fishes for compliments, but it would seem, Simon, that you were talking sweet about me." I smiled, knowing my face was breaking into a pink glow. I'd started for the bedroom when I heard a soft knocking at the door. I walked back to unlock and open the door without looking through the peephole. I had a strong feeling I knew who was on the other side.

There he stood, phone cradled to his ear, holding his duffel bag and smiling a big, toothy grin.

"I told her you were lovely, but the truth is, you're more than lovely," he said, bowing his head toward mine and bringing his face to within inches of my own.

"More?" I asked, barely drawing breath. I know my grin matched his.

"You're exquisite," he said.

And with that, I invited him in. While wearing only my button-down. From far away, the O cheered...

An hour later, we sat together at the kitchen table, a decimated loaf in front of us. In between his frantic pawing, I'd managed a bite or two. The rest now lived in Simon's tummy, which he proudly thumped like a melon. We'd talked and eaten, gotten caught up, watched Clive as he finished his hunt, and now relaxed as the coffee brewed. Simon's bag rested by the front door still—he hadn't even gone to his apartment yet. I was still in my button-down, feet curled beneath the chair as I stared at him. We were so comfortable, and yet that low-level hum, that electricity always sparking and snarking between us, continued.

"Fantastic touch by the way—the raisins? Loved them." He smirked at me, poking one more in his mouth.

"You're terrible." I shook my head, stretching up out of my chair and collecting the plates and the few crumbs that hadn't been inhaled. I could sense him watching me as I moved about the kitchen. I grabbed the pot of coffee and raised my eyebrows at him. He nodded. I stood next to his chair to fill his mug, and I caught him peeking at my legs below my shirt.

"See something you like?" I leaned across him to the sugar bowl.

"Yep," he answered, leaning toward me to take it.

"Sugar?"

"Yep."

"Cream?"

"Yep."

"That all you can say?"

"Nope."

"Gimme something, then. Anything." I giggled, walking back around to my side of the table. Once again he watched me as I arranged myself in the chair.

"How about this?" he finally said, resting on his elbows, face intense. "As I mentioned earlier, I broke it off with Lizzie."

I stared back, barely breathing. I tried to play it cool, so cool, but I couldn't stop the grin sneaking across my face.

"I see you are not at all broken up by this," he scoffed, sitting back in his chair.

"Not so much, no. Want the truth?" I asked, the grin ushering in a sudden surge of confidence.

"Truth would be good."

"I mean *truth* truth, back-and-forth truth. No witty comebacks, no snappy banter — although we do give great banter."

"We do, but I could go for some truth," he said, his voice quiet as his sapphire eyes blazed away at me.

"Okay, truth. I'm glad you broke things off with Lizzie."

"You are, are you?"

"Yes. Why did you? Truth now," I reminded him. He regarded me for a moment, sipped his coffee, ran his hands through his hair in a maniacal way, and took a deep breath.

"Okay, truth. I broke it off with Lizzie because I didn't want to be with her any more. With any other women, in fact," he finished, setting his cup down. "I'm sure we'll always be friends, but the truth is, I've been finding lately that three women? It's a lot for me to handle. I'm thinking of paring things down a bit, maybe trying just one for a while." He smiled, the blue getting dangerous.

Knowing I was a grin and a clench away from total embarrassment, I stood quickly and went to dump my coffee in the sink. I paused there for a second, only a second, thoughts whirling. He was single. He was...single. Sweet mother of pearl, Wallbanger was *single*.

I felt him move across the kitchen and come to stand behind me. I froze, feeling his hands gently brush my hair away from my shoulders and slip down to my hips. His mouth — his ever-loving mouth — barely touched the shell of my ear, and he whispered.

"Truth? I can't stop thinking about you."

Still facing away from him, my mouth dropped open and my eyes went wide, torn between fist pumping and actual kitchen sex. Before I could decide, his mouth moved more purposefully, pressing into the skin just below my ear and making my brain burn and parts below dance a jig.

His hands gripped my hips, and he turned me toward him—to face that body and grin—I quickly composed my face, trying desperately to keep it together.

"Truth? I've been thinking about you since the night you banged on my door," he whispered, bending down to kiss the hollow of my neck with breathtaking precision. His hair tickled my nose, and I fought to keep my hands to myself. He pushed me to the side a little and surprised me by lifting me onto the counter. My legs automatically opened to allow him between them, the Universal Law of Wallbanger superseding any actual thought I had in my head. Not to worry, my thighs knew what to do.

One of his hands snuck around to the small of my back, while the other gripped the back of my neck. "Truth?" he asked one more time, pulling my hips to the edge of the counter, which forced me to lean back as my legs once more went on auto-pilot and wrapped themselves around his waist. "I want you in Spain," he breathed, then brought his mouth to mine.

Somewhere, a kitty began to call...and an O finally began her journey home.

"More wine, Mr. Parker?"

"No more for me. Caroline?"

"I'm fine, thank you." I stretched out luxuriously in my seat. First class to LaGuardia, then first class all the way to Malaga, Spain. We'd be taking a car from there to Nerja, the small coastal town where Simon had rented a house. Scuba diving, spelunking, hiking, beautiful beaches, and mountains, all set in a quaint village.

Simon squirmed in his seat and shot an angry look over his shoulder.

"What? What's the problem?" I asked, looking behind and seeing nothing out of the ordinary.

"That kid keeps banging my seat," he grumbled through clenched teeth.

I laughed for a solid twenty minutes.

chapter sixteen

"We did it too soon. We should have waited."

"We waited long enough — are you kidding? You know I was right. It was time to do it."

"Time to do it, what a crock! We could have waited just a little longer, and then we wouldn't be in the mess we're in now."

"Well, I didn't hear you complaining at the time. You seemed pretty pleased, as I recall."

"I couldn't complain, my mouth was full. But I had a feeling. I just knew this was wrong, what we were doing was inherently wrong."

"Okay, I give up. You tell me how to fix this."

"Well, for starters, you're holding it upside down," I shot back, grabbing the map and turning it right side up. We'd been parked along the side of the road for five minutes, trying to figure out how to get to Nerja.

After landing in Malaga, navigating customs, navigating the rental car system, and finally navigating our way successfully away from the city center, we were now lost. Simon drove, so I was in charge of the map. And by that I mean he took it away from me every ten minutes or so, looked it over, hmm-ed and hawed, and then thrust it back my way. He didn't actually listen to anything I had to say, instead relying on his innate man-map. He also refused to turn on the GPS that had been provided for us, determined to get us there the old-fashioned way.

Which is why we were now lost. Taking a train would have been too easy. Simon needed a car to get around for his photos, which *was* ultimately why we were here. After flying through the night, we were both exhausted, but the best way to fight jet lag, allegedly, was to get on local time as quickly as possible. We had both agreed not to nap until we could go to sleep that night.

Now we argued about where we took the wrong turn. I'd been devouring some churros from a roadside stand when the wrong turn supposedly took place, and so we played "Place the Blame."

"All I'm saying is that if someone hadn't been stuffing her face and was watching for the turn, we wouldn't be — "

"Stuffing *my* face? Seriously? You were stealing *my* churros. I told you to get your own when we stopped!"

"Well, I wasn't hungry at first, but then you were smacking your lips and licking that chocolate, and well...I got distracted." He looked up from the map, which he'd spread out on the hood of the car, and grinned, breaking the tension.

"Distracted?" I grinned back, leaning a little closer. As he looked at the map, I looked at him. How could someone who'd been on a plane for the last hundred years look as good as he did? But there he was, faded jeans, black T-shirt, dark blue North Face jacket. Twenty-four hours of stubble begging to be licked. Who licked stubble? Me, that's who. He braced himself on his arms as he studied the map, his lips moving silently as he tried to figure it out. I snuck underneath his arms, draping myself across the hood of the car as shamelessly as a pinup girl in a garage calendar.

"Can I make a suggestion?"

"It is a lewd suggestion?"

"Surprisingly no. Can we please turn on the GPS? I'd like to make it there before I have to leave in a few days," I moaned. Due to my last-minute booking, I had to fly back a day before Simon. But five days in Spain...I was not complaining.

"Caroline, only pussies use GPS," he scoffed, turning to the map again.

"Well, this pussy is dying for some dinner, and a shower, and a bed, and to get rid of this jet lag. So unless you want to see me reenact *It Happened One Night*, Spanish version, turn on the GPS, Simon." I grabbed him by the North Face and pulled him down to me. "Did that sound harsh?" I whispered, giving him the tiniest of kisses on the chin.

"Yes, I'm terrified of you now."

"Does this mean GPS?"

"It means GPS." He sighed resignedly, leaning back and pulling me off the car with him. I gave a little cheer and started for the door.

"No, no, no, you were harsh, Nightie Girl. I'm gonna need some sugar," he instructed, eyes twinkling.

"You need some sugar?" I asked.

He tugged on my arm, bringing me back to him. "Yes, I require it."

"You're twisted, Simon." I leaned into him, slipping my arms around his neck.

"You have no idea." He licked his lips and waggled his eyebrows like an old-timey gangster.

"Come get your sugar," I teased as he brought his lips to mine.

I would never get tired of kissing Simon. I mean, how could you? Since the night he "truthed" me right up on to my kitchen counter, we'd slowly been exploring this new side of our relationship. Underneath all the snark and spark, there'd been some serious sexual tension building these many months. And we were letting it all out—albeit slowly. Sure, we could've raced right back to the bedroom that night and let the sex ring out across the city for days, but Simon and I, without saying a word, seemed to be on the same page for once, and were content to let this unfold.

He was wooing me. And I was letting him woo. I wanted the woo. I deserved the woo. I needed the wow that would surely follow the woo, but for now, the woo? It was whoa.

And speaking of woo…

My hands slipped into his hair, tugging and twisting and trying to pull his entire body inside my own. He groaned into my mouth, I felt his tongue touch mine, and I fell apart at the seams. I sighed, the tiniest whimper, and it became harder and harder to kiss him due to the giant grin overtaking my face.

He pulled back a little and laughed. "You sure look happy."

"Keep kissing me, please," I insisted, bringing his face back to mine.

"It's like kissing a jack 'o' lantern. What's with the grin?" He smiled down at me with a grin that looked as wide as my own.

"We're in Spain, Simon. Grinning is implied." I sighed contentedly, messing with his hair.

"And here I thought it was all to do with my kissing," he answered, kissing me again, gently, sweetly.

"Okay, cowboy, ready to see where the GPS takes us?" I asked, stepping away. I couldn't keep my hands on him for too long or we'd never leave.

"Let's see how lost we really are." He smiled and we were on our way.

"I think this is the turn…Yep, this is it," he said.

I bounced in my seat. Turned out we were closer than we thought, and we'd gotten a bit antsy. As we made one last turn, we looked at each other, and I squealed. We'd seen bits of the ocean for the last few miles or so — peeking out behind a stand of trees or over a cliff. Now, as we turned down a tiny cobblestone drive, the realization that Simon had rented a house not just *near* the beach, but *on* the beach washed over me, and I was silenced by the sight.

Simon pulled up to the house, the tires crunching on the rounded stones. When he turned the car off, I could hear the waves crashing against the rocky coast about a hundred feet away. We sat for a moment, just taking it all in and grinning at each other, before I scrambled out of the car.

"This is where we're staying? This entire house — it's yours?" I exclaimed as he grabbed our bags and came to stand next to me.

"It's ours, yeah." He smiled and gestured for me to walk ahead of him.

The house was charming and magnificent all at the same time: white stucco walls, clay-tile roof, clean lines, and soft archways. Orange trees lined the walkway from the drive, and bougainvillea climbed the garden walls. The house was a classic cottage, built to weather the sea and cocoon those inside. As Simon looked under the flowerpots for the key, I inhaled the citrus scents and the distinctly salty air.

"A-ha! Got it. Ready to see the inside?" He struggled with the door for a moment before turning to face me.

I reached for his hand, threading my fingers through his, and leaned in to kiss his cheek. "Thank you."

"For what?"

"For bringing me here." I smiled and kissed him square on the lips.

"Mmm, more of that sugar you promised me." He dropped the bag and pulled me close.

"Sugar this! Let's see the house!" I cried, wiggling free and charging past him through the door. But as soon as I made it past the entryway, I stopped cold. Close on my heels, he bumped into me as I took it all in.

A sunken living room, dotted with plush white sofas and comfy-looking chairs, opened up to what I assumed was the kitchen. French doors at the back of the house opened to several large, terraced patios, which sunk down toward the rocky beach. But what had stopped me cold was the ocean. All across the back, through the giant windows, was the deep blue of the lazy Mediterranean. The coastline curved back to the town of Nerja, where the lights were just beginning to sparkle as twilight drifted over the beach, illuminating the other white houses that clung to the cliffs. Remembering how to move, I ran to push open the doors and let the soft air spill over me and into the house, blanketing everything in the evening's perfume.

I walked to the wrought iron railing, which perched at the edge of an earthen tile patio flanked by olive trees. Placing my hands on the warm metal, I looked and looked and looked. I felt Simon walk up behind me and without a word place his arms around my waist. He nestled in to me, resting his head on my shoulder. I leaned back, feeling the angles and planes of his body fit against my own.

You know those moments when everything is exactly the way it was meant to be? When you find yourself and your entire universe aligning in perfect synchronization, and you know you couldn't possibly be more content? I was inside that very moment, and fully conscious of it. I giggled a little, feeling Simon's smile stretch across his face as he pressed into my neck.

"It's good, right?" he whispered.

"It's so good," I answered, and we watched the sunset in spellbound silence.

After watching the sunset until it was totally gone, we explored the rest of the house. It seemed more and more beautiful with every room, and I squealed once again at the sight of the kitchen. It was as if I'd been transported to Ina's home in East Hampton, with a Spanish flair: Sub-Zero fridge, gorgeous granite countertops, and a Viking stove. I didn't even want to know how much Simon was paying for this house. I'd decided to just enjoy. And enjoy we did, running back and forth, laughing like kids when we found the bidet in the hallway bathroom.

And then we entered the master bedroom. I came around the corner and saw him standing at the end of the hallway, just outside the door.

"What the hell did you find that has you so qui—oh my. Would you look at that?" I stopped next to him, admiring from the doorway.

If my life had a soundtrack, the theme from *2001: A Space Odyssey* would have been playing right now.

There, in the middle of a corner room, with its own terrace overlooking the most beautiful ocean in the world, was the biggest mother-loving bed I'd ever seen. Carved out of what looked to be teak, it was as big as football field. Thousands of silky soft white pillows stacked against the headboard, spilling down over a white duvet. It was folded down just so, the million or so thread count sheets shining, actually shining, as though they were lit from within. Sheer white curtains hung from rods suspended over the bed, creating a canopy, while even more curtains hung in the windows overlooking the sea below. The windows were open and all the curtains blew gently in the breeze, giving the entire room a billowy, flouncy, windblown effect.

It was the bed to end all beds. It was the bed that all the little beds aspired to be when they grew up. It was bed heaven.

"Wow," I managed, still in the hallway next to Simon.

It was hypnotic. It was like a bed siren, luring us in so we could crash.

"You could say that again," he stammered, his eyes never leaving the bed.

"Wow," I repeated, still staring.

I couldn't stop, and I was suddenly very, impossibly, excruciatingly nervous. I had a lovely case of performance anxiety, party of one.

Simon chuckled at my weak joke, and it brought me back to him.

"No pressure, huh?" he said, eyes shy.

Huh? Nerves? Party of two? I had a choice. I could go with conventional wisdom, said wisdom being that two grownups on vacation together in a gorgeous house with a bed that was sex incarnate would immediately begin nonstop sexing...or, I could let us both off the hook and just enjoy. Enjoy being together and let things happen when they happen. Yeah, I liked this idea better.

I winked and took a running leap on to the bed, bouncing pillows all over the room. I peeked over the remaining mound to see him leaning in the doorway, a sight I had seen so many times before. He looked a little nervous, but still beautiful.

"So, where are you sleeping?" I called, and his face relaxed into a smile, my smile.

"Wine?"

"Am I breathing?"

"Wine it is," he snorted, selecting a bottle of rosé from the generously stocked wine fridge. Simon had arranged to have some basic groceries delivered to the house before our arrival, nothing fancy but enough to nosh on and make us comfortable. It was now fully dark, and any thoughts we'd had about going into town faded away as the jet lag loomed. Instead we'd stay in tonight, get a good night's sleep, and head into town in the morning. There was a roast chicken, olives, a wedge of Manchego, some gorgeous looking Serrano ham, and enough other little odds and ends to make a meal. I assembled plates while he poured the wine, and soon we were sitting on the terrace. The ocean crashed below, and the wooden walkway down to the beach was strung with tiny white lights.

"We should go down to the beach before bed, at least take a little walk."

"Done. What do you want to do tomorrow?"

"Depends, when do you need to start working?"

"Well, I know some of the places I need to go, but I need to do a little scouting still. Want to come along?"

"Of course. Start in town in the morning and see where that leads?" I asked, nibbling on an olive.

He raised his glass and nodded. "To seeing where it leads," he toasted.

I raised my glass to his. "I'll second that." Our glasses clinked and our eyes locked. We both smiled, a secret smile. We were finally alone, all to ourselves, and there was no place else on the planet I wanted to be. We ate our dinner, stealing little glances at each other throughout, and sipped our wine. It made me drowsy, and a little touchy feely.

After that we'd picked our way carefully over the rocky shoreline to the beach. We'd grasped hands to navigate but never let go. Now we stood at the edge of the earth, the strong, salty wind whipping through our hair and clothes, buffeting us back a bit.

"It's nice, being with you," I told him. "I, um, well, I like holding your hand," I admitted, feeling brave from the wine. Witty banter had its place, but sometimes, all you need is the truth. He didn't respond, simply smiled and brought my hand to his mouth, placing a small kiss.

We watched the waves, and when he pulled me to his chest, snuggling me to him, I breathed out slowly. Had it really been so long since I'd felt — Oh, what was it I was feeling? — cared for?

"Jillian told me you know what happened to my parents," he said so softly I could barely hear him.

"Yes. She told me."

"They used to hold hands all the time. Not for show, though, you know?"

I nodded into his chest and breathed him in.

"I always see these couples that hold hands and make such a show of it, calling each other Baby and Sweetie and Honey. It seems like, I don't know, false somehow. Like, would they be doing it if they weren't in front of anyone?"

I nodded again.

"My parents? I never thought much about it at the time, but when I think about it now, I realize their hands were practically sewn together, *always* with the hand holding. Even when no one was looking, right? I'd come home after practice and find them watching TV, at either end of the couch, but with their hands propped up on a pillow so they could still be touching…It was just…I don't know, it was nice."

My hand, still tucked into his own, squeezed, and I felt his strong fingers squeeze back.

"Sounds like they were still a couple, not just a mom and dad," I said, hearing his breath speed up a bit.

"Yes, exactly."

"You miss them."

"Of course."

"Might sound weird, since I never knew them, but I feel like they would be so proud of you, Simon."

"Yeah."

We were quiet another minute, feeling the night around us.

"Want to go back to the house?" I asked.

"Yeah." He kissed the top of my head as we began to make our way back—hands stuck together like someone had spread Krazy Glue on them.

I'd left Simon to clean up the mess from dinner. I wanted a quick shower before bed. After washing away the days of airport and travel, I threw on an old T-shirt and boy shorts, too tired for the lingerie I had packed. Yes, I had packed lingerie. Come on, I was no nun.

I stood in front of the mirror in my bedroom (yep, I had totally claimed the big one) after blow-drying my hair when I saw him appear in the doorway. He was on his way to his room after his own shower, wearing pajama pants and a towel wrapped around his neck. I was exhausted, but not so exhausted I didn't appreciate the form in front of me. I watched him in the mirror as he appraised me as well.

"Have a good shower?" he asked.

"Yes, it felt amazing."

"Heading to bed?"

"I can barely keep my eyes open," I replied, yawning hugely to punctuate.

"Can I get you anything? Water? Tea? Anything?"

I turned to face him, as he stepped inside. "No water, no tea, but there is one thing I'd like before I go to sleep," I purred, taking a few steps his way.

"What's that?"

"Goodnight kiss?"

His eyes darkened. "Oh, hell, is that all? That I can do." He closed the distance between us and slipped his arms easily around my waist.

"Kiss me, you fool," I teased, falling into his embrace as if in an old-time melodrama.

"One kissing fool, coming up," he laughed, but within seconds no one was laughing. And within minutes, no one was standing.

After falling into Pillow Town, we scrambled about, arms and legs twisting this way and that, kisses becoming more and more frantic. My shirt bunched up around my waist, and the feeling of his hi-there against my hoohah was indescribable. He rained kisses down upon my neck, licking and sucking as I moaned like a whore in church.

To be fair, I'd never actually heard a whore moan in church, but I had a feeling it sounded a lot like the unholy sounds pouring forth from my mouth.

He flipped me about like a rag doll and settled me on top of him, my legs on either side, the way I'd wanted to be for so long. He sighed, gazing up as I impatiently pushed my hair away from my face so I could truly appreciate the magnificence I was perched on.

We slowed our movements, then stopped altogether, staring unabashedly at each other, appraising each other without shame.

"Incredible," he breathed, reaching to gently cup my face as I nuzzled his hand.

"That's a good word for it, yes. Incredible." I turned to kiss his fingertips. He stared into my eyes again, those sex sapphires doing their voodoo that made me a puddle of voodoo goo. For him to woo. See what he did to me?

"I don't want to screw this up," he said suddenly, his words breaking me from my Seussian rhymes.

"Wait, what?" I asked, shaking my head to clear it.

"This. You. Us. I don't want to screw this up," he insisted, sitting up underneath me, my legs wrapping around to his back.

"Okay, so don't," I ventured, unsure where this was going.

"I mean, you need to know, I have no experience with this."

I raised an eyebrow. "I have a wall back home that would disagree with that..." I laughed, and he crushed me to his chest, inexplicably hard. "Hey, hey…what's up? What's going on?" I soothed, my hands rubbing up and down his back.

"Caroline, I, Jesus, how do I say this without sounding like an episode of *Dawson's Creek*?" he stumbled, talking into my neck.

I couldn't help it, I chuckled a little as Pacey flashed into my head, and that brought him back. I pulled away a bit so I could see him, and he smiled ruefully.

"Okay, *Dawson's* be damned, I really like you, Caroline. But I haven't had a girlfriend since high school, and I have no clue how to do this. But you need to know, that what I feel for you? Shit, it's just different, okay? And, whatever your wall would say back home, I need *you* to know that this? What we have, or will have? It's different, okay? You know that, right?"

He was telling me I was different, that I was no replacement for the harem. And this, I knew. He looked at me so earnestly, so seriously, and my heart opened even more. I pressed a gentle kiss to his sweet lips.

"First of all, I *do* know this. Second of all, you're better at this than you think." I smiled, pressing his eyes closed and kissing each eyelid. "And, for the record, I loved *Dawson's Creek*, and you did the WB proud." I laughed as his eyes sprang back open and relief rushed in. I tucked him into my nook and held him there as we rocked back and forth, the rush of the earlier hormones subsiding as we found this new space, this quiet intimacy that was becoming almost as addicting.

"I like that we're taking things slow. You give good woo," I whispered.

He tensed underneath me. I could feel him shaking a little.

"I give good woo?" he laughed, tears springing to his eyes as he tried to control his laughter.

"Oh, shut up," I cried, smacking him with a pillow. We laughed for a few more minutes, falling back into the lush bed, and as the jet lag finally overtook us, we settled in. Together. There was no question in my mind now about sleeping in separate rooms. I wanted him here. With me. Surrounded by pillows and Spain, we nooked. The last thought I had, before slipping into sleep with his strong arms wrapped around me…I might be falling in love with my Wallbanger.

chapter seventeen

I was awakened this morning by a great rumbling. Forgetting where I was for a split second, I automatically assumed I was home, and we were experiencing a tremor. I was halfway out of bed with one foot on the floor before I noticed that the view outside my bedroom window was decidedly more blue than it was at home, and decidedly more Mediterranean. And the rumbling? That was no tremor. It was Simon snoring. *Snoring.* Snoring to beat the band, and by beat the band I mean beat that band up with his nose—which was emitting the most unearthly sound. I clapped my hands over my mouth to hold in the laughter and crept back into bed, the better to appraise the situation.

True to form, I'd taken over most of the bed in the night, and he'd been relegated to the far corner, where he was now curled into a little ball with a pillow tucked between his legs. But what he lacked in square footage, he made up for in sound. The sounds pouring forth from his nasal passages registered somewhere between grizzly bear and exploding tractor trailer. I wiggled across the mile-wide bed, curling myself around his head and looking down at his face. Even while making these horrific sounds, he was adorable. I carefully placed my fingers next to his nose, and plugged. And then waited.

After about ten seconds, he inhaled and shook his head, looking around wildly. He relaxed when he saw me perched on the pillows next to him. He smiled a sleepy smile.

"Hey, hey, what's up?" he mumbled, rolling into me and wrapping his arms around my waist, resting his head on my tummy. I ran my hands through his hair, delighting in the casual freedom we finally had in touching each other.

"Just woke up. Someone was quite noisy on this side of the bed."

He closed one eye and looked up at me. "I hardly think someone as flaily as you can complain about anything."

"Flaily? That's not even a word," I huffed, enjoying his arms around me more than I wanted to admit.

"Flaily, as in, one who flails. As in, one who, even though she is sleeping in a bed the size of Alcatraz, still needs almost the entire mattress to spread out and kick," he insisted, accidentally-on-purpose pushing my shirt up so he could rest his head on my naked tummy.

"Flailing is better than snoring, Mr. Snorey Pants," I teased again, trying not to notice the way his stubble scraped against my skin in the most delicious way.

"You flail. I snore. Whatever will we do about this?" He smiled happily, still half asleep.

"Ear plugs and shin guards?"

"Yep, that's sexy. We can suit up before bed each night," he sighed, pressing the tiniest of kisses just above my belly button.

A noise that sounded sadly like a whimper escaped my lips before I could pull it back, and my ears burned as I took in what he'd said about "each night," as in sleeping together *each night*. Oh my…

We ate a quick breakfast at the house, then headed into town. I fell in love with the village instantly: the old stone streets, the whitewashed walls glimmering in the blazing sunlight, the beauty that poured forth from every open archway. From every speck of azure that peeked through from the coast to the friendly smiles on the sweet faces of the people who called this enchanted spot home, I was hooked.

It was market day, and we wandered in and out of stalls, picking up fresh fruit to snack on later. I've seen beautiful places on this earth, but this town was heaven for me. I'd truly never experienced anything like it.

Now, I had been traveling alone for years, finding my own company quite pleasant. But traveling with Simon? It was…cool. Just, cool. He was quiet, the way I am when I'm seeing something new. He never felt the need to fill a silence with chattery words. We were content to soak up the scenery. When we did speak, it was to point out something we thought the other shouldn't miss, like the puppies playing in a dooryard, or an old man and woman talking back and forth over their balconies. He was a great companion.

We strolled back to the rental car, the afternoon sun toasting through the thin cotton covering my shoulders, when my hand tangled with his in the most unassuming way. And when he took the time to open my door for me, and leaned down to kiss me in the warm Spanish sunshine, his lips and the smell of olive trees were the only things I needed in the entire world.

In the time I'd known Simon, I'd committed several images of him to memory: Seeing him for the first time, clad only in a sheet and a smirk. Driving back across the bridge with him the night of Jillian's housewarming, when we called a truce. Warped and blurry Simon as seen from inside an afghan. Backlit by tiki torches, wet, and looking devilishly handsome by hot tub. And a recent addition to my Best of Simons? The sight of him underneath me as he clutched me close, his warm skin and sweet breath all over me as we nooked in the Giant Bed of Sin.

But nothing, and I mean nothing, was hotter than watching Simon work. I mean it. I actually had to fan myself a little—which he took no notice of, because when he was working he was delightfully focused.

And now here I sat, watching Simon work. We'd driven up the coast to get some test shots at a place a local guide had told him about, and the perilously handsome Simon now concentrated completely on the task at hand. As he'd explained to me, it wasn't about the actual pictures he was taking, it was about testing the light and the colors. So as he scrambled his way from rock to rock, I sat on a blanket we'd dug out of the trunk and observed. Perched on cliffs high above the sea, we could see for miles. The rocky shoreline stretched and curled back in on itself as millions of waves poured in from the deep sea. And while the scenery was gorgeous, what had my attention was the way the tip of Simon's tongue poked out as he surveyed the scene. The way he bit down on his lower lip as he puzzled over something. The way excitement broke over his face when he saw something new through his lens.

I was glad I had something to do, something to fixate on, as the beginning of a battle was starting to wage inside my body. Ever since we'd acknowledged the pressure that giant bed could have placed on us, all I could think about was that very pressure. As well as the pressure of an O long denied, waiting patiently—and sometimes impatiently—for her release. The pressure was so strong, so intense, that every single part of me could feel it.

Currently taking sides in this internal debate were my brain, Lower Caroline (speaking for the distant O), Backbone, and although she'd mainly kept quiet lately, letting Brain and Nerves take control, Heart was now weighing in.

It should be noted that LC (Lower Caroline wanted a hip but abbreviated name) had somehow drafted Simon's penis into the fray, and even though his penis didn't have direct access to her yet, LC felt it necessary to speak up on his behalf. While I didn't much like the term *penis*, internally I felt strange about calling him dick or cock, so penis it was...for now.

Now, Backbone and Brain were solidly in the wait-for-sex camp, believing this essential to the foundation of this burgeoning relationship. LC, and therefore Simon's penis, were in the have-sex-with-him-as-soon-as-possible society, obviously. O, while not officially in residence, could be counted among LC's supporters. But I felt a twinge, and just a twinge, of her floating above both camps, along with Heart, who was currently singing songs about everlasting love and warm, fluffy things.

Take all this into account and what do you have? One totally confused Caroline. A Caroline divided. No wonder I had sworn off dating. This shit was tough. So was I glad to have something to think about other than the pressure cooker of sex indeterminate? Yes. Could I spend a little more time trying to come up with a more clever name for Simon's penis? Probably. It deserved it. Mammoth Male Member? No. Pulsating Pillar of Passion? No. Back Door Bandit? Hell no. Wang? Sounded like the noise those doorstopper things made when you flicked 'em...

I said it out loud to myself a few times, cracking myself up a little. "Wang. *Wang.* Waaaang," I muttered.

"Hey! Nightie Girl! Get yourself over here," Simon called, breaking me out of my wang study. I left behind the mental battle, picking my way carefully across the craggy rocks to where he was poised.

"I need you."

"Here? Now?" I snorted.

He lowered his camera just enough to raise one eyebrow. "I need you for *scale*. Get over there." He pointed me toward the edge of the cliff.

"What? No-no. No pictures, huh-uh." I backed away toward my blanket.

"Yes, yes, pictures. Come on. I need something in the foreground. Get over there."

"But I'm a mess! I'm all windblown and sunburned, see?" I pulled down my v-neck just a little to show him how I was beginning to pink up.

"While I always appreciate you showing me your cleavage, save it, sister. This is just for me, just to give me some perspective. And you don't look windblown. Well, only a little." He tapped his foot.

"You're not gonna make me pose with a rose in my teeth, are you?" I sighed, shuffling over to the edge.

"Do you have a rose?" he asked, looking serious except for the shit-eating grin.

"Shut it, you. Take your pictures."

"Okay, just be natural. No posing, just stand there — facing the water would be great," he instructed.

I complied. He moved around me, trying different angles, and I could hear him muttering about what was working. I admit, even though I was shy about having my picture taken, I could almost feel his eyes, through the lens, watching me. He moved around for only a few moments, but it felt longer. The internal war was beginning to wage again.

"You almost done?"

"You can't rush perfection, Caroline. I need to get the job done right," he warned. "But yes. Almost done. You getting hungry?"

"I want those clementines in the basket — grab me one? Or will that mess with your masterpiece?"

"Won't mess with it. I'll call it Windblown Girl on a Cliff with a Clementine." He laughed and headed back over to the car.

"You're funny," I said wryly, catching the tiny orange he threw me and starting to peel.

"Are you sharing?"

"I suppose so, the least I could do for the man who brought me here, right?" I laughed, biting into a wedge and feeling the juice dribble down my chin.

"You got a hole in your lip?" he asked, capturing the moment as I rolled my eyes at him.

"Do you actually *think* you're funny, or are you just assuming you might be?" I countered, beckoning him over with the peel. He shook his head, laughing as he took a wedge. Of course, he took a bite and no dribble. He opened his eyes wide in feigned amazement, and I took the opportunity to smash another wedge in his face. His eyes remained wide open, as juice now ran freely off the tip of his nose and on to his chin.

"Messy Simon," I whispered as he looked at me. In a flash, he pressed his lips to mine, getting juice all over both of us as I squealed into his mouth. "Sweet Caroline," he whispered through his grin. He turned us so the sea was behind us, held up the camera, and took a picture: us covered in orange mush.

"By the way, why were you saying 'wang' earlier?" he asked.

I just laughed harder.

"This is it. This is now officially the single best thing I have ever had in my mouth," I announced, closing my eyes and moaning.

"You've said that about everything you've eaten tonight."

"I know, but I seriously can't handle how good this is. Smack me, pinch me, throw me overboard, this is too good," I moaned again. We sat at a little table in the corner of a small restaurant in town, and I was determined to try everything. Simon, showing off his language skills, had ordered for us. I told him to go for it, that I was in his hands and I knew he wouldn't steer me wrong. And the boy did good. We feasted.

We went with traditional tapas, of course, accompanied by glasses of the house wine. Little bowls and plates showed up at the table every few minutes after that: tiny pork meatballs, slices of ham, marinated mushrooms, beautiful sausages, grilled squid with fruity local olive oil. With each bite, I was sure that I had just eaten the best thing ever, then another wave of gorgeous food would show up and convince me once again. And then these prawns arrived. Unreal. Fried crispy in olive oil with tons of garlic and parsley, smoky paprika, and just a hint of heat. I swooned. I actually swooned.

Simon? He loved it. He ate it up. My reactions as much as the food, I think. He ate it up.

"Honestly, I can't handle any more," I protested, dragging a piece of crusty bread through the olive oil. He smiled as he watched me shamelessly enjoy another piece of bread before finally pushing back from the table with a groan.

"Best meal ever?" he asked.

"It really might be. That was insane." I sighed, patting my full tummy. Ladylike, schmadylike, I'd pounded that meal down like someone was going to take it away from me. A waiter appeared with two small glasses of a local wine. Sweet and crisp, it was the perfect after-dinner drink. We sipped slowly, the breeze coming in through the windows lightly scented with the sea air.

"This was a great date, Simon. Really. Couldn't have been more perfect," I said, taking another sip of my wine.

"Was this a date?" he asked.

My face froze. "I mean, no. I suppose not. I just—"

"Relax, Caroline. I know what you meant. It's just funny to consider this a date: two people traveling together, but only *now* on a date." He smiled, and I relaxed.

"Hmm, we haven't really followed the traditional rules so far, have we? This might even be our *first* date, if we wanted to get technical."

"Well, technically speaking, what defines a date?" he asked.

"Dinner, I suppose. Although we've had dinner before," I began.

"And a movie—we've already had a movie," he reminded me.

I shuddered. "Yes, and that was definitely a ploy to get me to snuggle with you. Scary movie, so obvious," I scoffed.

"It worked, didn't it? In fact, I do believe I slept with you that night, Nightie Girl."

"Yes, I'm cheap and easy, I admit it. I suppose we really did do this whole thing backward." I grinned, sliding my foot across the floor under the table and kicking him lightly.

"I like it backward." He smirked.

I narrowed my eyes. "Not touching that one."

"Seriously, though. As I've mentioned, I have no experience with this stuff," he said. "How does this work? What if we were doing this…not backward? What would happen next?"

"Well, I suppose there would be another date, and another after that," I admitted, smiling shyly.

"And bases. I'd be expected to try to round some bases, right?" he asked seriously.

I spluttered my wine. "Bases? Are you for real? As in, cop a feel, over the shirt, under the shirt, those bases?" I laughed incredulously.

"Yes, exactly. What am I allowed to get away with? As a gentleman, I mean. If this were truly a first date, we wouldn't be going home together, would we? Dating now, not hooking up. Remember, apparently I give good woo," he said, eyes twinkling.

"Yes, yes, you do. We wouldn't be going home together, that's true. But to be honest, I don't want you sleeping in the bedroom down the hall. Is that weird?" I could feel my ears burning as I blushed.

"It's not weird," he answered quietly. I slipped off my sandal and pressed my foot against his, rubbing lightly along his leg.

"Nooking is good, right?"

"Nooking is most definitely good," he agreed, nudging back with his own foot.

"As far as your bases are concerned, I think you could definitely plan on a little under the shirt action, if you were so inclined," I answered. Internally, Brain and Backbone gave a little cheer, while LC and Wang kicked a few chairs. Tatas were just glad someone was considering them for once, instead of being just a stopover on the way to points south. Heart? Well, she was still flitting about, singing her song.

"So, we go a little traditional, but not totally traditional. Take it slow?" he asked, his eyes burning, the sapphires beginning to do their little hypnotic dance.

"Slow, but not too slow. We are grownups, for goodness sake."

"To under the shirt action," he announced, raising his glass in toast.

"I'll drink to that." I laughed as we clinked.

Fifty-seven minutes later we were in bed, his hands warm and sure as he slipped each button through, revealing my skin. He went slowly, purposefully, and he let my shirt fall open as I lay beneath him. He gazed down at me, his fingertips lightly drawing a line from my collarbone to my navel, straight and true. We both sighed at the same time.

I can't explain it, but knowing we'd set some boundaries for the evening, silly as it may be, made it so much more sensual, something to be truly savored. His lips hovered around my neck, whispering tiny kisses against my skin, below my ear, under my chin, in the dip between my neck and my shoulder, and working his way down to the swell of my breasts. His fingers swept out, lightly, reverently, ghosting across the sensitive skin as I inhaled and then held my breath.

As his fingers gently grazed my nipple, every nerve ending in my entire body reversed and began to pulse in that direction. I exhaled, feeling months of tension begin to simultaneously flow out of me *and* build up even more. With sweet kisses and soft touches, he began the process of getting to know my body, and it was exactly what I needed. Lips, mouth, tongue — all of it on me, tasting, stroking, feeling, and *loving*.

As his lips closed around my breast, his hair tickled my chin in the cutest way, and I wrapped my arms around him, holding him close. The feeling of his skin against mine was perfection, and something I'd never experienced before. I felt...worshipped.

As we explored that night, what started out as funny and cute and part of our classic banter became something more. What was crassly called "under the shirt action" became part of a romance, and something that could have been merely physical became something emotional and pure. And when he cradled me to him, bringing me into his nook with tender kisses and breathless giggles, we fell into a contented sleep.

Flaily and Mr. Snorey Pants.

For the next two days, I luxuriated. Truly, there isn't another word in the English language to articulate the experience I indulged in. Now for some, the definition of a luxurious vacation might be endless shopping, spa pampering, expensive meals, elaborate shows. But to me, luxurious meant spending two hours napping in the sun on the terrace off the kitchen. Luxurious meant eating figs dripping with honey and dotted with crumbles of local cheese while Simon poured me another glass of Cava, all before ten a.m. Luxurious meant time alone to wander through the small, family stores of Nerja, poking through bins of beautiful lace. Luxurious meant exploring the nearby caves with Simon while he photographed, losing ourselves in the colors under the earth. Luxurious meant gazing at Simon dangling from a rock face while he searched out another foothold, shirtless. Did I mention shirtless?

And luxurious most certainly meant that I got to spend each night in that bed with Simon. Now that's a priceless luxury, not offered on every grand tour. We rounded another base or two, teasing each other with a little over-the-panties encounter. Were we being ridiculous, waiting until the last night in Spain to consummate this "thing"? Probably, but who the hell cared? He spent almost an hour kissing every inch of my legs one night, and I spent about the same amount of time having a conversation with his belly button. We just...enjoyed.

But with all this enjoyment came a certain amount of, well, how shall we say, nervous energy?

Back in San Francisco, we'd spent months engaged in verbal foreplay. But now, here? The actual foreplay? It was not to be believed. My body was so in tune with his, I knew when he walked into the room, and I knew when he was about to touch me, seconds before he did. The air between us was sexually charged, vibes zinging back and forth with enough energy to light up the entire town. Sexual chemistry? Had it. Sexual frustration? On the rise and getting close to critical.

Oh, hell, I'll say it. I was H-O-R-N-Y.

Which was why after we spent the afternoon in the caves, we found ourselves in the kitchen, kissing madly. We were both a little tired from the day, and I'd been wanting to test out that beautiful Viking range. I was preparing vegetables for the grill and stirring some saffron rice when he came in after a shower. It's almost impossible for me to explain the sight of him: worn white T-shirt, faded jeans, barefoot, scrubbing at his wet hair with a towel. He grinned, and I began to see double. I literally couldn't see through the haze of lust and need I suddenly felt surge through me. I needed my hands to be on his body, and I needed it to happen immediately.

"Mmm, something smells good. Want me to get the grill started?" he asked, walking over to where I was chopping vegetables at the counter. He stood behind me, his body only inches from mine, and something snapped. And it wasn't just the pea pod I was holding...

I turned around, and my tummy actually fluttered at the sight of him. It freaking fluttered. I pressed my hand against his chest, feeling the strength there and the warmth of his skin through the cotton. Reason waved bye-bye, and this was now purely physical. An itch that needed to be scratched, scratched, and then scratched again. I slid my hand up around the back of his neck, and pulled him down to me. My lips crashed against his, my intense need for him pouring into his mouth and down to the tips of my toes. Toes that kicked off their flip-flops and started shamelessly rubbing themselves across the tops of his feet. My body needed to feel skin, any skin, and needed it now.

He responded, matching my rough kisses with his own, his mouth covering mine as I groaned at the feel of his hands on the small of my back. I quickly spun him around and pressed him up against the counter.

"Off! I need this off, now," I muttered between kisses, yanking at his T-shirt. In a great whoosh of fabric, his shirt was thrown across the room as I maneuvered my body against his, sighing as I felt the contact. I was alternately trying to hug him and climb him, the lust now running freely through my body like a freight train. I reached between us and palmed him through his jeans. His eyes caught mine, and they crossed a little. I was on the right track. Feeling him getting harder by the second under my fingertips, suddenly all I wanted, all I needed, all I had to have to function in life, was him. In my mouth.

"Hey, Nightie Girl, what are you—oh God—"

Moving instinctively, I snapped open his jeans, dropped to my knees before him, and brought him forth. My pulse raced, and I think my blood actually boiled within me as I saw him. My breath drew in with a hiss as I regarded him, faded jeans pushed down just enough to frame this luminous sight.

Simon does commando. God bless America.

I wanted to be gentle, I wanted to be tender and sweet, but I simply needed him too badly. I glanced up at him, his eyes clouded but frantic, as his hands came down to brush my hair back from my face. I took his hands in my own and placed them back on the counter.

"You're gonna want to hold on for this," I promised. He groaned a delicious groan and, doing as he was told, leaned back a little. He pushed his hips forward, but kept his eyes on mine. Always on mine.

My lips purred as I slipped his length inside my mouth. His head dropped back as my tongue caressed him, taking him in deeper. The pure pleasure of this, the absolute pleasure of feeling his reaction to me was enough to make my head split in two. I drew him back out, letting my teeth just barely graze his sensitive skin as I saw him grip the edge of counter even harder. I ran my nails up the inside of his legs, pushing his jeans farther down for more access to his warm skin. Pressing kisses across the tip of him, I let my hands come up to grasp him, stroking and massaging. He was perfect, all smooth and taut as I took him in again, and again, and again. I felt crazed, drunk on his scent and the feel of him inside me.

He moaned my name over and over again, his words drifting down like molten chocolate sexy times, pouring inside my brain and dedicating every sense I had to him, only to him. On and on I went, making him crazy, making *me* crazy, licking, sucking, tasting, teasing, *luxuriating* in the madness that was this luscious act. To have him here, in this way, was the very definition of luxury.

He stiffened further, and his hands finally came back to me, trying to make me pull back.

"Caroline, oh, Caroline, I'm…you…first…you…oh, God…you," he stuttered. Luckily, I was able to interpret. He wanted me to have something as well. What he didn't realize is that this total abandon he was giving me was all I needed. I released him only for a moment, to place his hands once more on the counter.

"No, Simon. You," I replied, taking him in deeply once more, feeling him hit the back of my throat as my hands tended to the rest of him that my mouth could not. His hips moved once, then again, and with a shudder and the most scrumptious groan I've ever heard, Simon came. Threw his head back, closed his eyes, and let go.

It was wonderful.

Moments later, crumpled into me on the floor of the kitchen, he sighed contentedly. "Good Lord, Caroline. That was…unexpected."

I giggled, bending down to kiss his forehead. "I couldn't control myself. You just looked way too good, and I…well…I got carried away."

"I'll say. Although I don't think it's fair that I'm somewhat exposed here, and you're still fully clothed. We *could* remedy that pretty quickly, though." He pulled at the drawstring on my pants.

I stopped him. "First of all, you aren't *somewhat* exposed, you are hanging free on the kitchen floor, and I quite like it. And this wasn't about me, although I admit I enjoyed it immensely."

"Silly girl, now I want to enjoy *you* immensely," he persisted, running his fingers along the edge of my pants, dancing across the skin there.

Nerves began to dance the flamenco, demanding more time—more time! Not ready! LC kicked some things. "No, no, not tonight. I want to make you a nice dinner. Let me take care of you a little bit. Can't I just do that?" I removed his devil hands and kissed them.

He smiled up at me, his hair messy and a goofy grin still adorning his face. He sighed in defeat and nodded. I started to climb off the floor when he caught me around the waist, pulling me back down.

"A word, please, before you leave me—what did you say? Hanging free on the kitchen floor?"

"Yes, dear?" I asked, earning a raised eyebrow.

"So, using the base-rounding point of reference we've applied to this week, I'd say we just skipped ahead a few dates, yes?"

"I should say so." I laughed, patting him lightly on the head.

"Then I think it's only fair to warn you…Tomorrow night? Your last night in Spain?" he said, his eyes blazing through the twilight.

"Yes?" I whispered.

"I'm gonna try to steal home."

I smiled. "Silly Simon, it's not stealing if I wave you in," I purred, kissing him solidly on the lips.

Later that night, as I lay wrapped thickly in Simon, LC began to prepare. And Brain and Backbone began to chant...O...O...O. Wang? Well, we knew where he was, pressed rather closely against Backbone.

Heart continued to float above, but was circling ever closer to home. However, an additional entity began to assert herself once again, trying to influence the others. She tinted my dreams with her quiet whispering.

Hello, Nerves.

My sleep was most decidedly...flaily.

chapter eighteen

"Did you always know you wanted to take pictures for a living?"

"What? Where did that come from?" Simon laughed, sitting back in his chair and looking at me over the rim of his coffee cup.

We were enjoying a lazy breakfast on my last day in Spain. Dark coffee, tiny little lemon cakes, freshly cut berries and cream, and a side of sunny coastline. Clad in Simon's shirt and a smile, I was in heaven. Nerves seemed very far away this morning.

"I mean it," I insisted. "Did you always want to do this? You seem, well, you're very intense when you're working. You seem like you really love it."

"I do love it. I mean, it's a job so it has its tedious moments, but yeah, I love it. It wasn't something I always planned, though. In fact, there was a different plan altogether," he replied, a dark look passing over his face.

"What does that mean?"

"For a long time I planned on following my father into his business." He sighed, a rueful smile slipping into place.

My hand was in his before I even realized I'd offered it. He squeezed, and then took another sip of his coffee.

"Did you know Benjamin worked for my father?" he asked. "Dad hired him right out of school, mentored him, taught him everything. When Benjamin wanted to go out on his own, you'd think Dad would've been pissed, but he was so proud of him."

"He's the best." I grinned.

"Don't think I don't know about the crush you girls have on him. I'm aware." He gave me a stern look.

"I'd hope so. We're not exactly subtle in our admiration."

"Parker Financial Services was getting big, really big, and Dad wanted me to come onboard as soon as I was done with college. I honestly never thought I'd leave Philadelphia. It would have been a great life: working with my dad, country club, big house in the 'burbs. Who wouldn't want that?"

"Well…" I murmured. It was an idyllic life, for sure, but I couldn't picture Simon there.

"I worked on our high school newspaper, taking pictures. I took the class as an easy A. You know, good for my transcript? But even though I got assignments like covering the women's field hockey tryouts, I really liked it. Like, *really* liked it. I just figured it would always be a nice hobby. Never really thought about it as a career. My parents supported me, though, and my mom even got me a camera for Christmas that year—the year that…well…" He paused, clearing his throat a bit.

"Anyway, after everything happened with Mom and Dad, Benjamin came out to Philadelphia for the, um, for the funeral. He stayed for a while, got things in order, you know. He was the executor of my parents' will. And since he was living out on the West Coast, well, the idea of staying behind in Philadelphia didn't sound so great. So, long story short, Stanford accepted me, I started studying photojournalism, I got really lucky with some internships, and then right-place-right-time, and bam! That's how I got into this gig," he finished, dunking his cake and taking a bite.

"And you love it." I smiled.

"And I love it," he agreed.

"So what happened to your dad's company? Parker Financial?" I asked, spooning up a bite of berries.

"Benjamin took over some of the clients for a while, and over time he quietly closed up shop. The assets were transferred to me, per the will, and he manages it for me."

"Assets?"

"Yep. Didn't I tell you that, Caroline? I'm loaded." He winced, looking out to sea.

"I knew there was a reason I was hanging out with you." I topped off his coffee.

"Seriously. Loaded."

"Okay, now you're just being an ass," I said, trying to lift the tension that had settled over the table.

"Well, people get weird about money. You never know," he said.

"When we get home you're buying our building and installing a hot tub on the landing, that's all," I joked, which earned me a small smile.

We sat and looked at each other, deep in our own thoughts. He'd done so much alone. No wonder he always seemed a little lost to me. Living out of a suitcase, not allowing himself to be tethered to anyone, no real sense of belonging—could it really be that simple? Wallbanger had haremed because he couldn't stand to lose anyone else? Paging Dr. Freud…

Freudian or no, it made sense. He was attracted to me, *had been* attracted to me since the beginning. But what was different this time? Clearly he'd been attracted to all the other women as well. Wow, no pressure at all…With a toss of my head, I tried to change the subject.

"I can't believe I'm leaving tomorrow. I feel like we just got here." I leaned forward on my elbows. He smiled, likely noticing my not-so-subtle way of changing the subject. But he seemed grateful.

"So stay. Stay with me. We can spend a few more days here, and then who knows? Where else do you want to go?"

"Pfft. You'll recall that I'm leaving before you because it's the only flight I could get. Besides, I have to be back at work, organized, and in the right time zone on Monday. You know how many jobs Jillian has lined up for me?"

"She'll understand. She's a sucker for a good romance. Come on. Stay with me. I'll stash you in the overhead bin for the flight home." His eyes twinkled over his coffee mug.

"Overhead bin, my foot. And is this what this is? A romance? Shouldn't you be embracing me on the beach? And ripping my bodice?" I placed my bare legs in his lap, and he took full advantage of this, massaging between his warm hands.

"Lucky for you, I'm a bodice-ripper from way back. I could probably even throw together a pirate costume, if that's what you're into," he replied, the sapphires beginning to smoke.

"It has been quite a romantic tale, hasn't it? If someone would've told me this story, I doubt I'd have believed it," I mused, groaning as I finished my last bite.

"Why not? It's not that strange how we met, is it?"

"How many women do you know who would voluntarily go to Europe with a man who'd been banging the plaster right off her walls for weeks?"

"True, but you could also spin me as the guy who played you all those great records through the wall, and the guy who gave you, and I quote, 'the best meatball ever'?"

"I suppose you did begin to wear me down with the Glen Miller. That got me." I sunk into my chair as his hands did delicious things to the bottoms of my socked feet. Socks I had also appropriated from his side of the room.

"I got you, huh?" He smirked, leaning closer.

"Oh, shut it, you." I pushed his face away, smiling big as I contemplated what he said. Did he have me? Yeah. He totally had me. And would have me, sometime later that night.

At that thought, a whoosh of nerves hit my tummy, and I felt my smile falter a bit. Nerves had set up shop big time, and no matter where Brain went, eventually Nerves invaded every thought, every idea I had about where the night would go. I was ready, Lord knows I was ready, but I was damn nervous. O would come back, right? I knew she would. Did I mention I was nervous?

"So, are you almost done with your work? Do you still have a lot to do tomorrow?" I asked, changing the subject once again. As was always the case when he talked about his work, Simon's eyes lit up. He described the shots he still needed of the Roman-style aqueduct in town.

"I wish we had time to go scuba diving. I hate that we ran out of time." I frowned.

"Again, something that would be solved if you stayed here with me." He frowned back, making a big deal of mimicking my eyebrows.

"Again, some of us have nine-to-five jobs. I have to get home!"

"Home, right. You know there's gonna be a firing squad to face when we get home. Everyone is going to want to know what happened here between us," he said seriously.

"I know. We'll handle it." I cringed at the grilling I'd receive from the girls, to say nothing of Jillian. I wonder if a kitchen blowjob was what she had in mind when she said *take care of him in Spain.*

"We?"

"What? We what?" I asked.

"I could we with you." He smiled.

"Aren't we already we-ing?"

"Yeah, we're we-ing on vacation. It's quite a different thing to be we-ing back home, in the real world. I travel all the time, and that takes its toll on the we unit," he said, his brow knit together.

It took all my power, all of it, not to make a joke about the *we(e) unit.*

"Simon, chill. I know you travel. I'm well aware. Keep bringing me pretty things from faraway places, and this girl has no problem with your we, okay?" I patted his hand.

"Pretty things I can do. Guaranteed."

"Speaking of, where are you off to next?"

"I'll be home for a few weeks, and then I'm headed down south for a bit."

"Down south? As in LA?"

"No, a bit more south."

"San Diego?"

"Souther."

"Stanford educated, right? Where are you going?"

"Promise you won't be mad?"

"Spit it out, Simon."

"Peru. The Andes. More specifically, Machu Picchu."

"What? Oh, man, that's it. I officially hate you. I'll be in San Francisco, planning rich people's Christmas trees, and you get to go there?"

"I'll send you a postcard?" He looked like a kid trying to get out of trouble. "Besides, I don't know what you're so pissy about. You love your job, Caroline. Don't even try to tell me you don't."

"Yeah, I love my job, but right now I wish I was headed south," I huffed, snatching my feet away.

"Well, if you want to head south, I can think of something—"

I placed my hand in front of his mouth. "No way, buddy. I'm not machuuing your pichu now. Huh-uh," I stated firmly, not wavering one bit when he began pressing open mouth kisses against my palm. Not one little bit...

"Caroline," he whispered against my hand.

"Yes?"

"One day," he began, removing my hand and leaving tiny kisses up the inside of my arm. "One day..." Kiss. "I promise..." Kiss kiss. "To bring you..." Kiss. "And my woo..." Kiss kiss. "To Peru," he finished, now kneeling in front of me and dragging his mouth across my shoulder, peeling the fabric away to linger along my collarbone, his lips making me hot and shivery.

"You wanna woo me in Peru?" I asked, my voice high and stupid and not fooling him for a second. He knew exactly how he was affecting me.

"True." His fingers tangled in my hair and brought my mouth to his. I tried for a second to come up with something that rhymed with true, but I gave up and kissed him back with all I had. And so, I let him make out with me on the terrace, overlooking the ocean. Which was...blue. *Ahem.*

All week long, we'd been seeing signs of a festival coming together around town. It started tonight, as if celebrating my departure, and we were headed out to dinner, to somewhere considerably more fancy than the places we'd been eating all week. I'd discovered Simon and I were very similar in many of our tastes. I was all for getting dressed up from time to time, but I much preferred smaller, casual places, as did he. So tonight, getting dressed up and going out someplace a little fancy, and then maybe hitting the festival, had a special feel to it. I was definitely looking forward to this evening, in more ways than one.

They say when a soldier loses a leg in battle, sometimes, late at night, he can still feel twinges of that leg—phantom pain, they call it. I lost my O in battle, the battle of Cory Weinstein—that machine-gun fucker—and I was still feeling the aftershocks. And by aftershocks I mean nothing at all. But there was an end in sight. I'd been feeling twinges of the phantom O all week long, and I was very much looking forward to her return later this evening. The Return of the O. Of course I would see it as a title of some kind of action film in my head—but truly, if she was returning, I would capitalize anything. Any Thing.

Because tonight, sports fans, I was gonna get me some. Not to put too fine a point on it, I was ready for some serious Simon Wang.

I ran my fingers through my hair once more, noticing how the strong sun had brought out the natural honey tones. I smoothed the front of my dress, white linen with a little swing to the skirt. I paired it with some turquoise jewelry I'd bought in town and little snakeskin sandals. I was the most dressed up I'd been all week, and—undercurrent of nerves aside—feeling pretty good. I took one last look at myself in the mirror, noticing that my cheeks were pretty pink, and I hadn't even added blush tonight.

I went to the kitchen to pour myself a quick glass of wine and wait for Simon. As I poured the Cava, I saw him on the terrace, facing the ocean. I smirked when I saw he was wearing a white linen shirt. We'd be quite matchy-matchy tonight. Khakis completed his look, and he turned just as I was walking out to meet him. My heels clicked across the stone as I sipped my bubbly wine, and he leaned back on his arms across the wrought iron railing. As a photographer, he was innately aware of the kind of imagery he was creating, I felt certain. Anytime he leaned, he oozed sex. I just hoped I didn't fall in my heels…sex ooze could be slippery.

I offered my wine to him, and he let me bring the glass to his lips. Slowly, he sipped, his eyes on mine. When I removed the glass, he quickly wrapped an arm around my waist and pulled me to him, kissing me deeply, the taste of wine heavy on his tongue.

"You look…good," he breathed, pulling away from my lips to press his mouth against the skin just below my ear, his scruff tickling me in the most fantastic way.

"Good?" I asked, tilting my head back to encourage everything he was doing.

"Good. Good enough to eat," he whispered, grazing my neck with his teeth, just enough to make me aware of them.

"Wow," was all I could manage as I wrapped my arms around his neck and sank into his embrace.

The sun was beginning to set, casting a warm glow all around, making the terra cotta blaze red and orange, coating us in fire. My eyes were drawn to the cool blue of the sea crashing against the rocks below, the salt in the air actually present on my tongue. I clung to him, letting myself feel and experience everything. His body, hard and warm against my own, the feel of his shaggy hair against my cheek, the heat of the railing against my hip, the rush of every cell in my body curling toward this man and the pleasure he would surely bring me.

"You ready?" he asked, his voice gruff in my ear.

"So ready," I moaned, my eyes rolling back in my head at the nearness of him, the feel of him.

And then Simon took me to town.

After Simon had driven me to the brink with his kissing on the terrace, he'd literally driven me to the brink. We were now at a restaurant overlooking the water, which was easy to do in a coastal town. But where the little hole-in-the-wall places we'd been frequenting this week had their cozy charm, this was a romantic restaurant with an emphasis on romance. Romance was served on a platter here. It was in the wine, the pictures on the walls, the floor beneath our feet, and in case you missed the romance, it was also being piped in through the air. If I squinted, I could see the word romance floating through the air on the sea breeze…I had to really squint, but it was there, I tell you.

Floor-to-ceiling window panels had been rolled back to let in the briny coastal air, and hundreds of tiny tealights sparkled in hurricane glasses. Each table was dressed in white, with low tumblers spilling over with dahlia blooms in rich shades of crimson, pomegranate, and lusty fuchsia. Tiny white Christmas lights twisted into the wooden beams overhead cast a magical sepia tone over the entire scene. In this restaurant, there were no children, no tables of four or six. No, this restaurant was filled with lovers, old and new.

Now we sat, pressed closely together at an epic mahogany bar, slowly sipping wine and awaiting our own tiny table. Simon's hand settled against the small of my back, claiming me quietly and succinctly.

The bartender placed a tray of oysters on the bar in front of us. Twisted and craggy, they glistened, with slices of lemon nestled here and there. Simon raised an eyebrow, and I nodded as he squeezed the lemon, his strong and elegant fingers making short, erotic work of the oysters. He pried one from its home and brought it to my mouth on a tiny fork.

"Open up, Nightie Girl," he instructed, and I surely did as I was told.

Cold, crisp, like a burst of seawater in my mouth, I moaned around the fork as he slipped the tines back out. He grasped his own oyster and tossed it back like a man, licking his lips as I watched this little bit of food pornography play out. He winked at me as I looked away, trying not to let on how desperately turned on I was. The entire day had been like one giant, controlled ball of sexual tension, a slow burn that was now igniting into a wildfire. He slurped two more in quick succession, and as I watched his tongue dart out to lick his lips, I felt the sudden urge to help him. With no shame or sense of social propriety, I closed the distance between us and kissed him, hard.

He grinned in surprise, but kissed me back with equal intensity. The sweetness and tenderness that had been marinating between us all week now quickly deteriorated into full-on touch-me-touch-me-now, and I was all for it. My entire body turned toward him, my legs nestling in between his as his fingers found my skin—the skin just above the hem of my dress. We were kissing, kissing all-out Hollywood style. Slow, sloppy, wet, and wonderful. My head tilted so I could kiss him more deeply, my tongue sliding against his, leading and then letting him lead. He tasted like sweet and salt and lemons, and it was all I could do not to grab him by his pretty linen shirt and have my way with him on top of the bar—but in a very lady-like way, mind you.

I heard someone clearing their throat, and I opened my eyes to see my sexy sapphires, then an embarrassed host.

"Excuse me, señor, your table is ready?" he asked, carefully averting his eyes from our display in his very romantic, but still very public, restaurant.

I might have moaned a little as Simon removed his hands from my legs and turned my chair so I could stand. Taking my hands and pulling me, he smirked as I wobbled on my feet a bit. He grinned at the bartender.

"Oysters, man, oysters." Simon laughed a little as we shuffled off to our table. I was ready to let out an indignant huff until I saw him discreetly adjust himself. I was not the only one feeling the slow burn...

I stuffed my huff and smiled serenely, lowering my eyes just enough so he knew I knew. As we arrived at our table, Simon pulled out my chair for me. As he scooted me in, I let my hand drift back just enough to accidentally-on-purpose graze him, feeling how worked up he was. I heard him hiss, and I smiled inwardly. Just as I went in for graze number two, he grasped my hand tightly in his own, pressing himself against me. My breath caught in my throat as I felt him harden further under our hands.

"Do I need to change your name to *Naughty* Girl?" he murmured, low and thick in my ear. I closed my eyes and tried to get control as he sat across from me, grinning in a devilish way. As our waiter busied himself around us, straightening the linens and presenting menus, I only had eyes for Simon, cocksure and beautiful, across the table from me. This meal was going to take forever.

The meal did take forever, but as much as I was aching to get Simon alone again, I also never wanted this night to end. We were served a beautiful paella, coastal style with chunks of prawns and spiny lobster, chorizo, and peas. Made in the traditional way, almost impossible to recreate, the simple shallow dish it had been cooked in allowed the saffron rice on the bottom to become crunchy and nutty—delicious in every sense of the word. We'd finished a lovely bottle of rosé and were now lazily sipping tiny glasses of Ponche Caballero, a Spanish brandy with hints of orange and cinnamon.

The liquor was spicy as I rolled it around in my mouth. I was pleasantly warm and more pleasantly tipsy. Not drunk, just heady enough that I was hyperaware of my surroundings and found anything and everything sensual: the way the smooth brandy slipped down my throat, the feel of Simon's leg against my own under the table, the way my body had begun to hum. The entire population, it seemed, was out and about tonight and in a celebratory mood for the festival kicking off in the center of town. The energy was raw and a little wild. I sat back in my chair, teasing Simon with my big toe, a silly smile on my face as he stared at me hard.

"I ate your paella once," he said suddenly.

"Pardon me?" I sputtered, catching the drop of brandy on my lip before it rolled off onto my dress.

"In Tahoe, remember? You made us all paella."

"Right, right, I did. Not like we had tonight, but it was pretty good." I smiled, thinking of that night. "As I recall, we polished off quite a bit of wine as well."

"Yes, we ate paella and drank wine, got the others together, and then you kissed me."

"We did, and yes, I did." I blushed.

"And then I acted like an ass," he replied, his blush present now as well.

"You did," I agreed with a smile.

"You know why, right? I mean, you have to know that I, well, that I wanted you. You do know that, right?"

"It was pressed against my leg, Simon. I was aware." I laughed, trying to play it off, but still thinking of how I'd felt when I ran away from him in that hot tub.

"Caroline, come on now," he chided, his eyes serious.

"Come on now, yourself. It really was pressed against my leg." I laughed again, a little weaker this time.

"That night? Jesus, it would have been so easy, you know? At that moment even I wasn't totally sure why I stopped us. I think I just knew that..."

"You knew that?" I prompted.

"I knew with you, it would be an all or nothing kind of thing."

"All?" I squeaked.

"All, Caroline. I need all of you. That night? Would have been great, but too soon." He leaned across the table and took my hand. "Now, we're here," he said, raising my hand to his mouth. He laid kisses across the back then opened my palm and pressed a wet kiss at its center. "Where I can take my time with you," he said, kissing my hand once more as I stared back at him.

"Simon?"

"Yes?"

"I'm really glad we waited."

"Me too."

"But I really don't think I can wait any longer."

"Thank God." He smiled and signaled the waiter.

We laughed like teenagers as we paid the bill and began our trek up the hill to the car. The festival was in full force now, and we passed through part of it on our way back. Lanterns lit up the sky overhead as a heavy drum beat pulsed, and we saw people dancing in the streets. That energy was back, that sense of abandon in the air, and the brandy and that very energy knocked Nerves back down, way down to my gut, where LC and Wang threatened to beat her within an inch of her life. LC and Wang, it sounded like a rap duo…

As we reached the car, I went to grab the door handle when I was whirled suddenly by a very intense Mr. Parker. His eyes burned into mine as he pressed me against the car, his hips strong and his hands frantic in my hair and on my skin. His hand slid down my leg, grasping my thigh and hitching it around his hip as I moaned and groaned at the strength I was about to let run wild across my body and soul.

But I slowed him down, my hands pulling at his hair, making him moan in turn. "Take me home, Simon," I whispered, pressing one more kiss against his sweet lips. "And *please* drive fast."

Even Heart seemed pleased, floating around above. She was still singing, but a song that was infinitely more dirty.

chapter nineteen

I looked at my reflection in the mirror, trying to look objectively. When I was a kid, especially in those charming early-teen years, I used to see myself very differently. I saw dishwater-blond hair and pale, uninteresting skin. I saw flat green eyes and knobby knees that bisected skinny, bird-like legs. I saw a slightly upturned nose and a bottom lip that looked like I might trip over it if I wasn't too careful.

When I was fifteen, one afternoon my grandmother told me she thought the pink dress I was wearing looked nice against my skin. I scoffed and immediately disagreed with her. "Thanks, Grandma, but I got about three hours of sleep last night, and the last thing I look today is nice. Tired and pale, but not nice."

I rolled my eyes in that way teenage girls do, and she reached for my hand.

"Always take a compliment, Caroline. Always take it for the way it was intended. You girls are always so quick to twist what others say. Simply say thank you and move on." She smiled in that quiet and wise way she had.

"Thanks." I smiled back, busying myself with the spaghetti sauce and turning my face so she couldn't see my blush.

"It breaks my heart the way young girls pick themselves over, never thinking they're good enough. You make sure you always remember, you're exactly the way you're supposed to be. Exactly. And anyone who says otherwise, well, poppycock." She giggled, her voice lowering a bit at that last word, the closest she would ever come to swearing.

Grandma had a list of bad words and really bad words, and *poppycock* came close to approaching the latter.

The next day at school I mentioned to a friend that I thought her hair looked great, and her answer was to run her hands through it with disgust.

"Are you kidding? I barely even had time to wash it today."

Even though it did look fantastic.

Later on after gym class, I was changing in the locker room when I observed another friend touching up her lip gloss. "That's pretty. What's the name of that color?" I asked as she pursed her lips in the mirror.

"Apple Tartlet, but it looks terrible on me. God, I have no tan left over from summer!"

Grandma was right. Girls really *didn't* take compliments well. Now, I'm not gonna lie and say after that day I magically had no more bad hair days or never picked the wrong lipstick again. But I *did* make a conscious effort to see the good before the bad and really look at myself in a more clear way. Objectively. Kindly. And as my body continued to change, I became more and more aware of features I could look at positively instead of negatively. I never thought of myself as lethally gorgeous, but I did clean up well.

And so now, as I stared into the mirror in the bathroom, knowing Simon was waiting for me, I took the time to take a little inventory.

The dishwater-blond hair? Not so much dishwater. It was shiny and golden, a little wavy and curly from the saltwater it had been cooking in all week. The pale skin? Nicely browned up and, dare I say, a little glowy? I winked at myself, holding back a maniacal giggle. My mouth had that slightly pouty lower lip, just full enough to trap me some Simon *and not let him go*. And the legs I saw peeking from below the lace just covering my thighs? Well, not so bird-like anymore. In fact, I think they were going to look pretty spectacular wrapping around Simon's…whatever I felt like wrapping them around.

And so, as I smoothed my hair once more and mentally ran through all my internal checklists, I was wildly excited about the night ahead. We'd raced back to the house, practically disrobed each other in the entryway, and after begging a few moments of girl time, I was now ready to go out and claim my Simon. Because who was kidding who? I wanted this man. Wanted him for my own, and did not, would not, share him with anyone else.

Brain for once was finally in agreement with LC. Especially since she'd crawled up Backbone and slapped Brain right in the stem, telling her in that special way only she could that we needed this. We deserved this, and we were ready. Nerves, well, they continued to circle in my tummy, but that was to be expected, right? I mean, it had been a long, long time, and a little bit of nerves was normal, I expect. Had I been stalling all week? Maybe.

Kind of.

A little.

Simon had been more than patient, content to take things slow, at my pace, but for crying out loud, he was only human.

I was adamant that Nerves not be allowed to turn another Spanish night into the land of cuddle and coo. I turned in the mirror, trying to see myself as Simon might see me. I smiled in what I thought was a seductive way, flipped off the light, took one more deep breath, and opened the door.

The bedroom had been transformed into something from a fairy tale. Candles flickered on the dresser and nightstands, bathing the room in a warm glow. The windows were open, as well as the door to the little balcony overlooking the sea, and I could hear the waves crashing, romance-novel style. And there he stood: hair tousled, body strong, eyes blazing.

I watched as he took me in, dragging his gaze down my body and back, a smile spreading across his face as he appraised my outfit of choice.

"Mmm, there's my Pink Nightie Girl," he sighed, holding out his hand. And when I stalled for just the tiniest second, Backbone picked up my hand and gave it to him.

We stood in the darkened room, a few feet apart but connected by our woven fingers. I could feel the rough texture of his thumb as he traced circles on the inside of my hand, the same circles he'd traced weeks and weeks before when I began to fall under his spell. Our eyes full of each other, he took a deep breath.

"It's criminal how good you look in that," he said, drawing me toward him and giving me a little spin so he could better see the pink baby doll nightie. As he spun me, the lacey edges flipped up just a little, showing off the accompanying ruffled panties. A low noise sounded in his throat, and if I wasn't mistaken, it was a growl? Damn...

He spun me back closer, grasping my hips and pressing me against him, my breasts crushing into his chest. He placed a tiny kiss below my ear, letting me feel just the tip of his tongue.

"So there are some things I need you to understand," he murmured, nuzzling with his nose, his hands brushing up under my nightie to fluff my ruffles and grab a handful of backside, catching me by surprise. I gasped.

"You listening? Don't get distracted on me now," he whispered again, flattening out his tongue and dragging it up the side of my neck.

"It's kind of hard to focus with your distraction poking me in the thigh," I groaned, letting him bend me backward just enough so that my entire lower body was pressed against him, his hard places perfectly content to mold my soft places around them. He chuckled against my neck, now dotting my collarbone with his trademarked baby kisses.

"Here's what you need to know. One, you're amazing," he said, his hands now traveling up to the small of my back, fingers and thumbs massaging and manipulating. "Two, you're amazingly sexy," he breathed.

My hands now hurriedly unbuttoned his shirt, pushing it back off his shoulders as our pace began to transition from slow and easy to fast and frantic. Now his hands were sneaking around front, his nails lightly scraping along my tummy, lifting my nightie so we were skin to skin, nothing left between us. I ran my hands up and down his back, my nails much more aggressive, digging in and anchoring him against me.

"And three, as amazingly sexy as this pink nightie is, the only thing I want to see for the rest of this night is my Sweet Caroline, and I *need* to see you." He panted in my ear as he picked me up, straight up, and my right leg went around his waist on its own.

Once again, the Universal Law of Wallbanger dictated that legs went around hips when they were offered.

He walked me backward to the bed and set me down gently. Leaning over, he pushed me backward on to my elbows. Shirt hanging down off his shoulders, he winked at me, nodding at his state of undress. I reached forward, crooked one finger behind the button on his khakis, and snapped it open. Seeing no peek of boxers, I gently nudged his zipper down just an inch or so, exposing the happy trail that led down, down, down to where all good things were found. Sweet mother of pearl. Commando.

"You got something against underpants?" I whispered, raising one knee and forcing him between my hips. Forcing. *Right.*

"I'm against *your* underpants, and isn't it a shame they're still there?" He smirked, pushing his hips into me, letting me feel everything.

I dropped my head back, silently pushing down Nerves when she threatened to bubble up just a smidge. Piss off, Nerves. This was happening.

"No shame. I have a feeling they won't be on for long." I sighed, laying back to stretch my arms over my head, lengthening my body against his and encouraging his lips to further dance along the hollow at the base of my collarbone. I could feel him licking and sucking between my breasts. I arched into him, anxious to feel more. I needed more. He began peeling the straps of my nightie down, baring me and allowing him the access he needed to make me orbit the planet.

Feeling his mouth on me, on my breasts, hot and wet, tickling and sloppy, was unreal. So I told him so.

"That feels unreal," I moaned in to the top of his head as the scruff from his light beard roughed my skin pleasantly. His lips closed around my right nipple, and my hips went off on a tangent of their own, bucking wildly beneath him, both of my legs now wrapped firmly around his waist. Lips and tongue and teeth now lavished across my cleavage, which spilled out over the edge of the nightie as he alternated between breasts, loving them equally. I was surrounded by Simon, and even his scent was turning me on, equal parts peppery spice and thick Spanish brandy.

Nonsensical words poured from my mouth. I was aware of a few "Simons," and one or two, "Yes, that's good," but mostly what I overheard from myself were things like "Mmph," and "Erghh," and a rather loud "Hyyyyaeahhh," for which, frankly, there is not a correct spelling.

Simon sighed over and over again in to my skin, his actual breath a turn on as I felt it wash over me. My hands had been left free to roam in the wonderland that was his hair, and as I swept it back from his face I was rewarded with the amazing sight of his mouth on me, his eyes closed in clear worship. He bit down lightly, closing his teeth around my sensitive skin, and my hands almost tore the hair from his head. It felt phenomenal.

His other hand was running up and down my leg, encouraging me to grasp him tighter between my thighs as his wondrous fingers began to come ever closer to the edge of the lace. It was the last boundary we had yet to cross: the lace frontier.

I felt my breathing still as he went on final approach, his fingers brushing just under the edge of my panties, barely brushing. His breathing slowed as well, and as he continued to touch me gently, his face came back up to mine, and we had this moment, this quiet moment, where we just…stared. Awe—it's the only way I can describe the feeling of his hand ghosting over me, delicately, reverently. Our eyes locked as he eased his hand further underneath the lace and then, with achingly perfect precision, he touched me.

My eyes fluttered shut, my entire body awash with so many sensations. My breathing started back up again, the intense pressure that had been circling all around and inside and out was now like a low-level hum, just beneath the surface of my skin. I moved with him, feeling his fingers begin to explore me, and I let out the tiniest moan. It was all I could let out. The feelings were so intense and the energy—oh my goodness, the energy that surrounded us in that moment.

I was sure Simon was unaware of the entirety of the emotion that flew around behind my closed eyelids. The poor man was just finally getting a little touch. But as his fingers became more deft and sure of themselves, something incredible began to happen. That teeny tiny little bundle of nerves, which had been dormant for centuries, began to spark to life. My eyes flew open as a very specific warmth began to move through me, starting at the center of my being and working its way out.

Simon was most certainly enjoying this. His eyes were hazy and crowded with lust as I writhed underneath him. I knew he could feel me tense and come alive.

"God, Caroline, you're so…you're beautiful," he murmured, his eyes now crowding with something a bit more than lust, and I felt tiny pinpricks behind my eyeballs.

I threw my arms around his neck and held him close, tearing at his shirt to get it off, get it off him so I could feel everything. He lifted himself from me for only seconds, ripping off his shirt in an exaggerated way that made me giggle but yearn for him even more.

Lowering himself back on to me, he slipped further down, his lips tracing a path down to my belly button. Circling it with his tongue, he laughed into my tummy.

"What are you laughing at, mister?" I giggled, squeezing his ear. He was below the nightie now, his face hidden from me. Poking his head back out, he let loose a slow grin that made my toes point.

"If your belly button tastes this good—fuck, Caroline. I can't wait to taste your pussy."

There are certain things a woman needs to hear at different times in her life:

You got the job.

Your ass looks great in that skirt.

I would love to meet your mother.

And when used in the just the right context, in just the right setting, sometimes, a woman needs to hear the P-word.

This could be better than Clooney.

The moan that came out of my mouth when he said that word, well, let's just say it was loud enough to wake the dead. He let his tongue trace a path from my belly button down to the edge of my ruffles, and then with loving precision, he hooked his thumbs underneath the lace and dragged them down my legs.

There I was, spread out on top of PillowTown with a pink nightie bunched up around my midriff, all pertinent parts on display, and damn happy about it. He pulled my hips just to the edge of the bed and dropped to his knees. Sweet Jesus.

As he ran his hands up and down the tops of my legs, I lifted up on my elbows so I could watch, needing to see this wonderful man tending to me, taking care of me. Kneeling between my thighs, with his khakis unbuckled and halfway unzipped, hair at atomic heights, he was stunning. And on the move.

Once again letting his tongue lead, he planted open-mouth kisses along the insides of my thighs, one side and then the other, with each pass getting closer and closer to where I needed him most. Carefully lifting my left leg, he hitched it over his shoulder as I arched my back, my entire body now aching to feel him.

He gazed at me for a moment longer, maybe even just a few seconds, but it felt like a lifetime. "Beautiful," he breathed one more time, and then he pressed his mouth to me.

No quick licks, no tiny kisses, just incredible pressure as he surrounded me with his lips. It was enough to make me drop back on the bed, unable to support myself any longer. The feel, the exquisite feel of him was all-consuming, and I could barely breathe. He worked me slow and low, bringing one hand up to open me further to him, letting his mouth and fingers and perfect tongue gently and methodically coax me into the stratosphere, rising up, filling me with the sense of awe and amazement I had been missing for so long.

I allowed one hand to drift down to him and tangle in his hair, running my fingers through it with as much feeling as I could. The other hand? Useless. It was fisting the sheets into some kind of ball.

He lifted his head from me once, just once, to press another kiss against my thigh. "Perfect. Jesus, just perfect," he whispered, so quietly I could barely hear him over my own sighs and whimpers. He returned to me almost immediately, an urgency now to his movements, his lips and tongue twisting and pressing as he groaned into me, the vibration riding straight through.

I opened my eyes for a second, just a second, and the room was glowing, almost incandescent. All of my senses came alive, and I could hear the crashing of the surf, see the candlelight flickering on our bodies. I could feel my skin break into gooseflesh, the very air caressing me and announcing what I had been missing for months, years even.

This man could very possibly love me. And he was about to bring back the O.

Snapping my eyes closed again, I could almost see myself, standing at the edge of a cliff, staring down into the raging ocean below. Pressure, enormous pressure was building behind me, nudging me toward the edge where I could fall, fall freely into what was waiting for me. I took one step, then another, closer and closer as I could feel Simon grasping my hips. But wait. If the O was coming for me, I wanted Simon inside. I *needed* him inside me.

Tugging on his shoulders, I pulled him up my body, feet kicking at his khakis until they lay defenseless on the floor.

"Simon, I need, please, inside, now," I panted, almost incoherent with lust. Simon, schooled in Caroline shorthand, understood this completely and was poised between my legs, hips nuzzled up into mine within seconds. He leaned down, kissing me wantonly, the taste of me all over him. And I loved it.

ALICE CLAYTON

"Inside, inside, inside," I kept chanting, my back and hips alternately arching, desperately trying to find what I needed, what I had to have, to push me off that cliff. He left me for only seconds to fumble in his khakis, which I had kicked halfway across the room. The telltale crinkle let me know that I was safe, that we were safe.

Finally I felt him, exactly where he was meant to be. He barely nudged inside, but just the feeling of him entering me was monumental. My own needs quieted for the moment, and I watched as he began to push into me for the first time. His eyes bore into mine as I cradled his face in my hands. He looked as though he wanted to say something. What words would we speak, what wonderfully loving things would we say to commemorate this moment?

"Hi," he whispered, smiling as though his life depended on it.

I couldn't help but smile back. "Hi," I answered, loving the feel of him, the weight of him, above me.

He slipped gently into me, and at first my body resisted. It had been a long time, but the little pain I felt was welcome. It was that good kind of pain, a pain that let you know something more was coming. I relaxed a bit, allowing my legs to wrap around his waist, and as he pressed farther into me, his smile became infinitely more sexy. He bit down on his lower lip and tiny frown lines appeared on his forehead. I breathed in, inhaling his scent as I watched him pull back just the smallest bit, only to thrust once more. Now fully inside, I welcomed him the only way I could. I gave him that little internal hug, which made his eyes flash open and peer down at me.

"There's my girl," he murmured, raising one rakish eyebrow and thrusting into me again, with more conviction this time. My breath caught in my throat and I gasped, unwittingly rocking my hips into his with a motion as old as the waves crashing down below.

Slowly he began to move within me, sliding against me with a fantastic pressure, each new angle and sensation giving way to more of that warm tingly feeling working its way out to the tips of each finger and toe. The feeling of having Simon inside me, inside my body, was more than I can articulate. I groaned, and he grunted. He moaned, and I mewed. Together. His hips pushed me higher on to the bed, up toward the headboard. Our bodies were slick with sweat, crashing and smashing into each other. I threaded my hands deeply into his hair, tugging and writhing beneath him.

"Caroline, so beautiful," he sighed between kisses across my forehead and nose.

I closed my eyes and could see myself, once again, on the edge of that cliff, ready to jump, needing to jump. Again, that pressure began to build, that crackle of energy spinning itself wild and frantic, pulsing with every thrust, every slip and dip of his hips into mine, driving him, unrelentingly, in and out of my body.

I took one final step, one foot now dangling off the edge of the cliff, and then! I saw her…O. She was in the water down below, her hair like fire dancing along the waves. She waved and I waved and just like that, Simon brought one hand down between our bodies, just above where we were joined, and he began to trace his little circles.

Little circles from a perfect hand, and I jumped. I jumped free and clear and loud and proud, announcing my approval with a lusty "Yes!" as I rushed toward that certain high.

And I fell.

And fell.

And fell.

And crashed. Crashed and smacked into the unforgiving surface of the water, and I didn't come up. I fell for what seemed like an age, but instead of O meeting me at the bottom with open arms, I floundered, alone and wet. Every muscle in my body, every cell was concentrated on the return of the O, as if I could will her back. I strained, body tight and taut as I caught sight of her, just the very tips of her hair, like fire under the water, slipping away from me. She was so close, so very close, but no. No.

I scrambled after her, trying with sheer will to make her reappear, but nothing. She was gone, and I was left underwater. With the most beautiful man in the world inside me.

I opened my eyes and saw Simon above me, saw his beautiful face as he made love to me, and that *is* was this was. This wasn't sex. This was love, and I still couldn't offer him all that I had. I saw his eyes heavy and thick and half closed in passion. I saw a bead of sweat running down his nose and watched as it splashed lazily on to my breasts. I saw as he bit down hard on his lower lip, the strain on his face as he delayed his own well-deserved climax.

He was everything I had hoped he would be. He was a generous lover, and I could feel my heart beat to within bursting out of my chest to be nearer to him, to love him. He was everything.

I lifted his hand from between us and kissed his fingertips, then wrapped my legs tighter around his waist and anchored my hands on his back. He was waiting for me. Of course he was. I adored him. I closed my eyes once more, steeling myself for all I was able to give him.

"Simon, it's so good," I panted, and I meant every word of it. I bucked my hips. I clenched in all the right places, and I called his name, over and over again.

"Caroline, look at me, please," he begged, his voice rife with pleasure. I allowed my eyes to open again, feeling one tear spill down my cheek. A strange look stole over his features for only a second as his eyes searched mine, and then? He came. No thunder, no lightning, no fanfare. But it was stunning.

He collapsed onto me, and I took his weight. I took it all as I cradled him to my chest and kissed him over and over again, my hands soothing his back, my legs hugging him as tightly as I could. I whispered his name as he nuzzled into the space between my neck and my breast, simple touches and caresses.

Heart sat to the side and quietly sighed. Nerves? You motherfucker. Don't even think about showing your face here.

We lay for a while, listening to the ocean in our own little haven, this romantic fairy tale that could have, should have been enough. When his breathing returned to normal, he lifted his head and kissed me very softly.

"Sweet Caroline," he smiled, and I smiled back, my heart full.

Sex could be amazing, even without the O.

"I'll be right back," he said disentangling from me and walking to the bathroom, naked backside a sight to behold. I watched him retreat, and then sat up quickly, pulling the straps of my nightie back up around my shoulders. I rolled on to my side, away from the bathroom, and curled around my pillow. This had been the single best sexual experience of my life. Every *i* had been dotted, every *t* had been crossed. And yet, I was still no-go for O. What the hell was wrong with me?

I will not cry.

I will not cry.

I will not cry.

Even though he'd only been gone from the bed a few minutes, when he came back, I panicked and pretended to be asleep. Childish? Yep. Totally childish.

I felt the bed dip as he climbed back in, and then his warm and still very naked body was up against me, spooning. Arms wrapped around my middle, and then his mouth was at my ear, whispering.

"Mmm, Nightie Girl back in her nightie."

I waited, not speaking, just breathing. I felt him shake me a little bit and let out a little chuckle.

"Hey, hey you, are you sleeping?"

Should I snore? Whenever people faked sleep on sitcoms, they snored. I let out a tiny one. He kissed my neck, my traitor skin pebbling in the wake of his mouth. I sighed in my "sleep," snuggling closer to Simon, hoping he would let me pull this off. The fates were kind tonight, as he simply hugged me tighter to his chest and kissed me once more.

"'Night, Caroline," he whispered, and the night settled around us. I fake snored for a few more minutes until his actual snoring took over, and then I sighed heavily.

Confused and numb, I was awake until dawn.

chapter twenty

I had faked it.

Faked it with Simon. There must have been a rule written somewhere, maybe even chiseled into a stone tablet: Thou Shall Not Fake It With Wallbanger. So let it be written, so let it be done. I faked it, and now I was doomed to wander the planet forever, O-less.

Was I being overly dramatic? Oh my, yes. But if this didn't call for a little drama, what did?

That next morning, I was up and out of bed before Simon was even awake, something I hadn't done the entire time we were on our trip together. Usually we stayed in bed until the other one was awake, and then lounged for a while, laughing and talking. And kissing.

Mmm, the kissing.

But this morning I ran quickly through the shower and was in the kitchen making breakfast when a sleepy Simon came in. Shuffling across the floor in his socks, with boxers low on his hips, he grinned through his sleep haze and burrowed into my side as I sliced melon and berries.

"What are you doing out here? I was a little lonesome. Big bed, no Caroline. Where'd you go?" he asked, planting a quick kiss on my shoulder.

"I needed to get moving this morning. Remember the car is coming for me at ten? I wanted to make you some breakfast before I left." I smiled, turning to give him a quick kiss.

He stopped me from turning away and kissed me more thoroughly, not letting me hurry through anything. I could feel myself closing off, and I was almost unable to stop it. I needed some time to process this, to understand how I was feeling—other than miserable. But I adored Simon, and he didn't deserve this. So I let myself fall into the kiss, be swept away by this man once more. I kissed him back feverishly, passionately, and then pulled away just before it could become something more than a kiss.

"Fruit?"

"Huh?"

"Fruit. I made fruit salad. Want some?"

"Oh, yeah. Yeah. Sounds good. Coffee made?"

"Water is boiling. French press is all ready to go." I patted him on the cheek as I waved him toward the pot. We coexisted in the kitchen, talking quietly, and Simon stole a kiss or two here and there. I tried not to show how messed up my brain was, tried to act as normal as I could. Simon seemed to sense something was up, but he took his cue from me, let me lead this morning.

We sat outside on the terrace one last time, eating our breakfast together and watching the breakers roll in.

"Are you glad you came?" he asked.

I bit down on my lip at the obvious. "I'm so glad. This trip was amazing." I smiled, reaching across the table for his hand and giving it a squeeze.

"And now?"

"And now what? Back to reality. What time does your flight get in tomorrow?" I asked.

"Late. Really late. Should I call you or…" He left off, seeming to ask me if he should come over.

"Call me when you get in, no matter what time, okay?" I replied, sipping my coffee and watching the ocean. He was quiet now, and this time when I bit down on my lip it was to keep from crying.

I had packed early, so when the driver got here, I was ready to go. Simon had tried to tempt me to join him in the shower, but I begged off, making an excuse about finding my passport. I was panicking and pulling away just when we'd been getting so close, but this had really thrown me for a loop.

I had put all my Os in one basket, and the problem wasn't Simon. It was me. The sex had been unreal, amazing, perfection even with a condom on, and yet still, no.

Simon walked my bags out to the car and placed them in the trunk. After speaking to the driver for a moment, he came back to me as I walked through the house one last time. It truly had been a fairy tale, and I had enjoyed every moment.

"Time to go?" I asked, leaning back against him when he approached me at the terrace railing. I was glad for the feel of him against me.

"Time to go. You have everything you need?"

"I think so. I wish I could figure out a way to get some of those prawns home, though." I laughed, and he snorted into my hair.

"I think we can find something at home that will be suitable. Maybe we can have the others over next weekend and recreate some of the stuff we ate here?"

I turned to face him. "Make our debut?" I grinned.

"Yeah, sure. I mean, if you want to," he added sheepishly, looking at me carefully.

"I do," I answered. And I did. Even without the stupid, blessed O, I wanted to be with Simon.

"Okay, debut over prawns. That sounds weird."

I laughed as he hugged me to him. The driver honked, and we shuffled toward the car.

"I'll call you when I'm back, okay?" he said.

"I'll be there. Get some good work done," I instructed.

He brushed my hair back from my face and leaned in to kiss me once more.

"Bye, Caroline."

"Bye, Simon." I got in the car. And drove away from the fairy tale.

Once I was ensconced in my first-class seat, I had nothing but hours to contemplate. Strike that. I had nothing but hours to sit and stew and grumble. I'd cried in the car on the way to the airport, trying all the while to assure the driver I was fine and not stone-cold crazy. I cried because, well, there was sure as shit a lot of tension in my body, and it had to come out some way. And so it did, through my eyeballs. I was sad, and I was frustrated. Now I was done crying.

I tried to read. I'd stocked up on trashy magazines in the airport in Malaga. As I paged through them, titles of articles jumped out at me:

"How to Know If You're Having the Best Orgasm You Can Have"

"Kegel Your Way to Multiples"

"New Weight Loss Plan: Orgasm Your Way to a Thinner You!"

Lower Caroline, Brain, Backbone, Heart were all lined up and throwing stones at Nerves, who was trying her best to hide.

I slammed down all my new magazines, throwing them into the seatback in front of me. I grabbed my laptop, powered it up, and put in my earbuds. I'd loaded some movies on before the last flight. I could let my brain escape into a film. Yes, I could do that. I scrolled through some of the movies I had on file... *When Harry Met Sally*? Nope, not with that scene in the deli. *Top Gun*? Nope, that scene where they do it, and it's all lit blue with the breeze blowing through the gauzy curtains? No, too close to my fairy tale.

I found a movie I could safely watch, took three Tylenol PM, and was asleep before Luke learned how to use his lightsaber.

Somewhere between the connection at LaGuardia and the flight across the US, I downshifted from sad to mad. I'd caught up on my sleep, was done with the crying bullshit, and now I was good and mad. And on a plane where pacing was discouraged. I had to stay in my seat and try to rationalize what to do with this anger—and how I was going to live my entire life with no hope of an O. And again, overly dramatic? Perhaps, but with no O in sight, it's easy to have tunnel vision.

Finally, we touched down at SFO and as I followed the crowd to baggage claim, physically and emotionally exhausted, I looked up into the face of someone I never wanted to see again.

Cory Weinstein. That machine-gun fucker.

Plastered across the newsstand was his stupid face in a giant ad campaign for Slice o' Love Pizza Parlors. I stood in front of his giant head, which wore the biggest shit-eating grin as he posed with a giant pepperoni slice, and my anger bubbled over. It now had a face. My anger had a face, and it was a stupid face. I wanted to punch it in the face, but it was only a picture.

Unfortunately, that didn't stop me.

Not a smart thing to do, have a fit in an international airport. Turns out they frown on that. So after a strongly worded warning from TSA, and a promise that I would never attack a poster again, I packed myself into a cab, stinking of airplane, and went back to my apartment. I kicked my own door this time, and as I threw my bags down, I saw the only two things that could make me smile.

Clive and my KitchenAid.

With a strongly worded *meow*, he came running to me, actually jumping into my arms and showing the affection he reserved for moments exactly like these. Somehow his little cat brain knew I needed it, and he lavished attention on me as only he could. Shaking his tail and purring incessantly, he butted his head up under my chin and wrapped his big paws around my neck, giving me a tiny kitty hug. Laughing into his fur, I held him close. It was good to be home.

"Did Uncle Euan and Uncle Antonio take good care of you? Huh? Who's my good boy?" I cooed, dropping him to the floor and grabbing a can of tuna, his treat for behaving while I was gone. Turning now from Clive, who had focused solely on his bowl, my eyes laser-locked on my KitchenAid. I was going to shower, and then I was going to bake. I needed to bake.

An unknown amount of time later—although I will say the sun had set and risen while I floured and stirred—I heard knocking at my door. I'd been baking so long I felt my back creak and squeak as I lifted my head from slicing some of Ina's Outrageous Brownies. They took a few extra steps, but oh boy, were they worth the trouble. What the hell time was it? I looked around for Clive and didn't see him.

I shuffled to the door, noticing there was sugar all over the floor, brown and white, and I was performing an accidental soft-shoe dance. There was another knock at the door, more insistent this time.

"Coming!" I shouted, rolling my eyes at the irony. As I raised my hand to open the door, I noticed melted chocolate all over my knuckles. Not one to waste, I gave them a heavenly lick as I opened the door.

There stood Simon, looking exhausted.

"What are you doing here? You're not supposed to be home until—"

"Not supposed to be home until late tonight, I know. I took an earlier flight." He pushed past me into my apartment.

As I closed the door and turned to face him, I smoothed out my apron a bit, feeling bits of cookie dough clinging to it. "You took an earlier flight. Why?" I asked, soft-shoeing across the floor to him.

He looked around with an amused grin, noting the piles and piles of cookies, the assorted pies on the windowsills, the aluminum-wrapped bricks of zucchini bread, pumpkin bread, and cranberry orange bread, stacked like the foundation of a house all along the dining table. He grinned once more, then turned to me, picking a raisin off my forehead that I didn't even know was stuck there.

"Are you gonna tell me why you faked it?"

chapter twenty-one

Dumbstruck, I stood with my mouth hanging open as he walked farther into the room to contemplate the baked goods. He shuffled through the sugar and paused to swipe a finger through a bowl lined with melted chocolate. I sighed heavily as I returned to the counter to face him *and* the music as I removed a ball of dough from another bowl where it was rising.

How did he know? How could he tell? I flipped and kneaded the dough—a fluffy, clingy brioche—feeling my face flame. I thought I'd played it pretty well. I chanced a look up at him as he licked the chocolate from his finger, his eyes growing more concerned as my thoughtful kneading turned into punching. I took my frustration out on the brioche dough as I pondered an O-less life. Dammit.

His finger now clean, he brushed a lock of hair behind my ear as I continued to punch/knead and flip. I winced when he touched me, the glorious image of him perched on top of me impossible to ignore.

"We gonna talk about this?" he asked quietly, dipping his nose to my neck. I leaned into his body for a scant second, then caught myself.

"What is there to talk about? I don't even know what you're talking about. Are you delirious from the time change?" I said cheerily, avoiding his eyes as I wondered if I could pull this off. Could I convince him *he* was crazy one? God*damnit*, how did he know?

"Nightie Girl, come on. Talk to me," he prodded, nuzzling into my neck. "If we're gonna do this, we need to talk to each other."

Talk? Sure, I could talk. He should probably know what he was in for with me, doomed to wander the planet without an O for the rest of my life. I picked up the dough one more time and threw it against the wall. It dripped and rolled down, sticky like those creepy crawly things I used to play with as a kid. I whirled to face him, my face still red but beyond caring now.

"What was that going to be?" he asked calmly, nodding to the dough.

"Brioche. It was going to be brioche," I answered quickly, my tone frantic.

"I bet it would have been good."

"It's a lot of work—almost too much."

"We could try it again. I'd be glad to help."

"You don't know what you're offering. Do you have any idea how complicated it is? How many steps there are? How long it might take?"

"Good things come to those who wait."

"Christ, Simon, you have no idea. I want this so badly, probably even more than you."

"They make croutons out of it, right?"

"Wait, what? What the hell are you talking about?"

"Brioche. It's like, some kind of bread, isn't it? Hey, quit banging your head against the counter."

The granite felt cool against my defeated, hot skin, but I banged with less force when I heard the edge of panic in his voice.

He knew, and he was still here. He was here in my kitchen in that blue North Face pullover that made his eyes smoky sapphires and his entire body look cuddly and warm and sexy and virile and kick-me-the-in-head gorgeous. And here I was, covered in honey and raisins, banging my head on the countertop after killing my brioche.

Killing my brioche. What a great name for a—*focus, Caroline!*

Heart had damn near leapt out of my chest when she saw him at the door. LC was close behind, involuntarily clenching at the sight of him. Brain had shut down in shock and denial for a moment, but was now analyzing the situation and leaning toward pronouncing him a worthy candidate, noting the time and distance he'd committed to discovering the cause of concern. Backbone straightened now, knowing innately that proper posture created a better-looking rack—could you blame her? Nerves...fluttered.

Why. Why. He wants to know why. I examined him between bangs...ahem...and saw he was getting concerned. As was I—my head was really starting to hurt. I was tired, overwhelmed, and underorgasmed. And a touch slaphappy?

After one last bang, I straightened up, then listed a little left. I caught my balance, drew in a breath, and let fly.

"You want to know why?"

"I'd like to. Are you done banging?"

"God bless it, no more banging. Okay, why. Why? Here goes..." I paced in a tight circle, dodging the chocolate chips and pecans that had congregated close to the counter on the floor. I spied Clive in the corner, batting a few walnuts back and forth between his paws. Nuts all over the floor, nuts in my head. Fitting. "Know anything about pizza parlors, Simon?"

To his great credit, he listened. He listened as I went on and on, circling the kitchen island as I ranted and raged. I could barely make sense of it myself: "Weinstein...one night...machine gun...It went away!...night off...Jordan Catalano...Not even Clooney!...hiatus... Oprah...lonely...single...Not even Clooney!...Jason Bourne...almost Clooney...Pink nightie...banging..."

After a while he looked as dizzy I was beginning to feel. But I was determined to get it all out. He tried to grab me on one pass around, but I dodged his hands, almost slipping in a patch of crushed pecans, which I had crushed further in my circling. I had worn a path through the clutter.

I made one last pass, this time muttering, "Spanish fairy tale with prawns," when I tripped over a muffin tin and fell into his arms.

He held me close, breathing me in, kissing my forehead. "Caroline, babe, you gotta tell me what's going on. The mumbling? It's cute and all, but we're not really getting anywhere." He pressed his hands into the small of my back, holding me in place. I pulled away a little, resisting his embrace, and looked him straight in the eyes.

"How did you know?" I asked.

"Come on, sometimes guys know."

"No, really. How did you know?" I asked again.

He kissed my nose gently. "Because all of a sudden, you weren't my Caroline."

"I faked it because I haven't had an orgasm in one thousand years," I stated matter of factly.

"Come again?"

"I'm going across the hall to kick your door now," I sighed, pulling away and shuffling through the sugar.

"Wait, wait, wait, you what? You haven't had a what?" He grabbed for my hand as I turned back to him, with everything out in the open now.

"An orgasm, Simon. An orgasm. The Big O, the climax, the happy ending. No orgasms. Not for this Nightie Girl. Cory Weinstein can give me a five-percent discount whenever I want one, but in return, he took my O." I sniffled, tears now coming to my eyes. "So you can go back to your harem. I'll be entering the convent soon enough!" I cried, the dam finally breaking.

"Convent? What? Come here, please. Get your dramatic ass over here." He pulled me unwillingly back to the kitchen and wrapped me in his arms. He rocked me back and forth as I let out ridiculous sobs and wails.

"You're so...so...great...and I can't...I can't...you're so good...in...bed...and everywhere else...and I can't...I can't...God...you're so hot...when you came...so hot...and you came home...and I killed my brioche...and I...I...I think...I love you."

All stop. Breathe. *What did I just say?*

"Caroline, hey, stop crying, you gorgeous girl. Mind running that last part by me again?"

I'd just told Simon I loved him. While my snot soaked into his North Face. I breathed in his scent, then peeled myself off of him and headed to the wall to peel off the dough stuck there. Nerves sprang to life, for once working for us. Could I cover? Could I rally?

"Which part?" I asked the wall—and Clive, who had stopped playing with his nuts to listen in.

"That last part," I heard him say, his voice strong and clear.

"I killed my brioche?" I hedged.

"You really think that's the part I'm asking about?"

"Um, no?"

"Try again."

"I don't wanna."

"Caroline—wait, what's your middle name?"

"Elizabeth."

"Caroline Elizabeth," he warned, in a deep voice that unexpectedly made me giggle.

"Brioche is really good, when it's not flavored with wall," I blurted, my exhaustion mixing with my confession for an odd buzz. I actually felt a little relieved.

"Turn around, please," he asked, and so I did. He leaned against the counter, unzipping his snotty North Face. "I'm a bit jetlagged, so a quick recap, if I could. One, you seem to have lost your orgasm, yes?"

"Yes," I mumbled, watching as he took off his fleece, throwing it over the back of one of my chairs.

"Two, brioche is really hard to make, yes?"

"Yes," I breathed, not able to take my gaze away from him. Underneath the North Face was a white button-down. Which was good enough on its own, but couple that with the way he was slowly and methodically rolling up the sleeves? It was mesmerizing.

"And three, you think you love me?" he asked, his voice deep and thick, like molasses and honey and all things afghan—blanket, not country.

"Yes," I whispered, knowing it was one hundred percent the truth. I loved Simon. Big, giant *dur*.

"You think, or you know?"

"I know."

"Well, now. That's something to consider, isn't it?" he replied, his eyes dancing as he drew near. "You really have no idea, do you?" He spread his hands along my collarbone, brushing his thumbs across the very tops of my breasts.

My breathing quickened, my body sparking to life in spite of myself. "No idea about what?" I murmured, allowing him to press me against the wall.

"How thoroughly you own me, Nightie Girl," he said, leaning in to whisper this part in my ear. "And I *know* I love you enough to want you to have your happy ending."

And then he kissed me—Heart was in heaven—kissed me like it was a fairy tale, even though in this fairy tale I had dough sticking to my back and a cat with a pawful of nuts. But that didn't stop me from kissing him back as though my life depended on it.

"Did you know I started falling for you the night you banged on my door?" he asked, kissing my neck. "And that I as soon as I started to get to know you, I wasn't with anyone else?"

I gasped. "But I thought, I mean, I saw you with—"

"I know what you thought, but it's true. How could I be with anyone else when I was falling in love with you?"

He loved me! But wait, what's this? He was backing away…where was he going?

"And now, I'm going to do something I never thought I would do." He sighed mournfully, looking at the stacks of bread on the table. With a deep breath and a grimace, in one fell swoop he knocked them all to the floor. Bread rained down in foil-covered bricks around us, and I can't be sure, but I think I heard a tiny whine escape as he watched them hit the floor. But then he turned to me, eyes dark and dangerous. He grabbed me and swung me up on the table before him, nudging my legs apart to stand between them.

"Do you have any idea how much fun we're going to have?" he asked, slipping his hands inside my apron, warm and a little rough on my tummy.

"What are you up to?"

"An O has been lost, and I'm a sucker for a challenge." He grinned, pulling me to the edge of the table and snugly in to him. With his hands behind my knees, he wrapped my legs around his waist, kissing me again, lips and tongue hot and persistent.

"It's not going to be easy. She's pretty lost," I protested between kisses, worrying his buttons open and exposing his Spanish suntan.

"I'm done with easy."

"You should print that on cards."

"Print this—why do you still have clothes on?"

He laid me back across the table as I grinned up at him. My foot hit the flour sifter and sent it crashing to the floor, dusting us thoroughly in the process. Simon's hair looked like a biscuit, powdery and puffy. I coughed and a plume of flour came out, making Simon laugh out loud. The laughing stopped when I reached down for him, finding him hard, yet still covered in denim. He groaned, my favorite sound in the world.

"Fuck, Caroline, I love your hands on me," he said through his teeth, dipping his mouth to my neck and leaving a trail of white-hot kisses across my skin. His tongue swept out across me, underneath the edge of my apron. Hands quickly found the bottom of my tank top, and it went sailing across the room, into the kitchen sink. Within seconds, a pair of shorts found themselves swimming alongside, quickly followed by a pair of jeans and a white button-down.

The apron? Well, we were having a little trouble with that one.

"Are you a sailor? Who tied this knot, Popeye?" he seethed, struggling to get it undone. In his struggles, he managed to knock over a bowl of orange marmalade glaze, which now dripped down the table and on to the floor. My contribution was to flip over a carton of raisins while I craned my neck trying to see the knot behind me.

"Oh, screw the apron, Simon. Look here," I insisted, snapping the front of my bra and tossing it to the floor. I pulled down the top of the apron, arranging and propping up my cleavage. Pie eyed, he looked at my now-naked breasts and went in for the kill. I was pushed roughly back on to the table once more, his insistent mouth now dragging down my neck, attacking my skin like it had done something personal to him and he was exacting his revenge. And a lustful revenge it was.

Dipping a finger into the marmalade puddle, he traced a path from one breast to the other, circling and pressing the sticky into my skin. Bending his head, he tasted one, then the other, both of us groaning at the same time.

"Mmm, you taste good."

"I'm glad I wasn't making hot wings. This could be a different story—wow, that's nice." I sighed as he responded to my smart-assery with an actual bite.

"These would be extra spicy."

He laughed as I rolled my eyes.

"Want me to get some celery to cool you down?" I asked.

"No one's cooling down in this apartment, not anytime soon," he promised, grabbing the jar of honey from the nearby counter and pulling aside my apron. Without missing a beat, he got my panties all wet. And not in the way you think, although there was that...

As I watched, he poured the honey all over me, covering my panties and making me squeal. He stood back to admire. "Look at that, those are ruined. They're going to have to come off," he said as he came close again. I stopped him with a marmalade foot.

"You first, Mr. Man," I instructed, nodding at his flour-covered boxers. He raised an eyebrow, and dropped the boxers. Standing naked in my wreck of a kitchen, he was insanely cute.

In that instant, Heart, Brain, Backbone, and LC lined up on one side of the playground. They beckoned for Nerves, waving her over like a game of Red Rover. I looked at Simon, naked and floury and perfect, and I sighed with a giant smile. Nerves finally, blessedly, scampered over, and we were finally all on the same page.

"I fucking love you, Simon."

"I love you too, Nightie Girl. Now lose the panties and gimme some sugar."

"Come and get it," I laughed, sitting up and sliding my panties down my honey-dripped legs. I threw them at him, and they hit his chest with a loud thwack, the honey dripping everywhere.

"We're going to need one helluva shower after all this," I remarked as he wrapped me in his sticky arms.

"That'll be round two." He smiled, picking me up and carrying me to the bedroom, my body aligned with his, only the apron between us. And that wasn't going to keep us apart for long.

Did I need an O? I mean, was it necessary for life? Being near Simon, being so close to him, wrapped up in his arms and feeling him move inside me, was it enough?

For now, it was. I loved him, you see...

He dropped me on the bed, and I bounced a little, rolling sideways and making the headboard bang a bit.

"You gonna bang my walls, Simon?" I laughed.

"You have no idea," he promised, and scrunched my apron out of the way as I sighed and threw my arms over my head. I lazed backward, with a giant smile on my face. His fingers walked down over my tummy, my hips, my thighs, finally reaching me. After a gentle nudge, I let my legs fall open. He licked his lips and sank to his knees.

He touched and tasted me as he had in Spain, but it was different. It still felt amazing, but *I* was different. I was relaxed. Twisting and turning his fingers, he found that spot, the one that made my back arch and my moans grow deep. He groaned into me, causing me to arch off the bed again, his lips and tongue finding me once more, deliberate. My hands sought my breasts, and as he watched, I teased my nipples, bringing them taut once more.

Again, I had the distinct honor of feeling his mouth, his wonderful mouth, on me. I seized up, my entire body tensing at the sizzle of energy that ran through me, and then I relaxed once more. I started to feel, really feel everything going on inside at that moment. Love. I felt love. And I felt *loved...*

Here in the daytime, where nothing could be hidden, everything was on display—and covered in messy stuff—I was being loved by this man. No fairy tale, no waves crashing, no flickering candles. Real life. A real life fairy tale where I was being loved by this man. And I mean *looooved* by this man.

Tongue. Lips. Fingers. Hands. All of it dedicated to me and my pleasure. A girl could get used to this.

I could feel the sweet tension begin to build, but this time my body received it differently. My body, perfectly in tune for once, was ready, and in my mind, behind closed eyes, I saw myself begin to approach that cliff. In my head, I grinned, because I knew this time I was gonna catch that bitch. And then? Really amazing things began to happen down below. Long gorgeous fingers pressed inside me, twisting, and curving, and finding that secret spot. Lips and tongue encircled that other spot, sucking and licking, pressing and pulsing. Tiny pricks of light began to dance behind my eyelids, intense and wild.

"Oh, God...Simon...that's so...good...don't...stop...don't...stop..."

I groaned loud, louder, and then louder still, unable to contain the sounds I was making. It was so good, so good, so very, very good, so close, so close...

And then the screaming began. And it was not my own.

Out of the corner of my eye, I became aware of some kind of furry missile racing across the floor.

Like some kind of pussified dive bomb, Clive ran at Simon, leaped, and dug into his back, attacking him from behind.

Simon ran from the bedroom into the hallway, then back in again, Clive still latched on like some kind of rabid coonskin back cap that would not shake off. He had his arms—does a cat have arms?—wrapped around Simon's neck in a way that under other circumstances would have seemed like an adorable cat hug. But right now, he meant business.

I ran after them, naked except for my apron, trying to get Simon to slow down, but with those ten claws digging deeper in, he continued running from room to room.

The irony that Simon was literally trying to run away from pussy was not lost on me.

If I could have watched from outside, rather than being involved, I would have peed myself. As it was, I was having a hard time stifling myself listening to Simon's screams. I really must love him.

Finally, I backed them both into a corner, turned Simon around, resisted the urge to squeeze buns, and pried Clive loose. I quickly headed out to the living room and deposited him on the sofa with a thunk, patting him on the head once as a thank you for the defense, unwarranted as it was. Clive responded with a prideful meow and began licking his whiskers.

I went back into the kitchen to find Simon, still huddled against the wall. I appraised him, his eyes wild as he leaned against the wall, wincing at his back. My gaze was drawn lower. Unbelievable.

He

Was

Still

Hard.

He saw my eyes travel down his body, reminiscent of the first time we met face to face. He nodded sheepishly.

"You're still hard," I blurted, breathing heavily as I tried once more to untie my apron.

"Yeah."

"That's amazing."

"You're amazing."

"Ah, fuck," I huffed, giving up on the knot.

"Yes, please."

I paused for a split second, then whirled the apron around to my back in one swift movement. I leaped across the room, my apron flying behind me like a low-rider cape and crashed into him, driving him up against the wall as I assaulted him. He caught me as I wrapped around him like a feisty blanket, kissing him furiously. My nails raked down his chest, and he gasped.

"Your back okay?" I asked between kisses.

against his, my cries getting louder as we sped up our rocking, both of us, in tune and right there. Right there. Right, right, right…there…

"Caroline, Jesus, you…are…amazing…love…you…so…much…killing…me…"

And that's the little extra I needed.

In my head, I took one step back, then dove. Not jumped. Dove. Executed a perfect swan dive, thank you very much, straight into the water. Clean and true, I grabbed onto her and didn't let go as I slipped into the water.

The O had returned.

White noise filled my ears as my toes and fingers got the news first. They tingled, tiny fizzles and sparks of energy spinning up and out, driving through every nerve and every cell that had been starving for this for months. These cells told other cells, communicating to their sisters that something fantastic was happening. Color exploded behind my eyelids, bursting brightly into tiny little sensory fireworks as the feeling continued to spread to every corner of my body. Pure pleasure shot through me, pulsing and slicing, filling me up as I shook and shimmied on top of Simon, who hung on through the entire thing.

I don't know if he could see the choirs of dirty angels singing, but no matter. I could. And it was the definition of bliss.

O came back, and she brought friends.

Wave after wave crashed through me as Simon and I continued to press and twist, arching into every single one of them. My head was thrown back as I continued to scream lustfully, not caring who or what could hear me in my own House of Orgasm.

I opened my eyes at one point to see Simon below me, frantic and happy, smiling big as he stayed with me through it all, his strenuous effort clear across his face as the flour in his hair turned into a wonderful little paste.

He was becoming papier-mâché.

Still onward I thrashed, passing through the land of multiples and into some kind of no man's land. Passing six and seven, my body became limp with ecstasy.

But O brought one more friend. She brought along G, the Holy Grail.

Stuttering like an idiot, I grasped hold of Simon, holding on for dear life as the biggest tidal wave of love and toe-curling heat hit me like a ton of bricks. Sensing I needed help for this one, Simon sat up, which positioned him even more uniquely. He found a spot deep inside, hidden to most, and he leaned into me, driving himself over and over again as I held my breath and hung on tight.

I finally opened my eyes again, seeing light spark around the room as oxygen rushed back into my system. I babbled incomprehensibly into his chest as he rocked into me again and again, finally finding his own kind of amazing somewhere deep inside me.

I held onto him, feeling the waves finally retreat, both of us shaking now. As we panted, the pleasure left and the love simply rushed in, filling me back up again. My mouth was too tired to move. He had taken my breath away. So I did the best I could, I placed his hand over my heart and kissed his sweet face. He seemed to understand, and kissed me back. I hummed with happiness. Humming didn't take as much effort.

Utterly spent and exhausted, punch drunk and covered in sticky sweat, I lay back against his legs, not caring a bit how contorted and ridiculous I looked as tension tears ran down the sides of my face and into my ears. Sensing this was not the most comfortable position for me, Simon moved out from under me and helped to unbend my pretzel legs before cradling me in his arms on the kitchen floor.

We lay quietly, not speaking for a while. I noticed Clive sitting just inside the doorway to the bedroom licking his paws quietly.

All was good.

When movement seemed possible, I tried to sit up, the room spinning a little. Simon kept one arm around me as we appraised the situation, the overturned bowls and bottles, the scattered bread, the chaos that was my kitchen. I laughed quietly and turned to him. He watched me with happy eyes.

"Should we clean this up?" he asked.

"No, let's shower."

"'Kay," he answered, helping me up.

I cracked my back like an old lady, wincing at the good hurt my body felt. I started for the bathroom, then changed direction, heading for the fridge. I grabbed a bottle of Gatorade and tossed it to him. "You're gonna need it." I winked, flouncing my apron on my way to the shower. Now that the O was back, I planned to waste no time in summoning her again.

As Simon followed me to the bathroom, taking a swig of Gatorade, Clive suddenly flopped onto the floor, rolling over on his back. He seemed to be waving Simon over with his paws. Simon looked at me, and I shrugged. We both looked at Clive, who wiggled on his back, continuing to wave him over. Simon knelt right next to him, cautiously extending one hand. Winking at me — I swear to Christ he did — Clive wiggled a little closer. Knowing this could still be a trap, Simon cautiously reached down and rumpled the fur on his belly. Clive let him. I even heard a tentative purr.

I left the two boys alone for a moment and went to turn on the shower so it could heat up. I finally got the apron knot undone and was able to abandon it on the floor. Stepping under the spray, I moaned at the feeling of the warm water hitting my still-sensitive skin.

"You coming? 'Cause I sure did," I called over the rush of the shower, laughing at my own joke. A moment later Simon poked back the corner of the shower curtain to watch me naked and covered in bubbles. He smiled like the devil as he climbed in. I drew in a breath at the sight of ten tiny punctures in his back, but he laughed it away.

"We're good. I think we just made friends," he assured, pulling me against him and joining me under the water.

I sighed, relaxing. "This is nice," I murmured.

"Yeah."

The water beat down around us. I was in the arms of my Simon, and it couldn't get any better.

He pulled back a little, a question on his face. "Caroline?"

"Hmm?"

"Is any of that bread I threw on the floor...well..."

"Yes?"

"Is any of it zucchini?"

"Yes, Simon, there's zucchini bread."

Silence once again, but for the water.

"Caroline?"

"Hmm?"

"I didn't think I could love you more, but I really kind of do."

"I'm glad, Simon. Now gimme some sugar."

chapter twenty-two

"Is that the soap? Don't slip on the soap."

"I won't slip on the soap."

"I don't want you to slip. Be careful."

"I won't slip on the soap. Now turn back around and be quiet."

"Quiet? Not possible, not when you...mmm...and then when you...ooohhh...and then when you—ow, that hurt, Simon. You okay back there?"

"I slipped on the soap."

I started to turn around to see if he was indeed okay when he suddenly pressed me up against the shower wall, holding my hands flat against the tile. Lips tickled and water sprinkled down my skin and across my shoulders as his body flexed against mine. Thoughts of runaway soap slipped from my mind as he slipped inside me, hard and thick and delicious. My breath left me in a gasp, amplified by the tile walls, made sexy by the water falling, and quickly followed by another gasp as he proceeded to thrust into me, achingly slowly and purposefully, his hands now gripping my hips.

I threw my head backward, turning my face to find the sight of Simon, naked and wet. His brow was furrowed, mouth open as he invaded completely and without apology. I spiraled fast, awareness and clear thought narrowing down to a pinpoint before exploding, wordless words falling out of my mouth and down to the water, circling the drain.

Now that O was back, she didn't dally. So far, at least, she arrived promptly and without question, shattering the memory of days and weeks and months of waiting and crying, begging and pleading. She'd rewarded me with a steady, constant parade that left me scrambled and silly, boneless and ready for more.

Groaning into my ear, shivering and pulsing, Simon failed to slow his roll. He knew inherently, as I knew, that his girl was good for a few more. And so, with agonizing dexterity, he planted a wet kiss on my neck, left my body, spun me quickly, and was back inside before I could say, "Hey, where'd you go?"

"Nowhere, Nightie Girl, not anytime soon," he muttered, roughly grabbing my bottom and lifting me against the wall, using his weight to crush me against the tile, holding me to him and holding me inside. His body flexed while mine flattened, our slippery skin feeling indescribable against each other. How had I stayed away from this man as long as I had? No matter. He was here, inside me, and about to deliver another O parade throughout. I pressed back against him just enough, opening the space between us just enough to gaze down, lust clouding my vision but not so much that I couldn't see him entering me, over and over again, filling me up like no man ever had.

Now glancing down himself to see what had me so transfixed, he was captivated as well, and a sound rather like "Mmph" left his mouth. His movements sped up, chasing it down, that feeling, that tipping point that felt so close to pain and so close to perfection. Those blue eyes, now filled with lust and fire, flew back up to mine as we both threw ourselves off that cliff again together.

Seizing. Freezing. Locked and unloaded. We came together with a roar and a grunt and a groan that left my throat raw and my hoo-hah thrilled.

Thrilled hoohah…what a great name for a…Mmmm…

6:41 p.m.:

Walking around my apartment in only a towel, dodging flour piles and raisin clumps, Simon was a sight to behold. When he skidded on a patch of marmalade and bumped into the counter, I laughed so hard I had to sit down on the couch. He now stood in front of me with a slice of zucchini bread as I laughed, an amused look on his face. I continued to laugh, and my towel slipped down, revealing more than a little of my assets. At the sight of boobs, two things happened. His eyes popped, and something else popped. Popped out. I raised an eyebrow at this latest development.

"You realize you are turning me into some kind of machine?" he noted, nodding down at his HiThere poking through the towel. Simon took the time to place his zucchini bread safely on the coffee table.

"How cute is that? It's like he's poking his head out from behind a curtain!" I clapped my hands.

"You may not be aware, but as a general rule, no man likes the word *cute* in the same sentence as his junk."

"But he is cute—uh-oh, where'd he go?"

"He's shy now. Still not cute, but shy."

"Shy, my ass. He wasn't so shy in the shower a little bit ago."

"He needs his ego stroked."

"Wow."

"No, really. I think you'll find he is quite receptive to stroking."

"Now see, I was thinking maybe he just needed a good tongue lashing, but if you think stroking will suffice…"

"No, no, I think a tongue lashing is quite in order. He—God-*damn*, Caroline!"

I leaned in, brought the shy one forth, and immediately surrounded him with my mouth. Feeling him grow harder still, I settled myself on the edge of the couch, wrapped my arms around him and dropped the towel. Pulling him closer, and therefore deeper into me, I hummed in satisfaction as I felt his hands come up into my hair and trace my face. Reverently, he placed his fingers on my eyelids, cheeks, temples, finally burying one hand in my hair and the other, well, wow. He held himself. As I concentrated all my attention on the tip of him, he stroked himself at the base, something that was quite possibly the sexiest thing I'd ever seen. Seeing his hand, wrapped around himself as he moved in and out of my mouth…oh my.

Sexy isn't the right word for it. It is inadequate in the face of the pure erotica playing out in front of me. And speaking of in front of me, I hummed again in appreciation, feeling myself getting worked up just at the play my mouth was getting. Lucky mouth.

I fell back against the couch and pulled Simon with me. He responded by using both hands to brace against the back of the couch, thrusting in and out of my mouth with conviction. The angle allowed him to penetrate more deeply, and made it easier for me to take more of him in. I grabbed his backside, feeling the thrill of attending to him, knowing it was me, only me, who got to have him in this way.

I could feel him getting close. I was already beginning to know his tells intimately. I wanted him again. I was selfish this way. Releasing him with a final strong pull, I pushed him down on to the couch and straddled him. Feeling me against him, he thrust upward as I sank down, and there was that moment—you know that moment? When everything feels stretched and pulled in the most delicious way? Your body reacts: something that shouldn't be inside is now inside and for a split second, it's alien, unknown. And then your skin senses a returning champion, your muscle memory takes over, and then it's so good, that feeling of fullness, of wonder and awe.

And then you begin to move.

Grabbing his shoulders for leverage, I rolled my hips into his, noticing not for the first time that he'd been intelligently designed with my exact measurements in mind. He fit inside me perfectly, two halves of a whole, some kind of sexual Lego. He sensed it too, I could tell.

He placed his hand flat against my chest, directly on top of my heart. "Stunning," he whispered as I rode him, sweet and hot. He kept my heart in his hand as I rocked into him, his other hand on my hip, guiding me, positioning me, feeling me attend to us both. He struggled to stay with me, to keep his eyes open as his release rushed in. I took his hand from my heart and placed it further down, where he began to trace those damnable perfect circles.

"Jesus, Simon...oh, God...so...soooo good...I...mmm..."

"I love watching you fall apart," he groaned, and I did. And he did. And we did.

I collapsed into him, watching until the room stopped spinning and the feeling returned to my fingers and toes, warmth snaking through my body as he held me to him.

"Tongue lashing. What an idea," he snorted, and I giggled.

8:17 p.m.:

"Ever think about changing the paint color in here?"

"Are you serious?"

"What? Maybe a lighter shade of green? Or even a blue? Blue might be nice. I'd love to see you surrounded by blue."

"Do I tell you how to take pictures?"

"Well, no…"

"Then don't tell me how to pick paint colors. And as it happens, I'm planning to change the palette in here, but it's going darker. Deeper, you might say."

"Deeper, you say? How's this?"

"That's pretty good. Mmm, that's really good. Anyhow, as I was saying, I'm thinking of maybe a deep slate gray, with a new creamy sugar marble countertop, deepening the cupboards to a rich, dark mahogany. Holy shit, that feels good."

"Noted. Deeper is good, and very deep is even better. Can you put your foot on my shoulder?"

"Like that?"

"Christ, Caroline, yes, like that. So…new countertop, you say? Marble might be a little cold, don't you think?"

"Yes, yes, yes! What? I mean, what? Cold? Well, since I'm not usually laid out like a jelly roll on the counter, the cold won't bother me. Besides, marble countertops are the best for rolling out dough."

"Don't," he warned, turning his face to kiss the inside of my ankle.

"Don't what, Simon?" I purred, my breath hitching as I felt his pace begin to quicken slightly, unnoticeable to anyone but me, the one he was currently inside of.

"Don't try to distract me with dough talk. It won't work," he instructed, letting go of the countertop with his left hand and running it lightly over my breasts, back and forth, teasing my nipples into hard peaks with his fingertips.

A frantic energy began to settle low, low in my hips and in my thighs, the pit of my stomach and points in between. "No dough talk? No dirty dough talk for Simon? Mmm, but don't you think a little distraction is good from time to time? I mean, can't you just imagine me, bent over the countertop, working so hard for you…"

I trailed off, running my fingers through his hair, bending him to me to kiss him with a wet mouth, tongue and lips and teeth intent on bringing him deeper into me.

I was perched on the edge of my kitchen island, very much naked, as was our fair Mr. Parker, buried inside and determined to make this last as long as possible. We wanted to see how long we could carry on a conversation while…well…doing it. So far seventeen of the most intense, sensual, fantastic minutes of my life, and that wasn't counting the foreplay. O was dancing in the periphery, wondering why she wasn't being granted immediate access. But now I had control of the bitch, and this sweet torture was incredible. Worth enduring.

That is, until Simon asked me to place my foot on his shoulder. Holy hell, he was wrecking me. One leg on his shoulder, the other leg he held open to one side, his hips rotating in maddeningly tiny circles, increasing in the smallest of increments. He was the one who insisted on the conversation, and I'd been able to keep up, until the foot on shoulder. Suddenly, parts that hadn't really been a part of it before were now being stimulated, and it was getting harder and harder to keep my wits about me. But really, who needed wits? I could be witless. As long as I could be under Simon, I was okay being witless.

But I could still play this game right now, while a few lingering wits remained.

"Don't test me, Naughty Girl. I will dirty talk you right off this island."

"Mmm, Simon, can't you just see me? Bent over, little apron with nothing underneath, rolling pin in hand, and a bowl full of apples?"

"Apples? Oh boy, I love apples," he groaned, picking up my other foot and placing it on the opposite shoulder, his hands roughly pulling me even farther toward the edge, his pace picking up again just a bit.

"I know you do, with cinnamon? I could bake you a pie, Simon. Your very own apple pie, even a homemade crust…all for you, big guy. You know all you have to do is ask me…" I smirked, trying to keep my eyes from crossing as he sped up again, the sound of skin slapping not even funny at all. There went another wit.

"How does that feel, Caroline. Good?" he asked, surprising me.

"Good? It feels amazing."

"Amazing? Really?" He pulled out almost all the way before sliding back into me all at once, making me feel every single inch.

And the wit stands alone. "You know, it does, but back to the apples. Would you like your pie served hot with vanilla ice cream? Warm and melty with—oh my God..."

"You really want to talk about this right now? Because if you keep this up, I'm going to be forced to get really dirty myself."

"Dirtier than apple pie talk?" I asked, stretching and pointing my toes toward the ceiling, creating a new sensation.

"How about this, if you don't stop all this apple pie talk," he started, leaning down to place his mouth against my ear, making me shiver. One hand grasped my breast, roughly turning and tweaking my nipple. The other snuck down, feeling against me until he found the spot that made me tense and cry out. "If you don't stop, I'm going to stop fucking you, and believe me when I say I haven't even begun to ravage you in all the ways I've dreamed about."

He stood back up and thrust. Hard.

Last wit? Bye-bye. I ain't too proud to beg. "God, Simon, I give. Just fuck me."

"Apple pie for me?"

"Yes, yes! Apple pie for you! Oh, God..."

"That's right, apple pie for me, apple pie for—God, you're tight this way." He groaned, switching both of my legs to one side, holding them up as he pounded into me, again and again, never retreating, only advancing, looking down at me, watching as my back arched and my skin flushed, heat creeping as my climax broke over me, stunning me silent in its intensity as I was shaken to the very core of my being.

"I love you, Caroline, I love you, I love you, I love you," he chanted, thrusting erratically now as he sped toward his own release, sweat breaking over his brow as he clutched at my hips as I clutched him from the inside, holding him as long as I could, feeling his solid weight on me as he laid his head on my breast. How could his warm weight feel so good? It should have made it hard to breathe, constriction of the lungs and all that, but it didn't. Holding him, cradling his face as I swept his hair back, it felt the opposite of heavy.

"You're going to kill me, sure as I'm lying here," he moaned, kissing everywhere he could.

"I love you too," I sighed, gazing at my kitchen ceiling. I could feel a smile as big as the bay across my face. The O was going to be around for a very long time.

No way am I painting my kitchen blue.

9:32 p.m.:

"I can't believe this is the second time we're cleaning flour and sugar off each other. What's wrong with us?"

"The sugar is good for exfoliation," I explained. "Not sure what good the flour is doing us, though."

"Exfoliation?"

"Yeah, I figure every time we sex it up out there, all that sugar helps us remove dead skin cells."

"Really, Caroline? Dead skin cells? That's hardly sexy."

"You weren't complaining earlier."

"Well no, how could I? You promised to bake me an apple pie. Don't forget that part."

"I won't forget, but I was somewhat under duress."

"You were under me, not under duress, under *me*."

"Yes, Simon, I was under you."

"Wash your back?"

"Yes, please."

We lay on opposite sides of the tub, relaxing and soaking off yet another round of kitchen goo. At some point, I was going to have to clean all that mess up, but right now the only thing I could concentrate on was this man in front of me. This man, up to almost his neck in fragrant bubbles, strong arms snaking out now to bring me closer. I spun in the tub like a buoy, bobbing back and forth and arranging myself in front of him. He used a washcloth to gently remove the last of the sticky that covered me. Then he pulled me to his chest, leaning back against the edge of the tub. Arms encircled me, tucking me in, surrounding me with warm water and warmer Simon. I closed my eyes, relishing the feel of it all. The safety, the sweetness, the sexiness. I shifted, trying to get impossibly closer, and then I felt him against my bum. Growing.

"Why, hello there, friend," I murmured, sneaking my hand through the bubbles to find him, wanting and wanton.

"Caroline..." he warned, laying his head back on the edge of the tub.

"What?" I asked innocently, trailing my fingers along the sides of him, feeling him react.

"I'm not seventeen, you know." He chuckled, his voice growing husky and needy in spite of his words.

"Thank goodness, or I would have to answer for my actions—corrupting a minor and all that," I whispered, slowly turning over to rub myself along the length of him, soap and bubbles and water making me slippery.

He hissed slightly and smiled. "You're going to break me, you know this, right? I swear on all that's holy, I'm not a machine—Christ, don't stop doing that," he groaned, thrusting into my hand without thought.

"Ah, break schmake. I just want to fuck you until you can't see straight," I purred, tightening my fist as he splashed water over the side a bit.

"I can barely see as it is. There seem to be three of you," he moaned, pulling my legs apart and positioning me above him.

"Aim for the one in the middle, Simon," I instructed and slid down.

Yeah, we had some water to clean up.

11:09 p.m.:

"I'm just going to get the food. I need sustenance, woman."

"Get it, then hurry back to me. I need you, Simon. Why are you crawling on the floor?"

"I don't think I can actually stand at this point. The machine needs a break. The machine may very well need repairs. The machine, wait, what're you doin' there, Caroline?"

"What, this?"

"Yeah, yeah, it looks like you're—wow, do you touch yourself like that a lot?"

"I haven't lately, why? Looks good to you, yes?"

"Yes, that's...wow...um...that's the door...the guy with the Thai is here. I...and I...Thai...I..."

"Are you really rhyming right now, Simon? Mmm, that feels nice…"

"Hello! Hello, anyone there? Someone called in an order for—dude, how am I supposed to give you your change?"

"Keep the change."

"Dude, you shoved a fifty under the door. You know that's like a thirty-dollar tip, right?"

"Keep the change. Leave the Thai. Caroline, get on that bed."

"Mmm, so close, Simon. Sure you don't…want…me…to…mmm…finish…oooh. I love when you do that."

"Mmph, mumph, hah, hooo…"

"Don't talk with your mouth full, Simon, Simon, Simon, Simon, Siiimmooooon…"

"Okay, dude. I'm totally setting your food out here. Um, thanks for the tip."

1:14 a.m.:

We lay in bed, limp and a little stupid. My poor Simon, I'd ridden him to the brink of extinction. He wasn't a teenager, but even he was surprised by his…hmm…stamina. After the last round of crazytown, he crawled back to the hallway, retrieved the food, and we ate Thai sitting in the middle of the bed. I'd quickly stripped the sheets because raisins and flour clouds lingered from earlier. The amount of work I was going to be faced with in the kitchen tomorrow was daunting, but it was worth it. All of it. All of it was worth it.

Now we lounged, settled but not settling. Still wrapped around each other but now clad in a pink nightie and a pair of sweatpants. To be clear, I wore the pink nightie. We lay side by side, facing each other, legs tangled and hands held.

"When do you have to go back to work?"

"I told Jillian I'd be back Monday, although that is the last thing I can think about right now."

"What *are* you thinking about?"

"Spain."

"Yeah?"

"Yeah, it was amazing. Thank you so much for taking me, and then taking me." I nudged him with my elbow.

"It was my pleasure, on both counts. I'm glad you could...come," he snorted.

Now that the O had returned, we could joke about it. We were quiet for a moment, just enjoying the music. Simon had hobbled next door a little while ago to put on a record. Even hobbled, he was sexy.

"When are you leaving for Peru? Ass, I still hate you a little for getting to go, but when are you leaving?"

"About two weeks. And no hating on the photographer. I have to go, but I'll always come back."

"Oh, to be clear, I don't hate you for leaving. I hate you because I want to go too. But I digress. I love you more than I hate you, so we're good."

"We're good?"

"Yes, of course. You have to travel for your job. It's not like I didn't know this."

"Well, knowing about it and then being the one left behind are two different things," he said, eyes getting a little cloudy. I smoothed my hand across his cheek, feeling his scruff and skin and watching him lean into my touch. His eyes closed, and he hummed a contented hum.

"You're not *leaving me behind*. We live busy lives and will continue to do so. Just because you get to stick your dick in me now, that isn't going to change us," I replied.

A slow grin spread across his face. Eyes still closed, but grinning. "Sometimes dicks change people," he said through the grin.

"Sometimes dicks change what needs to be changed. Sometimes dicks make it better."

"Sometimes dicks make it better—what an odd thing to say."

"Stick around, who knows what I'm gonna say next."

"Sticking."

"Stuck."

"Going to kiss you now."

"Thank Christ." I giggled as he wrapped his strong arms around me. We kissed quietly, thoughtfully. I settled down into his nook, perfectly shaped and smelling like heaven.

"I adore this nook."

"Good."

"No one else gets this nook."

"It's yours."

"Yes, yes it is. Make sure you tell that to all those gorgeous Peruvian women who will try to seduce the hot American."

"I'll make sure to tell them my nook is spoken for."

I smiled and yawned hugely. It had been an exhausting few days. I was jet lagged and had been rocked to within an inch of my life. Tended to make a girl tired. Simon leaned across me to shut off the light and tucked me back into the nook.

1:23 a.m.:

"Simon?"

"Mmm?"

"Are you asleep?"

"Mm-hmm..."

"I just wanted to say, well, I'm really glad you came home early."

"Mm-hmm, me too."

"And I'm pretty smitten with you."

"Mm-hmm, me too."

"Smitten like a kitten."

"Mm-hmm, me too."

"Who's lost her mittens."

"Mittens, mm-hmm..."

"Simon?"

"Mm-hmm?"

"Are you asleep?"

"Mm-hmm..."

"I love you."

"I love you too."

…

…

…

"Caroline?"

"Mm-hmm…"

"I'm really glad I came home early too."

"Mm-hmm…"

"And I'm really glad you came."

"Enough."

"'Night, Caroline."

"'Night, Simon."

And as Count Basie and his orchestra played us off into dreamland, we curled around each other and slept.

Text between Simon and Caroline the following Tuesday:

Talked to a buddy of mine. I think I figured out how to do those prawns you went so crazy over in Spain.

Perfect, they'll fit in with the Spanish feast I am planning for Saturday. Everybody's coming, even Jillian and Benjamin.

Sure you don't want to have it at my place?

No, it'll be easier at mine. I have the island, which is better for prepping, but I'm commandeering your oven.

Can I commandeer you on the island?

That's not the correct use of the word commandeer.

Please, you know what I meant.

I did, and you may.

Sweet. Have you seen my running shoes?

Yep, they're in my bathroom where you left them. I tripped over them this morning.

Is that the thump I heard?

You heard that?

Yep, woke me up.

And yet you didn't come see if I was okay?

Didn't want to disturb Clive.

I can't believe he's been sleeping on your side. Traitor cat.

We're friends now…well, almost friends. He peed on my sweatshirt again.

HA! I have to get back to work, cat stealer. We still watching a movie tonight?

If that's what you want to call it.

Makes it seem like we actually have plans.

I have plans. Oh man, do I have plans.

As do I…

I'm sitting here eating your apple pie…think about that.

That's all I can think about now…hating you.

You don't hate me.

That's true. Now go eat my pie.

…choking…

Text between Mimi and Caroline on Thursday:

You sure I can't bring anything Saturday?

Nah, Sophia is bringing drinks, and we're taking care of the rest.

So good to hear you in a we again.

Yes, I'm enjoying the we.

And the we-we?

What are we, 7? Yes, the we-we is good.

Good to hear it. So have you slept in the bed of sin yet?

No, we seem to be staying at my place. I think I'd feel weird in that bed.

Many walls were banged from that bed...

Exactly. That's my point, feels strange.

Maybe it would be nice to make your mark on his bed, so to speak. New era, new girlfriend, new banger?

I don't know, we'll see...I know at some point I'll sleep there, just not yet. Besides, he's having too much fun bonding with Clive.

WHAT? Clive hates guys! Except gay guys.

They've come to some kind of weird kitty/man understanding. I'm not questioning it.

It's like a new world order.

I know.

Want me to come over early Saturday and help?

You just want to get into my drawers again.

They need to be reorganized...

Come over early.

WAHOO!

Get some help...

Thursday evening all was quiet. Simon and I sat on my couch, working. I was sketching a holiday concept for someone's ballroom. Yep, ballroom. This was the world I visited. Just visited, not lived in. I was still in my yoga clothes. Simon cooked, using my kitchen, in which he was becoming very much at home. He said it would be easier since we'd just end up at my place anyway, but I caught him lifting

Clive up onto the counter so he could "watch." I put that in quotes because the actual word was spoken by Simon to Clive. The entire sentence, I believe, was "Here ya go, buddy. This way you can watch! You can't see too well from down on the floor, I bet, right? Right?"

And Clive answered. I know it was technically impossible, but the meow he uttered sounded like, "Thanks."

My boys were bonding. It was nice.

So here we sat, me sketching and Simon making his travel plans for Peru online. He had something like seventy billion frequent flyer miles, and he loved to flaunt them in my face.

So quiet it was, save the scratching of my colored pencils on the page and his clickety-clack on the keyboard. And the clicking from Clive. Most stubborn kitty hangnail in the free world.

Simon finished and closed up his laptop, stretching his arms over his head and exposing his happy trail. I may have drawn outside the lines a bit. He laid his head against the back of the couch, eyes closed. Within a few moments, the tiniest of snores began, and I grinned silently. I continued my sketching.

Ten minutes later I felt his hand reach out across the pillows, and grasp my hand.

I only needed one hand for sketching after all.

"Holy shit, Caroline, these prawns are sick!" Mimi moaned in a way that made Ryan readjust the way he sat.

It was Saturday night, and we were all gathered around my dining room table, full of Spanish food and Spanish wine. I'd had a blast trying to recreate all the wonderful food Simon and I had eaten. Not as good certainly, but pretty close. And of course we were without the coastal ambiance, but instead had the coziness only an autumn evening in foggy San Francisco can provide. The city lights twinkled through the windows, a fire crackled in the fireplace, courtesy of Benjamin, and laughter filled the apartment.

I sat in my chair, tucked in to Simon's side as we laughed with our friends. I'd been a little nervous that we'd be subjected to some kind of hazing, since our inevitable getting-together had been the topic of conversation for so long. But it was good, everyone settled into the evening with only minimal teasing. Simon and I had stuck pretty close together most of the evening, but I could already tell we would morph into one of those couples that *didn't* need that.

I never wanted to be *that* couple, the one that was entirely codependent and in constant need of reassurance. I loved Simon, that much was clear. One of us traveled, for goodness sake, so we needed to roll with it. And I thought we would. I felt him next to me, and I moved just a little closer. He slipped an arm around my waist, his hand patting my arm, squeezing and just making me more aware of him. I was aware. His fingertips traced little circles around my elbow, and I sighed as he pressed a quick kiss to my forehead.

I would never need the Honey and the Baby. I just needed him and his little circles. Just needed to feel him at my side, whenever he was here. Jillian caught my eye from across the table and winked.

"What was that for?" I asked, sipping my second glass of brandy. Simon was going to have no trouble getting me into bed later that night, not that he ever did.

"Things worked out well, didn't they?" she asked, looking back and forth between Simon and me.

"Couldn't have worked out better. Subletting your apartment to me was the best decision you ever made." I smiled, leaning into Simon as he rubbed my shoulder.

"Jillian giving me your number so I could text you from Ireland, now *that's* the best decision she ever made," he added, winking at Benjamin from across the table.

"Oh, I don't know. Pretending I didn't know your mysterious neighbor was a damn good decision too," she said, a mischievous grin lighting up her face as Simon coughed into his brandy.

"Wait, what? You knew all along I was the one living next door?" he asked, sputtering as I handed him a napkin. "But you've never even been to my place!"

"She hasn't, but I have," Benjamin spoke up, clinking his glass with his fiancée's.

Simon and I sat pie eyed as we watched them laugh and congratulate themselves.

Well played...

"Okay, that's the last of it. No more dishes," Simon announced, closing the dishwasher. After everyone finally left, we decided to clean up the rest of the mess instead of leaving it for the morning after.

"Thank goodness. I'm beat."

"And I have dishpan hands." He winked, showing me how red they were.

"That's the mark of a good housewife." I just barely sidestepped his grabby hands.

"Just call me Madge and bring that fantastic ass back over here," he fired back, snapping a dishtowel in my direction.

"This ass? This ass right here?" I asked, propping myself against the island just so, leaning forward on my elbows.

"You want to play now, is that it? Thought you were beat," he murmured, catching my bottom in his dishpan hands and giving me a light smack.

"Maybe I'm catching my second wind." I giggled as he promptly swept me up over his shoulder in a fireman's hold and headed for the bedroom. Upside down, I beat my fists against his bottom and kicked, though not so much as to actually get away. His feet stopped at the bedroom door.

"Forget something today?" he asked, turning so I could see inside: stripped bed, no sheets.

"Damn, I forgot to put the sheets in the dryer. They'll still be soaked!" I grumbled.

"Problem solved. Slumber party at Simon's," he announced, pulling open my lingerie drawer. "Pick a nightie, any nightie."

"You want to stay at your place tonight?"

"Yeah, why not? We've been sleeping here since we got back from Spain. My bed's lonely." He ruffled through piles of lace and peekaboo.

Hmm, his bed was probably lonelier that it had ever been before.

"So, pick one." He gave my ass another slap.

"Eh, you pick out something you like. I'll model it for you." I grinned, talking myself into this. Come on, I could certainly spend the night in his bed. Could be fun. I saw a familiar something pink and lacy make its way under his arm, and then we were off across the hallway. I managed to kick his door on the way in, something pretty hard to do while upside down.

Once more, I found myself in a bathroom, putting on lingerie for Simon. He really liked everything I wore. Whether it was actual lingerie or one of his old shirts, he didn't seem to care. And it was rarely on for very long.

Without meaning to, I thought of all the women who'd come before me, all the women he'd enjoyed and had enjoyed him. But I was here now, and I was who he wanted. I smoothed the silk over my body with a deep breath, my skin already beginning to tingle in anticipation of his hands.

I heard him messing about with his record player — the telltale crackle and pop of needle on vinyl such a comforting sound.

Glenn Miller. "Moonlight Serenade." Sigh.

I opened the door, and there he was. Standing by the giant Wallbanger bed of sin. His slow grin overtook me, and he looked me up and down.

"You look good," he murmured as I walked in.

"You too."

"I'm wearing the same clothes I was wearing earlier, Caroline."

He smirked as I encircled his neck with my arms. His fingertips dragged up and down my arms, tickling the inside of my elbow.

"I know," I replied, placing a wet kiss under his ear. "You looked good then, and you look good now."

"Lemme get a better look at you," he whispered, responding with his own wet kiss at the base of my throat. I shivered. The room wasn't at all cold.

He spun me out, as if on a dance floor, and held me at arm's length for just a moment. The pink nightie, his favorite. He'd neglected to bring the matching panties, and I neglected to notice. He spun me back into him, and I immediately began to work the buttons on his shirt.

"Quite a night tonight," he remarked.

Two buttons down.

"You're telling me. I can't believe those two were matchmaking from the very beginning! Although I don't think they can take credit for the other two couples. That was all us."

"Who knew love was in the air when you banged on my door?"

Another button down.

"Luckily, you were so taken by my charms, it was inevitable."

"It was the nightie, Caroline. It was the nightie that did me in. The charms were a bonus. I had no idea I'd be getting a girlfriend out of the deal."

Shirt untucked and on its way off.

"Really? And here I thought we were just messing around!" I giggled, scrambling to get his belt buckle poked through.

"Well, then, here's to messing around with my girlfriend!" Belt buckle undone, jean buttons popped. Thank goodness for the old-fashioned button fly. He picked me up, by my naked bottom I might add, and walked me to the bed as I pushed his shirt off. It hung from him by the sleeves.

"I like the sound of that," I whispered in his ear as he lay me down on the bed.

Hovering over me, placing kisses across my chest, he kept saying the word over and over again. Girlfriend, then kiss. Girlfriend, girlfriend, then kiss.

"Did you know Mimi and Neil are thinking about moving in together? Isn't that a little soon? I hope they know what they're getting into," I reported, arching up to meet his kisses.

"I know what I'm getting in to."

"What's that?"

"You, silly," he said, and I heard the blessed sound of his belt buckle hitting the floor. "I'm only concerned with our happy ending. Or two, or three even. Drank that ginseng tea you left me this morning—watch out." He chuckled, lifting one of my legs on to his shoulder and kissing a path down the inside of my calf.

"Happy ending, huh?"

"Don't you think we've earned it?" he asked, kneeling now, lips trailing along the top of my thigh as I panted.

"Oh, hell, yes," I laughed, throwing my arms over my head and arching up to meet him. Hello, O! Nice to see you again. With his lips, he brought me one. With his tongue, he brought me another. And when he slid into me and pushed me high up on to the bed, I almost had another on contact.

Clothes now discarded, skin on sweaty skin, my legs wrapped solidly around his hips, which pushed against mine. His eyes burned as I felt every inch of him. Inside. Outside. All around the town.

"Oh, God," I moaned. And then I heard it.

Thump.

"Oh, God," I moaned again.

Thump thump.

I giggled at the sound. We were banging.

He looked down at me, raising one eyebrow. "Something funny?" he asked, pausing his movements. He pushed back into me slowly, very, very slowly.

"We're banging the walls." I giggled again, watching his eyes change as he registered my giggling.

"We sure are," he admitted, chuckling a little as well. "You okay?"

I wrapped my legs even tighter around his waist, making sure I was as close to him as I could be. "Bring it on home, Wallbanger." I winked, and he complied.

I was being driven up the bed with the strength of his thrusts. He drove into me with unflinching force, giving me exactly what I could take, then pushing me just past that edge. He stared down at me, hard, flashing that knowing smirk. I closed my eyes, letting myself feel how deeply I was being affected. And by deep, I mean deep…

He grasped my hands and brought them above my head to the headboard.

"You're gonna wanna hold on for this," he whispered and threw one of my legs up over his shoulder as he altered his hips.

"Simon!" I shrieked, feeling my body begin to spasm. His eyes, those damnable blue eyes, bore into mine as I shook around him.

He called out my name, and no one else's.

A little while later, almost asleep, I felt the mattress dip as Simon left the bed. Hearing him flip over the record, I snuggled deeper into the pillow. My body was deliciously tired, having been worked to within an inch of total exhaustion. We banged that wall, yes indeed. I owned both sides of that wall now.

I heard him bumble down the hall and half wondered what he was up to. Thinking in that tired, half-awake way that he must be getting some water, I slipped back down to sleep.

A few moments later I was awoken by his arms sliding around me, pulling me against his warm body. He kissed me on my neck, then cheek, then forehead as he got settled. Then I heard…purring?

"What's that?" I asked, looking around.

"I thought he might be lonely," Simon admitted sheepishly. Looking over my shoulder, I saw Simon, and then Clive. Simon had gone over to get him. Clive was purring very loudly, quite pleased with all the attention he'd been receiving lately. He poked his nose in to me and settled into the nook between us.

"Unbelievable," I muttered, rolling my eyes at the two of them.

"Are you that surprised? You know much I love pussy," Simon deadpanned. Then his silent laughter shook the bed.

"You're very lucky I love you," I added, letting his arms hold me tight.

"I'll say."

And then, as the laughter faded and sleep took hold, I pondered what the future might hold for me and my Wallbanger.

I knew it wouldn't always be this easy. But it sure as hell would be a good time.

*A*ll was quiet as I set out on patrol, making sure the perimeter was secure. I padded through my new territory, taking notice of any loose Q-Tips. They would need to be dealt with if unruly. If allowed to run unchecked, they would multiply. I'd seen it happen.

I came upon a curious shelf with nothing but glass bottles on it. I batted at one, watching as it fell to the floor. I would have to come back to this location, but for now I had rounds.

Checking the view from the front window I saw that I could retain control of my neighborhood from this vantage point. I scouted a possible napping station in another window with southern exposure, then stopped for a stare-off with an owl outside. Neither of us gave in willingly, and it was another fifteen minutes before I continued on to check on my people. They had finally quieted down after several rounds of caterwauling. Honestly.

The Feeder was, predictably, taking up most of the sleeping quarters. The Tall One, aptly named because he was taller than The Feeder, was making that noise again—the noise I simply could not tolerate. The Feeder was beginning to toss and turn. She was not sleeping soundly. Without enough sleep, she would be unlikely to play with me the following evening, so this situation would have to be remedied. She did seem to enjoy our games, so I would once more take matters into my own paws.

Jumping from the floor to the bed with a natural grace—a grace that was not fully appreciated by my people, I felt—I navigated my way through knees and legs, arms and elbows, until I reached the pinnacle and came to rest just beneath his chin. Stretching out one paw, I placed it over his breathing holes, stopping the noise momentarily. The Tall One brushed away my effort, although once he rolled onto his side, the noise stopped. He curled in to himself, in the one corner The Feeder had allowed him. As he had done so, I remained standing, doing my best log-rolling impression and maintaining perfect balance. Again, my people just didn't get it.

Settling into the nook between them, I rested. Our home was secure, and I now watched over The Feeder and The Tall One, so I allowed myself to dream. Of her. The one that got away...

acknowledgments

There are so many people I have to thank for helping me bring this story back out there. To Lauren, who edited this from the very beginning and always told me when I was getting it right. To Sarah M Glover for her San Francisco insight and her insistence that I do have a voice and I should be encouraged to use it. To Elizabeth for allowing me to be crazy. To Brittany and Angie for recognizing that I was one of them and allowing me to play with the curvy girls. To Deb for being the best dirty cheerleader on the planet. To my real life mentors, Staci and Janet, upon whom the character of Jillian is entirely based. To the fantastic Banger Nation, those wonderful ladies who were there from the very first chapter and enjoyed the ridiculous with me. To the Filets for their support in the wee hours and their constant gut checks. To all of the wonderful readers and friends on Twitter who make it a pleasure to communicate in 140 characters. To authors like Laura Kaye, Ruthie Knox, Jennifer Probst, Michelle Leighton, Tiffany Reisz, Karen Marie Moning, and Jennifer Crusie for writing some of my favorite stories of all time. I have always been a reader first and a writer second, and nothing makes me happier than telling a friend about a great book I just finished and can't stop thinking about.

To the online writing community that allowed me the grace and space to create something I could truly be proud of.

To Keili and Ashley for making me funny again and starting something as silly as Not Your Mother's Podcast with me.

Special thanks to my editor, Jessica, who is the perfect blend of smart and sassy. You are a perfectionist, you are a sounding board in a padded room, you are the colon to my semi.

Very special thanks to Enn for bringing me back into the fold, listening to my rants, and putting up with my commas. For working your ass off. For always having my back. There is a taco in heaven with your name on it.

And of course big fat thanks to Peter for always taking such good care of me. I adore your giant thumbs.

Thank you to all the readers, to all the Nuts Girls, to all the Bangers, to all the chickens. Thank you.

Alice

xoxo

about the author

Novelist Alice Clayton makes her home in St. Louis where she enjoys gardening but not weeding, baking but not cleaning up after, and is trying desperately to get her long-time boyfriend to make her an honest woman — and please buy her a Bernese Mountain dog.

After working for years in the cosmetics industry as a makeup artist, esthetician, and educator, Alice picked up a pen (read laptop) for the first time at 33 to begin a new career: author. Having never written a thing, she soon found writing to be the creative outlet she'd been missing since walking away from the theater 10 years before.

She has a great time combining her love of storytelling with a sense of silly, and she was shocked and awed to be nominated for a Goodreads Author award in 2010 for her debut novels, the first two installments of The Redhead Series — *The Unidentified Redhead* and *The Redhead Revealed*.

Additionally, Alice loves spending time with her besties on Not Your Mother's Podcast (check them out on iTunes). She also enjoys pickles, Bloody Marys, and eight hours of sleep

Young Adult

Shades of Atlantis and *The Ember Series: Ember* and *Iridescent* by Carol Oates
Breaking Point by Jess Bowen
Life, Liberty, and Pursuit by Susan Kaye Quinn
Embrace by Cherie Colyer
Destiny's Fire by Trisha Wolfe
Streamline by Jennifer Lane
Reaping Me Softly by Kate Evangelista

Historical Romance

Cat O' Nine Tails by Patricia Leever
Burning Embers by Hannah Fielding

Erotic Romance

Becoming sage by Kasi Alexander
Saving sunni by Kasi & Reggie Alexander
The Winemaker's Dinner: Appetizers by Dr. Ivan Rusilko & Everly Drummond

Anthologies and Singles

A Valentine Anthology including short stories by Alice Clayton, Jennifer DeLucy, Nicki Elson, Jessica McQuinn, Victoria Michaels, and Alison Oburia

It's Only Kinky the First Time by Kasi Alexander
Learning the Ropes by Kasi & Reggie Alexander
The Winemaker's Dinner: RSVP by Dr. Ivan Rusilko
The Winemaker's Dinner: No Reservations by Everly Drummond
Big Guns by Jessica McQuinn
Concessions by Robin DeJarnett
Starstruck by Lisa Sanchez
New Flame by BJ Thornton
Shackled by Debra Anastasia
Swim Recruit by Jennifer Lane
Sway by Nicki Elson
Full Speed Ahead by Susan Kaye Quinn
The Second Sunrise by Hannah Downing
The Summer Prince by Carol Oates
Whatever it Takes by Sarah M. Glover
Clarity by Patricia Leever
Glimpse of Light by Jennifer DeLucy

coming soon from
OMNIFIC PUBLISHING

16 Marsden Place by Rachel Brimble
Blood Vine by Amber Belldene
The Winemaker's Dinner: Entrees by Dr. Ivan Rusilko and Everly Drummond
All American Girl by Justine Dell
Divine Temptation by Nicki Elson
The Englishman by Nina Lewis
Tangled by Emma Chase
Corporate Affair by Linda Cunningham